The bright figure draws a sword that shines like all the stars and the moon and the sun.

A single dark ruby in its hilt. The dark figure rushes onwards, screeching something. Meets the bright figure with a clash. White light and blue fire. Blue fire and white light. His eyes hurt almost as he watches. But he cannot bear to look away. The two struggle together. Like a candle flame flickering. Like the dawn sun on the sea. The silver sword comes up, throws the dark figure back. Blue fire blazes, engulfing everything, the shining silver armor running with flame. Crash of metal, sparks like a blacksmith's anvil. The shining figure takes a step back defensively, parries, strikes out. The other blocks it. Roars. Howls. Laughs. The mage blade swings again, slicing, trailing blue fire. Blue arcs in the evening gloom. Shapes and words, written on the air. Death words. Pain words. Words of hope and fear and despair. The shining figure parries again, the silver sword rippling beneath the impact of the other's blade. So brilliant with light that rainbows dance on the ground around it. Like a woman's hair throwing out drops of water, tossing back her head in summer rain. Like snow falling. Like colored stars. The two fighters shifting, stepping in each other's footprints. Stepping in each other's shadows. Circling like birds.

WITHDRAWN

Praise for
The Court of Broken Knives

"Gritty and glorious! A great read."
—Miles Cameron, author of The Traitor Son Cycle

"Fierce, gripping fantasy, exquisitely written; bitter, funny, and heart-rending by turns."
—Adrian Tchaikovsky, Arthur C. Clarke
Award winner for *Children of Time*

"Grim, gritty, and fast paced; with great battle scenes! Anna Smith Spark is one to watch."
—Andy Remic, author of the Blood Dragon Empire series

"Anna Smith Spark writes in a unique voice with such pace and veracity your imagination has to struggle to keep up with your eyes."
—Adrian Collins, *Grimdark Magazine*

"On a par with R. Scott Bakker."   —*Grimdark Alliance*

"Captivating."
—Marc Turner, author of the Chronicles of the Exile series

"Holy crap, this is good!"   —*Grim Tidings Podcast*

"All hail the queen of grimdark fantasy!"
—Michael R. Fletcher, author of *Beyond Redemption*

By Anna Smith Spark

EMPIRES OF DUST

The Court of Broken Knives
The Tower of Living and Dying

THE COURT OF BROKEN KNIVES

EMPIRES OF DUST: BOOK ONE

ANNA SMITH SPARK

www.orbitbooks.net

*This book is dedicated to my father,
who introduced me to fantasy and history and
mythology, and who taught me how to write.*

PART ONE

BRONZE WALLS

Chapter One

Knives.

Knives everywhere. Coming down like rain.

Down to close work like that, men wrestling in the mud, jabbing at each other, too tired to care any more. Just die and get it over with. Half of them fighting with their guts hanging out of their stomachs, stinking of shit, oozing pink and red and white. Half-dead men lying in the filth. Screaming. A whole lot of things screaming.

Impossible to tell who's who any more. Mud and blood and shadows and that's it. Kill them! Kill them all! Keep killing until we're all dead. The knife jabs and twists and the man he's fighting falls sideways, all the breath going out of him with a sigh of relief. Another there behind. Gods, his arms ache. His head aches. Blood in his eyes. He twists the knife again and thrusts with a broken-off sword and that man too dies. Fire explodes somewhere over to the left. White as maggots. Silent as maggots. Then shrieks as men burn.

He swings the stub of the sword and catches a man on the leg, not hard but hard enough so the man stumbles and he's on him quick with the knife. A good lot of blood and the man's down and dead, still flapping about like a fish but you can see in his eyes that he's finished, his legs just haven't quite caught up yet.

The sun is setting, casting long shadows. Oh beautiful evening! Stars rising in a sky the color of rotting wounds. The Dragon's Mouth. The White Lady. The Dog. A good star, the Dog. Brings plagues and fevers and inflames desire. Its rising marks the coming of summer. So maybe no more campaigning in the sodding rain. Wet leather stinks. Mud stinks. Shit stinks, when the latrine trench overflows.

Another burst of white fire. He hates the way it's silent. Unnatural. Unnerving. Screams again. Screams so bad your ears ring for days. The sky weeps and howls and it's difficult to know what's screaming. You, or the enemy, or the other things.

Men are fighting in great clotted knots like milk curds. He sprints a little to where two men are struggling together. Leaps at one from behind, pulls him down, skewers him. Hard crack of bone, soft lovely yield of fat and innards. Suety. The other yells hoarsely and swings a punch at him. Lost his knife, even. Bare knuckles. He ducks and kicks out hard, overbalances and almost falls. The man kicks back, tries to get him in a wrestling grip. Up close together, two pairs of teeth gritted at each other. A hand smashes his face, gets his nose, digs in. He bites at it. Dirty. Calloused. Iron taste of blood bright in his mouth. But the hand won't let up, crushing his face into his skull. He swallows and almost chokes on the blood pouring from the wound he's made. Blood and snot and shreds of cracked dry human skin. Manages to get his knife in and stabs hard into the back of the man's thigh. Not enough to kill, but the hand jerks out from his face. Lashes out and gets his opponent in the soft part of the throat, pulls his knife out and gazes around the battlefield at the figures hacking at each other while the earth rots beneath them. All eternity, they've been fighting. All the edges blunted. Sword edges and knife edges and the edges in the mind. Keep killing. Keep killing. Keep killing till we're all dead.

And then he's dead. A blade gets him in the side, in the weak point under the shoulder where his armor has to give to let the joint move. Far in, twisting. Aiming down. Killing wound. He hears his body rip. Oh gods. Oh gods and demons. Oh gods and demons and fuck. He swings round, strikes at the man who's stabbed him. The figure facing him is a wraith, scarlet with blood, head open oozing out brain stuff. You're dying, he thinks. You're dying and you've killed me. Not fair.

Shadows twist round them. We're all dying, he thinks, one way or another. Just some of us quicker than others. You fight and you die. And always another twenty men queuing up behind you.

Why we march and why we die,
And what life means...it's all a lie.
Death! Death! Death!

Understands that better than he's ever understood anything, even his own name.

But suddenly, for a moment, he's not sure he wants to die.

The battlefield falls silent. He blinks and sees light.

A figure in silver armor. White, shining, blazing with light like the sun. A red cloak billowing in the wind. Moves through the ranks of the dead and the dying and the light beats onto them, pure and clean.

"Amrath! Amrath!" Voices whispering like the wind blowing across salt marsh. Voices calling like birds. Here, walking among us, bright as summer dew.

"Amrath! Amrath!" The shadows fall away as the figure passes. Everything is light.

"Amrath! Amrath!" The men cheer with one voice. No longer one side or the other, just men gazing and cheering as the figure passes. He cheers until his throat aches. Feels restored, seeing it. No longer tired and wounded and dying. Healed. Strong.

"Amrath! Amrath!"

The figure halts. Gazes around. Searching. Finds. A dark-clad man leaps forward, swaying into the light. Poised across from the shining figure, yearning toward it. Draws a sword burning with blue flame.

"Amrath! Amrath!" Harsh voice like crows, challenging. "Amrath!"

He watches joyfully. So beautiful! Watches and nothing in the world matters, except to behold the radiance of his god.

The bright figure draws a sword that shines like all the stars and the moon and the sun. A single dark ruby in its hilt. The dark figure rushes onwards, screeching something. Meets the bright figure with a clash. White light and blue fire. Blue fire and white light. His eyes hurt almost as he watches. But he cannot bear to look away. The two struggle together. Like a candle flame flickering. Like the dawn sun on the sea. The silver sword comes up, throws the dark figure back. Blue fire blazes, engulfing everything, the shining silver armor running with flame. Crash of metal, sparks like a blacksmith's anvil. The shining figure takes a step back defensively, parries, strikes out. The other blocks it. Roars. Howls. Laughs. The mage blade swings again, slicing, trailing blue fire. Blue arcs in the evening gloom. Shapes and words, written on the air. Death words. Pain words. Words of hope and fear and despair. The shining figure parries again, the silver sword rippling beneath the impact of the other's blade. So brilliant with light that rainbows dance on the ground around it. Like a woman's hair throwing out drops of water, tossing back her head in summer rain. Like snow falling. Like colored stars. The two fighters shifting, stepping in each other's footprints. Stepping in each other's shadows. Circling like birds.

The silver sword flashes out and up and downwards and the other falls back, bleeding from the throat. Great spreading gush of red. The blue flame dies.

He cheers and his heart is almost aching, it's so full of joy.

The shining figure turns. Looks at the men watching. Looks at him. Screams. Things shriek back that make the world tremble. The silver sword rises and falls. Five men. Ten. Twenty. A pile of corpses. He stares mesmerized at the dying. The beauty of it. The most beautiful thing in the world. Killing and killing and such perfect joy. His heart overflowing. His heart singing. This, oh indeed, oh, for this, all men are born. He screams in answer, dying, throws himself against his god's enemies with knife and sword and nails and teeth.

Why we march and why we die,
And what life means...it's all a lie.
Death! Death! Death!

Chapter Two

"The Yellow Empire...I can kind of see that. Yeah. Makes sense."

Dun and yellow desert, scattered with crumbling yellow-gray rocks and scrubby yellow-brown thorns. Bruise-yellow sky, low yellow clouds. Even the men's skin and clothes turning yellow, stained with sweat and sand. So bloody hot Tobias's vision seemed yellow. Dry and dusty and yellow as bile and old bones. The Yellow Empire. The famous golden road. The famous golden light.

"If I spent the rest of my life knee-deep in black mud, I think I'd die happy, right about now," said Gulius, and spat into the yellow sand.

Rate sniggered. "And you can really see how they made all that money, too. Valuable thing, dust. Though I'm still kind of clinging to it being a refreshing change from cow manure."

"Yeah, I've been thinking about that myself, too. If this is the heart of the richest empire the world has ever known, I'm one of Rate's dad's cows."

"An empire built on sand...Poetic, like."

"'Cause there's so much bloody money in poetry."

"They're not my dad's cows. They're my cousin's cows. My dad just looks after them."

"Magic, I reckon," said Alxine. "Strange arcane powers. They wave their hands and the dust turns into gold."

"Met a bloke in Alborn once, could do that. Turned iron pennies into gold marks."

Rate's eyes widened. "Yeah?"

"Oh, yeah. Couldn't shop at the same place two days running, mind, and had to change his name a lot..."

They reached a small stream bed, stopped to drink, refill their water-skins. Warm and dirty with a distinct aroma of goat shit. After five hours of dry marching, the feel of it against the skin almost as sweet as the taste of it in the mouth.

Running water, some small rocks to sit on, two big rocks providing a bit of shade. What more could a man want in life? Tobias went to consult with Skie.

"We'll stop here a while, lads. Have some lunch. Rest up a bit. Sit out the worst of the heat." If it got any hotter, their swords would start to melt. The men cheered. Cook pots were filled and scrub gathered; Gulius set to preparing a soupy porridge. New boy Marith was sent off to dig the hole for the latrine. Tobias himself sat down and stretched out his legs. Closed his eyes. Cool dark shadows and the smell of water. Bliss.

"So how much further do you think we've got till we get there?" Emit asked.

Punch someone, if they asked him that one more time. Tobias opened his eyes again with a sigh. "I have no idea. Ask Skie. Couple of days? A week?"

Rate grinned at Emit. "Don't tell me you're getting bored of sand?"

"I'll die of boredom, if I don't see something soon that isn't sand and your face."

"I saw a goat a couple of hours back. What more do you want? And it was definitely a female goat, before you answer that."

They had been marching now for almost a month. Forty men, lightly armed and with little armor. No horses, no archers, no mage or whatnot. No doctor, though Tobias considered himself something of a dab hand at field surgery and dosing the clap. Just forty men in the desert, walking west into the setting sun. Nearly there now. Gods only knew what they would find. The richest empire the world had ever known. Yellow sand.

"Not bad, this," Alxine said as he scraped the last of his porridge. "The lumps of mud make it taste quite different from the stuff we had at breakfast."

"I'm not entirely sure it's mud..."

"I'm not entirely sure I care."

They bore the highly imaginative title The Free Company of the Sword. An old name, if not a famous one. Well enough known in certain select political circles. Tobias had suggested several times they change it.

"The sand gives it an interesting texture, too. The way it crunches between your teeth."

"You said that yesterday."

"And I'll probably say it again tomorrow. And the day after that. I'll be an old man and still be picking bloody desert out of my gums."

"And other places."

"That, my friend, is not something I ever want to have to think about."

Everything reduced to incidentals by the hot yellow earth and the hot yellow air. Water. Food. Water. Rest. Water. Shade. Tobias sat back against a rock listening to his men droning on just as they had yesterday and the day before that and the day before that. Almost rhythmic, like. Musical. A nice predictable pattern to it. Backward and forwards, backward and forwards, backward and forwards. The same thinking. The same words. Warp and weft of a man's life.

Rate was on form today. "When we get there, the first thing I'm going to do is eat a plate of really good steak. Marbled with fat, the bones all cracked to let the marrow out, maybe some hot bread and a few mushrooms to go with it, mop up the juice."

Emit snorted. "The richest empire the world has ever known, and you're dreaming about steak?"

"Death or a good dinner, that's my motto."

"Oh, I'm not disputing that. I'm just saying as there should be better things to eat when we get there than steak."

"Better than steak? Nothing's better than steak."

"As the whore said to the holy man."

"I'd have thought you'd be sick of steak, Rate, lad."

"You'd have thought wrong, then. You know how it feels, looking after the bloody things day in, day out, never getting to actually sodding eat them?"

"As the holy man said to the whore."

Tiredness was setting in now. Boredom. Fear. They marched and grumbled and it was hot and at night it was cold, and they were desperate to get there, and the thought of getting there was terrifying, and they were fed up to buggery with yellow dust and yellow heat and yellow air. Good lads, really, though, Tobias thought. Good lads. Annoying the hell out of him and about two bad nights short of beating the crap out of each other, but basically good lads. He should be kind of proud.

"The Yellow Empire."

"The Golden Empire."

"The Sunny Empire."

"Sunny's nice and cheerful. Golden's a hope. And Yellow'd be good when we get there. In their soldiers, anyway. Nice and cowardly, yeah?"

Gulius banged the ladle. "More porridge, anyone? Get it while it's not yet fully congealed."

"I swear I sneezed something recently that looked like that last spoonful."

"A steak...Quick cooked, fat still spitting, charred on the bone...Mushrooms...Gravy...A cup of Immish gold..."

"I'll have another bowl if it's going begging."

"Past begging, man, this porridge. This porridge is lying unconscious in the gutter waiting to be kicked hard in the head."

A crow flew down near them cawing. Alxine tried to catch it. Failed. It flew up again and crapped on one of the kit bags.

"Bugger. Good eating on one of them."

"Scrawny-looking fucker though. Even for a crow."

"Cooked up with a few herbs, you wouldn't be complaining. Delicacy, in Allene, slow-roasted crow's guts. Better than steak."

"That was my sodding bag!"

"Lucky, in Allene, a crow crapping on you."

"Quiet!" Tobias scrambled to his feet. "Something moved over to the right."

"Probably a goat," said Rate. "If we're really lucky, it'll be that female goa—"

The dragon was on them before they'd even had a chance to draw their swords.

Big as a cart horse. Deep fetid marsh rot snot shit filth green. Traced out in scar tissue like embroidered cloth. Wings black and white and silver, heavy and vicious as blades. The stink of it came choking. Fire and ash. Hot metal. Fear. Joy. Pain. There are dragons in the desert, said the old maps of old empire, and they had laughed and said no, no, not that close to great cities, if there ever were dragons there they are gone like the memory of a dream. Its teeth closed ripping on Gulius's arm, huge, jagged; its eyes were like knives as it twisted away with the arm hanging bloody in its mouth. It spat blood and slime and roared out flame again, reared up beating its wings. Men fell back screaming, armor scorched and molten, melted into burned melted flesh. The smell of roasting meat surrounded them. Better than steak.

Gulius was lying somehow still alive, staring at the hole where his right arm had been. The dragon's front legs came down smash onto his body. Plume of blood. Gulius disappeared. Little smudge of red on the green. A grating shriek as its claws scrabbled over hot stones. Screaming. Screaming. Beating wings. The stream rose up boiling. Two men were in the stream trying to douse burning flesh and the boiling water was in their faces and they were screaming too. Everything hot and boiling and burning, dry wind and dry earth and dry fire and dry hot scales, the whole great lizard body scorching like a furnace, roaring hot burning killing demon death thing.

We're going to die, thought Tobias. We're all going to fucking die.

Found himself next to pretty new boy Marith, who was staring at it mesmerized with a face as white as pus. Yeah, well, okay, I'll give it to you, bit of a thing to come back to when you've been off digging a hole for your superiors to shit in. Looked pretty startled even for him. Though wouldn't look either pretty or startled in about ten heartbeats, after the dragon flame grilled and decapitated him.

If he'd at least try to raise his sword a bit.

Or even just duck.

"Oh gods and demons and piss." Tobias, veteran of ten years' standing with very little left that could unsettle him, pulled up his sword and plunged it two-handed into the dragon's right eye.

The dragon roared like a city dying. Threw itself sideways. The sword still wedged in its eye. Tobias half fell, half leaped away from it, dragging Marith with him.

"Sword!" he screamed. "Draw your bloody sword!"

The dragon's front claws were bucking and rearing inches from his face. It turned in a circle, clawing at itself, tail and wings lashing out. Spouted flame madly, shrieking, arching its back. Almost burned its own body, stupid fucking thing. Two men went up like candles, bodies alight; a third was struck by the tail and went down with a crack of bone. Tobias rolled and pulled himself upright, dancing back away. His helmet was askew, he could see little except directly in front of him. Big writhing mass of green dragon legs. He went into a crouch again, trying to brace himself against the impact of green scales. Not really much point trying to brace himself against the flames.

A man came in low, driving his sword into the dragon's side, ripping down, glancing off the scales but then meeting the softer underbelly as the thing twisted up. Drove it in and along, tearing flesh. Black blood spurted out, followed by shimmering white and red unraveling entrails. Pretty as a fountain. Men howled, clawed at their own faces as the blood hit. And now it had two swords sticking out of it, as well as its own intestines, and it was redoubling its shrieking, twisting, bucking in circles, bleeding, while men leaped and fell out of its way.

"Pull back!" Tobias screamed at them. "Get back, give it space. Get back!" His voice was lost in the maelstrom of noise. It must be dying, he thought desperately. It might be a bloody dragon, but half its guts are hanging out and it's got a sword sunk a foot into its head. A burst of flame exploded in his direction. He dived back onto his face. Found himself next to new boy Marith again.

"Distract it!" Marith shouted in his ear.

Um...?

Marith scrambled to his feet and leaped.

Suddenly, absurdly, the boy was balanced on the thing's back. Clung on frantically. Almost falling. Looked so bloody stupidly bloody small. Then pulled out his sword and stabbed downwards. Blood bursting up. Marith shouted. Twisted backward. Fell off. The dragon screamed louder than ever. Loud as the end of the world. Its body arched, a gout of flame spouted. Collapsed with a shriek. Its tail twitched and coiled for a few long moments. Last rattling tremors, almost kind of pitiful and obscene. Groaning sighing weeping noise. Finally it lay dead.

A dead dragon is a very large thing. Tobias stared at it for a long time. Felt regret, almost. It was beautiful in its way. Wild. Utterly bloody wild. No wisdom in those eyes. Wild freedom and the delight in killing. An immovable force, like a mountain or a storm cloud. A death thing. A beautiful death, though. Imagine saying that to Gulius's family: he was killed fighting a dragon. He was killed fighting a dragon. A dragon killed him. A dragon. Like saying he died fighting a god. They were gods, in some places. Or kin to gods, anyway. He reached out to touch the dark green scales. Soft. Still warm. His hand jerked back as if burned. What did you expect? he thought. It was alive. A living creature. Course it's bloody soft and warm. It's bloody flesh and blood.

Should be stone. Or fire. Or shadow. It wasn't right, somehow, that it was alive and now it was dead. That it felt no different

now to dead cattle, or dead men, or dead dogs. It should feel…
different. Like the pain of it should be different. He ached the
same way he did after a battle with men. The same way he did
the last time he'd got in a fight in an inn. Not right. He touched
it again, to be sure. Crumble to dust, it should, maybe. Burn up
in a blaze of scented flame.

If it's flesh and blood, he thought then, it's going to fucking
stink as it starts to rot.

There was a noise behind him. Tobias spun round in a panic.
Another dragon. A demon. Eltheia the beautiful, naked on a white
horse.

New boy Marith. Staring at the dragon like a man stares at his
own death. A chill of cold went through Tobias for a moment. A
scream and a shriek in his ears or his mind. The boy's beautiful
eyes gazed unblinking. A shadow there, like it was darker suddenly.
Like the sun flickered in the sky. Like the dragon might twitch
and move and live. Then the boy sighed wearily, sat down in the
dust rubbing at his face. Tobias saw that the back of his left hand
was horribly burned.

"Pretty good, that," Tobias said at length.

"You told me to draw my sword."

"I did."

There was a long pause.

"You killed it," said Tobias.

"It was dying anyway."

"You killed a bloody dragon, lad."

A bitter laugh. "It wasn't a very large dragon."

"And you'd know, would you?"

No answer.

"You killed it, boy. You bloody well killed a bloody dragon.
Notoriously invulnerable beast nobody really believed still existed
right up until it ate their tent-mate. You should be pleased, at least.
Instead, you're sitting here looking like death while Rate and the
other lads try to get things sorted out around here." Wanted to

shake the boy. Moping misery. "At least let me have a look at your hand."

This finally seemed to get Marith's attention. He stared down at his burns. "This? It doesn't really hurt."

"Doesn't hurt? Half your hand's been burned off. How can it not hurt? It's the blood, I think. Burns things. It's completely destroyed my sword. Damn good sword it was, too. Had a real ruby in the hilt and all. Bloke I got it off must have thought it was good too, seeing as I had to kill him for it." Rambled on, trying to relieve his racing mind. At the back of his racing mind this little voice basically just shouting "fuck fuck fuck fuck."

"The blood is acid," Marith said absently. "And boiling hot. Once it's dead it cools, becomes less corrosive." He turned suddenly to Tobias, as if just realizing something. "You stabbed it first. To rescue me. I did nothing, I just stood there."

Absurd how young the boy seemed. Fragile. Weak. Hair like red-black velvet. Eyes like pale gray silk. Skin like new milk and a face like a high-class whore. Could probably pass for Eltheia the beautiful, actually, in the right light. From the neck up at any rate.

Couldn't cook. Couldn't start a fire. Couldn't boil a sodding pot of tea. Could just about use a sword a bit, once someone had found him one, though his hand tended to shake on the blade. Cried a lot at night in his tent. Emit had ten in iron on him one day breaking down crying he wanted his mum. Eltheia the beautiful might have made the better sellsword, actually, in the right light.

"You just stood there. Yeah. So did most of them." And, oh gods, oh yeah, it's the squad commander pep talk coming unstoppably out. Let rip, Tobias me old mucker, like finally getting out a fart: "Don't worry about it. Learn from your mistakes and grow stronger and all that. Then when we next get jumped by a fire-breathing man-eating dragon, you'll be right as rain and ready for it and know exactly what to do."

Marith shook himself. Rubbed his eyes. "I could really, really do with a drink."

Tobias got to his feet. Sighed. Boy didn't even need to ask things directly for you to somehow just do them. A trick in the tone of voice. Those puppy-dog sad eyes. "You're not really supposed to order your squad commander around, boy. And we haven't got any booze left, if that's what you mean. There's water for tea, as long as it's drawn well up river of...that. Seeing as you're a hero and all, I'll go and get you some." He started off toward the camp. "Want something to eat while I'm at it?"

An attempt at drinks and dinner. Get the camp sorted so someone with a particularly iron stomach could get a bit of sleep in that wasn't mostly full of dreams of blood and entrails and your tent-mate's face running off like fat off a kebab. The final butcher's bill on file: Jonar, the man who had hacked the thing's stomach open, had disappeared completely, his body totally eaten away; four others were dead including Gulius; one was dying from bathing in fire and hot steam. Skie finished this last off cleanly by taking off his crispy melted black and pink head. Another four were badly wounded: Tobias suspected two at least would be lucky to survive the night. One, a young man called Newlin who was a member of his squadron, had a burn on his right leg that left him barely able to stand. Tobias had already decided it would be a kindness to knife him at the earliest opportunity. One of the other lads was bound to make a botch of it otherwise.

They'd only lost three men in the last year, and they had largely been the victims of unfortunate accidents. (How could they have known that pretty farmer's daughter had had a pruning hook hidden under her cloak? She hadn't even put up much resistance until that point.) Losing ten was a disaster, leaving them dangerously approaching being under-manned.

Piss poor luck, really, all in all, sitting down for lunch in front of a convenient bit of rock and it happening to have a dragon hiding behind it. Even if it wasn't a very large one.

They were still pitching the tents when Skie's servant Toman appeared. Reported that Skie wanted to see Marith Dragon Killer for a chat.

"Hero's welcome," said Tobias with a grin. Though you never could tell with Skie. Could just be going to bollock the boy for not killing it sooner.

Marith got up slowly. Something like fear in his eyes. Or pain, maybe.

Tobias shivered again. Funny mood, the boy was in.

Chapter Three

Skie's tent was beautiful old leather, well cured, unlike the smelly, greasy cloth things the men slept under, embossed with a design of looping flowers. The colors of the paint still showed in places, even some touches of gold leaf. Looted from somewhere, Marith was certain. Probably part of a lady's hunting pavilion. Although they usually had a little jeweled flag on the top. Skie's had a skeletal hand.

Skie himself was a small, thin man, gray and hard, his head bald. A straggly gray beard, which he'd look much better without, a scar across the bridge of his nose. Nothing exceptional, until he moved, and you saw he had lost his left arm at the elbow. Marith looked down at the ragged burns on his own left hand.

"So." Skie fixed him with cold eyes. "The dragon killer himself. I suppose we all owe you our lives." He gestured to Marith to sit down opposite him outside the tent entrance. "Rather more than I assumed you were capable of when I first encountered you, I must admit. Out of interest, how'd you know where to stab it?"

"I know how to kill dragons."

"That seems unarguable. I was asking how you knew. Not a common piece of knowledge."

"I'd have thought that was obvious."

Skie made a snorting sound, possibly a laugh. "You're either a very determined liar or the worst fool I have ever met, dragon killer. And watch how you speak around me, lad." Marith shrank for a moment under his gaze. The dark eyes stared at him, measuring him. Mocking him. The look his father used to give him. Judging. Knowing. Scornful. Don't judge me, he thought bitterly. You've not exactly made much of life yourself, from the look of you.

There was a small leather book on the ground between them, very old, battered and ripped in places, the thick leather cover faded to an indeterminate shade of brown-green-gray. Skie licked his fingers, began thumbing through it carefully. Some of the tension between them released; Marith looked at the book with interest, breathing in its musty scent. A memory: curling into a chair with a pile of old books, stories, poems, histories, travelogs. Simple pleasures. Good, honest things. He shook his head and the memory faded. At least the geography might finally start coming in useful, he thought. Almost laughed in pain.

Skie expertly manipulated the book with his one hand until he found the right page. He produced a pen and an ink stone from his pack. Licked the pen to begin.

"What is it?" Marith asked.

The gray face creased in an angry frown. "You don't ask questions of your commander, boy. You need to remember that. Speak when spoken to. Otherwise, shut up and obey. It's a record of the company's more notable deeds. Battles won, cities looted, that kind of thing. It's not been written in much in the last few years. 'Small village pillaged, two old men killed' isn't exactly the stuff of legends. The Long Peace hasn't been kind to the likes of us. But I think a dragon and a dragon killer deserve noting."

Skie's writing was blotchy, the careful, uncertain script of a man who was only semi-literate. Though, actually, thinking about it, that was perhaps unfair. Perhaps impressive he could write at all, especially one-handed. Marith's own hand itched with impatience watching the shaky progress of the words across the page.

"*Lundra, twenty-seven Earth,*" said Skie slowly, sounding out every word. Marith pulled his mouth closed over the misspelling of the word "Erth." "*On this day, did Marith, the newest recruit to the noble Company, valiantly slay a dragon in the deserts east of Sorlost. Reward: six iron pennies.* Should be a silver mark, but we're down on provisions and there's nothing to spend it on out here anyway." He smiled coldly at Marith. "Certainly nothing that would interest you, boy. Go and see Toman about the money. He might even give it to you."

I killed a dragon, Marith thought bitterly as he walked back to his own tent. I killed a dragon, you ungrateful old man. You should be thanking all your gods and demons for it. Not laughing at me. There was an itchy feeling in his body, he felt raw and sick. Shut his eyes, breathed deeply. Keep calm, he thought. Just keep calm. Everything will be all right. When he opened his eyes again the light was brilliant, leaving him momentarily blind. Blinked, staring, rubbed at his eyes. It's all right. It'll be all right. It's better than it was. It is. The harsh dun landscape seemed almost unreal. He looked around the encampment. Fires were being tended, more soupy porridge prepared. Someone with more luck than Alxine had caught and butchered a crow and was trading it for tea and salt. Two men sat dicing in the shade of a scrubby thorn tree; another two argued heatedly over the price of a battered cook pot. The six iron pennies were sticky in his hand. He sighed and shoved them into his jacket pocket. There was indeed nothing to spend them on out here.

When he got back to his tent, he found that Alxine had kindly cut him a square of the dragon's skin as a souvenir.

They marched the next morning, walking fast to get as much distance as possible between themselves and the dead dragon. In the morning heat, it had indeed begun to stink, rotten and rancid and with the dry pungency of boiled metal, and had started to draw crows. Insects. Even a scrub eagle. Small corpses now littered the ground around it.

"You'd think they'd have some natural aversion to it," said Rate curiously. "Smelling like that and all. Things round my cousin's farm know to avoid bad meat."

Tobias gestured around at the empty landscape. "Isn't exactly too much to eat around here. Probably desperate for anything with blood in it. Meat smells like meat, if you're hungry enough. Besides"—a grin and a wink at Marith—"I don't suppose they've encountered a dead dragon very often, them being notoriously difficult to kill."

Two more men had died in the night from the unfortunate complication of not being able to walk well enough to keep up with the troop. One of them was Newlin. Marith felt rather sorry for him, especially as they'd been sharing a tent, but perhaps it had been for the best. Also the man had been asleep at the time, so it wasn't like he'd realized what was happening.

Alxine seemed surprisingly upset about it though, his deep copper-colored face dark with concern. "He was a comrade," he said repeatedly. "We shared a tent. He trusted us."

"He wasn't a comrade, he was a member of my squad," said Tobias shortly. "And he was a liability, state his leg was in. It would probably have gone bad anyway. Spared him, like."

True enough. Made more space in the tent, too.

Mid-afternoon, they crested a small hill and found themselves looking down on a small, scrubby village, five houses huddled around a central barn. The largest population center they'd encountered for days now. Several of the men cheered.

After much discussion, Skie sent a handful of men down into the village to buy or trade for provisions. They returned with a particularly scrawny dead goat, a sack of onions and five good-sized clay bottles of something liquid. As nobody in the village spoke Immish, the last five hundred years having apparently entirely passed them by, and almost nobody outside the Empire spoke more than the most basic Literan, its grammar and syntax being possibly the most complex things known to man, the drink's exact nature remained a mystery. It was brownish, frothy and smelled alcoholic so was declared to be beer, though it might equally well have been weed-killer from the taste of it. Though, as far as Marith could see, they were lucky to have managed to acquire anything, the foraging party having been reduced to the well-known language of pointing at their bellies and holding out a couple of coins while shouting "food" and "money" in Immish, Pernish and even Aen. If they were really, really unlucky, the stuff in the bottles was a local cure for the gripe.

"Couldn't buy more," Tobias pointed out to them in the face of grumblings, "village is too big to raid without drawing notice, this near, and it would rather give the game away if we start buying supplies for forty men." He seemed to think for a moment. "Thirty men, I mean."

The probably-beer was carefully divided up between the men in a makeshift wake for the dragon's victims. Disgusting, but surprisingly strong: the small cup Marith had gulped down was making his head feel pleasantly muzzy after several weeks of brackish water and tea. His eyes began to itch again. Breathe, he thought desperately. It's all right. Just breathe. He clenched his hands tightly. Concentrated on the feel of his nails digging into the skin of his palms. Pain. Calm. Breathe.

He must have made some kind of twitching movement, because a couple of the other men turned to look at him.

"You all right, lad?" Alxine asked. Sounded genuinely concerned.

"I'm fine." Clenched his hands more tightly, took a long sip of water.

"Boy can't take the taste of proper beer, that's all," said Emit. He couldn't be more than five years older than Marith. I'll kill him one day, Marith thought. I'd kill him now, if Skie wouldn't have me beheaded for it.

He rubbed his eyes again, harder this time. Pain. Calm. Breathe. Everything will be all right. Just stop thinking these things.

Rate burst out laughing. "Oh, come on, Emit, drop the whole 'real beer' shtick. The stuff tastes like donkey's piss and you know it. Goat's ready, anyone wants some."

"Going begging, is it?"

"Think this goat was past begging long before we started on it. Worse state than the porridge, this goat."

"Delicacy, in Allene, slow-roasted goat guts."

"I'm not entirely sure that's its guts..."

Alxine carved them all portions, serving them elegantly on beds of thin oat porridge flavored with rotten onion. It tasted debatably worse than the beer. "Gods, imagine living out here, drinking donkey piss and eating rancid goat's dick every day of your life," he said cheerfully. "At least we've got violent death to look forward to in a few days' time."

"I think the beer's making you maudlin," said Rate. "Lucky for everyone, it's run out. Anyone know any thank-all-the-gods-I'm-no-longer-drinking songs?"

Such empty things. Pointless. That they could live so fiercely, in the shadow of the certainty of their death. That they could live at all, and feel contentment in it. Marith got up, walked a little away from the others, out into the dark. The air was very cold, pure and dry in his mouth. He breathed it in in great gulps. Stars blazed overhead, a thousand blind eyes. Gods. Beautiful women. Dead souls. The Crescent. The White Lady. The Dragon's Mouth. The Fire Star.

It had been a long time since he'd looked up at the stars like this. He and Carin used to watch them sometimes, lying back side by side on mossy grass or the damp sand of a beach, hands circled together, hair entwined. Carin had known all their names. In the starlight his hair had been pale as ashes. Stars reflected in his eyes.

"There's your star, Marith, and there's mine. Look! And there's the Worm, and the Maiden, and the Crown of Laughing, and that big green one is the Tear. You see it?"

"I see it." Spinning, flickering in his vision, a blizzard of light. His star.

But he mustn't think about Carin.

The weight of the stars felt crushing on his body, the endless remorselessness of them, the sheer number of them. Looking up into them was like a death, an annihilation of the self. The great abyss, yawning over everything. The dark. All there really was was the dark. The one true thing. He could feel it, deep inside his skin. It knows you. Knows what you are. Stared upward, letting his mind empty. Utterly silent, the desert. A man could walk forever out here until he went mad from thirst or loneliness. A man could live out here, in peace, away from everything. Just sit and stare up at the stars until his mind gave way. A man could die out here, slowly, painfully, burned up by the heat of the sun and the dry dust. He pressed his hand into his pocket, where the six iron pennies still sat. I killed a dragon yesterday, he thought. The words exalted him. I killed a dragon.

He walked back toward the campfire. In his tent, he wrapped himself in his cloak and settled down to sleep, gazing up again through the tear in the canvas at the stars. The others were still sitting by the fire talking; he could hear their voices without understanding, as though in delirium or dream. It was strangely comforting. Like being a child again, hearing voices murmuring across the room as he slept.

Woke with a start to the feel of water. He sat up in a confused panic, momentarily uncertain where he was or why his face was wet. His movement woke Alxine, who sat up too, his hand going instinctively for his sword.

"It's only me," Marith hissed. "It's all right."

Alxine muttered something unintelligible, lay down, then sat up again. "What's that sound?" he asked, a note of fear in his voice. They were all on edge, after the dragon.

"Rain. It's rain."

"Rain?"

Astonishingly, gloriously, it was raining. Great, heavy, thick drops of summer rain, warm and fragrant, pounding on the walls of the tent like horses' hooves. Marith crawled out and stood still, letting the water stream down his face and soak into his clothes and hair. Almost dawn: the sky was pale with the light coming. Men stumbled out of their tents, staring at the rain, laughing or cursing where the dust was turning to mud beneath them. They looked like ghosts in the half-light, veiled by the sheet of water. A little gulley burst into life, water rushing down it, carrying stones with it that knocked together as they went.

Rate leaped out of his tent with a shout of delight. He knelt down by the newly made stream, pouring water over his head and shoulders, threw himself backward, soaking his head and torso, clambering out again a moment later shivering in the cold air but gleaming clean. Some of the other men joined him, so that the stream was filled with shouting, shivering, jostling bodies. Alxine, who had crawled out of the tent grumbling at the noise, stood and watched them with a grin.

"You're not going to bathe?" Marith asked him. After time spent sharing a tent, the idea of Alxine washing was remarkably appealing. The great advantage of Newlin dying was that there'd been a bit more space last night between his head and Alxine's feet.

"Maybe once they're done." Alxine retreated under the cover of the tent, lay down wrapped in his cloak. "Rain madness, the desert folk call it." He shook his head. "Never thought I'd see grown men so excited about getting wet."

The sun rose, and plants began to unfold in the desert. The thorn bushes unraveled, releasing tiny green leaves soft as kittens' ears; coarse patches of sickly yellow delft grass put forth brilliant pink flowers with crimped edges like torn silk. A flock of jewel-green birds descended to bathe and drink in the puddles. Insects burst out from the cracked earth, iridescent beetles the size of a man's thumb, yellowish grasshoppers with huge brown eyes. Even a couple of small dark-colored frogs that splashed frantically in the shallows of the pool.

Marith stared at it all in wonder. So much life. So much life in this dead place. The air smelled of life. The stream sang of life. The sky was luminous with life, colorless, liquid. He felt a wild peaceful happiness inside him, like when he was a child, standing on a high rock looking down into the sea, arms raised aloft in triumph.

"*Emmna therelen, mesereth meterelethem
Isthereuneth lei*

Isthereuneth hethelenmei lei.
Interethne memestheone memkabest
Sesesmen hethelenmei lei.
In the midst of the desert,
You came to me like water,
Your face gazing, like water.
So quickly my love came, like flowers," he said quietly.

"You what?" said Alxine with a start and a stare at him. "What was that you just said?"

"Maran Gyste. The opening lines of *The Silver Tree*. The original Literan, then Daljian's translation. It just seemed...appropriate."

"Oh." Alxine shook his head. He thought for a moment. "It's meant to sound dirty, I assume?"

Marith laughed. "You should read the later bits."

The light shimmered around him, the sand like new silver, the air clean as glass. One day, he thought. One day it will all burn, and there'll be no more living.

When they made camp that evening, Skie ordered proper watches set and kept to. They'd not bothered, previously, so deep in the desert, letting two or three men guard the entire troop. Now there were to be three shifts of five, and a proper guard kept while they marched. No fires lit, not even a small one for a kettle of tea. From this alone, it was clear that they were approaching their destination. The great disadvantage of campaigning in the desert: smoke or fire, even the flash of reflected light on polished metal, would show for miles. Caught out here, such a small body of men would be annihilated. Nowhere to run even if you ran: without water, a man would survive two days, perhaps three; without cover, he would be spotted and hunted down. Sound, too, carried astonishingly—anyone within twenty miles must have heard the dragon attack like a thunderstorm—so they were ordered to march and camp in near silence, communicating by gestures, voices whispering in each other's ears. It would be a long, dark couple of nights from now on.

It surprised Marith more than he had realized how cheerfully the men accepted the new regime. Where the previous night they had been an unruly huddle, grousing about the size of their portions of beer, singing and joking, then shouting and whooping in the fresh cold water that morning, cheerfully ignoring Skie's angry shouts that it was potential suicide to swim in a storm channel, now they were silent, disciplined, uncomplaining. He understood for the first time that they truly were hardened soldiers, men who would follow Skie's command to the letter unthinkingly, men who would kill at Skie's word.

Strange, it felt, to see that in them. To understand that. The power something held over them, that Skie could lead them to that and they would obey.

They ate a dinner of raw oats soaked in cold water, augmented with scraps of meat and cheese. Neither exactly improved by having got soaking wet and then dried out again. Drank cold water with a few tea leaves floating in it "for flavor." Amazing how quickly you could miss rancid goat and vile beer. There was only a sliver of moon, thin clouds obscuring the stars: they crawled into their tents in silence by feel and memory, blind like birds in the dark. Marith simply lay down to sleep fully dressed rather than struggle out of his clothing. It wasn't like he hadn't had plenty of practice sleeping in his clothes.

It took him a long time to fall asleep, staring into the night through the rent in the canvas. He could hear Alxine breathing hoarsely, the sound hypnotic and loud as a heartbeat. Other than that there was silence, an awful empty silence broken by the occasional cry of some night creature, sad and angry and wild. Marith shivered. His skin and eyes itched. When we get there, he thought suddenly, when we get there, I have six iron pennies to spend. There would be things there that would interest him. The thought comforted him, some of the fear drained out of him. He lay awake trying to force himself to sleep before he had to wake up. He would probably be dead in a few days. It would be nice to get some sleep in first.

＊　　＊　　＊

He must have slept, because suddenly Tobias was in the tent, waking him for the dawn watch. It was utter, pitch black. The stars had disappeared completely, hidden by thicker clouds. Marith flailed around trying to collect himself and scramble out of the tent, tripped over Alxine who cursed him. They crawled out into the cold air, trying to see in the dark. It reminded Marith of playing blind man's catch as a child, a thick velvet scarf bound over his face. The claustrophobia of seeing nothing, like being dead—he had screamed once, playing it, and his brother had laughed at him. The stars frightened him but he wished they would come back, so that he could see something. Pretend something was there. He put his hand to his pocket, trying to cling to the feeling of security he had felt. Six iron pennies to spend. But it was so dark now. The darkness pressed on his shoulders, smothering him. Calling him. Knowing him. His eyes itched so much that his hands shook and he clawed at the skin of his face.

And then finally he saw the light coming up in the east, the sun rising, the sky changing from black to soft deep blue. In the west the clouds blew over so that stars appeared, the last stars of the early morning, the Maiden, the Dog, the Tree; the Fire Star that burned even in the full light of day. A soft pink sun blossomed in the sky like the delft grass flowers unfolding. He turned his face to it, tears running down his face, because it was beautiful and alive.

After breakfast, they lined up for orders, Skie standing to address them. "We're approaching the city now." He had the trick of keeping his voice low but clearly audible, a good voice for battle commands. It was deep, rather pleasant, a nice low bass. Marith thought: I wonder if he can sing. "Another two days or so now. As I said last night, from now on it gets serious. The desert's safe: it's virtually uninhabited—"

"Except for a bloody dragon," Rate muttered.

"—not well traveled; anyone coming, we can see them. The desert stops, now. We get to good-sized villages, towns, farmlands.

Soldiers on maneuvers, local watches. People. Thirty armed men aren't exactly inconspicuous. You know all this." Skie nodded at them. "You've done this kind of thing before. We've done this kind of thing before.

"We'll be splitting into the different squadrons, taking different routes in. We leave the tents here." There was a chorus of half-ironic cheers. "If we can come back for them, we will. I'd like to come out the way we came in to pick them up. But the payment includes money for new.

"If anyone is caught, you're on your own. You're a small band of laborers looking for work in the city. Villagers turfed off your land by your local bigwig and thinking the streets of the Golden Empire are still paved with gold. Thieves. Murderers. Wandering bloody musicians for all I care. What matters is that you're alone, and know nothing about any other groups of men on the roads. Got it?"

The men nodded, rumbled acknowledgment. Skie dismissed them and tramped back to his tent, signaling to the squadron leaders to join him. The men fell to sorting and stowing the gear, organizing small travel packs, engaging in a final buying, selling and bartering of oddments and goods. A large pit was dug in the sand. It was carefully lined with the tent cloths, then the tent poles were carefully arranged above. Skie's tent and its meager contents went in last, before another layer of tent cloth and a final covering of sand. A stone was placed on top as a marker.

Marith thought: it looks like a grave.

"We'll never come back here to get it, of course," said Alxine cheerfully. "And even if we do, some bastard will be bound to have moved the stone. But it keeps you hopeful, pretending we'll be picking them up again anytime soon."

They began moving out, very small against the great expanse of desert. Heading down into the farmlands, the townlands, the fields and houses, the human world.

Heading down into the great city, the undying, the eternal, the city of dreams, Sorlost the Golden, the most beautiful, the unconquered, the unconquerable, the decaying capital of the decayed remnant of the richest empire the world had ever known.

Marith rubbed his eyes, and sighed, and walked slowly. Tobias walked slowly beside him, watching his face.

Somewhere far off in the distance, something that might have been a hawk screamed.

Chapter Four

The Imperial Palace of the Asekemlene Emperor of the Sekemleth Empire of the eternal city of Sorlost the Golden is clad in white porcelain. Its towers are gilt in silver, its great central dome in gold. Its windows are mage glass, shining like sunrise. Its courtyards are hung with yellow satin, its balconies are carved of gems. Its gates are ivory and whalebone and onyx and red pearl. Its walls enclose lush silent gardens of lilac trees where green flightless birds dart and sing. Tall marble columns create cool loggias, opening onto perfumed lakes to form shaded bathing places of pale sand and dark water, purple irises and silver fish. Lawns run down to tangled bushes with flowers that smell like human skin. Apples and apricots and cimma fruit grow in profusion, perfect and uneaten; when the trees are not in season, servants in black turbans hang brightly painted wooden fruits from their boughs. The fruits were jeweled, once, but these were sold or stolen long ago. It is commonly known as the Summer Palace, though there is no Winter Palace and never has been one. Sorlost is a city without seasons: perhaps some ancient incarnation of the Emperor in the youth of empire once thought it fitting of his status to make a differentiation that is not needed and cannot indeed exist. Perhaps a Winter Palace was planned, once, before time passed too quickly and money was borrowed that could not be repaid and building works were delayed and abandoned and forgotten, in the richest empire the world has ever known.

A beautiful building. Sorrow radiates off it, and corruption, and hope. The center and symbol of an empire of dreaming, where men live in the dry desert and count their meaning only in gold. An absurdity. Of course an absurdity. An Emperor who rules forever, in a palace built on sand. A thing sacred to eternity, dead and rotted, encrusted with dust. A hive of insects crawling to achieve divinity, the sublime pointlessness of absolute rule. No one cares. No one wonders. Time ceases. Dust settles. The Empire and the Emperor and their servants go on.

This is Sorlost, the eternal, the Golden City. The most beautiful, the first, the last. The undying. The unconquered. The unconquerable.

The mummified heart of an empire of dust and desert villages, half forgotten by half the world.

In a small room at the top of one of the silver towers, two men were talking. The room was furnished in green and silver, small round windows giving a view of the whole sprawling city beneath. The pale evening sky already lit with the first stars. In the west the sky would be fading crimson. Such melancholy! And always a perilous time, this borderline between the realms of life and death. The younger of the two men shivered despite the heat. A rational man, but he hated the dusk. A bell tolled, the room sat still and tense, then the bell tolled again. Night comes, he thought. We survive. The room seemed immediately darker. Shadows falling in the corners, twisting on the green-gray walls.

On one wall, a map caught the lamplight, the world picked out in a mosaic of tiny gems. The Sekemleth Empire gold and yellow diamonds. Immish looming over them to the east, its borders shiny bright. Allene to the south smiling peacefully. Chathe and Theme squatting west and north. Immier a sad empty whiteness, Ith in shadow, the Wastes done in floor scrapings, Illyr carefully hidden behind a lamp sconce. The rich terrifying lumps of the White Isles at the far eastern edge glaring over at them all.

The younger man looked at the map. Shivered again. Looked away.

A joke, that this room was where they were meeting. That damned map staring at them.

"A cup of wine?" the older man asked him. Without waiting for an answer, he poured pale wine from a crystal bottle into two porcelain cups. He was pale like the wine and dressed in silk. His hair was gray and receding, thin curls clinging to the sides of his head; his eyes pouched and tired, his nose long and broad. His hands were delicate, small in proportion to his wide body, bitten fingertips above several large old rings. His hands shook slightly as he placed the bottle back on the table.

The younger man was dark-skinned and slender, his hair long and black, his eyes brown. He took a small sip from his cup. "It's an excellent wine," he said.

"You think so? I personally find it a little dry. It's fifty years old, the estate no longer produces, I'm afraid. The cask was originally broached for the Emperor's birthday, but he didn't like it. Bad taste, I'd say. But what does one expect from a man brought up by fishmongers?"

"That his adviser should have corrected his tastes better?"

"How can they? He knows everything about taste, having such a superb knowledge of all possible varieties of dried fish."

"Yes, yes, of course. Very witty. Let's assume I've now made a pointed suggestive response. So can we just come to the point, please, Tam?"

The older man, Tamlath Rhyl, Lord of the Far Waters, Dweller in the House of the Sun in Shadow, Nithque of the Ever Living Emperor and the Undying City, the Emperor's True Counselor and Friend, smiled blandly. "There's always a point, Orhan. If you think about it." He pushed his cup aside and spread his hands on the table, rings glittering. "Very well, then. You are of course quite correct, I did not ask you here simply to compare tasting notes. Or indeed to discuss the failings of the current incarnation of His Eternal Eminence, oenologically or otherwise. Ten years,

I've held this post. Ten years! And now March Verneth is dripping poison in the Emperor's ear. We can't wait, Orhan. We need to make it happen now."

The younger man, Orhan Emmereth, Lord of the Rising Sun, Dweller in the House of the East, the Emperor's True Counselor and Friend, sighed. "We've been over this, Tam. We can't make it happen any quicker. It's not exactly easy as it is."

"If March persuades the Emperor to dismiss me—"

"If March persuades the Emperor to dismiss you, it hardly matters. We'll just reappoint you afterward."

"March—"

"March is an irrelevance." The younger man, Orhan Emmereth, Lord of the Rising Sun, thought: Your post is an irrelevance. We're all irrelevant. That's why we're doing this. You still don't see that, do you? He tried to keep his irritation out of his voice. "The Immish have raised another troop levy. Another five thousand men. Who gets to hold your titles is of no concern if the city's burning." You haven't managed to persuade anyone in the palace to do anything except laugh, he thought. Your great power and authority as Nithque! So it hardly matters whether you hold on to your power or not. As I would have thought was obvious. A wise man who's ignored is about as effective as an idiot who's listened to.

"All the more reason to act more quickly, then," said Tam waspishly.

"Quickly, yes. Too quickly, no. The last thing we want is chaos."

Tam sipped his wine. "Sometimes I still wonder whether this is even real, Orhan. Anything more than your mind looking for excitement and a desire for something to interest you since Darath... well... Oh, don't frown like that! Twenty years, the Long Peace has held. Why would the Immish be looking to cause trouble now? And even if they are, why should it be directed at us?" His eyes flicked to the map on the wall. "Surely one of their northern borders—Theme, say, or Cen Andae."

Orhan sighed. Because they can. Because they see no reason not to. Because they've finally looked at the graveyard of our Empire with open eyes. Because they're fools and madmen and like the art of war. Because their children go hungry and we piss gold and jewels into the dust.

"Twenty thousand troops, now, they've raised in two years... Don't you feel it, Tam?" he said after a moment. "A new mood coming? You hear the same things I do. A fight in Gray Square between apprentice boys and Immish caravan guards, four men killed. The Immish were mocking us, the apprentice boys said. Mocking our fidelity to the God. Three of our merchants stoned to death in Alborn, accused of false trade."

"And a firewine drunk stood in the center of the Court of the Fountain yesterday and proclaimed himself the true incarnation of the Emperor, before his drinking companion knifed him in the heart. These things happen, Orhan. You're oversensitive."

"God's knives, Tam, it's a bit late to start questioning things now, isn't it?"

Tam smiled again. "Oh, I'm not questioning anything, Orhan. Just suggesting you look at your own motives for what you're doing, and why." He drained his cup. "Another drink? As I said, fifty years old and the estate no longer produces. A shame to waste it."

"I'm fine, thank you."

"You're sure? Yes? You refuse to move the timetable up, then? Even by a few days?"

Orhan sighed again. "A few days. Just a few days. No more."

"Now you sound like a fish merchant. Shall we start haggling over the price again?" Tam refilled both their cups anyway and sipped from his. "You always look so morally aggrieved, Orhan. This was your idea, remember, not mine. You only brought me in to hide your own squeamishness. Someone else to blame." He bent forward, drawing his head closer to Orhan. Old man smell on his breath beneath the wine. Sour and fat. "I'll tell you something, Orhan. Something I know. Something the Emperor doesn't. You're quite right. The Immish are planning something." A smile and a wink, the small chewed hands moving. "Does that make you feel any better about it all?"

Orhan started. "What?"

"Oh, just March. Irrelevance that he is. He's had...meetings. With someone who I have it on very good authority is a close agent of the Immish High Council. Money has been exchanged. Promises of aid. He wants more than my role as Nithque, I should think. The Immish want more than to give it to him, I should also think."

"What authority? You have proof?"

The small hands moved again. Lamplight flashed on the rings. Thin curls bobbed as the old man's head shifted. "My dear Orhan, I know the man is an agent of the Immish High Council because he's been paying me for years as such. Ah, don't look so shocked! He could have been paying you too, if you'd let yourself be open to such things. As you know perfectly well. He's probably been paying March for years too. But recently he started paying him a lot more."

Orhan looked at him. Angry. Humiliated. All this dancing around, even though they were on the same side, seeking the same ends. He frowned and drank his wine. "A week, then. We'll bring the timetable forward by one week. No more."

"I knew you'd see sense."

"If you'd started this conversation telling me that..."

Tam drained his cup and rose. Pale silk swirled around him, making the lamp flicker, as though a moth had flown into its flames. "But that wouldn't have been how we do this, would it, Orhan? You had to decide for yourself, not because I asked you to. It's your idea, remember, not mine. What I know or don't know is...irrelevant."

"I am aware it's my idea, Tam, thank you." Impossible to forget, indeed. Might as well engrave it in letters of fire over his bed. Orhan sipped his wine. It was too dry, now he'd had a couple of cups of it. Tam could probably have chosen better, if he didn't believe quite so much in thrift.

"I'll be leaving then. You're going to March's party, I assume?"

"It seems a good idea, in the circumstances." Though he'd rather not. But he'd better, now. "Are you?"

Tam sniffed. "I wasn't invited. March is so pathetically crude one could almost laugh. Watch out for Immish agents and don't eat anything someone else hasn't eaten first. Keep alert to things. Signs and portents, since you seem so keen on them. Firewine drunks. Dreams. And do give March my regards." He pushed open the door and went out in a rustle of cloth. "Enjoy yourself."

Hot, scented air, spices and lilac flowers. A fluttering of wings as a flock of ferfews darted overhead, flashing brilliant green wings. White stone gleamed in the moonlight. A woman laughing in a tinkle of bells.

Orhan walked quickly, his guards following him with drawn knives. Amlis, red and sandy; Sterne, dark-skinned and tall with vivid blue eyes. Amlis had obviously passed the time at the palace cajoling the kitchen maids: his breath smelled of raw onions and there was a grease stain on his shirt. House Emmereth. Such style. Such sophistication. Such beauty and elegance in a city of dreams.

He should probably change himself, really, put on something a bit more elaborate, wash off the dust. But he really couldn't be bothered. The streets were full of dust anyway. He'd only get dirty again.

In the Court of the Fountain, two young men were fighting. A handful of spectators leaned against the wide marble bowl of the fountain, cheering on one or the other. A street seller wandered among them, holding out a tray of preserved lemons. Orhan stopped to watch. The spectators seemed to favor the taller of the two men: he was certainly the better looking, his skin smooth black, his hair deep gold, shining in the torchlight. His opponent was his opposite, fair skin and dark hair, shorter and stockier. Both were dressed in fine white silks. They were real street blades, then, not simply bored young men quarreling. White was the color men wore when they were serious about fighting. It showed up every scratch of the knife.

The dark-haired man made a powerful lunge and knocked the golden-haired man backward. Blood gushed up from golden-hair's right leg and the audience groaned. With a curse, he went down on one knee for a moment, then rallied and lashed out at dark-hair. Dark-hair skittered back out of reach, sending several spectators running. He was the stronger and technically the better fighter. Golden-hair had more grace and flair, a more elegant turn of his body. But golden-hair was more likely to die. Obviously limping now, his face pained.

Dark-hair lunged again and again golden-hair stumbled backward. He was panting, sweating heavily. Those watching began to mutter. Disappointed. They obviously wanted golden-hair to win. Golden-hair stepped back several paces, trying to give himself room to recover and breathe. Dark-hair pressed forward, sensing his opponent's weakness and growing fear. Knife blades crashed heavily into each other as the two men closed again. They grappled together for a long moment, then with a cry dark-hair broke backward as golden-hair somehow managed to twist sideways and strike out hard with his left fist. A cheer rang out from the audience. Golden-hair seemed to rally at the sound and brought his knife down, slicing at dark-hair's arm. The audience cheered again as dark-hair stumbled. Blood was streaming down from his elbow to his wrist and he struggled to raise his own blade. Grinning, golden-hair struck again. More blood spurted up, not just a scratch wound but brilliant inner blood. Heart blood. Dark-hair muttered something and retreated backward, then roared desperately and flung himself at golden-hair. The audience shouted and clapped as the two tussled together, grunting, panting. Both filthy with blood and grime. There was blood on the ground, making the stone slippery. If either fell, it would be fatal. Not an elegant fight, now. They were too close even for knife work, they wrestled, trying to break the other's grip and set him off balance. Their feet scuffled and sent up the dust.

Suddenly there was a roar and dark-hair reeled backward, his face contorted in pain. Golden-hair leaped on him, his knife flashing, stabbing out and down. The blade bit home into the soft hollow in the throat where the pulse beats. Blood sprayed up. Dark-hair swayed on his feet, his face astonished. Crashed to the ground and lay still.

Golden-hair stood staring, as if he suspected a trick. A pool of blood began oozing out from under dark-hair's body. Dead. Golden-hair panted deeply. Dropped his knife. It clattered onto the worn stones. He raised his hands in victory, turning to acknowledge the crowds around him. They clapped and cheered again. Golden-hair bowed elegantly, then walked off across the square. Another young man, also black-skinned and golden-haired, bent to retrieve his knife and then followed him.

Muttering. The audience began to disperse. Three men exchanged money between them, obviously settling bets. The sweet-seller jingled his tray enthusiastically; one man bought a bag of preserved lemons with his winnings and wandered off chewing, his lips puckered with the taste. They looked like good lemons. Orhan bought a bag and offered one to Amlis. The salt-and-sour might disguise the smell of onions. The rich golden yellow of their skins made him think of the victor's hair.

Dark-hair lay in the dust by the fountain in a pool of black blood. Flies were beginning to settle on his body. Without really knowing why he was doing it, Orhan bent down and tucked a silver dhol inside the dead man's shirt. The traditional reward for whatever scavenger removed the body. A dead man's clothes and a silver piece, in exchange for digging a decent grave somewhere outside the city walls. Those who wore white out after dusk in the streets of Sorlost had no one left who would care to bury them for any reason beyond a coin.

"He fought well," said Amlis. "He deserved to win." The bondsman prodded the slumped body with his foot, then swore under his breath as he realized he'd got blood on his shoe. "He should have won."

Sterne shook his head. "The crowd was behind the other. He gave up believing he could win. Decided that his opponent was better, despite knowing it not to be true. He lost because the other was better looking."

That's absurdly melodramatic, Orhan thought. But the truth. He'd judged dark-hair the superior fighter, but he'd have bet on golden-hair even so.

"Are we going on, now, then?" Amlis asked.

Orhan thought for a moment. It was tempting just to return home and go to bed. He'd watched a half-decent fight and bought a bag of excellent preserved lemons. A good night, all told.

"We'll go on," he said at last. The Verneths did indeed need closer watching. Tam was possibly right. Probably right. And perhaps it would give him some comfort, later, if he could convince himself of it. Amlis shrugged and wiped his shoe clean on dark-hair's white silk trousers.

They strolled down the wide sweep of Sunfall and crossed the Court of the Broken Knife. A single pale light flickered beneath the great statue in the center of the square, too small in the dark. A woman sat beside it, weeping quietly. A place where someone was always weeping, the Court of the Broken Knife. We live, Orhan thought, looking at her. We die. For these things, we are grateful. The statue was so old the man it depicted had no name or face, the stone worn by wind and rain to a leprous froth tracing out the ghost of a figure in breastplate and cloak. A king. A soldier. A magelord. An enemy. Even in the old poems, it had no face and no story and no name. Eyeless, it stared up and outward, seeing things that no man living had ever seen. In its right hand the broken knife pointed down, stabbing at nothingness. In its left hand it raised something aloft, in triumph or anger or despair. A woman's head. A helmet. A bunch of flowers. It was impossible to tell.

A man in white circled the square, looking for an opponent. Folly, or bravado, or ignorance: it was ill luck to fight there. A tall woman in a silver dress made wide eyes at Orhan as he passed her, tossing her black hair. Her legs were hobbled with thin cords, giving her a creeping, sinuous movement like a charmed snake. Orhan shook his head gently. Painfully slowly, she crept back across the square to her waiting place. There was a weary look on her face, as if she had been there a long time.

"Pretty," said Amlis.

"Probably diseased," said Sterne. "And look at her face. Keep clear."

"Easy for you to say," Amlis grunted. Sterne shot him a look like daggers. Orhan almost laughed.

"Sterne's right," he said. "Keep clear."

"You'd know, would you? My Lord."

"About disease, yes."

A litter swept past them, shining red silk lit from within by candles. The bearers wore dark clothes and hoods, blurring them into the night so that the body of the litter seemed to float, a glowing red world. Shadows moved and danced on the surface of the silk. Two women, hair loose, one with long trailing sleeves and a headdress that nodded like horses' plumes as she twisted her head. The shadows they cast were distorted by their movements and by the flickering of the candle flames, making them grotesque, tangles of limbs and hands and huge heads. The woman with trailing sleeves raised her arm for a moment and her long fingernails writhed in the light.

"I'd assume they're headed where we're headed," said Amlis.

"Almost certainly."

Twelve or fourteen bearers, six feet square of fine silk. A very expensive means of transport. And remarkably impractical, given the width of some of the city's streets. Lucky for the owner that House Emmereth wasn't in the habit of throwing parties. They'd have to demolish several buildings to get it down Felling Street.

They followed the litter into the courtyard of the House of Silver. It was not large, as such places went, neat and square, without porticoes or columns but faced and roofed entirely in silver, tarnished and murky, mottled with rainbows, light and reflections shifting. A dream of water in the desert. A dream of heat haze. The blurred vision of dusty light. The blazing red of the litter standing before it cast it in soft crimson, beating like a heart.

"Lady Amdelle." Orhan gave a delicate half bow.

"Orhan." Celyse Amdelle, wife of the Lord of the High West,

opened her golden-brown eyes very wide. "How lovely. I really hadn't thought you'd be here. And arriving at just the same time."

Orhan took his sister's arm and they walked toward the open doorway. Amlis disappeared into the servants' quarters; the other woman in the litter, presumably an insignificant Amdelle girl Celyse was trying to marry off, followed them in silence, five paces behind. Celyse walked slowly, her body very erect to support the weight of a headdress of silver wire and tiny mirrors that chimed and glittered as she moved.

"And how's your dear wife?" asked Celyse sweetly. "Not accompanying you? She doesn't seem to go out so much these days. The last time I saw her, she looked horribly tired. Nothing wrong, I trust?"

"She's already here. She's had a bit of a cold, that's all."

"Oh! What a shame for her. I was worried it was something more than that."

"She's neither pregnant nor dying, if that's what you're after. I'd tell you if she were."

"Of course you would. So unfortunate for you, Orhan. You make a marriage of convenience that's really anything but."

Orhan sighed. Poor Bil. "Your own marriage, of course, being so much more successful."

"Oh, I'd say it probably is." Celyse smoothed her dress with long fingers. "I get some happiness out of mine, at least."

Colored light broke onto them as they entered the inner court-yard of the House of Silver. A fire burned in the center of the court, enclosed in a great framework of multi-colored silks that cast shifting patterns of light over the people around it.

"Ahhh," Celyse said with real pleasure, "it's even prettier than my litter." The mirrors of her headdress shone and danced, swirling the colors around her like a cloak. Tasteless, but undeniably striking. She must have found out about it in advance and themed her entire outfit accordingly.

"Something of a fire risk, I'd have thought," Orhan muttered.

Celyse laughed. "Eloise has hired a mage, of course, to control it."

Orhan stared at her. "She's hired a magician to stop her party piece burning down?"

"You make him sound like a cheap conjuror. He works with the craftsman who makes the things, keeping them fire-safe, protecting them. Made my litter: it has bindings in it, to stop it catching if a candle tips. He did a demonstration before I bought it. Eloise is quite charmed by him, she's thinking of keeping him."

The things the high families felt the need to waste money on... Orhan gazed around the courtyard, looking out for friends and enemies. Saw Bil almost immediately, sitting on a low bench on the other side of the court, near the firebox, talking to a young woman with fair hair and a pale face. He ought to at least tell her he was there. He wandered over to her, was half surprised to see her look almost pleased to see him.

"Orhan," Bil said with a bright smile. "What a surprise. Landra: my husband, Lord Orhan Emmereth, Lord of the Rising Sun. Orhan: Lady Landra Relast. Her father is lord of a small rock somewhere in the far east. She only arrived here two days ago. I've promised to show her around a bit."

The woman nodded her head in greeting and they exchanged pleasantries. No, she'd only been here a few days, not seen much of the city yet. Yes, the Great Temple was indeed beautiful, she'd seen that. No, she had no particular purpose being here. Just come to...*nenenthelesal*? "Get away from things"? Was that the right word?

Ah, indeed, Sorlost the Golden, city of dreaming, the greatest city on the face of the earth, where people came to wander around aimlessly, gawp, point, laugh!

Her Literan was poor, heavily accented with the soft bell chimes of Pernish. She was young, only in her mid-twenties, but had a hard, tired look to her. Sorrowful. Orhan had to admire the tact with which she readjusted her face after involuntarily glancing at Bil and then back to him.

Bil is a lovely creature, he thought sadly. If you look beyond the skin. She is almost beautiful. Almost desirable. The cruelty in people's eyes, when they look at her and me. Do I love her despite it? Desire her because of it? Did I marry her for money? Were we plighted at birth? The question was so obvious, there in every eye that looked at them together. Should have it carved on her tomb.

She was dressed exquisitely, as always, in a deep blue gown with a mesh of diamonds in her red hair. Her white arms were bare and painted with spiraling patterns of gold flowers; she wore little gold bells on her wrists that tinkled prettily as she moved her hands. Fingernails an inch long, gilded and studded with pearls.

Yes, she was almost beautiful. Apart from the scars. The gold paint swirled over them, like cracking mud or leprosy. Eruptions of skin. Molten wounds.

If she was Lord Rhyl's wife, the fashion would be for long sleeves and veils and high necks to cover. Or perhaps women would wear false scars, in clay and paint. All the women of Sorlost would copy every detail of the Nithque's wife's costume. But Lady Bilale Emmereth's husband had no power, thus she must be grotesque and pretend she didn't care.

A girl approached with a tray of cups. Orhan took one. Cold wine, mixed with snow. Very refreshing in the heat of the fire. More entirely pointless magery: it must have cost a fortune to transport and store the snow and keep it from melting even when being served. House Verneth was undeniably trying to prove something to someone tonight. Eloise would be melting down gold thalers in the candle flames by midnight, the way things were going. There was a story about an Imperial banquet where the food had been crushed gemstones, mixed with wine and honey to make a thick paste and shaped to resemble fruit, meat, bread. The Emperor had insisted his guests eat their fill, gorging themselves on rubies and diamonds until their guts ached and their mouths were cut and running with blood. The story embodied Sorlost: the great houses shat gold and pissed gems. In the version of the tale Orhan's nurse had told him as a child, the night-soil men had scraped clean the sewers and built themselves great palaces of marble and cedar wood.

Bil fluttered away to stand in the coterie of Eloise Verneth. His sister and her grotesque headdress seemed to have disappeared. The sad-eyed young woman sat silent, watching the shifting colors of the fire-box dance. Orhan sat beside her for a while. The silks fluttered and swirled, alive, spelling out secret words. He thought of the knife-fighter, gleaming black skin and golden hair, the way his eyes had stared as he thrust his blade, the panting breath as he watched his opponent die. The colors beat in his vision, red, green, yellow, blue, red, green, yellow, blue, red, green, yellow, blue, red...

"Mesmeric, isn't it?"

Orhan turned round, startled. The handsome, hawk-nosed face of Darath Vorley looked down at him.

"Mind if I join you?"

"No...no..." His mouth tasted dry. The wine was mildly dosed with hatha syrup, he realized, to enhance the effect of the fire and the colored silks. He had no idea how long he'd been sitting gazing at it. The young woman whose father was lord of a small rock had gone.

Lord Vorley, Lord of All that Flowers and Fades, seated himself beside him and stretched out his legs. Colored light danced on his copper-black skin.

"Please don't tell me you're surprised to see me here," Orhan said after a while. "It's getting repetitive. I'm surprised to see myself here, I don't need constant reminding of it."

"Offended might be a better word. I had a party myself a little while ago. To my inconsolable grief, you didn't attend."

"I was busy." Colored light danced in Darath's gold-black hair.

Darath waved down a passing servant and relieved him of a tray of candied dates. "Want one? Lovely and fat and sticky looking."

"I'm fine." Orhan shook his head, trying to clear it. Really didn't need this right now. Shouldn't have come. Really shouldn't have come.

"You always are. Bloodless bastard." Darath smiled at him lazily, honey on his lips. "So. Been seeing a lot of old Tam, haven't you? I've noticed. So have others." He leaned closer, his breath in Orhan's ear. Made Orhan shiver. "But whatever others might assume, I've been making some enquiries. Purely for political reasons, of course, don't fret yourself. Imperial assassination. Really, Orhan, you have fallen off your pedestal, haven't you?"

They walked away into a corner of the gardens, where the darkness was dimly illuminated by colored mage glass globes. Bats called at the very edge of hearing, sad and painful, hunting white moths with glowing wings. Strings of bells hung between yellow rose trees; Orhan brushed one and it sang like a child's laugh.

"I want in," said Darath.

"Absolutely and completely not. No. No."

"Oh, come on. I know what you're doing. I can guess why. I might as well be involved already, frankly. I just need you to tell me when and how."

"Ask your spies, then. Or better yet, ask mine. They're so badly paid they'll tell you anything for a gold talent."

"A talent? My dear Lord Emmereth, they charged six dhol the last time I asked."

"For six dhol, I'm not sure you should trust a word they said. At that price, I've probably ordered them to tell you a pack of lies then throw the money to the nearest beggar."

"Ah, but they give me special rates. They all know me so well, after all." Their eyes met for a moment, like they were going to start really arguing. Ah, Darath. Moths' wings flickering around his hair. "You don't want me in. Fine. But I'll find out. I might even be forced to take steps against you. Tell someone."

Pause. Orhan's heart pounding. You wouldn't, he thought. You couldn't. Even after everything. No. Please.

"God's knives. I'm sorry." Darath lowered his gaze from Orhan's face. Read things there Orhan wasn't sure he wanted him to see. You're sorry. I'm sorry too. "I didn't mean that. But I want in. In. Come on. I can help you. You know I can. God's knives, you can trust me, Orhan." He looked vaguely embarrassed. "Despite what I just said."

"I'm tired. This isn't exactly a private place to be talking. Neither of us is exactly sober. I really don't want to do this now."

"I'll contribute to the funding, even. You can't ask fairer than that. Don't tell me you couldn't do with some financial support here. You're poor and Tam's a skinflint."

This is turning into a farce, thought Orhan. Change the date, change the cast list, get financial contributions toward it like it's a family wedding and the bride's parents need help with the cost of the food. Shall we just change the target too? It's in motion, Darath. It's all in motion and you want to turn everything upside down because you're bored and nosey and—

He sighed heavily. Knowing he was making a mistake. But whatever way he went, he'd regret it. Why did you have to find out, Darath? You just complicate bloody everything. And it's dangerous. Orhan sipped his drink and felt the hatha further clouding his mind. Shouldn't have come. If he hadn't come...

"Give me a few days to think about it. Then we'll talk again."

"Think about it? I know what you're doing and in a few days I'll know when and how. I'll wager you three thalers I'll know when and how, in fact. And you're hardly going to think about it and say no, are you? Unless you've sunk so low you're planning on knifing me too to keep me from talking."

Orhan shuddered. Don't say that. Not...not like that. Not from you to me. You put it so crudely. There are so many reasons. You know some of them. We used to talk about this, after all. But I don't want to put it on you. Tam can stomach the guilt. Live with it. But not you.

"A few days, Darath." He sighed again and chewed a candied date. Sticky and cloying in his mouth. We eat sweets and drink wine and plan murder in the dark. The pinnacle of urban sophistication. The great cities are built on this. Barbarians come with fire and the sword, yelling obscenities; we smile and sip a drink and laugh as we discuss killing a man.

"A few days. I'll tell you everything in a few days. Once things are settled. Not here."

Darath smiled. "Three thalers says I find out before you tell me."

We are incapable of taking anything seriously, Orhan thought sadly. So inured to everything, we've forgotten a world exists beyond our walls. Darath waved down a servant to get them another drink. Bil flitted past in a tinkle of bells, laughing.

He sipped his wine again, felt lumps and spat. A moth had blundered into his goblet and drowned there. A clear sign he needed to go home.

"Suit yourself." Darath laughed, drank, looked down and fished an insect out of his own cup. "This really wasn't the best place to sit, you know. All your plans thought through?" He licked his fingers. "I'm going on to Faleha's, myself. I'll kiss something pretty for you."

Always knew how to make him hurt.

Chapter Five

A few days later.

Bil was already seated at the table in the breakfast room, eating flatbread topped with almonds and honey. She smiled at Orhan as he joined her. Bread crumbs and beads of honey stuck to the scar tissue erupting from the corner of her mouth. Orhan wondered sometimes if he would ever cease to notice.

The room opened onto the east gardens, one wall a sweet-wood trellis overgrown with jasmine. The flowers were out, the scent almost overpowering. The thick mass of their leaves cast a green tinge to the light, making the room seem smaller and more elegant than it really was, hiding the scuffed floor and the old damp stain on the wall. A pleasant room. Orhan helped himself to an apple from a silver bowl in the center of the table, indicated to the waiting servant girl to bring him some bread. The perfume of the jasmine made the food taste almost flowery. He drank a cup of water drawn from the well in the corner of the garden, a coppery tang to it that lingered in the mouth.

Bil finished eating and dabbed her mouth with a silk napkin. The honey smeared across her scars, gleaming slightly, as though she were dusted with pollen or powdered gold. She wore a loose yellow dress, embroidered with a design of peacock feathers in dark blue and green. Like a hundred little eyes looking at him.

"I need to tell." She looked at him curiously, with a mixture of eagerness and fear. "I'm pregnant."

"Pregnant?" Orhan stared back at her. "You're sure?" he said at last. His heart beating fast.

"As sure as I can be, this early."

"How early?"

"Three months, maybe. It won't be born until well into next year. Around the Emperor's birthday, perhaps, Janush thinks."

One serving girl present, standing inconspicuously in the corner, watching her mistress with big dark eyes. She presumably knew most of Bil's doings, and the nature of his marriage and his and his wife's lives was hardly a secret. But no reason to allow the household too much free rein. A man must have some dignity, in his own home. Orhan waved her away sharply and she retreated beyond the green walls of the jasmine. Sat back in his chair and smiled warmly at Bil.

"Well done, Bilale," he said loudly, addressing the green leaves of the jasmine. "An Emmereth heir."

"You're pleased? Truly?" Bil came over and stood next to him, her face flushed and bright.

As if he didn't have enough to worry about. "Of course I'm pleased." He looked at her gently. Why else did I marry you? his eyes said to her, cool and honest. Why else would I marry at all, yet alone you? The fact that you're rich was useful, of course, but we both know what this marriage is about. Bil got a title that reopened doors closed to her by her disfigurement. He got a wife who expected nothing more from him than his name, and who would magic him up an heir with enough discretion no one would ever know where it came from.

"We should go to the Temple," Bil said. "Give thanks. It's a child sacrifice tonight, so it's propitious."

Orhan frowned. "Is it? Yes, of course, I suppose it must be. If you want, then." If he was going to do this, he'd have to do it properly, no half measures. A child would certainly merit a public show of prayers, and probably a generous offering. He'd need to find the money for a name day feast too, later. An expensive business, children.

"I'll go and change," he said, for need of something to say. He was aware of Bil looking at him, seeing his thoughts in his face. It was odd, how well in some ways she knew him. "You've got some honey around your mouth, you should probably wash it off."

"Janush says I should eat honey every day. To make the baby sweet-tempered." She sounded happy. She wants this baby, Orhan realized. She wants to be a mother and to have a child. She has wanted this for a long time now. She knew him, but he knew so little about her.

They traveled to the Temple in a litter, reclining uncomfortably close to each other behind thin yellow curtains that showed the city beyond like flies in amber, Amlis and Sterne walking before them in the soft blue livery of House Emmereth, knives drawn to clear their path. Sterne's face was fixed and blank. So my parents once traveled, Orhan thought, to give thanks for my birth. So my father's parents, before that. The same streets, the same turnings in the road, old bricks and old stone, old as his family were old, old as Sorlost itself. It gave him an odd kind of start to realize how much he was fulfilling the demands of his history, and how much he was betraying it. The child would be an Emmereth in name, if not in blood, he thought. And what does blood matter? What matters is that it will be strong, and healthy, and born at all. He eyed the ripples of muscle across Sterne's back. Strong...

They came down the Street of Flowers and turned into Gray Square. In itself unimpressive, not large, its flagstones worn. Not even marble, just cheap soft gray stuff that turned greenish in the rain. Cracked and blackened in places, as though they had once been subject to intense heat. A mighty duel was once fought there between two great magelords, grandmothers told their grandchildren, so powerful the stones were melted in the fire of their hate. But the names and the reasons varied, and the story had no basis in truth that Orhan could ever find. The stones were cracked and blackened simply because the square was old. The marketplace and meeting place of a desert village, untouched since the first days of Sorlost. In itself unimpressive, not large, its flagstones worn.

But behind it stood the Great Temple. It too was old. Not old like the square was old, but old like the stars are old. Old like the sea is old. Old like the cut of a knife.

It had stood before Sorlost was a village. It had stood before the desert dried. It had been built by gods, by demons, by dead men quarrying stone with their bare hands. It was vast and terrible, and once a man stared at it he could not stop staring. It gaped like a diseased wound in the center of the city, holy and blind. If a man left Sorlost for a while, he saw it every night in his dreams.

The first inhabitants of Sorlost had built it, or found it, or dreamed it into being, and then they had built their marketplace and their houses and their shops around it, as though it was a human thing. Their descendants had taken a village in the desert and built or dreamed it into an empire. Their descendants in turn had lost an empire and retreated into their dreams. But the Temple still stood as it had always stood. It was the most perfect thing in all Sorlost. Perhaps the most perfect thing in all the world.

A square of black marble, in which blood was shed and the living kept alive.

The litter stopped. The square was crowded, people milling around, merchants and shoppers, street sellers offering flowers and cakes and skewers of roast meat, beggars, a mendicant magician pulling green fire from a young boy's ears, a poet with the hatha sores selling little scrolls of his work. Their arrival attracted a general degree of attention, the fine quality of the litter's silks and the uniforms of the bearers indicating the wealth and status of its occupants even before Bil's shimmering gown and jeweled headdress caught the morning sun. She, at least, was recognizable to some of the onlookers. Might have been the subject of poems herself, if they were not too cruel to write.

As they walked toward the Temple, Orhan realized that he had assured his sister only a few days before that Bil was certainly not pregnant. Mildly vexing. She'd be irritated with him, even think he had lied to her. And disappointed, too: at the moment, her sniveling little son was the de facto Emmereth heir. Please let it be a boy, he thought again. A good strong boy with Sterne's good clean peasant strength.

They mounted the six steps to the doorway of the Temple, so old and worn that they dipped unsteadily in the center, ground away by the tread of endless, countless feet. The great door was closed—was always closed—but moved easily on its pivots as Orhan pushed. Taller than a man, taller than two men standing one on the other's shoulders, but narrow, so that only a single man could walk through at one time. It put one in mind of a great rat-trap, or a blade coming down. Black wood, hard as stone, uncarved, unadorned, the grain dark stripes like animal fur, the knots like watching eyes, like the eyes on Bil's dress. Three long claw marks ran down the door at the height of a man's head.

The door gave onto a long black tunnel, thin and tall as the door itself. Bright light shone at the end of it. The sensation of walking through the narrow dark was stifling, the high ceiling magnifying the sense of oppression, the dead air above a great weight pressing down. Crushing. Drowning. Eating one alive. It could hardly be a long corridor, perhaps ten paces' walk, but it seemed very long. Orhan shuddered, felt Bil shudder too behind him, walking very close to him.

This is what it feels like to die, the thin dark corridor whispered, and then they stepped out into the Great Chamber and the light whispered that this is what it feels like to live.

The Great Chamber of the Great Temple was vast. Its walls and ceiling were lined with bronze tiles, making it shimmer and glitter and burn with light, the light as tangible and oppressive as the dark from which they had come. Orhan thought of the firebox at Eloise's party, of the mirrored facade of the House of Silver, of his sister's red silk litter: they had shone and danced with fire; this was fire, like being in a fire, like being burned. The floor was black stone, worn like the steps with a thousand years of reverential footsteps.

Thousands of candles made the air sweet. They burned in sconces on the walls, on black stone altars, in trailing patterns like dances across the black floor. Hushed voices muttered prayers, the same words repeated over and over. Like birdsong. Like rainfall.

"Dear Lord, Great Tanis Who Rules All Things, from the fear of life and the fear of death, release us," Bil said slowly, bowing her head. Orhan hesitated then took her hand. They walked across the room, their footsteps ringing on the hard floor. A well-dressed young woman kneeling before a small side altar turned and looked at them.

The Lord of the Rising Sun seen publicly holding hands with his wife in the Great Temple. The news would be around the gossip-mongers of the city in the time it took to light a flame.

They approached the High Altar. It was closed off from the rest of the room by a bar of iron that glowed red in the light. Behind this, the High Priestess knelt in prayer. Her black hair hung down around her face, veiling her from prying eyes. A night and a day, she must kneel there, before the evening's sacrifice. She was still as something carved from stone, the only decorated thing in the Temple. Her eyes fixed on a single lamp that burned deep red like a pool of blood. She looked very small and slight, bent on her knees before the great monolith of the altar stone.

Just visible behind the High Altar was the curtained entrance to the room beyond. The room one did not speak of. The room in which a child would already be lying, waiting to die.

Orhan turned away. Don't look. It is necessary. But don't look. God's great hunger for lives was a mystery of which he and most other educated men did not speak. As a boy he had thought briefly of volunteering, as all children briefly did. The greatest and most sacred choice, his teacher had told him. But he had known, even then, that to choose it would have been somehow wrong, that his teacher and parents would have been outraged if he did. The greatest and most sacred choice, unless someone you knew made it, when it became something else. Something shameful, although he still could not quite say why. A bad thing.

Death is a bad thing. What a profound man you are, Orhan Emmereth.

A young priestess bustled up to them, smiling. "My Lord, My Lady," she said sweetly, "are you looking for something? Would you like to see someone?"

"Yes." Orhan fidgeted. They were here now. No going back. "My wife and I, we would like…My wife is newly with child. We would like to make a prayer and an offering, and seek a blessing." He pitched his voice clear. Loud.

The priestess smiled more broadly. Happiness in her eyes. "It is an auspicious day for it," she said, glancing toward the High Altar, and the kneeling figure, and the curtained doorway beyond. "I will fetch one of the senior priestesses." She slipped away, returned a few moments later with another priestess.

"My Lord Emmereth. Helase tells me that you have great joy to make known to our Lord." Bil flushed with pride and happiness at her words. "Come." The woman indicated a low altar to the left of the great iron bar, topped with three yellow candles, two almost burned down to stubs, one new and tall. "Kneel."

Orhan knelt uncomfortably on the cold floor, helping Bil down. She moved awkwardly in her heavy dress. The old priestess held out a candle to Bil.

"Place it on the altar."

Bil contemplated the altar for a moment before placing the candle carefully at the very center.

The priestess said slowly and loudly, "Great Lord Tanis. These two come before You, to ask Your blessing of the child they bear. Grant that it will live and die, as all things must live and die. Grant that it will know sorrow, and pain, and happiness, and love. Grant that it will endure Your blessing and Your curse. Grant that it will be alive, as we are alive in You. Dear Lord, Great Tanis Who Rules All Things, from the fear of life and the fear of death, release us."

"Dear Lord, Great Tanis Who Rules All Things, from the fear of life and the fear of death, release us," Bil repeated, her voice shaking.

"Place your hands on the candle," the priestess instructed. Bil glanced at Orhan, then reached out and placed the palm of her right hand on it, fingers pointing up toward the unlit wick. Hesitantly, Orhan did likewise. Bil's skin was rough and warm beneath his. Whorls and twists of scar tissue, like the molten wax on the altar.

"Good. Now remove them again, and ask for His blessing."

Bil bowed her head, her lips moving silently. Her hands folded over her stomach.

The candle flickered into flame, bright and beautiful, its light dancing on the bronze wall.

Chapter Six

"I hear we should congratulate you." Darath Vorley gave Orhan a lazy smile as he slid into his seat. The Temple business had gone on rather longer than he'd expected and he was slightly late. The assembled High Lords of the Sekemleth Empire turned to him irritably and shifted round slightly to make more room. The power and brilliance of an Imperial meeting: eight backstabbing men in various states of ignorance, boredom or general decay gathered round a slightly too small table in a room that hadn't been redecorated in nigh on a century.

"Congratulate him?" echoed Cammor Tardein. Always quick on the uptake, that one.

"Lady Emmereth is with child," Darath said. "Or did you want to break the joyous news yourself, Orhan? I'm terribly sorry for stealing your thunder if so. But you did announce it in such a very public manner this morning."

"Congratulations," said Holt Amdelle stiffly. "And I'm sure my wife will be equally delighted." Oh, come on, thought Orhan wearily. Don't pretend you didn't both know. Your spies are so good, you probably knew before I did. You probably knew before Bil did. Celyse's questions at the Verneth party: *nothing wrong, I trust?*

"Quite an achievement," said Elis Vorley. "A most unexpected piece of good news, I must say."

"That was rather cheap, brother dear," said Darath. Smiled elegantly at Orhan. "We all knew Orhan had it in him. And his wife is after all so dedicated to the family name."

Lord Aviced ground his teeth and muttered something, his face scarlet. Orhan shot him an embarrassed glance. You married her to me. No need to look quite so shocked. But it smarted, still, that they should mock so openly.

They were interrupted by the crash of metal on the doors of the room. A rich strained voice calling them to worship: "The Emperor! All kneel for the Ever Living Emperor! Avert your eyes and kneel and be thankful! We live and we die! The Emperor comes! The Emperor comes!" The High Lords of the Sekemleth Empire got carefully to their feet and assumed kneeling positions on the floor around the table. Small but aching differentiations of rank in the postures they adopted: Lord Emmereth and Lord Verneth knelt upright, heads bowed but bodies erect. The Lords Vorley were crouched lower, Lord Aviced so low his gray hair almost brushed the floor. The minute graduations of status in the high families, mapped out in a man's closeness to the dirt on the Emperor's marble floors.

The Emperor entered slowly, a youngish man with a heavy face and a heavy stomach, dressed in black that drained the color from his skin. He was not a handsome man, and knew it. He was not a clever man, and knew that too. The thin band of yellow silk round his forehead dominated him but improved his looks. "The Emperor! The Emperor comes! Kneel and be thankful! The Emperor comes!" Nodded to his lords and gestured absently for them to rise. They did so slowly, elegantly, a subtlety in their manner, as if they simply happened to be rising at that moment, not because their Emperor had commanded it. Whether the Emperor noticed this or not was uncertain. Probably not. So the great lords of the Sekemleth Empire had risen for centuries, before the fishmonger or stable hand or innkeep's boy whom the High Priestess in her wisdom had recognized as the next incarnation of the Asekemlene Emperor, the Ever Living, the Eternal, the Husband of the City, he who had watched Sorlost grow from a desert village to an all-powerful empire to a gold-sodden husk.

A servant poured goblets of honeyed wine. "You are all well, My Lords?" the Emperor asked absently, playing with his cup. Eyes flickered, looking at his cup moving, his hands, anywhere but his face. Eyes down and averted. The Golden Emperor, the Sun As It Rises, the World's Dawn, the King of Golden Life. A youngish man, not handsome, not clever. One should not fear such a man. The High Lords of the Sekemleth Empire, who had once been richer and more powerful than gods: they should not fear such a man. A fish merchant's son! But their hands shook, beneath the careful perfect nonchalance of their poise.

The Secretary coughed, flinched at the tension, shuffled silver paper, coughed again, began. A domestic issue: the guard house at the Maskers' Gate to the east of the city was crumbling, should an extra tax levy be imposed on the few merchant caravans still daring the old road to Reneneth in order to fund repairs? Orhan agreed without interest that they should, as did most of the other lords. A petty concern, almost below their notice, except that as Lord of the Rising Sun and thus somehow intimately connected with the eastern edge of the city he might otherwise be called upon to pay for the repairs himself. He spoke shortly to nod the plan through, his mind mostly occupied by the striking new serving boy fussing with the wine jug.

"Prince Heldan has reached marriageable age," the Secretary said. Orhan blinked and realized they'd moved on to foreign affairs. Rather more interesting, although usually equally depressing. The Emperor's attention wandering, also eyeing the servant and the wine jug. The High Lords of the Empire relaxed a little, now they were onto less important things.

"I know," said March Verneth. "My mother's been talking about it for months. He can have one of my girls. Both, if he promises to be nice to them."

Laughter at that. The Secretary flushed. "What I mean, My Lords, is that King Rothlen seems to be looking for a marital alliance with Ith or Immish."

Holt Amdelle shuddered. "Ith? I wouldn't marry a Calboride if you paid me twice her weight in diamonds."

"Ith would be preferable, however," said Darath. "If he won't take one of your girls, of course, March."

"I agree," said Orhan thoughtfully. "Chathe and Immish in close alliance would be catastrophic, as things stand. We'd be hemmed in badly." The other men half rolled their eyes. Harping on about Immish again, Lord Emmereth? Can't you find anything more interesting to think about? They've only raised twenty thousand men in two years, tripled our trade levies and crushed the Telean uprising so savagely even we felt upset about it for a few weeks. Anyone would think you suspected them of something untoward... "Though a half-Calboride heir to Chathe probably isn't ideal, either..."

"Oh, come on," Elis Vorley snorted. "The Calborides haven't been different from any other great family for centuries now. Whatever his ancestors might have been or done, Selerie has always seemed perfectly reasonable; in fact, his brother was quite charming when he was here."

"Blood's blood," said Holt darkly.

Elis laughed. "I'd rather be descended from a false god than a well-documented money-lender."

"There's also been news from the east," said the Secretary loudly. "The Altrersyr Prince is dead."

"Took him long enough," Tam Rhyl murmured. "I'm amazed he lasted this long."

"The younger boy's already been named as heir. King Illyn is reported to be rather pleased, as you can well imagine."

"For the best, I suppose," said Darath. "Though it would have been interesting to see how things turned out, if he'd survived long enough to rule." He stroked his chin thoughtfully. "The younger boy was here a few years ago, seemed to like it... We should make overtures."

"Overtures?" said Tam Rhyl darkly. "An assassin would be more like it."

Ah, yes. Of course. That. Not really the kind of thing someone forgot or forgave. Pathetic stupidity, the whole thing. But still... The High Council looked sympathetically at Tam, trying not to snigger. Orhan gave the man what he hoped was a soothing smile.

"I can appreciate your feelings, Tam. But even you must agree it's a better outcome politically."

"We'll need to send some kind of formal missive of, uh, condolence and congratulation," said Cammor. "Carefully crafted, of course. Sensitive subject, children."

The Secretary gave him a crisp smile. "It's already been written and dispatched, My Lord."

"His mother was a Calboride, wasn't she?" said Lord Amdelle, still stuck in his previous musings. "Calboride and Altrersyr blood...bad combination, that, if ever there was one."

God's knives, the man was obsessed with genealogies. Terrible overcompensation: anyone would think he was ashamed of his own. As if blood meant anything. Your great-great grandfather did something nasty and suddenly you had bad blood. Nobody ever spoke about the peasantry like that. They were just people, good or bad, fat or thin, mad or sane. But one of the curious things about being high-born was the way you were entirely defined by your ancestors. Thus interesting to see how the next Lord or Lady Emmereth turned out.

"And there's been another outbreak of deeping fever in the southern Chathe," the Secretary went on hurriedly. "Reports are confused, of course, but at least three villages seem to have been affected. No known survivors, although one can't be certain."

"Put extra soldiers on the gates, question anyone travelling from the north. Have them dispatch anyone traveling from the north who seems sick," said Tam quickly. Orhan nodded agreement. He'd read several accounts of deeping fever.

"That's a little extreme, isn't it?" Holt Amdelle began, just as the Secretary said, "It's already been ordered, My Lord. If the number of villages affected grows beyond six, they're to kill anyone with a Chathean accent or garb, whatever their state of health."

"Might finally have an effect on the hatha merchants," said Samn Magreth. Orhan was pleased to see that March had the decency to look embarrassed. He'd felt vile for the best part of a day after Eloise's party.

The Secretary flashed Orhan a cold smile. "Finally, my lords, a curious rumor has reached us. Perhaps My Lord Emmereth could enlighten us further...It would appear someone or something has killed a dragon out in the desert to the east. A caravan driver lost the road, followed a flock of crows and claims to have found a very large corpse. He was irreparably insane with sun exposure by the time he was found, of course, but still..." He gazed blandly in Orhan's direction.

A dragon killer in the eastern desert? Orhan flushed. "I'll... look into it," he said hurriedly. The particular absurdity of his title as Lord of the Rising Sun. He should have known about it. And it was not ideal having people talking about certain places right now. Someone or something with a sword...

"Man's been busy with his beloved wife," said Darath. Flashed a nasty grin at Orhan.

"Thank you, My Lord," said the Secretary in a smooth voice. "Any other business, My Lords? Your Eminence?" He bowed in the direction of the Emperor, who had sat silent throughout, dozing over the prattling of his lords. A show, this meeting of the Emperor and his Friends and Counselors, a piece of fiction drawn out for weary centuries, since the days when the high families of Sorlost were as powerful as emperors and their Emperor more powerful than gods. All faded now, like the frescos on the wall. The high families ruled a city of crumbling plaster, the Emperor an empire of empty sand. What could they do now, these god men? Refuse to levy a tax to pay for repairs to a gate?

The Emperor rose and his counselors rose with him and swept back onto their knees. The Emperor walked slowly out of the room, the Secretary following him. The guards pulled the doors closed behind him, the harsh voice called out distantly "The Emperor! All kneel for the Ever Living Emperor! Avert your eyes and kneel and be thankful! We live and we die! The Emperor comes! The Emperor comes!" in case a stray servant should cross his path without groveling in the dust.

The great lords of the Sekemleth Empire got up neatly and brushed down their silk-clad knees.

Orhan and Darath Vorley strolled down the Street of Closed Eyes together, heading in a general way toward the House of the East. Sterne and Amlis and Darath's escort followed at a respectful distance, knives drawn.

"I think it fair to say Holt won't be receiving an invitation to His Eminence's next private banquet," said Darath. "Most unfortunate. 'Blood's blood'! Did you see the Emperor twitch?"

"Your brother was on rather dangerous ground, too, as far as I can see."

"My brother knows it and doesn't care. Holt Amdelle doesn't know it and does. Care. Vile upstart man." Darath laughed. "I've got Calboride blood myself, you know."

"Have you? I didn't know. Your divinity shines through you but darkly, then," said Orhan.

"You didn't used to say that." Darath shot him a smile. Their eyes met and Orhan smiled back. "My great-great-great grandmother. But still. My honor demands I should feel offense. Unless you feel offense on your sister's behalf that I am offended?"

Orhan sighed. "She knew what she was getting into. We Emmereths have pride enough we can happily sell ourselves and not care about it."

"That what you did, is it? And I always imagined you just lay back and thought of the state of your roof. Oh, don't frown like that. I fully appreciate my own intense good fortune in having a younger brother to churn out little Vorleys for me when necessary."

They turned into the Court of the Fountain. The crowds milled around them, bright and thick in the evening light. The air smelled heavily of grilled meat and perfumes and sweat. Slanting sunlight caught the water of the fountain, flashed on the beaded headdress of a woman dancing beside it, hands twisting and fluttering like butterflies. Her bare feet pounded out her rhythm, the sound of her bells and the sound of the water her only accompaniment. Across the square, a piper played a tune at a different pace to the dancing woman, mournful and slow.

Black skin and golden curls, arms raised in triumph...

"Can we talk seriously now?"

"I thought we were." Darath wandered over to a woman selling grilled meats, bought two skewers. He gave the woman a talent and smiled at her brilliantly. She stared back at him.

"Here." He passed a skewer to Orhan. "Harder to lip-read if someone's got a mouthful of rancid grease."

Orhan bit down on the meat. Stringy and overcooked but well-seasoned, with the pleasant sweetness of honey and cinnamon and a bitter tang of vervain that clung in the mouth. They continued walking, slowly but purposefully, gazing around them at the sights and spectacles of the square. No one seemed to be following them directly, although there were always watchers of one kind or another. It had been absurdly, typically reckless of Darath to even mention it at Eloise's party.

"So..." Darath said through a mouthful of meat, "you owe me three thalers, Lord Emmereth."

"Oh, come on. You can't possibly have found out." Not even managed to tell the people actually doing it the new date yet, following all Tam's messing around.

"What do you want me to do, shout it out loudly in front of all these people? If you really want me to prove it..." Darath's voice rose: "Ladies and gentlemen of Sorlost, the Lord of the Rising Sun has some burning news he would like to impart to you..."

"Lord of Living and Dying, Darath, you are the most insufferable man alive." Orhan dug his hands into his purse. "Here, you can have a talent and three...four dhol."

Darath took the coins, grinned triumphantly at Orhan then tossed them to the nearest beggar. They missed and skipped across the paving stones. Two hollow-eyed children dived for them, shrieking. The beggar, crippled in both legs, half blind, blinked dazedly after them.

"It's happening soon," said Darath over the hubbub. "Very soon, I'd guess. Weeks? Yes, look at your face, weeks. And you'll choose Tearday, because you always choose Tearday to do things... Two weeks this Tearday, then. In the evening, obviously, gives you the whole night to consolidate, you hope, while everyone else is running around trying to work out what's going on. How... that seems obvious enough. The big question is why. Immish, I'm guessing. Though why that should drive you to this extreme suddenly...You really think you can change the world like this, Orhan? Through blood?"

"There's another way, is there?" Was he really that predictable? Hadn't realized, still, after everything, how much Darath knew him. How much Darath had listened, when Orhan himself had assumed it was all just a game for him. "The city's dying, Darath. The Empire's a joke. An empty desert and a few villages. A wasteland. The Yellow Empire, we're known as! The Yellow Empire! Cowards! Weak! The richest empire the world has ever known, and look at us! Petty cowards! Fools! Starving children crawling in filth in our streets! We should have been swept away long ago. The Immish will come with twenty thousand men and a mage, and we'll fall in days. Or if not the Immish, someone else. Chathe, Eralad, Allene...They see what we are, even if we don't."

"Or barbarians from Ae-Beyond-the-Waters, with well-hung stallions gripped between over-muscular thighs, set on rape and pillage and fun for all?"

"God's knives, Darath!"

"Yes, yes, I'll be serious...The Empire has survived like this for centuries, Orhan. Unconquered. Unconquerable. The Godkings, the World Conqueror, the Salavene Wars...none of them have ever touched us. The Seven Years War ended in stalemate and no one even looked at us the whole time. So why in Great Tanis's name now? Twenty years, the Long Peace has lasted."

That's exactly why, Darath, Orhan thought wearily. Can't you

see? Can't you see? There's been peace for too long. We're so
smug and certain. So convinced nothing will ever change. They
won't even need twenty thousand. Certainly not a mage. All this
is illusion. One touch and we'll crumble to dust. Orhan sighed and
chewed on roast meat. A nasty gristle feeling between his teeth.
But Tam's right, too, he thought. The Immish are just a pretense.
An easy way to say what I can't explain. I'm afraid, Darath. I
don't know why, or of what, but I'm afraid. Shadows. Sorrow.
Death. Something's coming. I don't know...But I'm afraid. We're
too weak, the way we are, sitting on our piles of gold pretending
nothing exists beyond our walls. We need to be ready. And yes,
that does mean blood. We're too far gone for anything else.

"It was them who killed the dragon, of course," said Darath.

Orhan started, lost in his own thoughts, visions of flames.
"What? Who? Oh. Yes. Yes, I imagine so. Unless there are two
lots of armed men out wandering around the eastern desert. Of
all the wretched luck..."

"They probably thought so at the time, too." Darath prodded
at him with a meat skewer. "Three thalers. I told you I'd find
out when and how. Enough blades to kill a dragon, Orhan? A
bit much for one man, even an immortal one, I'd have said." His
face changed. "Lord of Living and Dying, you really are going to
do it, aren't you? You really are trying to change the world..."

"Not the world. Sorlost."

"Sorlost is the world. And what in Great Tanis's name does
Tam Rhyl think this is about? He's not looking to change the
world, surely?"

Tam? Change the world? "He just wants power. And March
Verneth humiliated. But I couldn't do it alone."

"You could have come to me," Darath said.

"Could I?"

"Ha. No. Probably not."

They turned into Felling Street, still strolling slowly, gazing idly
in the shop windows at expensive sheets of silk paper, old books,
pretty silverware with a patina of refined age.

"But now that I know…If we're doing it, we're doing it properly. If I'm in, I'm in. So…how many men? And where did you find them? Even I've not bought that kind of service before. Wouldn't know where you even begin, or what a likely price would be. I'd imagine it's rather more complicated than buying a new coat, somehow."

Orhan snorted. "Even you…! So daring and wicked and corrupt your very name is a byword for idleness. It is strangely like buying a new coat, to be quite honest, if that doesn't disappoint you. Get a recommended name, describe what you want and by when, negotiate over details and price, sit back and wait and hope the man cuts your cloth straight and knows where to stick his pins. Forty men. The Free Company of the Sword, they're called. Absurd name. They were recommended by one of my acquaintances in Immish, ironically enough. The High Council has used them a couple of times. They were key to the Immish recovery of Telea during the Winter War. Specialize in…interesting work like this."

"And you trust them?"

"Of course I don't trust them. I don't expect to trust them. That's what they do. Betray people for money. They're inherently untrustworthy, in fact. Except that I'm paying them, and they don't get paid if they betray me. That's how they operate."

"Like buying a whore, then. They'll get a bad reputation if they don't go through with it, or pick your pocket or whatnot."

"If you really must put it that way, probably, yes, I imagine it is."

Darath grinned at him again. "Now I've put you out, haven't I? So sweetly fastidious as always. Even plotting murder you have to be purer than I am…They're arriving soon, then, I take it?"

"I had word yesterday. They're coming in in small groups. Two or three days, it will take."

"Hmmm…This doubling of the guard. Dangerous. Very bad timing. Why in the God's name did Tam suggest it? And why in the God's name did you agree?"

"Because I don't particularly want to die of deeping fever, probably." Orhan took a last bite of meat and spoke as he chewed. "And it's actually extremely fortuitous, as far as I can see. Excellent timing. The guards will be so preoccupied looking out for Chathean accents, they won't look too closely at anything else."

"I suppose so... You've got a lump of gristle on your chin, by the way."

Orhan rubbed at his face in irritation. The spices were beginning to sting his lips. "We could have just had this conversation in my study. Without the need for all this flim-flamming about."

"Your study... Now that's somewhere I haven't been for a while. What would people say? Quite an eventful day you'd be having. And I don't trust even your men not to be peeping at the keyhole. Especially your men, if they really do only charge six dhol."

They paused in the street, standing with the charred skewers in their hands, sticky with grease. Before them the small green square flanking the House of the East. A magnolia tree bloomed in its center, its petals were beginning to fall and lay like skin on the marble ground. The air was very still, as though the city had stopped breathing. A bell tolled over in the west. Dusk. A ferfew called loudly; he heard a woman laugh. A dog barked and the bird flew up with a frantic beating of wings. Orhan thought: a little way over to the west, a child is dying. Always a perilous time, the border between day and night. He looked at his ex-lover, who was more worn now, more haggard, more alive.

"Why don't you come in, Darath?" he said.

Darath looked back at him. The tension that was between them flickered like the tongue of a snake. "Damned erotic thing, plotting the overthrow of one's Emperor. Or did the pretty serving boy earlier stir you up? I saw you eyeing him. Lovely lips, he had."

They turned together in through the gates of the House of the East, which opened smoothly at Orhan's approach. Amlis and Sterne and Darath's escort followed behind them, knives drawn.

Chapter Seven

They line up in long rows, stretching away into the horizon. Rank upon rank of them. Gleaming silver armor, silver-gilt bronze over fine white cloth. The blood shows through the white and marks them as His soldiers, who will fight until they've lost every drop of blood in their bodies and beyond.

They carry the long spear, the sarriss, its jagged point a thing to rip flesh going in and coming out. A short wide-bladed sword that will stab and hack and cleave and tear. A broad cruel knife. No shields. His armies do not need shields. Shields are to stop a man dying. It does not matter how many of them die. Only that they kill as they do so. A shield is a coward thing.

Their helmets cover the eyes but leave the mouth bare, to bite and spit and scream. Ten times a thousand pairs of eyes stare through white-tempered bronze. They wear red horse-hair plumes that nod in the wind. He likes His soldiers plumed like birds in His colors. Seen from above, standing on the walls of a city looking down at them, they must look like a great field of flowers. Like the rose forests of Chathe must have looked, before they burned them.

They stand in perfect silence, still as standing stones, still as teeth in a dead mouth. Perfect order. Perfect discipline. He likes that. Demands that. His officers know the need for it, have passed the lesson on to their men. And they do not often need speech, anyway, when they march. They sing the paean and they sing the death song and they shout their allegiance to the skies. Anything else is unnecessary. What is there in the world to think of but Him?

Within their ranks are men and women and children and old men and cripples and the maimed and the half-dead. He does not care who they are. Whether they are strong or weak. Only that they will fight. If they have no other use, they will deflect an arrow or a sword. If they have no other use, they will die.

They are the army of Amrath, the World Conqueror, the King of Dust, the King of Shadows, the Dragon Kin, the Dragonlord, the Demon Born. For all eternity, they will fight for Him.

A command sounds, a great horn of silver. Music of paradise! The officers call out commands in clear voices. The ranks move forward, cavalry and infantry marching together, baggage wagons drawn by white oxen, camp followers with their meager lives packed on their backs. Dark red pennants flutter above them, bright in the wind. The war drums pound out a beat like that of the human heart. The terrible, awful sound of living, that one first learns to love and tremble at when floating in the womb. The sound they march to, slow and steady. They are in no hurry. They walk slowly to the pounding of a human heart.

In the first day they travel perhaps twenty miles. They stop and make camp with the efficiency of those who have done this a hundred times. Tents are raised. Fires built up. Food prepared. The camp is filled with the usual bustle of armies. Women tend children or tout for business. Gamblers and loan sharks and pawnbrokers ply their trades. Soldiers dice or drink or sit quietly talking. A few even read. But no matter how long they have fought for Him, how far they have marched with Him, they turn, now and again, every one of them, to the great red tent in the center of their encampment, where He sits. They say a baby can tell its mother by smell and texture, before its eyes are fully working, before it can see more than dark and light. So they know Him. So they feel Him. They whisper His name, sometimes, a prayer before any action taken.

No other god they have but Him. They are hushed and reverent, knowing He is there.

They march again the next morning. Days and days they march. It is neither too hot nor too cold for marching. Though they would march through drought and snow and raging storm for Him. A light wind blows from the west, smelling of cut grass. They hold their heads high and march into it, the sun warm on the backs of their heads. He rides at the very front, with His guard in red and silver, mounted on His great white horse. His armor is too bright to look at. His cloak flutters around Him red as blood. The column stretches behind Him for hours, ten times a thousand faces set. A second column, a second army of camp followers, behind them. A city, marching.

On the sixth day, they come to the borders of His Empire. Excitement burns through them. The enemy is awaiting them, gathered already, horses and footmen and archers and even a few great weapons of war. Impossible to keep the enemy ignorant that they are coming. The trample of their feet on the dry ground alone must signal their approach like the roar of water signals the coming of a flood. They make camp that night in sweet meadows where the grass is tall and golden, scattered with pink flowers that smell drowsily sweet. The stars shine down on them brilliant as daylight. The Maiden. The Tree. The single red star of the Dragon's Mouth. They sharpen their weapons and polish their armor and sing the paean. When the dawn comes they are roused and arranged in their lines. Birdsong all around them. Dew on the grass. His tent glows red in the morning. A second sun. The drums start up, beating out the rhythm of their blood pumping. The horses nicker and stamp. Leather creaking and shifting. The snap of their banners in the wind. All these sounds are graven on their hearts. They line up in battle order. Men. Women. Children. The old. The sick. The maimed. The half-dead. Red plumes bobbing on their helmets. Spears at their shoulder. Swords at their hip.

They are the army of Amrath, the World Conqueror, the King of Dust, the King of Shadows, the Dragon Kin, the Dragonlord, the Demon Born. For all eternity, they will fight for Him.

* * *

They wait.

Three days, they wait. The enemy is a coward who does not dare to engage them. A west wind blows, smelling of cut grass. A rich country, this, warm earth and tall trees and a fair sky. Good growing land. He wants it. Wants the orchards and the vineyards and the white-gold ripples of the wheat. Some to feed His armies, His cities, the march of His will across the world. The rest to burn and trample and sow with salt.

On the fourth day, they burn three villages, strip every leaf from the fruit trees and hang the inhabitants' bodies from the bare branches. On the fifth day, they dump the fly-blown bodies into the sacred River Alph, whose waters run clear as the evening sky. The water churns and boils and distant voices beneath the surface cry out in pain. Poison flows downriver, toward the rich towns and cities of the plains. Samarnath, city of towers. Tereen, city of the wise. The wheat fields of Tarn Brathal. Bloated bodies bringing disease.

On the eighth day, the enemy is forced to confront them. And so they march out in silence, heads held high, filled with pride. The drums beat slow and steady. Loud. The tips of their spears glitter in the sun. A light breeze blows the plumes of their helms, sets the horse hair nodding.

A blare of trumpets, bright and sparkling. He rides up and down the battle front, inspecting them, checking their lines, raising love and fearlessness in their hearts. They shift and tighten their grip on their weapons, hunger rising. They look over into the south and see the enemy waiting. They sing the paean. The enemy beat their sword blades on the bosses of their shields.

It is beginning to get hot. Sweat drips down their faces, runs inside their tunics and their bronze armor. Sticky on their foreheads beneath their helms. The two lines shift and stare at one another. They sing the paean again. The drums beat louder. A heartbeat. The first and last sound of a human life.

A trumpet sounds. They lower their sarriss and begin to move forward. A slow careful walk. The gap between the armies closes. Arrows shower down on them, clattering on their armor with a sound like rain. The enemy begins to march, coming toward them, a wall of spears. They put their weight behind their sarriss and grit their teeth.

The gap closes. The two lines meet.

The dust rises. The enemy line is broken. The enemy is surrounded and shattered and killed and destroyed. They are the army of Amrath. They will conquer the world. They were born for this. As indeed all men are.

Death! Death! Death!

Chapter Eight

The candle was still burning at the Low Altar that night, though it had melted down to a pool of golden wax. The Great Chamber still blazed and shone with light. A few worshippers still knelt in prayer, whispering praise and desperation, clinging on to the promise of hope or of a kind death.

In her bedroom high above, the High Priestess of Great Tanis the Lord of Living and Dying leaned out of her window, looking down at the gardens, her girl's face tired and drawn. Another priestess, also young, also tired-faced, sat cross-legged on her floor. They were drinking smoky-scented tea and eating small cakes flavored with cimma fruit: the High Priestess always craved sweet things after her long days of fasting. The room smelled of fresh mint and lavender oil.

"I really should go to bed," the other priestess said. She munched on a cake and gave no sign of moving.

"Yes..." The High Priestess gave no sign of moving either. "It went well, this evening, I think. The child cried a bit, at the end, but I think it went well enough."

"It went well. It always goes well. You should go to bed, Thalia. You must be exhausted."

The High Priestess, Thalia, came away from the window and sat down beside her friend. She was indeed exhausted, so tired her legs ached. Three days' fasting, a night and a day kneeling on the stone floor before the High Altar in the blazing light of the Great Chamber, and then the Small Chamber and the child and the knife. Her left arm was heavily bandaged: she had cut herself deeply, this evening, her hand had shaken a little on the handle of the blade as she raised it to her own skin. But she could never sleep, after. She felt wide awake, filled with a dizzy feeling that was part joy, part horror, part excitement, part shame. It took a long time to recover from it, to be able to think about sleeping and being alone.

"Yes." She frowned at the other girl. "You really think it went well? The child was…was so little."

"Of course it did. You worry too much. You looked so beautiful, kneeling before the altar. Like you always do." The other priestess, Helase, looked at her companion in envious admiration. "It's no wonder there are so many poems about you."

"They're not really about me," said Thalia. "I keep telling you that. I don't suppose some of the poets who say all those things have ever even seen me."

Helase picked up a book from a pile on the table and flipped through it.

"Beautiful as the dawn,
A willow tree beside clear water,
A flower in desert flood.
Her face blinds me,
Light too bright to bear.
I will dedicate myself tomorrow,
That I might see her close,
Hear her breathing, feel her skin,
My blood mingling with her bleeding,
Dying under her hand.

No one's ever likely to write anything like that about me."

Thalia laughed. "It's hardly *The Song of the Red Year,* is it? And I haven't actually seen the poets queuing up to offer themselves.

Even the *Red Year*: do you think Maran Gyste was really so madly in love with Manora he'd have cut off his manhood if she'd asked him to?"

Helase yawned. "Some very great people came to the Temple today. Lord Emmereth and his wife. She was horribly sad, she must have had the scab worse than anyone I've ever seen. I wouldn't dare show even the tips of my fingernails, if I looked like that. I think I'd rather be dead. But she didn't seem to care. Her dress was gorgeous, all yellow silk and embroidery like peacock tails. Her skin was whiter than doves' feathers. They were celebrating the fact she was pregnant. The candle lit so brightly. It was lovely."

"That's nice," Thalia said.

Helase said earnestly: "Because of you, Thalia. Because you keep life and death balanced. Those who need death dying, those who need life being born."

"You really think that?" Thalia frowned. "Yes. Yes, of course."

Helase yawned again. "Ah, I am tired. I will go to bed, now." She got up. "Good night, Thalia. It went well. Be pleased."

"Good night, Helase."

The door swung shut. Thalia went back to the window and gazed out again. A flock of ferfews darted past, wings shimmering in the light of her lamp. They called as they flew, sweet and low. Ghost birds, she'd heard one of the Temple servants call them. Dead souls. Superstitious nonsense, for which the woman should have been whipped. The dead had no souls. Still, the thought made her shiver.

She went over to her bed and sat down on it. Her hair was damp from bathing, twisted into a long thick plait bound with silver thread. Cool sheets, faintly scented with spice.

We all drew our lots, she thought. Helase's yellow, mine red. What would we rather, that we had drawn the black or the white? Fifteen years dead, both of us. And drowning is a hard way to die, they say. Maran Gyste drowned, she thought then. He grew old and fat and married and never cut off his manhood, and in the end he drowned swimming in a lake.

* * *

The day after a sacrifice was always a busy one in the Temple. After the sacrifice of a child, doubly so. People flocked to the Temple, offering small gifts of silver to buy candles, seeking blessing on a child born, a marriage contracted, an agreement made. A child was not sacrificed often, and was especially pleasing to the Lord.

Thalia felt tired and drawn still, her sleep heavy, broken with dreams. The extra day's fasting, she told herself. Drained her. The wound of her left arm ached. It never fully healed, a delicate pattern of scar tissue, silver, black, red and white. She thought momentarily of Helase's description of Lady Emmereth, scarred and grotesque. Her own scars a mark of her status. Words written on her skin.

She ate breakfast alone in the small room off the dining hall where the other priestesses sat. They were mostly silent, heads bowed, but smiles and nods and short exchanges passed between them. She ate a bowl of wheat porridge, sweet with milk and honey, studded with slivers of almond. It steadied her a little, gave her a little strength. The act of eating made what had gone before seem less real.

After breakfast, she was bathed and robed for her duties in the Temple. Her gown was gray, the color of thin high rain clouds. She liked this robe and this ceremony, a day of joy after the shedding of blood. Walked with slow steps to the Great Chamber, Samnel walking before her, old fat Ninia and another couple of priestesses behind. Not Helase, today.

It was still early enough that morning light shone through the high east windows of the Great Chamber. The great room resounding with light, so brilliant it sounded in the heart. Thalia stood before the High Altar and her body shone in the light. Samnel chanted in a dry voice, the other priestesses echoing her. Old words, recited in a long rhythmic drone of old cadences. Like birdsong. Like rainfall. Thalia knelt before the High Altar, gazing up at the single red light. Dear Lord, Great Tanis Who Rules All Things, from the fear of life and the fear of death, release us. We live. We die. For these things, we are grateful.

Afterward, she went back to her bedroom and sat by the window again, looking out at the gardens now bright with the midday light. The day was cool, a fresh breeze and a few clouds scudding in the golden-blue sky. The strange beautiful golden light of the desert that makes the air clear so that detail is picked out like the brush stroke of a painting, the soft wide shape of things blurred with wind-blown sand. A lovely day. Clean. She felt clean, bright as the sunshine, bright as the gardens. If she listened carefully, she could hear the bustle of the city, forever just out of reach beyond the high walls of the Temple. Laughter. Noise. The shouts of children, the clatter of a beggar's bowl, the stamp of sandalled feet. The great towers and domes of the palace loomed above her, gold and silver, the only other building she had ever seen. The pethe birds called and whistled, higher pitched than the ferfews, less melancholy. The Small Chamber seemed very far away now. It is necessary, she thought. So that the living remain living, so that the dead may die. A good life and a good dying. And the things beyond either kept back. The world is a good place. Even with pain in it. Even with death.

Somewhere in the shade beneath the trees, a slave of the Temple would be digging a tiny grave.

Chapter Nine

I was handed over to the Temple when I was three hours old. I am told that my mother cried, although why she should have done so, I do not know. We are born and bred to it, and whatever comes of us is decreed by fate. I was lucky beyond all things, for the lot I drew was that of High Priestess.

It is a curious thing, when I think of it. It is not the first thing that I remember—that, strange to say, is simply a blurred image of an old woman Temple servant, entirely insignificant to my life or any other's, who died when I was three or four—but it is the first thing I can hold before me with any meaning, understand all that took place and render the events clearly from my recollection of them. Unwanted girls, girls whose parents cannot afford to keep them, girls who have been promised, girls who should not have been born...they are handed over to the Great Temple, dedicated to Great Tanis Who Rules All Things. At five, each child is taken into a dark room at the back of the Temple, to draw a lot from a silver box. The room is briefly illuminated and the lot examined before being replaced in the box. If it is black or white, it means death by drowning. If green, death by sacrifice. If yellow, the child is dedicated as a priestess of the Temple. If red, the child is acknowledged as the new High Priestess, holy beyond all things. Needless to say, there are a great many black and white lots, but only one red. It had not been drawn for forty years, before it was drawn for me.

You will ask, I suppose, what happens to the High Priestess-that-is, when the red lot is drawn. A simple thing: the High Priestess-that-will-be kills her. There is a great deal of training and suchlike first, of course, for there is a great deal to learn and to know. And five is rather too young, for killing or for learning. But when the High Priestess-that-will-be reaches the age of fifteen, she stabs a blade into the heart of her predecessor and takes her place. It has been fifteen years now, since I drew my lot, and I have not yet seen the red lot drawn. Perhaps it will be drawn tomorrow. Perhaps it will not be drawn for a hundred years, and I will live until I am an old woman, and die quietly, and be without a successor.

The poets sing all the usual things of my divine beauty. As she is described in *The Song of the Red Year*, the High Priestess Manora had skin like white satin and hair as golden as the dome of the Summer Palace at dawn. The High Priestess Jynine, according to the *Book of the Moon*, had eyes the color of emeralds and a face like the bud of a rose. As to myself, my hair is like trees against the evening light; my skin is like rainwater in a garden; my eyes are like the sky after a storm. Which is to say, I have black hair, brown skin and blue eyes. I am tall, a good thing. Caleste, my predecessor, was so short she had to stand on tip-toe to reach the High Altar. I was taller than her as a girl of thirteen.

The day of my dedication was gray and hot. I spent the night before in prayer, fasting. I was not even permitted a drink of water in the heat. At dawn slaves came to bath me, dressed me in a robe of gold and a veil of silver net sewn all over with golden flowers. It was so heavy I could barely see through it; my reflection in the mirror when they showed me was distant and blurred like a figure seen through thick glass. Two acolytes had to hold my arms to lead me where I walked. On my feet I wore shoes of copper, raised up on wooden pads so that I did not touch the ground.

I was sat on a high-backed bronze chair with a curtain drawn around me while the priestesses and guests filed in; I could hear the chatter of voices and then the silence when the Emperor arrived. I sat hidden for a long time while the ceremony went on around me; priestesses chanted in high, sad voices, calling down the blessing of the Lord of Living and Dying upon me. After what seemed half an eternity, the curtain around me was pulled back and Samnel called upon Great Tanis to behold His servant in all her glory. More prayers, more singing, then, finally, slim cool hands lifted the great veil and revealed me to the assembled multitudes. The lords and ladies wore their best clothes, shining red and green and purple and white. So beautiful, they looked.

I looked first for the Emperor, of course, whom I had never seen. He sat at the front in the middle, flanked by his guards, young and striking in his black but disappointingly plain with a fat face. He looked bored, fidgeted with the clasp of his robe. Helase said later that it is because the Emperor must remain a virgin: it is harder for men to remain that way, she said.

More prayers, then Samnel approached me and raised me to my feet. It was strange to see her like that, masked in silver with lapis inlays around her lips and eyes, like the tiles on my bedroom floor. I stood awkwardly in the copper shoes. She helped me across to the High Altar, and two priestesses helped me to kneel before it. I'd been told to keep looking straight ahead, but the one on my right pinched my wrist and I glanced up into pale blue eyes: Helase, laughing at me behind her mask. I hadn't known, before, that she would manage to get a role in the ceremony.

Samnel's voice came lisping through the mask. I bowed my head and said the words after her. My voice was very loud. I had been afraid that it would stick in my throat. I was raised up again, a cup placed in my hand. Bitter in my mouth when I drank, salt water mixed with the tang of blood. The faces stared at me, a multitude of faces black and brown and white, bright eyes and golden jewelry. I rose and stood tall before the altar, in my robes and my crown, and I was the High Priestess, the Chosen of God, the Beloved of Great Tanis the Lord of Living and Dying, she who gives light and darkness and life and death and mercy and pain.

Chapter Ten

They would be in Sorlost the next morning.

The last few days had worn their patience, sleeping rough without tents, so close to their destination. Emit had argued with Alxine and Rate, Rate had snapped at Alxine, Marith had wandered along a few paces behind not speaking until Emit swore at him for nothing in particular except being alive and good-looking and not swearing at him first. The last of the bread had gone moldy. Rate had found a scorpion in his boot.

And it had been the birth night of Amrath, two nights past. That was going to make a man edgy, even if he wasn't sleeping on stones with nothing to eat but green bread. Emit had made a libation. Alxine had rolled his eyes. Rate had muttered words against ill omen, refused to watch.

"About a thousand years late for that, don't you think?" Emit had muttered back at him. "You Chatheans really need to let it go."

"Bit hard to let it go, when someone wipes out your entire population."

"It was a thousand years ago! And it can't have been your entire population. 'Cause you'd hardly be sitting here, would you, if it had?"

Marith hadn't spoken to anyone all night that night. Twitchy. Nasty sad face. Best left alone. But the boy was from the White

Isles, Tobias thought, to be fair to him. Biggest celebration of the year, there. Gods, the stories you heard of what went on! He'd be missing it. And it was lonely, being so far from home on celebration nights. Missing his mum especially badly, probably. Deep down the whole damn troop of them knew how that felt.

Being a good Immishman, Tobias had recited the story to himself in the starlight. His mother and his grandmother and everyone in the village had gathered to recite it every year. Light the lamps, stoke the fires, bar the door. *It begins with a woman, a princess, a descendant of the old gods, and she lived in a country called Illyr, on the shores of the Bitter Sea, on the edge of the world…*Amrath the World Conqueror, the son of Serelethe and…and, well, the gods and His mum alone knew who His father was, but He claimed that His father was a demon, and if any man who ever lived could claim that he'd been fathered by a demon, it was Amrath. By the time He was ten years old, He'd killed a man. By the time He was twenty years old, He'd conquered an empire. By the time He was thirty years old, He'd conquered the world. The greatest, the most terrible of all the Lords of Irlast. Merciless. Ruthless. King of Shadows. King of Dust. King of Death. The whole world feared Amrath. They were right to fear, too, since He was a bastard who killed like other men breathed air. His wife Eltheia was the most beautiful woman living. His armies were the wonder of the world. Whole cities, He ordered burned with a snap of His fingers. Whole kingdoms, He enslaved. And by the time He was forty years old, He was dead and gone without even an unmarked grave.

Not a good night to be out in, then, the anniversary of Amrath's birth day. Ill-omened. The dark was close around them, the light of their fire was thin and weak. Their feet ached from walking. The ground seemed especially hard and lumpy. Rate discovered wriggling worm things in his water bottle after he'd drunk half of it. Emit laughed until Rate punched him. Marith woke them all up crying in his sleep again. Alxine found two scorpions in his boots.

Ill-omened. Hell, yeah. Tobias had a suspicion that even apart from Marith's sobbing none of them had got much sleep.

Then the next morning the sun came up with a staggeringly pretty sunrise, and they found a tree full of ripe pink apples just sitting there waiting to be eaten, and a staggeringly pretty ripe pink girl waved at them, and Rate and Emit apologized to each other, and they'd finally been able to come down out of the wilderness into a town, and, glory of all the glories, spend the night in a cheap inn.

Amrath was born and died a thousand years ago. Ill omens could bugger off.

The inn had had hot food and hot water and a copious supply of not entirely undrinkable beer. Done them a world of good, Tobias reflected, watching them tramp along, mildly hung-over, Rate still eulogizing the fact he'd finally had a night in a bed. They seemed more comfortable around each other. Back to being a team. Even Marith: he'd fidgeted and hesitated, looked like he might cry again, refused to join them in favor of going straight up to sleep. Tobias had had to virtually drag him into the common room. But once there he'd relaxed quickly enough, to the point he either hadn't been bothered or simply hadn't noticed that Alxine had his hand on his leg. This in turn had cheered Alxine up enormously.

Good lads, Tobias thought. Basically good lads.

Shortly before noon he called a halt and ordered an early lunch. They could press on to the next village, but he'd rather they stop by the roadside, so he could talk to them properly. It was a lovely day, fresh and pleasantly warm after the searing heat of the high desert; they sat on scrubby grass and stretched out comfortably. Tobias shared out the food he had bought that morning, bread, cold meat and fresh golden apricots. The apricots in particular were delicious, sweet, ripe and perfumed, soft as skin.

"The plan for the next few days is simple," Tobias said after a while.

"That's good," said Emit.

"We'll reach Sorlost tomorrow morning. Tonight, we'll stay in a caravan stop outside the city and be in through the gates shortly after sunup. Then we'll be lodging in the city itself while we make final preparations. It's tight discipline from now on again, too, things might start up any time."

"What's the cover story?" asked Alxine.

"Good question." Tobias drew a breath. This was the bit of the plan he wasn't sure about, for all kinds of different reasons. Necessary, if anyone asked them what they were doing there and why. Always good to have a reason more than "because it's there", when you were about to shed blood in it. But it irked him. Uncomfortable, like a stone in his shoe. "We've got a few things to buy that might raise some eyebrows, if you know what I mean? Being bought by a load of hard men with funny accents. So. The story is that Marith here is a young Immish lordling come to Sorlost to sightsee, flash his cash and generally enjoy himself. We're his entourage." He looked at the men uncomfortably. Knew what they'd say. "Got it?"

Marith shifted slightly but said nothing.

"We're his bloody servants, you mean?" said Emit with a growl. "I'm not being his bloody servant. I'm not taking orders from a green bloody boy."

Alxine said hotly: "He killed a dragon. More than you've ever done."

"He's a green boy. You can follow him around all you like, I'm not."

Yes, indeed, knew what they'd say. Predictable as bloody cheese worms, this lot. "Stop it," Tobias said firmly over the top of them. "Be quiet, all of you. This is the plan. Skie's plan. You don't like it, you can have a whipping for insubordination." He looked at Marith, who was sitting on the grass a little away from them, his expression unreadable. The boy's eyes met his own. Flickered for a moment, like the shadow of a bird's wings passing before the sun. Tobias looked away.

"He's not really dressed for a noble," Rate said doubtfully.

Talk about Mr. Insightful. Never a truer word spoken by a man with no mouth and no tongue. Tobias sighed. "We'll buy clothes and things when we get to Sorlost. The story will be that we were set on by bandits somewhere on the Immish road. Lost our horses and baggage, had to run to escape. Explains why we need equipment and such." Turned to Marith. "It's plain as day you're high-born, lad. And you're obviously penniless, else you wouldn't have ended up with us. So playing at high-born and penniless shouldn't really be a problem for you, eh?"

Marith burst out laughing.

"Right then. We're agreed, yes?" Rate and Alxine nodded, followed after a moment by Emit. His eyes looked daggers at Marith, who stared blankly back. Emit turned away, spat in the dirt and cursed.

Rate stood up and performed a flourishing bow. "Sire," he said, doffing an imaginary hat in Marith's direction, "I am at My Lord's service. Anything he wants, I shall procure him. What does My Lord command? In wine and women I am afraid I am sorely lacking, but I should think I can rustle up a handful of dried goat shit."

Broke the tension. Marith smiled with rather more amusement than he'd laughed. Even Emit grunted something like he was entertained. Well handled, lad, Tobias thought, looking at Rate. A clever boy there, knew when to play the clown, when to be firm. How to manage grumpy bastards like Emit. He'd only joined the company the last summer past, but he was a key part of them, the others looked to him. I'll begin training him, Tobias thought. Pity to waste his potential. If he survives this, of course.

Marith, on the other hand... Yes. Well. The boy had a charisma of some kind. More than just his obvious high breeding, though that was part of it. But it went deeper, something in him that you couldn't put into words. The other men in the squad, even Rate, were men in the squad. Just men. Each with his own foibles and infuriating habits and passable good points if you squinted at them in the dark and ideally after about ten pints, but basically just men. Good lads. Marith was... something else. He'd sat quiet last night, hardly speaking. Nose down in his drink and those big sad eyes. The barmaid had pawed over him, not surprising, really, since the boy was considerably prettier than she was, and he'd ignored her completely. Not because he was shy of her, or not interested in her, he'd given the girl a thorough looking over at first, same as they all had apart from Alxine, but as though she had stopped meaning anything to him. As though nothing meant anything to him. He'd just sat there, in near silence, with that look on his face, far off and sad. And now he was sitting on the grass eating an apricot, legs drawn up before him, looking fresh as new cotton, sweet and young and innocent apart from his eyes.

"Let's get on then," Tobias said, standing up and wiping the remains of his meal off his hands. "We should be outside the gates by this evening." The men followed, shouldering their packs. "Not him. He's a lord now. From now on, he doesn't carry anything, do anything. We do it for him." Paused and glared round at them. "And no complaining, got it? No more than would be realistic, anyway."

"Bloody stinking gods and demons," muttered Emit.

"That's probably more than is realistic, Emit," said Rate.

They arrived in the environs of the city itself in the late afternoon, warm sunlight gleaming on the great bronze walls that loomed before them, perhaps another hour's swift walk. Unmistakable, even to those travelers who have never before seen them. *As long ago as tomorrow, beneath the brazen walls of Sorlost.* For the last couple of hours, they had been walking through an increasingly inhabited landscape, prosperous villages, market gardens and caravan stops, joining up with more people and trains of goods.

"We'll stop here," said Tobias. A caravan inn, large and wealthy and faded, on the edge of a small town that functioned as an entrepôt to Sorlost itself. Cheaper to stop outside the shadow of the city walls; easier too if one arrived toward evening. The great gates of the city were slammed shut at dusk, and no man might come or go until morning. Even at the city's zenith, when it had bought and sold half the world in its marketplace, the gates had closed every evening with the last rays of the setting sun. The merchants grumbled, but did not dare to ask that they be kept open after dark. The night was not a safe time for the crossing of boundaries, even boundaries made by man. And the walls were so high, and so heavy, who was to say who had made them, when the moonlight shone full upon them, or in the darkness of a night when there was no moon?

They entered the inn through a stone portico giving onto a small courtyard, faded frescos of birds on the walls, well-scrubbed flagstones, a lemon tree in a pot dying quietly in the corner. The smell of spice and bread and beer; laughter from a room opening off to the left, accompanied by the thrum of a lyre and a clapping of hands. A musician, maybe even a troop. Tobias nodded approvingly. Good distraction. People less likely to notice or remember them if there was a good story and a song to look forward to.

He accosted a young woman scurrying past with a tray of clean tea bowls. Cleared his throat and greeted her in three words of his best Literan. She sniggered and he switched hastily to Immish: "The innkeep, if you please, miss. We're in need of rooms." She nodded, scurried off and returned with a thin middle-aged man with bright, cold eyes.

"Rooms, you'll be needing, is it?" the man asked him, looking their tattered clothing over with a practiced eye. "We're a bit crowded right at this moment, I'll be telling you."

Tobias smiled at him, produced a small leather purse. "We have gold. Not much else, mind. This here—" indicated Marith with a jerk of his head "—this here is Lord Marith Cotas. Not much, he looks at the moment, I grant you—we were waylaid by bandits on the road ten days out from Reneneth. Bastards took almost everything. But he's rich. And I'm clever. So we've still got enough gold on us for rooms."

The innkeep hesitated. "Been rumors of bandits out in the borderlands. Roads are bad at the moment. Not good for trade, so not good for me. But few dare the desert road anyway, now. Your lord's a fool, traveling with so few men."

Marith frowned, a dark look in his eyes. Seemed about to say something.

"My Lord realizes that," said Tobias hastily. "Maybe best not to rub it in any further, yeah? Regardless: rooms. We'd like rooms and baths and a hot supper." He jingled the purse again. "Five dhol?"

"Six," the innkeep said in a grudging voice. "I've got two rooms, but one's small. Might be best if Your Lordship had that one, I'm afraid, less he wants to share with his servants. I can get baths drawn, though we've only got two so you'll have to take turns. Food served after the evening bell, there's music tonight too, you're lucky."

They were led upstairs. "My Lord's" room was tiny, an attic gable at the back of the building with a fine view of a scrubby field. The innkeep shifted awkwardly on his feet as he showed Marith in. Barely room for a bed. "Can't move one of my other guests for less than ten," the innkeep said shortly. "My Lord." Tobias, Rate, Alxine and Emit had a larger room, two beds and floor space for two more, overlooking the stable yard. Rate took a big lungful of the stinking air and grinned. "Smells like home. What say we dice for the beds?"

The bath was drawn up by the same young woman they'd encountered in the courtyard, clanking up and down the stairs with pails of steaming water till Marith felt vague guilt. She was far too small and slim for heavy lifting. The water was hot and scented with herbs, lemon thyme and basil, sharp and sweet. The soap was lye, but clean. There was even oil for the hair. Marith sank back into the water with a deep sigh. Hadn't had a bath like this for months. The feel of the hot water was wonderful. The girl smiled shyly at him and offered to stay and wash his hair, but he turned her down, then called her back and asked her to bring him a jug of wine.

His clothes were given a quick clean while he was bathing. His cloak looked wretchedly tatty still, but was a shade closer to its original rich red; his boots and belt, being good leather, had responded well to being polished. The silver buckle of his belt shone. Between a good wash and a proper shave, the cleaner clothes and the wine, he came downstairs feeling more like himself than he had done for a long time. Looked more like himself, too, he realized as he caught sight of his face in a small bronze mirror on one of the landings. If you ignored the heavy scarring to his left hand. The thought made him shiver. His eyes were itching, his skin beginning to burn. Last night had been the first time he'd been in a tavern since Skie had picked him up. Tonight would be worse.

Music and laughter were pouring out of the common room. He took a deep breath and walked in. A large clean room with more faded frescos decorating the walls. Two musicians, a lyre-player and a piper, playing at one side of the room. The girl was sitting already half in the lap of a laughing man in a fine red tunic. The inn the previous night had been small, rural, relatively harmless. This room made him shiver again, despite the warmth of the wine in his head. That had been foolish too. Last night hadn't gone so badly, considering how it might have ended. Tonight he needed to be more careful. So much more careful. Which was so much more difficult...

Tobias, Emit and Alxine were already sitting at a table, also scrubbed clean.

"My Lord." Rate rose as he entered and indicated a seat beside him with a gloriously overblown flourish.

"Would Your Lordship care for a drink?" asked Emit in a particularly servile voice.

Marith felt himself flinch despite himself. "Perhaps a cup of wine," he said. The others were drinking the pale, sweet beer they favored in Sorlost. "How's your room?" he asked, trying to find something to say to them. Strange how playing himself was so much more difficult than playing whoever he'd been for the last few months.

"Stinks," said Emit shortly.

"Bigger than yours," said Rate. "As the serving girl has already pointed out."

Tobias was just rising to order food when a bell sounded, loud and low and sad. The room fell suddenly silent, the musicians stopping playing, voices breaking off in the middle of a word. A long pause, a silence that hung in the air. Everything and everyone very still. Marith felt something between a laugh and a scream well up inside him. A dim confused memory of a silence like this.

On and on, drawn out painfully, tense as knives. Suddenly, finally, the girl laughed loudly, a high-pitched squealing sound. Something broke in the air. The bell tolled again. The drinkers turned back to their drinks, muttering. The musicians started to play.

"What the hell was that all about?" Emit asked.

"Twilight," said Tobias. "The bell marks the moment between day and night. Considered a dangerous time."

"*Seserenthelae aus perhalish,*" murmured Marith. "Night comes. We survive." Carin used to say it sometimes, his voice deep and solemn; they'd both laugh. It had all seemed almost funny, back then.

"Speak bloody Literan, now, do you?" Emit growled. Marith blinked back to the present. They were all staring at him. Speak bloody Literan, now, do you? Oh gods. He was getting careless. Slipping. Letting out things they shouldn't know. But it was so hard to think here. Shadows. Laughter. Carin. Ah gods, Carin... Pain, clawing at him. Something screaming, just out of reach. He rubbed his eyes and tried to smile at them. "Plain as day I'm highborn. You didn't think I'd be well educated as well?"

"Speak the lingo, know the customs..." Emit was glaring. "I'm starting to wonder about you, boy..."

"My Lord," said Alxine, trying for levity. "I'm starting to wonder about you, My Lord. He can recite dirty poetry too."

"Course he can," said Rate. "Basis of a good education, dirty poetry. '*My love is like a lily fair, With lice around her pubic hair.*' But can he recite dirty poetry in Literan?"

"Actually, yes," said Alxine helpfully. Emit snorted beer.

"The best dirty poetry is written in Literan." Marith's face felt hot. "Maran Gyste..." Digging a hole. Big as a latrine trench. He shut up. Tried not to look at Emit or Rate.

"Yes. Well. On that note. Yes." Tobias, trying to smooth things. Tobias went up to the bar, returned with a goblet of wine for him and the promise of food to be brought shortly. It was good wine, rich and heavy. Thank the gods. Marith drank it in small sips, trying to make it last. The food when it came was good too, cold meat in a hot sauce and fresh bread. They were finishing eating when the musicians put down their instruments and the piper addressed the audience in a loud voice. In Pernish, fortunately, like almost all traveling singers: Marith had a sudden image of Tobias forcing him to translate from Literan in time to the beat.

"Good gentlemen and ladies—" laughter from the girl, the only woman in the room "—tonight we bring you a story, a tale of telling old, of heroes, of dangers, of warriors fierce and bold, of Amrath, greatest lord of all, who caused all men to fear. So listen, my good audience, this mighty tale to hear." The drinkers groaned and cheered in equal measure.

Oh gods. Oh gods and demons. Marith's hands started to shake. He had a sudden fear he was going to be sick.

"And a happy birthday to Him," said Emit. "Just let it go, Rate, lad. Let it go."

The lyre-player struck a few chords while the piper licked his lips, adopted a dramatic pose and began to speak:

"This is a tale of the first days of Ethalden, before the wars came, when Serelethe and Amrath were still building the city's strength. A great fortress, they built, using Serelethe's magic and Amrath's power. All of white marble, it was, each block twice as tall as a man, and no mortar was needed to hold it together, so smooth were the joins. Five floors it went down into the earth, deep cellars and dungeons and secret rooms. And five floors it rose up into the air, council chambers and feasting halls and armories. It stood on the very top of the White Hill, and from its windows you could see for a hundred miles. Lost, it is, now, even the hill flattened into dust, but, then, ah then, then the fortress of Amrath was the greatest and the most beautiful and the most feared building in all the world.

"But great and beautiful and feared it may have been, but the fortress was also haunted, and Amrath could find no peace in it. Filled, it was, with Serelethe's spells and secrets, but this was something else. A thing that Serelethe herself could not understand, could not solve. For each month at the dark of the moon, a soldier or a serving maid or a noble was found dead in their bed, and not a mark on them but the burning marks of a great fire running all up the length of their right arm. But no smoke was smelled, and no cries were heard, and what was killing them and how they died no man knew. And the guards and the maids and the nobles began to lose faith in Amrath, if He could not keep His own people safe within His own walls.

"So Serelethe and Amrath were in despair, for try as they might, they could not find an answer to the mystery, and their people were dying and muttering against them. And Amrath had angry words with Serelethe, who had promised Him mastery of an Empire but could not defend His own men for Him. And so things went badly in Ethalden.

"Now, this had been going on for a year, and no man was any closer to finding the truth of it, when there came to Ethalden a young mage, a wandering sorcerer from Tarboran where the fires burn. And he stood before the throne of Amrath, and dared look even Amrath full in the face. And he promised Amrath that he knew the secret that was plaguing His fortress, and could destroy it. And all he wanted in return was a chance to stand beside Amrath, and be His lieutenant, and lead His armies with fire and blood.

"So Amrath roared a great roar of laughter, and promised the mage gold and silver and precious jewels, and a lordship, and the command of His armies, if he should only defeat the evil that was plaguing Him. For He saw in the mage a brother, and a comrade, and a tool to be used. He gave the mage a great chamber for lodgings, and put all of His wealth and His power at his disposal.

"The mage walked the corridors of the fortress, sniffing the air and looking at the stone. And at length he stopped in a certain place, a small room in the outer keep looking down over the city, and he gave a great cry and said, 'This is the place. And now we shall see what we shall see.' And he ordered the men with him to dig.

"The men dug and the men dug, and they broke open the great stones of the walls, and they found there buried the body of a young girl, with her right arm burned through to the bone from her wrist to her shoulder, and the marks of a knife on her throat.

"Well, Amrath, He ordered the body buried with full honor, as though the girl was His own sister. Ten horses, they burned over her grave. But still the dying did not stop, for at the next month at the dark of the moon one of the mage's very servants was found dead and cold with no mark on him but the burning marks of a great fire running all the way up the length of his right arm. And the mage knew then that he was dealing with no ghost but a gabeleth, a demon summoned up from the twilight places by the shedding of the girl's blood. And he was greatly afeared, for such a thing is very powerful.

"But the mage had promised Amrath he would destroy that which was harming His people. And he feared Amrath near as much as he did the gabeleth. So he locked himself away in his chamber with his books and his magics, and for three days he did not eat or sleep but only worked at his spells. And at the end of three days he went back to the room where he had found the girl's body, bringing with him his staff, and his sword, and a silver ring. And there he fought the demon.

"Three days and three nights they fought, and fire raged through the skies above Ethalden, and Serelethe herself cried out for fear. So terrible was the battle that every child birthed on those three days in all Ethalden and for thirty leagues beyond was born dead. So terrible was the battle that the sick died and healthy men went mad and ran screaming into the sea, or set themselves afire and were burned to death where they stood.

"But at the end of three days, the mage overcame the demon, and imprisoned it in the silver ring. He could not kill it, you see, for such things are not alive, and so cannot die. And Amrath and

Serelethe rejoiced, and Amrath made him His lieutenant, and gave him command over His armies, to lead them with fire and with blood."

The lyre-player struck a chord again with a flourish. "And now the tale I'll sing you, a story great and true, so listen all fine gentles, and pay attention too." The piper started playing and the lyre-player began to sing, flowery and beautiful in heavy old Pernish rhythms. Not often sung, the tale of the mage lord Symeon and the gabeleth. Complex, filled with half rhymes and strange cadences, twisted, barely used words. And it didn't show Amrath in the best light either. "He was Amrath, the Lord of the World, the Demon Born," Marith had asked his tutor after being set to study the song. "How could He have been defeated by a thing like a gabeleth?"

"Amrath perhaps wondered the same thing," his tutor had replied after a moment's thought. "Since He had Symeon executed six months later. Remember that. There's a lesson there."

Felt as though everyone in the room must be staring at him. The itching was painful now, stabbing fire in his face and hands. I want—I need—I don't—Help me, Carin. Make it all go away. Please, make it all go away. Help. Help me. He had one iron penny left after last night, which would probably buy him a half-cup of weak beer. It seemed unlikely Tobias would advance him the money to drink himself unconscious, so as quickly as seemed half decent he went upstairs to his room and lay awake in the darkness, weeping uncontrollably, trying to keep from scratching his face so badly it bled.

Chapter Eleven

Two young men, boys really, gallop over the crest of a hill and down toward a long stretch of pale yellow sand. One is slim and dark-haired, the other stockier and fair-blond. They are both riding expensive chestnut-colored horses. They laugh and shout triumphantly as the horses thunder onto the beach and splash out into the cold sea.

It is still early morning, the mist coming in off the gray water. Seabirds fly overhead. They wheel up before the rushing horses. Sad, lonely, painful cries. The sky is very pale, blurring with the sea and the dark hills, almost no color save the deep red flash of the dark-haired boy's cloak. A strange, bleak, melancholy winter light washes over everything, sorrowful as the birds' cries. Against this, the boys are bright and brilliant, faces radiant with laughter and the sheer joy of being alive. They spur their horses into the foam, kicking up the water, making them leap the waves. The dark-haired boy pulls on his reins and his horse rears up, hooves thrashing, treading the air. He draws his sword and brandishes it aloft, so that its blade catches the morning light.

The fair-haired boy brings his horse to a standstill, water breaking around its legs. He watches the other, smiling at him. The dark-haired boy's horse wheels and bucks, sending its rider's hair in a dance.

The dark-haired boy makes a gesture with his hand and they ride back onto the dry sand. For a moment they look at each other, grinning. Then together they dig in their heels and urge the horses on again, faster and faster, galloping madly along the beach. Birds scream and start up as they thunder past, the horses neck and neck, perfectly matched. On and on, like they could ride forever, crashing through the mist, splashing back into the sea and then up onto the sand.

"Amrath! Amrath!" the dark-haired boy shouts jubilantly as he rides.

"Amrath!" the fair-haired boy echoes, laughing.

Chapter Twelve

You will wonder, perhaps, whether I enjoy my life. I suppose I do. And I have known no other with which to compare it. But then, we can all say as much. All us mere mortals, anyway: I suppose the Emperor must remember his previous incarnations. Although, as he is always the Emperor, there may not be much difference between them.

I am the High Priestess of the Lord of Living and Dying, the most powerful and most sacred woman in all the Sekemleth Empire, second in importance only to the Asekemlene Emperor himself. I preside over the most sacred of the great ceremonies in the Great Temple. I, and I alone, am permitted to shed blood in the Temple. I, and I alone, may touch the High Altar. I, and I alone, know the true will of the God.

But sometimes my life seems very small, and the world around me even smaller. I have never left the Temple since I was brought here, so new born I was still marked with my mother's blood. I will never leave it, even in death. My body will be buried in the great pit beneath its precinct, and my bones lie where I lived. The confines of my life are so small, so narrow, walls and corridors and closed doors that I know so well I can walk them with my eyes closed.

The Temple itself is huge, of course. But most of it is holy rooms, or storerooms, or imposing empty space. Ten priestesses, five novices and three girls too young to have drawn their lots live here beside myself, and there are servants and guards and such to accommodate. So there are not then many places to go. I have a bedroom, small and clean with a large window and a balcony and stairs down to the gardens and the bathing house. I have a little dining room, in which I eat alone. When I can eat: often, I have to fast. Two days, before a killing. Three days, before the killing of a child.

The killing. You will wonder most about the killing, I suppose. How I can bear to do it. But it is what I was chosen to do. What I have been trained to do since I was a child. What I am and what I know. Life, and death, and the need for dying. It must be done. I must do it. As well ask a man if he enjoys the act of being alive.

Once, in the great days of Empire, a sacrifice was made to Great Tanis every evening, in the moment the light fades and the world is neither day nor night, alive nor dead. A man for the waxing moon, a man for the waning moon, a woman for the full moon, a child for when the moon is dark. How the High Priestess then did not die of hunger, I do not know. Perhaps she lived on water and the scent of blood. Or perhaps she did not have to fast. Perhaps the fasting only came later, as the Empire shrank and its people were less willing to die for their God.

Now, a sacrifice is made only every ten days. I am glad of this, I suppose, I do not think I would like to do it every day, even if I did not have to fast between times. Always the eyes look at me and beg me not to do it, always the victim realizes, at the last, that their choice was a wrong one, that they do not after all want to die. That they do not believe in the God they are dying for. Maybe it is in my eyes too, or will be, when one of the little girls draws the red lot. It has not been drawn yet: even if it were drawn tomorrow, I would have ten years of living left to me. A good while. But a while is never enough. I see that in the eyes of every sacrifice too. They would burn half the world for a few more moments of life.

I especially do not like the killing of children. They are so small, some of them.

But I have lived in the Temple all my life, been trained as High Priestess since I was five. It is all I have ever known and all I will ever know. For all my fine clothes and titles, I am a servant of the Temple, as surely as the women who scrub the floors. I am a tool of Great Tanis Who Rules All Things, His hands, His knife. You do not ask the women who scrub the floors whether they enjoy what they do. You do not ask your hand, or your knife. You see that they are necessary, and that they do what is needful of doing. You would not ask a soldier whether he enjoys his work. You would simply accept that in a war men must die and someone must kill them. If it is this man or that man who lives and this man or that man who is killed—well, that is war. Some must live and some must die. So I lived, and so others die. Another draw of the lot, it would have been reversed. Who am I to say it is wrong, or right?

There are two ways to die in Sorlost, if you seek death. The first is the white silks and the knife in the street, a brief glory of fighting and an unmarked grave. The knife-fighters are the heroes of the city, though they are nameless and forgotten as soon as they die. They walk the streets like corpses, already dead, waiting for someone to kill them, stealing women's hearts. That is the way of young men, brave men, fools. The second is the Small Chamber and the altar stone, a noble sacrifice and the city's gratitude that we may live and die for another few days without fear. That is the way of old men, sick men, women, children. Many that I kill are dying already, eaten up with disease or simply bored of their lives. They choose something good and noble in their dying. Or so we say.

My life is not all blood and sacrifice, besides. Most times, it is quite pleasant.

Four days out of ten, I officiate at the ceremony of the dawn. Helase hates it, for it means waking in the dark of the night to prepare, but to me it is worth the waking. I wear a robe of silver, that shimmers as I walk. The priestesses sing a hymn of praise so beautiful it makes the heart weep. I carry fresh flowers and place them before the High Altar, and the scent of them clings to my arms and my hair, the weight of them in my arms smears my skin with pollen and crushed petals and dew.

Other times I walk in the gardens or play with the children. They make me laugh, the little ones training to be priestesses; they look upon me with such awe. Only the very young ones, who have not yet drawn their lots, I avoid.

There is a fine library in the Temple: I read anything I wish. Poetry I especially enjoy, and histories. I have read several histories of the Temple and the High Priestess, which is curious. Reading about myself, it seems, for their lives can have been no different to my own.

Twice a year, at Year's Renewal and Year's Heart, we celebrate the Great Ceremony. Year's Renewal is more somber, Year's Heart wilder and more joyful. The Emperor and all the great families come to the Temple shining with gold and jewels; the ceremony lasts for hours; the people of Sorlost dance and sing in the streets, gather outside the Temple to light candles and offer flowers. Afterward, there are parties and banquets all over the city, and no one sleeps until the sun has risen the next day. Even we, in our cloister, have a fine meal and stay up to see the dawn, though we pray and sing rather than drink and dance. It is the one day of the year I am allowed to dine with the other priestesses. I wear a dress of cloth of gold for the ceremony, like the one I was dedicated in. It is heavy and stiff, but so very beautiful it pains me to take it off. I look like the High Priestesses from the old poems, Manora or Valdine. I look like a queen from an old book.

I have people I think of as friends: Helase, Ausa, even Samnel in her way. The woman who tends my rooms and helps me dress is kind and I talk to her of little things. I have people I suppose I would count as enemies, were I not what I am—Ninia, who talks of the old High Priestess-that-was as if everything I have done for the last five years has been failure and uselessness, as if the very way I kneel before the altar is wrong when compared to the way Caleste the High Priestess-that-was knelt; Tolneurn, the Imperial Presence in the Temple, who loathes the fact I do not have to do as he commands me, though he has never tried to command me and never will; one of the servants who serves the meals, who looks at me with hatred despite the fact I have never spoken to her.

Mostly, my life is as dull and repetitive as any other. I have seen old pictures of emissaries from half the world kneeling in the Great Temple, spellbound and trembling before the might of Great Tanis Who Rules All Things. Now I officiate to peasants and petty merchants, while foreign kings laugh at us for our beliefs behind fat fingers. Pointless, it seems sometimes. All the candles, all the gold and silver and bronze. Pointless, in the way most lives are pointless. A ritual motion we must go through, for want of anything else to do or believe.

But that is not true. It is not pointless. Nothing is pointless, as long as one is alive. One moment of beauty. One moment of happiness. One moment of pain.

Lives for living. Nothing less and nothing more.

Chapter Thirteen

"Big, isn't it?"

"Fancy, too. Must be a real bugger to keep clean."

"I like the way it shines like that. Very pretty, that is."

"Seems a bit...over the top, though, really."

"Well, if you're the richest empire the world has ever known, I suppose you need something to spend your money on. If you've exhausted your capacity for wine and women, might as well be a bloody massive wall made of solid bronze. Probably a slightly more useful way to chuck money away than just digging a big hole and burying it."

Alxine gestured to a small group of ragged, thin-faced men hanging about in front of them. "They could have given it to the poor."

"What, and have them waste it by spending it on things?"

"I'm slightly disappointed, to be honest. All you hear about it, I kind of expected it to be taller."

The bronze walls of Sorlost loomed before them. Five times the height of a man, shining in the morning sun. They had no seams or joins, a perfect ribbon of metal twisting around the city, punctuated only by the five great gates. The Maskers' Gate, the Gate of the Evening, the Gate of Dust, the Gate of Laughter, the Gate of the Poor. It was impossible to conceive who had built them, or how. They had never been breached: even Amrath Himself had dashed His armies to pieces against them to no avail and given up in despair.

Marith stood and gazed up at them in awe. It was still early, only a short while past dawn, and he could feel the cold radiating off them. In the heat of the afternoon, the sun beating down upon them, they must be hot as coals to the touch. The morning light flashed off them blindingly bright. Approaching from the east as the sun rose had been wondrous, the metal turning from inky dark to blazing fire, more beautiful and vivid than the dawn itself. The moment the light hit them had been like watching someone thrust a torch into a bowl of pitch. An explosion of light. Dragon fire. Joy. Hope.

There were no villages immediately outside of the city. No houses at all. The town where they had spent the previous night had been the last place before the gates, after that there was an hour's walk through empty country, barren grassland and scrubby thorns. No wealthy villas or shanty towns of starving untouchables, just bare ground as though they were in the remotest part of some abandoned kingdom, and, rising before them, the great walls.

A stillness, too, very few animals or birds to be seen. The air smelled of metal. The land around was a vast graveyard, for the people of Sorlost buried their dead in this silent place outside their walls. Most were unmarked. Once, they had passed a fresh grave, the earth still dark, a few flowers scattered on the hump of soil. Someone especially beloved: the people of Sorlost did not as a rule concern themselves with such things. To bury someone so close to the road, to offer flowers...Perhaps an only child, a new married wife, a beloved parent. The one joy of the mourner's heart. Marith looked, and then looked away.

He had studied Sorlost's history and culture, her language, her poetry and art. Well educated indeed. You need to know your enemy, his tutor had told him as he groaned over the complexities of Literan grammar, the tedious list of the Emperor's thousand tedious little lives. To be walking here before her walls was strange as dreaming. The others felt it too, he could tell from their laughter, their dedicated attempts at nonchalance. *As long ago as tomorrow, beneath the brazen walls of Sorlost.*

Within sight of the gatehouse, Tobias drew them to a halt.

"Everyone know what they're doing and saying?" he asked briskly. "Any last questions? No? Fine. Good." He gestured to Marith with a flourish. "Over to you then, boy. Your Lordship. Lead on."

Marith took a deep breath. Again, strange how unnerving having to act himself was. Far more frightening than acting someone else.

Four soldiers stood to attention outside a brick building straddling the road before the open gates. Two stories with a portcullis and towers, but it looked absurd beneath the vast bronze walls. A toy fort with toy soldiers. Old wooden gates, splintered and worm-eaten, carved with blank-eyed faces. Behind it, the great mass of the Maskers' Gate like a roaring mouth. They know, Marith thought madly. They see it. Help me. Help me. What would Tobias do, he wondered, if I stopped in the road and screamed? The soldiers stared at them, asked them a few bored questions, waved them on. Past the gatehouse they stepped into the great cavern of the wall. The air stank of metal. Their footsteps echoed, a ringing sound that was unpleasant to the ear. None of them spoke.

It took perhaps ten paces to walk through. A very long ten paces. Almost a death, or a rebirth. Then suddenly they were out in a great square, the Court of Faces, blinking in the light, surrounded by people and sound and noise and stink. Like a magic trick. More soldiers gave them cold glances. Traders and hustlers surged forward, offering guides and recommendations for a good lodging house. A crowd of thousands, hair and skin every possible color, clothing bright and dark and pale as water, glittering with gold. Color and texture and beauty roaring in the eyes. Shouts in every language, birdsong and music, dogs barking, bray of asses, buzz of flies, bleating of goats. Sweat and incense, spice and honey, wood smoke and rot and shit and vomit and piss. Vast buildings, white marble, yellow brickwork, gilt wood, red paint. Carved porticoes and stone columns and velvet awnings and jeweled domes. Clock-work toys and paper flowers and silk carpets and caged birds and silver jewelry and roast meat.

The decaying heart of a decayed empire.

Sorlost.

"Right." Tobias smiled at them warily. "We're in. Just got to find everyone else now."

"Friendly bunch, aren't they?" muttered Emit, glancing back at the soldiers. "Or maybe they just don't like His Lordship here." Can't say I blame them, his eyes continued.

What have I ever done to you? Marith thought bitterly. He felt again a vague desire to kill the man.

His eyes were itching, the skin of his face raw. He found he was rubbing at his mouth and forced his hands to drop to his sides. His body felt heavy, the armor he wore hot and awkward hidden under his shirt. The noise and the confusion was almost too much for him, after the long days of silence in the desert sand. He had liked the emptiness, the feeling of it like a pain in his body, fear and yearning and sorrow that cut like great claws. Dragon's claws, he thought with a bitter laugh. Everything had seemed briefly easier, with nothing between himself and his shadows, nothing to think about but walking onwards in the dust. Calm. Clean. Empty. This clamor and bustle of life made him uneasy, as though he were walking a high tightrope and might easily fall.

But there should be things here...He gazed around the square with nervous interest. Street sellers offered skewers of meat, thin cakes of sweet bread, flowers, drinks of lemon water, sherbet ice. Even this early in the day a few whores touted for business, worn and raddled in the fresh light. Two beggars with withered limbs and running sores jangled alms bowls. A drunk lay slumped against the base of a statue, sleeping in a puddle of vomit beneath rearing stone hooves. Almost nostalgic.

He eyed the whores with wary anticipation. A young woman noticed him staring and teetered toward him. Her legs were bound with tight cords to give her a mincing, hobbled gait; she wore bells at her wrists and ankles that tinkled irritatingly. Curious things, other people's sexual peccadilloes. Anywhere else, most men would have got bored and walked off by the time she got near. Marith took a half step toward her. So close... But she moved so painfully slowly...

Then Rate noticed the woman and whistled. Marith's heart sank. Taking risks. Letting things slip. I'm not so desperate, yet, he thought, though he knew that was a lie as he thought it. He shuddered and tried not to rub his eyes.

Tobias was looking at him with a frown. "Getting into character are we, My Lord?" he said scathingly. "She's a bit out of your price range, I'd have thought, unless she'll give credit. Leave off, girl," he shouted to the woman, who had now advanced a good half a yard toward them. "He's not interested."

The woman flinched, blinking her eyes and rubbing a hand absently across her mouth. A pinched, desperate expression came over her face. Marith shuddered. Pain in his eyes. So close. So close. Turned to Tobias, trying to look embarrassed and relieved. Tobias gave him a look then pointed to one of the streets off the square. "I think we should be getting on," he said firmly. "We need to go that way, I think. We're lodging at the Five Corners on the Street of the South."

"Sounds charming," said Rate. "Want to bring your new friend, My Lord?"

"Wouldn't know what to do with her," Emit muttered.

Marith trailed behind them, gazing back at the woman with hungry eyes.

Even equipped with a map, it took them over an hour of wandering before they found the Street of the South. It was a small, neat lane in an unremarkable area of the city that was not particularly rich, not particularly poor. Shoppers and merchants bustled about, engaged in their own honest business, assuming others did likewise. Flower boxes bloomed in many of the upper windows, a small garden square with a dried-up fountain was alive with birds. All bathed in the lovely soft golden desert light. Safe. Safe, and warm, and welcoming. Marith felt his heart rise within him. One could almost pretend, here, that the world was a good place.

The Five Corners itself was equally charming, a homely lodging house with faded yellow walls and honeysuckle growing around the door. From inside came the smell of fresh bread, the sound of a woman singing in a high sweet warbling voice.

It was run by three sisters, each prettier and friendlier than the last. Rate flirted with them shamelessly from the moment he set eyes on them; even Emit grinned at them and called them "ladies" in a cheerful voice. The rooms were small but clean. Again, "My Lord Marith" had his own room, the others shared two between them. He half wondered if the whole set-up was some elaborate joke of Skie's.

They sat down for lunch in a quiet corner of the house's common room. It opened onto a small garden with flowering trees in painted pots. The middle sister, Alyet, brought them eggs cooked with chicken, green leaves and spices, fresh bread still warm. To drink there was dry sharp wine mixed with lemon, fragrant and refreshing. Marith sat quietly, looking at the trees, enjoying the taste of the wine in his mouth and the sweet smell of the bread.

"Gods, we've lucked out here," said Rate through a mouthful of eggs. "The others can't possibly all have got lodgings as nice as this. Skie must have a solid gold bed or something, if he's staying somewhere nicer than this."

Tobias looked up from his plate, glared at Rate. Alyet came over to them smiling with another basket of bread and he said loudly, "You're too kind, miss, too generous indeed. The best bread I've ever eaten."

Alyet laughed sweetly. "I'm sure you say that to everyone."

"Why of course," Rate said. "Means it, too. I, on the other hand, would rather praise a lady's face than her baking. Your smiles are sweeter than the moon, Alyet, and far, far sweeter than this fine bread."

Alyet laughed again and bustled off to another table.

"We don't talk about the rest of them," Tobias said angrily. "They're spread out across the city and we don't know where they are and we don't run into them, and we don't look at them if we do. I shouldn't even have to tell you that." He passed the basket to Marith. "More bread, My Lord? Another drink?"

After lunch they went out for a look around the city, equipped now with Alyet's advice on where to go and where to avoid. Marith looked around him in fascination. This was the city that had escaped Amrath's armies, that had refused to recognize Turnain of Immier as a god on earth. The golden, the eternal, the most beautiful, the first, the last, the undying. The unconquered. The unconquerable. The richest city there had ever been. He had read more about this city than any other place in all the world. Dreamed of seeing it.

In some disappointing ways, it was just a city like any other. The streets weren't paved with gold, nor did they run with innocent blood. Most of the buildings were just shops and houses filled with ordinary shop and house things. The people out walking were engaged in the same business they would be in any other city. But a sense always of things beneath the surface. Things out of reach. They passed a dark alleyway that gaped like a mouth, in which shadows moved and from which a low noise came, a crying wail that made the skin on Marith's back crawl. They passed vast gates of ivory and silver, studded with diamonds that flashed in the sun. They passed hollow-eyed children in silks and satins, scrabbling for rubbish blown in the corners of the streets. *As long ago as tomorrow, beneath the brazen walls of Sorlost…*

They stopped in a large square, grand and ruinous, white marble and peeling gold leaf on the walls. A huge statue of a man dominated it, its face eaten away, a stone hand clutching an object too worn to be recognized.

"The Court of the Broken Knife," Tobias said, consulting his map.

"That's the knife, then?" said Rate brightly, indicating the broken blade in the statue's hand. "Looks more like a sword, I'd have said."

Two women were sitting beneath the statue, one old, one young. The young woman wore a veil of white silk through which her eyes showed large and dark. She was lighting a little candle, her hands shaking on the taper she held. The old woman sat weeping. A tiny child played at their feet. Marith looked at them a moment. Almost as though he remembered them. The child smiled back at him shyly, gestured something with its grimy fingers. He shuddered at the sight of it, as if the child's gaze might hurt him. The child's lips moved, as though about to speak.

There was a disturbance in the square, a shifting of people, a chattering of voices. The child pointed. A man. Tall, middle-aged, flabby in the body with a short graying beard and a balding head, dressed in the simple loose robes of the south. Entirely unprepossessing. But he carried in his right hand a tall staff of dark wood.

The mage positioned himself in the center of the square near the statue. Gazed around at the crowd and gestured for them to be silent. Tobias grunted almost as though he was pleased.

"He's just going to . . . perform?" asked Rate. Amazement in his voice. Awe. "Like a traveling musician?"

"He's probably a wanderer, seeking whatever it is people like him seek, and needing to raise a quick bit of cash," said Tobias. "Or he fell out of favor somewhere and is down on his luck. Just because he's a wonder worker, doesn't mean he's wealthy. Never heard the term hedge wizard?"

Rate shook his head. "Magery's punishable by death in Chathe. Don't have many hedges round my way either."

The mage gestured again for silence. The tip of his staff began to glow with a soft emerald light, delicate in the sunshine, growing brighter until his face and hands were tinted green. A ball of light rose up from the staff and floated across the square above the heads of the crowd. Another and then another, tracing out a complex pattern as they crossed and recrossed each other's paths, their colors shifting, rising and falling, dancing, alive.

After a while, the spectators began to lose interest. The mage gestured with his other hand. The lights changed direction, moving together, spinning faster and faster, the colors flashing and pulsing until they seemed all colors at once like the wings of a dragonfly. They came together above the faceless statue, one great dance of light that hung in the air and then exploded in a shower of sparks. When the sparks landed they froze, so that the audience was dusted with tiny, glittering colored stars.

Cheers. A smattering of applause. The mage twisted his staff and pointed toward the statue. Blue flames leaped up around it. They burned with a hissing noise, but gave off no heat. The radius of the flames expanded, covering the two women and the child. Fire licked their hair, blazed in their eyes and over their hands. The child shrieked in delight, waving his thin arms to see the flames dance. The young woman cried out in fear, then sat staring at the child, her veil a crown of fire. The old woman wept.

The fire retreated, licking the eaten stone of the statue's misshapen head. The flames grew darker, no longer blue but black. Hungry. For a moment they were almost frightening. Then they too died away. More applause. The mage smiled. He made a gesture with his hand and a thousand silver lights bloomed in the air like blossom on a tree. These, too, fell into the crowd, disappearing as they hit the ground. More lights, green and blue and gold, began to dance and race in the air, chasing around the statue, swooping and diving. They rushed together and shot up into the air before bursting with a great golden flash. A clap of brilliant white light filled the square. When Marith could see again, the mage had disappeared.

There was a short pause, then laughter and cheers.

Tobias grunted in satisfaction.

"Pretty good, that," said Alxine. "I assume he'll be passing a hat round later."

Rate seemed for once entirely lost for words. His mouth hung open, a dazed, shocked expression on his face. "That was... That was... I don't know what that was."

"It was a conjuring trick," said Tobias. "An illusion. A con. You ever see a mage fight in battle, then you'll see the real thing. It was quite good for what it was, though, I'll grant you."

Street sellers appeared in the square, capitalizing on the milling crowd to offer sweets, drinks and hot food. Alxine bought a bag of preserved lemons. They were tough and chewy, salt and sweet and sour all rolled into one. Marith found them rather enjoyable, though Tobias spat his out.

Tobias was looking around at the lengthening shadows. Already halfway through the afternoon. "I'm due to meet Skie," said Tobias. "So you lot need to go back to the house. I should be picking up some money, then we can get down to business."

Marith walked back slowly, trailing behind Rate, Emit and Alxine. Felt more vulnerable, without Tobias to accompany him. Adrift. It had been nice, following Tobias. No choices. No possibilities. Quietened his mind and took some of the fear away. Didn't have to be what he was. He thought of the statue burning, black flames licking its face. What must it have felt like, to have been bathed in the mage's fire? Transcendent? A world of light and flame? Or perhaps it had felt like nothing at all. Perhaps those who had stood in the fire would not have known anything was happening, had they closed their eyes. An illusion, Tobias had called it. A trick. A con.

I used to dream of this city, he thought. I used to dream of beautiful things. And I'm here now and none of this is real. None of it has ever been real.

I killed a dragon, he thought. I've seen the rain fall and the desert bloom. I'm staying in a house full of sunlight and women's smiles. But in the end it's all just darkness. A trick. Not real. Black fire, burning. Colored lights. A lie.

"Fuck," Alxine said suddenly.

They were walking down a narrow street, and Rate had just pointed out that they were lost, and that Tobias had taken the map.

Marith had seen and studied maps of Sorlost, but they were old in fact and old in his memory. Rate had never been anywhere even half as big before and found the city's sheer size baffling. Alxine had a poor sense of direction at the best of times. Emit looked almost satisfied that they'd got themselves into a mess. It was beginning to come on toward evening. There were four of them, but only lightly armed.

"We stick to the larger streets," Rate decided. "Safer, that way. The house is a good one, people should know it if we ask around."

But the first person they asked, a well-dressed man with a servant following him, did not know it. Nor did the next, a pair of stout middle-aged women on their way home from a market. Nor a messenger boy dawdling on his errand to make eyes at the women as they passed. Nor a beggar, who spoke neither Immish nor Pernish and simply grinned at them. The streets began to get more dilapidated and uncomfortable, the people harsher faced and tiredeyed. They tried to get back onto wider streets, but whichever way they went their surroundings seemed ever poorer and more threatening. A rich city. A very rich city. But even very rich cities have places it is dangerous to go. No, thought Marith, not even. It is because it is a very rich city that it has places it is dangerous to go. Here in this city built on dying, where life and death are sacred to their god. If they stop killing, the sun will cease to rise.

Three men came toward them. They outnumbered them. There were other people about, it was still almost daylight. But the men were large, and armed with swords. Rate drew a sharp breath, his hand going to his knife. The street seemed to empty. The men looked at each other, then at the four of them. Angry, hungry eyes.

The largest of the three went straight for Marith. He had a short, fat sword, ugly and ill-made. Swung it fiercely, not with any skill but with strength and need behind it. Marith stepped backward. Almost knocked into Rate. He drew his knife, which looked stupid beside the sword. Left their swords at the Five Corners. Only murderers carried swords, in Sorlost. Those of them that even had swords, after the dragon. They were supposed to be buying replacements tomorrow. The man sliced at him so that he had to jerk away and found himself up against a wall. There was a chance he might actually die. The absurdity of it struck him as almost funny.

The big man lashed out again. Marith couldn't get in close

enough to use his knife for anything more than parrying the worst of the sword thrusts. One solid strike and it would be knocked from his hand. The sword came dangerously close to his face and he couldn't parry it, twisted sideways, kicked out hard. A gratifying grunt of pain. He felt the sword crash into the stone beside him. Pain blossoming in his shoulder. Swung his arm up to block the sword's next stroke, the blade clashing on his knife with a force that made his body jolt. Kicked again, catching his opponent on the right kneecap. The man's leg buckled and he was momentarily unbalanced. Marith managed to get his knife in close and draw blood from a flesh wound to the left arm before the sword was against him again and he had to move back. More pain, sharp and sweet at his hip, the sound of cloth ripping.

He'd killed a dragon. He'd killed...But he'd never fought another man to the death before. Not like this. Not his life against another's, hacking away at each other, everything stripped down to this one thing between them, absolutely certain, dry and solid as boiled bone. The one thing that wasn't an illusion. The one thing that was real. Warm pleasure spread through him deliciously. Bright as stars. Why hadn't they told him? He'd spent so long running from things. *Help me. Help me, Carin. Help me blot it out...* What a fool! He'd kill this man, and kill him slowly, and feel his life leaving him. He must have been happy, sometimes, this man who would die before him under his knife. Must have looked at something once and thought "this is a good thing." Must have loved and wanted and desired and hoped. And all of that he'd take from him, like it had never been.

There was a howl from somewhere to his right, then a horrible choking, roaring sound. His opponent kicked him back and his head spun with pain. The sword swung at him. Ducked under it, the blade missing him by a breath, threw himself forwards, inside the reach of it, lashing with his knife and his fist. His opponent's breath stank, sweet and rotten. Their faces so close Marith could see the network of red blood vessels in the man's staring eyes, the sluggish blink of his pupils as the knife blade bit home. Die.

Just die. Just die. Kicked again and stabbed again, brought his left hand up and struck the heavy, sweaty face. Not a hard blow, but enough with the wound to the gut to send the man stumbling back. The sword clattered to the ground. Hollow sound as it hit the flagstones, like a new-shod horse. His opponent bent over, clutching his stomach, bleeding. Crying. Marith drove his knife into the man's neck, aiming for the great artery where the heart blood came. The blade slipped down, sticky with blood, leaving a gaping slash like the opened belly of a fish.

Break him. Crush him. Kill him. Kill! Kill! The man crashed to the ground. Marith kicked him in the wound in his stomach. Blood and air bubbled from the wound in his neck. His scream sounded as though it was underwater. Marith kicked him again. The body convulsed, alcohol vomit oozing from between its lips. Some of it seemed to be leaking out of the wound in its neck. Break it! Kill it! Kill! Kill! Marith kicked it a third time in the gut, then in the face, grinding his heel down where the bloodshot eyes stared up blind and frantic, suffocating in the warm afternoon air. A crunch of bone and blood as he pressed down. Break it! Kill it! Shatter its skull! Harder. Oh, harder! Break it beyond death! Kill! Kill! Kill!

"That's enough! Marith!"

He spun round, knife out. Rate, Alxine and Emit standing staring at him.

"He's dead! He's dead, Marith! Stop!" Alxine put his hand on Marith's shoulder. "Stop."

Rate's arm was bleeding and Alxine had nasty red marks on his cheeks. The two men they'd been fighting had disappeared.

"You killed them?" Marith asked slowly.

"They ran off once Emit stabbed one in the shoulder. They were just louts looking for money, Marith. You probably didn't need to do...that."

Looked down at the body on the ground before him, spilling guts and blood and puke and piss. One hand frozen reaching for the sword. So near it, only a few finger widths away. It looked much smaller, now, almost like a child. Shrunk down.

He'd done that. He'd taken something alive and made it dead. Bright as stars. Sweet as sunlight.

Oh gods, Carin, help me...

"He was trying to kill me," he said.

"Well, yeah, seeing as you were trying to kill him. I think he realized pretty quick it wasn't a good idea to just stop and apologize."

Marith bent and wiped his knife on the dead man's shirt. Shaking. His boots were covered in blood and vomit. He wiped them as well as he could on the dead man's trousers. His hands were sticky with blood. Looking at them, smelling the blood on them, he had a sudden desperate urge to lick it off. The stink of it was maddening, from his hands and from the dead man, lying face up in the dust with the tread of his boot crushed into its ruined flesh. Mouth sort of open, one eye visible looking up at the sky. Dead. Dead and empty. Nothing. Marith rubbed his eyes, trying not to scratch at his face. Such power a man had, to take something living and turn it into that. So easy. He almost wanted to weep. The scabs on his burned hand had opened up again, oozing and bleeding, pain spreading like water up his arm.

"I..." He closed his eyes, opened them to the warm golden dusty light. "I thought he was going to kill me."

They trudged back the way they had come, and found a wide street leading straight back to the Court of the Broken Knife. It took them a half-hour at most after that to find the Street of the South and the Five Corners. A couple of people looked at them curiously, but they attracted surprisingly little attention.

Chapter Fourteen

Tobias was to meet Skie in a wine shop called the Star in the Morning, nestled up near the Gate of Laughter. Like their lodgings it was certainly not poor but not especially rich either, neat and tidy, busy and noisy with cheerful drinkers and the smell of good hot food. Skie sat in a small alcove in the far corner, carefully positioned a little way away from the other tables with the walls and the droning of a lyre-player providing cover.

Seated with Skie was the other squad captain, Geth, and a man Tobias had never seen before, in his early thirties with a face the color of dark bronze.

"Good, good." Skie gestured to Tobias to sit. He spoke in Immish, less likely to be understood than Pernish, for all the Immish were Sorlost's nearest neighbors. "You had no trouble getting here?"

"No. Remarkably easy. We're in need of some cash, though."

The other man smiled at him. "This is an expensive city, I'm afraid."

Tobias nodded. Didn't particularly like the other man. He was cheaply dressed but everything about him was shouting that he was more important than he was trying to seem. His voice was smooth, his Immish faultless. Even better than Marith's Literan. Though to be fair to the boy, it was a rather less complex language.

Shorter words. Not so many weird sudden changes of tense. Tobias flicked Skie a questioning look from the corner of his eyes. They'd worked together a long time, Geth and Skie and him. He trusted Skie with his life, near as. Had to, in their line of work. He'd like to think Skie had a similar trust in him. So not good, being kept in the dark.

Skie gave no indication he'd noticed, but Geth drummed his fingers on the table tip tap tip tap tip tap. Ah. It wasn't a code exactly, no real meaning in it, nothing worked out, just a thing that had arisen between them over the years in situations like this. Don't ask questions. This man is important, more than just a go-between. Good, thought Tobias. Probably. Safer, in many ways, though not without risks in itself. Go-betweens talked, or demanded gold not to talk, or got scared and confided in someone stupid like their but-I-thought-he-loved-me-like-the-proverbial-how-was-I-to-know-he-had-a-major-league-gambling-habit brother or their it-was-just-unfortunate-she-turned-out-to-be-shagging-the-garrison-commander wife.

Though the important person knowing your face wasn't a great feeling either, when you were busy killing someone for them and they'd kind of prefer someone else not to know.

"I have money for you," Mr. Important said importantly. He looked at Skie for a moment, then turned to Tobias and Geth. "I can see you are beside yourselves wondering who I am."

"Maybe not beside myself, but interested, yeah."

"And I assume your commander will tell if I don't. So." The man smiled and pitched his voice lower. "I am Lord Darath Vorley, Dweller in the House of Flowers, the Emperor's True Counselor and Friend, Suzerain of the South Reaches and the Desert Sea. Wherever that was. And now you have the advantage of me, gentlemen."

Ah. Well. Yes. Indeed. There were several old ballads about the Vorleys, usually emphasizing how rich and indolent they were. This one looked to be no different from the way Tobias had imagined: handsome, oh so charming, naïve in that odd way the extremely rich and high-born tended to be. He'd assumed their employers were both very rich and very powerful, but it was good to be able to put a name to the enterprise.

Really didn't like giving the man his name in exchange, though. All kinds of danger in a man like this knowing his name. "Tobias," he said reluctantly. "And this is Gethen."

"Gethen. Tobias." Lord Vorley nodded his head elegantly at both of them. Pompous git. "How much money do you need, then?" He took advantage of a general stirring in the room as the lyre-player struck a few chords and rearranged himself on his stool to discreetly pass them both fat leather purses. "I trust this will be sufficient for now. You'll need, what, suitable attire, equipment, living expenses? We seem to have promised you a good deal, I find. The amount of planning all this took! A great many people have written about this kind of enterprise, and several have even managed it halfway successfully, but it seems a true labor of love to get the detail right."

His tone was mocking, world-weary. Gambling and whoring lost their appeal for you? Tobias thought. Or competitive poetry writing or flower arranging or child torture, or whatever else the big nobs do around here to pass the time? Decided you'd try a little light regicide to relieve the tedium of having more money than most gods? Geth nudged his foot meaningfully and drummed on the table again.

They all fell silent a moment as the lyre-player addressed the room. "My friends, listen and hear a story of great wrongs and great passions, the most powerful of all men laid low by love and a sweet face. The tale of Amrath and Eltheia, fairest of women, and of those that died that Amrath might possess her."

Oh, wonderful. Another story about birthday-boy. Two in two nights, and this one even more cheerful than the last. The bit about Amrath having His new in-laws boiled alive was always particularly pleasant as an accompaniment to a pint and a hot pie. Too much to hope the man would switch from Pernish to Literan and let them ignore it completely, of course. Every gory detail doubtless about to be described in glowing detail. Possibly even in rhyme.

The lyre-player struck a note and began to sing:

"Now Amrath's Empire reached from sunrise to sunset,
Mightier than life, than death, than birth or dying.
Every city in Irlast trembled beneath His power.
Two lands only stood unconquered:
Sorlost, the Golden, great city of the God, Lord Tanis,
Ith, land of silver, seat of Godkings, proud and unbowing.
Thus Amrath journeyed to Ith, war seeking, war bringing,
And thence came the ruin of Ith, the sorrow of her maidens."

Oh gods. Not even in rhyme. Tobias tried not to snigger, though the audience looked enraptured. Good thing Rate wasn't here, they'd have been listening to scatological ditties intoned in blank verse for days otherwise.

"The event will be in five days' time," Lord Vorley said quietly. Your ways in will be arranged closer to the time: one of my associates will provide that information a few hours before."

"How will we know who the targets are?" Geth asked. Indeed: it was hardly likely they'd be wearing signs round their necks saying "kill me." And half the troop was illiterate even then.

Lord Vorley smiled. "Oh, I thought perhaps small oil paintings. Or perhaps poetic descriptions would suit better? 'You're to kill a man with hair dark curling, bald spot concealing...' There are ten men who must not survive. Six others whose deaths would not be disastrous. So we're keeping the plan simple. Kill everyone."

"Everyone?"

A flash of irritation at that. "If it was just one person, we could have handled it ourselves. We're not going to the expense of hiring a small army for nothing. Chaos and death, I was told we were buying." He looked at them keenly, studying their faces. Wondering if he's shocked us, thought Tobias. Wondering if we really have the strength of will to butcher a load of unarmed men. When none of them spoke, Lord Vorley said: "Anything else you need to discuss now?" He seemed almost disappointed they took it all so calmly.

Skie thought for a moment, then shook his head. "No. It's sometimes best not to plan too much, keep things open. We go in, we do it, we go out." Tobias and Geth nodded. It was the going out that was usually the interesting bit, but that wasn't something you discussed in front of the important bloke. "Just ensure the gates remain unguarded."

Lord Vorley finished his drink and nodded politely at them. "Indeed. And on that note, I should be going. I can only apologize for the musical accompaniment. As I said, someone will be in contact with you soon. Good evening, gentlemen."

And he was gone.

"Wept she, the princess, torn 'tween love and love's desire,
Proud Amrath or her noble father for to lose,
Her own life, too, should Amrath she reject,
Yet the price so terrible, a crown and bridebed dearly sold."

"What do you make of him, then?" Tobias asked Geth. Skie frowned at him. Not really professional to discuss the employer quite so soon after meeting him. He'd quite possibly have left a spy watching over them to check they weren't laughing at him or meeting his chief creditor or ex-wife.

"Fine." Tobias stood up. "I'll get the stuff as planned. We'll talk after that, here again, say tomorrow same time?"

Skie nodded. Fine, fine, thought Tobias. It's all settled, don't tell me anything more. He was about to leave when Geth said, "This, um, music reminds me. I picked up interesting news from the east back in my inn. It seems the Altrersyr heir is dead. Murdered, some rumors have it. Might be worth looking into, don't you think?"

Skie frowned. Looked...uncomfortable? Seemed to think about it, then said, "Murdered? Boy was headed for death anyway, if the stories are true. Not much for us there, I'd have thought. More opportunity if he'd hung on a bit and got to rule."

Geth said, "Yes, I thought so too, at first. But...The boy's mother was Marissa of Ith. Selerie Calboride's sister. And the very interesting rumor I picked up in the inn is that King Illyn himself had him killed."

A snort from Skie: "Probably can't be blamed if he had."

"Well, no. But you can imagine what Ith has made of the whole thing. Not quite up there with parboiling most of the ruling family, especially as the boy was basically dying anyway, but you know how these things can go...And the new heir and his mother... Some of the other island lords are not best pleased at her family's influence either. Weren't happy when Illyn married her. Won't be happy now. Definitely worth looking into, I'd have thought."

"No..." Skie looked thoughtful. Still edgy, though. "No... You're right, there could well be...opportunities. It can be a dangerous crossing, this time of year. But something to think on, you're right."

Hmm. Something interesting in Skie's responses there...

Why, Tobias wondered, were the posh nobs so bloody keen on killing each other? Amrath had had the excuse He didn't want to be burdened with influential and semi-divine new relations—cue several thousand very tasteless mother-in-law jokes—but really, most of them just seemed to be children kicking something to see what would happen if it broke. Nothing good, usually, despite various best-laid plans. But it kept the company in employment, and between him and Geth they usually got out all right. The Whites were supposed to be nice enough, once this was over. Pork sausages. Good beer. Not so bloody hot.

He strolled back to his lodgings feeling almost relaxed about things, only to discover his men had somehow got themselves into a fight with a bunch of street thugs. Made him look bloody stupid, it really did.

Chapter Fifteen

City after city falls before them. Elarne, the magelord Nevet burns to ashes with a single word. Telea opens it gates to them and they enter to cheers. They are turned loose on it the next morning and the streets run red. Samarnath they find empty, its inhabitants fled into the wastelands. They tear down its temples, poison its rivers, raze its palaces to dust. If a city resists them, they besiege it until it breaks. If a city yields, they slaughter its people, to show others that surrender is an act of cowardliness. Lanth gives itself to them by treachery, a small group of its nobles opening the postern gate at the dark of the moon. They despise them for it. Ten days, it takes the betrayers to die.

They are the army of Amrath, the World Conqueror, the King of Dust, the King of Shadows, the Dragon Kin, the Dragonlord, the Demon Born. "Amrath the World Conqueror", they call their master. Their god. And they have conquered the world for Him. But they do not want to rule the world.

They want to destroy it. Burn it in fire. Drown it in blood. Make it hurt. Make it despair. Kill it all.

Chapter Sixteen

Rate's arm was a bloody mess. Alxine had made an attempt to clean and dress it, but it was cut deep. Needed stitching. Tobias gave Rate a large cup of brandy, stuck a wooden spoon in the lad's mouth and told him to bite down and sit still while he sewed it up. After three attempts he ordered Alxine to gag him and hold him firm. Rate went white, thrashed like a pig then vomited and fainted. Tobias sighed with relief and sewed him up neat as a well-made shirt. Should have just hit him on the head first off. He mended a tear in the lad's jerkin as well while he had the needle and thread out. Nice soothing job, after ranting at them until his throat hurt for being such complete bloody idiots.

Alxine's face was a mess too. Red and puffy looking, with the beginnings of a black eye. They were supposed to be going out to buy some of the gear they needed tomorrow morning. Nothing said "all fine and above board, nothing to see here" like a group of men buying weapons whilst nursing fresh fighting wounds. Marith had nearly disemboweled one of their assailants, apparently, so obviously it wasn't like that would have drawn much attention either. Bloody stinking gods and demons, as Emit might say. Good lads, his men. Good lads. Gods only knew what would have happened if he'd left them alone for the entire evening.

It was a sorry group that met him for breakfast the next morning.

Tobias surveyed them wearily. Alyet laughed musically at Alxine's face and asked him if he'd been uncomplimentary about her sister's cooking. Rate struggled to eat left-handed and ended up spilling porridge on Emit's boots. Emit swore at Rate and Rate swore back. Marith sat dead-eyed, not eating, rubbing his face in that incredibly irritating way he did when he thought nobody was looking at him. You'd have thought he had a skin disease, if he hadn't had skin like new-spun silk.

"Okay," Tobias said. "You lot fucked up totally yesterday. Let's try to get through today without killing someone, shall we?" Rate laughed, realized no one else was and went back to attempting to smear honey on a slice of bread. "The plan for today has been fucked up too. Rate can't go anywhere for the next day at least, and Alxine has a face you wouldn't trust to sell a fish knife to right now. So." He fixed Emit with a glare. "I'm sending Marith and Emit out for a few things. I have some things I need to do myself, so you'll have to manage without me. Think the two of you can handle going shopping without incident?"

Emit grimaced, saw Tobias's face and attempted to look cheerful. "'Spect we can manage, between us. Ever been in a shop before, Your Lordship My Lord?"

Marith flushed but said nothing.

"You'll need new clothes, first off," Tobias said with a sigh. The fight had finally marked the point of no return for Rate's last remaining shirt and Marith's jacket. They all looked tatty and worn anyway, they'd always planned to re-equip themselves once in the city, but it was still a part of their general stupidity that they'd managed to get themselves so thoroughly mucked up. Marith's jacket had survived a bloody dragon, for gods' sake. "Try to get something that doesn't make us look too much like brothel boys. And good quality cloth." He sounded like an old fish-wife. He sounded like his mum.

Emit glared at him then looked down and spooned up his porridge in silence. All mouth, he was. Marith was...like Marith, only rather worse. There were faint scratch-marks round his eyes. Like something had been clawing at him. All that bloody face- rubbing, must be. Made Tobias's own skin crawl to watch it. Maybe he should send the boy to a pox doctor...? But he looked healthy enough, just miserable as buggery with eyes like he'd been crying and a new status as someone who fileted people with a pocket-knife. The gods themselves probably couldn't understand that one.

Didn't really like sending the two of them out alone, Mr. Grumpy and Mr. Increasingly Frigging Weird, but there were things they needed that really couldn't wait. Clothes and whatnot. Things. And he could probably trust Marith. Yeah? The boy looked at him and smiled sadly, rubbed his eyes again, frowned.

"Here." He handed Marith the purse and the map. "Bloody well look after it, and don't get lost this time."

Rate was looking at him too. Seemed to be about to say something. Tobias fixed him with a glare and Rate shrugged and went back to his breakfast. Marith opened the purse, looked carefully at the money inside and tucked it away in his belt. He nodded to Emit. "Shall we get off, then?"

"Still need to finish my breakfast," said Emit, chewing so slowly the bread would probably go stale in his mouth.

They stopped at a tailor's shop first, recommended by Alyet. Marith felt a weight lifted from him. He ran his hands over the fine cloth heaped on the counter. Silk the color of pale roses. Heavy brocade winking with gold.

All for show, of course: the clothes actually for sale were cheaper and more practical. He bought two slim-fitting silk shirts and a pair of dark gray leggings. A deep blue jacket, entirely unnecessary given the city's warm climate but elegant, with a gray fur trim at the collar. If he had to play a role, he'd do it properly, at least. If Skie was mocking him, he'd make what he could of it. Would have liked new boots, too, the mixture of dragon's blood, rainwater and human entrails not having been particularly kind to his old ones, but Tobias's purse wasn't generous and there were other, more pressing things he needed to buy. Emit bought a shirt and leggings, a jerkin. Similar clothes were parceled up to be sent back to the Five Corners for the others. They might even just about fit.

"How about we stop for a drink?" Marith said casually as they left the shop. "We can spare a couple of coins, I should think, without Tobias noticing."

Emit looked at him, then grinned. "Most sensible thing I've ever heard you say, boy. Almost makes up for the fancy coat. Bit early, but I wouldn't say no."

They strolled down the street and came to a small, expensive-looking tavern. It was only just opening, it still being well before midday, and they were the only customers. Emit selected a table at the back and Marith ordered the drinks. Emit had a cup of beer. Marith had something else. Emit raised an eyebrow but didn't comment. They sat in silence for a while.

"What was all that fuss about black for?" asked Emit. Idiot had asked if they had a shirt in black and the tailor had been shocked and embarrassed enough it looked like he could have done with a drink himself.

He really didn't know? Although obviously he didn't. Astonishingly stupid thing to ask, here. Marith said, "Sumptuary laws. Only the Emperor is permitted to wear black cloth. He is only permitted to wear black cloth, in fact. It marks him out against everyone else in the city, signals his status. In Chathe, only the ruling family may wear pearls. In Tarboran, it was peacock feathers."

"Sumptuary laws... How d'you know all this stuff?"

"I—"

Emit sniggered at him. Vile man. "Your tutor, yeah, I remember. You going to lecture me on the name of the King of Chathe's pet dog, next? Bloody odd place, this, though. Sumptuary laws... An Emperor's an Emperor. He doesn't need to wear a different color to show it, I'd have thought. Sodding big crown and people groveling before him should be enough of a clue."

Old lessons. Repeated until he could chant them off by heart as a child. "The way power works is more complicated here. The Asekemlene Emperor and his court control the bureaucracy of the

Empire. Or did, rather, there not being an Empire any more to speak of. The great families control the wealth and the land. The Nithque to the Emperor liaises between the two. The sumptuary laws...I don't know, they mark out the difference. The great families hate the Emperor. The Emperor hates the great families. The Emperor wears black because the great families want to outshine him. Or the great families aren't allowed to wear black to show how much lower they are than the Emperor, who doesn't need the false trappings of money to show his power and prestige. One or the other. Maybe both. If anyone ever knew exactly why, it was forgotten centuries ago." Marith rubbed his face wearily and drained his drink. Glanced hopefully over at Emit's cup. It was still more than half full.

"Still odd, if you ask me. Emperors should wear cloth of gold. And it's the Yellow Empire. The Yellow Emperor. Why's he called the Yellow Emperor, if he wears black all the time?"

Oh gods. Marith remembered his tutor laughing at him for asking the same question. He'd been five or six at the time. "I think it's not quite as simple as that." "Not quite as simple" as in "a joke." *Sekemlenet*: golden dawn light. Yellow: so cowardly you're scared to fight. He said casually, "I'll get some more drinks."

Emit laughed. "There was me thinking you were a lightweight boy, Marith. No, we should be going."

Damn. "It wouldn't hurt. Just another one."

Emit frowned at him. "It's Company money and we're on Company business. And Tobias'll have us whipped if we fuck up again." Got up and headed for the door.

Damn. Damn, damn, damn. Misjudged the man. Marith gazed around the room with longing eyes. No point in trying to slip away, Emit would be after him in a moment. Emit didn't trust him. Didn't like him. He'd put him on his guard now, too.

They walked south in a rambling fashion, looking at the shops and the crowds. Marith had the map. Slowly, cautiously, he began to lead them away from the larger streets, back toward the squalid quarter they'd stumbled into yesterday. That had been a stroke of luck, now he thought about it. A good and hopeful place. He had a good memory for directions. The streets became dirtier and more run down, the air dustier. He lowered the map. Stared around him. Tried to look afraid.

"We're lost," he said.

"What?" Emit said stupidly. He stared about in turn. "Oh fuck. Fuck, Marith, you stupid bastard. Not again." He bent forward to grab the map from Marith's hands. Marith pulled his knife out from under it. Pressed it into Emit's gut, just under the ribs, breaking the skin.

"What the hell—?"

"Stay perfectly still and don't make a sound." Marith pressed a little harder. Felt Emit flinch. "If you try to shout or break away, I'll stab you. Understand? Now walk."

He guided Emit into a narrow alleyway. Dark. Cold even in the warmth of a sunny morning. The corpse of a cat lay stretched out near the entrance, writhing with maggots. Blank walls leaned together overhead, blocking out the light. Didn't look like much came in here. Didn't look like much left. He pushed Emit up against a wall. The brickwork was crumbling. Stank. Dust and mildew and rot grinding into Emit's face. He kicked Emit hard in the back of the knees and pushed him to the ground. Looked down at him and smiled. Emit looked back up.

"Don't say anything." He knelt down and placed the knife against Emit's throat. "This is going to hurt. A lot. And then you'll die. Are you ready?"

Emit made a horrible whimpering sound, deep in his throat.

Marith drove the knife in.

Emit screamed. And then he was dead.

He'd sworn to kill the man, Marith remembered. Only a few days ago, though it felt like months now. Maybe Emit had even deserved it. But…but…

But nothing, he thought then. I killed him. It doesn't matter whether he deserved it or not. I killed him and now he's dead.

I'm sorry, Emit, he thought.

He wiped his hands on Emit's nice new shirt and walked back out of the alley, stepping neatly over the dead cat. Glanced at the map and began to walk hurriedly. The streets were becoming more and more run down, the flagstones of the road broken and overgrown with weeds, the buildings dilapidated and decayed. The air stank. Dog shit and human shit and rotting filth. Nervous excitement building within him. Please. Oh, please. A group of children stared out at him from a doorway, then came out at a run behind him, throwing stones and dirt. A lump of something hit him on the back. He walked on hurriedly, barely noticing.

He came to a small square, centered on an ugly statue of a man holding a sword. A dead dog lay below the statue. Two girls played in the bowl of a broken fountain, splashing and laughing, their skirts soaked. A young woman came out of a boarded-up house, gaudily dressed in faded, mismatched clothes. She walked slowly around the edge of the square, holding on to the walls with her hands as if she was blind. Turned her head toward Marith for a moment and her face was covered in scratch-marks, raw red lines spiraling out from her eyes and mouth. Oh gods. He almost fell. Please. Oh please. Her head twitched and she raised her hand to rub at her eyes. Black fire on her skin, burning. Black flames on old stone. Shaking, he walked over to her. Finally. Finally. Finally. Please. Please. Please.

The woman stared at him. The whites of her eyes were yellow and blood-shot, her pupils mismatched. One hugely dilated, the other a pinprick of black. Marith stared back at her. Oh gods. Oh gods. So close. Please. He fumbled in the purse Tobias had given him and produced a gold talent.

"Hatha?" Hard to speak, he was so on edge. "You know where to get hatha? Quickly? Now?"

She frowned. Sighed. "Nobody. Nobody has hatha. Not for days now. Plague in Chathe, they say. Nobody has it." Her hands jerked, rubbing at her face. Fresh blood welled up as the scabs cracked. "Nobody."

No. No, no, no . . . A void in his mind. Blank dark. No. Oh gods, no. No. Fire in his head, screaming. No. He stared hopelessly at the woman. Kill her, he thought. Kill her. I can't go on. Not after yesterday. Not any more. Kill her. Make her hurt. It's not fair... Not fair. Please...Help me...

"Are you sure? I have gold. I can pay well." His voice shook.

She gave him a mournful look, staring at the coin. "Nobody has it for any price." Then she nodded. "But I could get you other things. Fire? Keleth seed?"

Marith almost laughed. Pressed the coin into her hand and then, feeling generous, gave her two more.

"Fire? Yes. That would be lovely." Keleth seeds were utterly boring. But fire...He licked his lips. "Now."

She nodded. "Come."

She could just be going to kill him. But he'd killed a dragon. He'd killed Emit. He'd killed better men than Emit. Could probably handle a young woman barely able to walk. The thought disappeared from his mind as she turned and started down a narrow street. She walked slowly, unsteadily. He danced impatiently behind her, clutching the purse Tobias had given him in shaking hands.

After a short while they came to a little court of buildings, falling over each other and half ruined, with a dank alley running beside them. The woman gestured toward a small low doorway where a man crouched scrabbling in the dirt in a pool of his own piss. She tapped on the door and pushed it open. Marith followed her eagerly, his eyes bright, his whole body shaking now with anticipation and fear and hope and happiness.

Tobias arrived back at the Five Corners around early in the afternoon. Marith and Emit didn't. It got too late in the afternoon and Tobias began to fret. They should have been back hours ago. It didn't take that long to buy shirts. He had to meet Skie again, couldn't show up and tell him he had no idea what had happened to half his squad.

"Where the bloody hell are they?" he shouted at Rate and Alxine. "They didn't say anything to you, did they?"

"Maybe they got lost again," said Alxine. "Or got in a fight. Or Emit finally snapped and lamped Marith one."

"We'd better go out and look for him." Tobias stood up wearily. "You two, come with me." If he left them alone, they'd probably manage to set fire to the building. He composed a message for Skie explaining he'd be delayed and asked the oldest sister, Navala, to send a message boy with it to the Star. All the boy had to say was "Will be late, meet at the Star tomorrow morning", so it was probably pretty safe. Not much else he could do anyway.

They must have been to the tailor's shop, a parcel of not entirely tasteless clothes having arrived just after midday, so the search started there. The two of them were fairly memorable, especially as Marith turned out to have bought an extremely expensive coat. An apprentice had been taking out some parcels at the time they left and thought he remembered them talking about going for a drink. Tobias almost kicked the wall with rage at this point.

There was a tavern just down the street. The landlady smiled wistfully at the memory of the beautiful boy who'd come in just after opening and bought a very large measure of extremely expensive brandy, as well, most generously in her opinion, as a cup of beer for his servant man. No, she didn't know where he'd gone, but she very much hoped he'd come back. Tobias did kick the wall then, and almost kicked Alxine too, for good measure.

They wandered the streets vaguely for a while, feeling increasingly lost. After an hour's searching, Rate was ready to conclude they were dead and give up. Moaning his arm hurt and he was fed up with walking round in circles. "They're probably dead in a ditch somewhere," he muttered repeatedly. "Or in prison, or run off together to start a new life as traveling musicians. We are not going to bloody find them."

"They can't have just run off," Alxine responded each time. "Emit wouldn't do that to us, and Marith..." But none of them could say what Marith would or wouldn't do, and each time Alxine would trail off emptily.

Why on earth did I trust him with the money? Tobias kept

asking himself. He just seemed so…so…Confident was the wrong word. Trustworthy was entirely and absolutely the wrong word. Frightening. Pitiful. Strange. Sad. Wrong and broken, in ways Tobias couldn't begin to understand. But he'd given him a bag of gold and sent him off without a backward glance. *Things they needed that really couldn't wait. Could probably trust Marith. Yeah?* What had he been thinking? What had he been bloody thinking? It was beginning to get dark, the sun red in the west and twilight drawing in. "Let's go back," he said wearily. Gods only knew what he'd tell Skie. The man was going to bloody well flay him alive.

They had almost reached the Street of the South when Alxine grabbed Tobias's arm and pulled him across the street. Tobias turned and saw a young woman in the midst of a violent argument in the doorway of a shop. "What—?"

"No," Alxine said urgently. "Listen."

The woman was hurling abuse at a well-dressed man, who was looking back at her in scornful disbelief. From what Tobias could gather from the jumble of Literan and Pernish, she was trying to buy a dress from the man, who was refusing to even let her enter his shop. Shouting that she had money enough to buy ten of his dresses, never mind one. To prove it, she thrust a talent piece in his face. Given she was currently dressed in rags, the shop-keeper promptly accused her of theft. She shouted even louder, yelling at the top of her voice that she'd been given it as a gift by a beautiful young lord with eyes like storm clouds and hair the color of dark wine. He'd given her more, in fact, but she'd already spent them. On drink, from the state of her. The shop-keeper burst out laughing. Asked if he'd also had lips as red as roses and a gold-plated cock.

Tobias's heart sank like a stone.

The shop-keeper finally succeeded in shoving the woman away from him and slamming his door shut. She stood transfixed in the doorway, hurling a stream of incoherent abuse at the dark wood. Finally she sank down onto the cobbles and began to cry. Tobias went over to her.

After a short discussion and the production of a couple of dhol, the woman agreed to show them where she'd taken her beautiful, generous, kind-hearted, charming young lord. They followed her warily, frowning at each other. Not looking particularly good, this. Hands on the hilts of their knives. The woman walked slowly; her voice slurred and stilted, the stress placed on the wrong words, with a rhythm to it like a body jerking on a noose. The skin around her eyes was raw and ragged, patterned with scratches and open sores; she rubbed at them as she walked and blinked constantly, as though the evening dark was blindingly bright. Tobias shuddered as she brushed against him. Made him think of worms and grave soil. Beetles burrowing into rotting flesh.

She led them at last to the mouth of a filthy alleyway. "There," she said with a hoarse laugh. "A beautiful palace for a beautiful boy."

She turned and headed slowly back into the gathering dark. Living dead, waiting for her heart to give out like her rotted mind and body, something eating her away from the inside. A kindness just to kill her now. Tobias realized suddenly and horribly that the way she itched her face was the same as Marith's habit of rubbing at his eyes. He and Rate and Alxine stared at the doorway she had indicated. A stream of raw sewage ran across the threshold. A man lay in the sewage, muttering something under his breath, the same meaningless syllables over and over again. There was blood around his mouth. His lips were stained black. The woman had been horrible. This was worse. Tobias pushed the door open hesitantly and stepped inside.

It was a wine shop, though poorer and more disheveled than any place Tobias had ever been in. Very dark, a single windowless room lit by a few lamps that gave off a rancid, fishy smoke. A handful of customers were slumped at dirty tables. A man with a face that was a mass of sores stood behind the bar, laughing mirthlessly at an old woman in a torn dress who twitched and jerked like a beetle on a pin. The air stank of puke and piss and raw alcohol, so strong it made Tobias's head spin. There were puddles on the floor he tried hard not to tread in. A large rat scuttered past, something hanging from its mouth that might be alive. Fat flies crawling on hands and faces and cups, clustering around eyes and open mouths. No talking. No singing. No arguments. No whores. Not a place where people came to drink, this. A place where people came to die.

Marith was in a corner at the back, the side of his head resting on the table-top. His eyes were open and staring, empty as stones.

Tobias sat down opposite him. Felt sick looking at him.

"Hello, Marith."

"...Tobias...?" Marith blinked and raised his head, made a strangled sound that might have been a laugh. After several attempts, he managed to sit up. His voice was thick and strange, coming from a long way off, like he was an animal trying to speak. He took a gulp of his drink. "Hello...Want to join me?"

"We've been looking for you for hours. Where the fuck have you been?"

"I've been...here." Waved his hand vaguely, knocked over his cup. Its contents splashed over the table with a hiss, scorching the wood. Tobias jerked backward.

"What in all hells is that?" Alxine asked in a horrified voice, hastily moving his hands off the table. The liquid was thick and dark and oily, deep red with a glossy sheen. Tobias could swear it was smoking slightly.

"Firewine," said Rate. "Blindness-in-a-bottle, it's sometimes known as. Sort of a cross between an alcoholic drink and the stuff used to poison wells in a siege." He looked quite impressed. "I've never managed more than a couple of cupfuls, myself. And then I was ill for a week."

Would the boy's prowess never cease? "You were supposed to be with Emit," Tobias growled at Marith. "Where in the gods' name is he?" Entirely pointless. Something of a surprise if the boy had any idea where he was at this particular moment, let alone anyone else. But he had to ask.

"Emit..." Marith blinked at him. "Emit...he's...in an alley. Somewhere." His eyes flickered for a moment. Something like a smile passed over his face. "I can't remember where." He poured himself another drink and carefully set the bottle back down on the table. Alxine flinched as it rocked.

Tobias grabbed Marith's arm. "I think you've maybe had about enough now, boy," he said, to sniggers from Rate and Alxine. "Time to stop, don't you think?"

Marith's eyes seemed to clear for a moment. Like he finally understood what Tobias was saying to him. "I've had nothing like enough. I don't intend to stop until I'm unconscious." His voice was raw with hatred. Pushed Tobias's hand away, took a long drink. "Or dead."

The last time something like this had happened, it had been Gulius and Alxine, and they'd come fairly peacefully after Tobias had yelled at them enough. There was something else here. Shadows crawled on the walls, like the shadows in Marith's eyes. The boy looked like a demon. A wraith. A thing undead, steeped in hate and grief. The room was full of pain, soaking into the bones, despair beating around them. Ruin and dust and dark. The drinkers coughed and whimpered, waiting for death.

"I'm your commanding officer, Marith," Tobias said firmly, keeping his voice low. "This is an order. We're leaving. Now."

Marith's face went dark. He frowned at Tobias, then laughed and took another drink. "No."

"You don't refuse to obey orders, boy. You follow them. Get up." Marith laughed again.

"You're drunk, you've misused Company money entrusted to you, and you're committing an act of insubordination. That's a whole world of trouble. Get up. Now."

Marith picked up the bottle and very carefully topped his cup up to the brim.

"Get up, boy, or I'll have Rate and Alxine drag you out of here."

Marith blinked and smiled and something dark and rotten climbed out from behind his eyes. The background noises in the room faded. A sound from far off like a sword being drawn.

"No."

"This is an order. We leave, now, and tomorrow you'll be whipped."

"I said no." Marith raised his cup, drained it, refilled it, drained it again. "I am a prince of the line of Amrath the World Conqueror, kin to the dragons and to the Living Gods of Immier and Caltath. In my veins flows the blood of gods and demons from beyond the realms of life and death. My family has ruled over empires the likes of which the world had never known. We have been kings since the land rose from the sea and men first crawled from the mud to do our bidding." He bared his teeth, his voice an angry hiss. "I do what the hell I like."

The dramatic effect was spoiled slightly when he slumped sideways and was violently sick all over his lovely new coat.

Chapter Seventeen

Two young men, boys really, stumble down a dark street. One is slim and dark-haired, the other stockier and fair-blond. They are both expensively and elegantly dressed, torchlight flickering on the embroidery of their coats. The dark-haired boy leans heavily on the fair-haired boy's arm. He might perhaps charitably be described as more than a little drunk.

They stop walking. The dark-haired boy falls over. Lands in a dirty puddle. Doesn't get up.

"I can't walk any more," he moans. He crawls forwards a few paces, curls up with his head resting in the muddy water. "I told you that stuff would finish me," he mutters in a slurred voice.

"You've just got to get used to it. Then you'll be fine." The fair-haired boy sits down beside him and passes him a vicious-looking black glass bottle. The dark-haired boy hesitates, then sits up and drinks.

"I was. Fine...I'm tired...Can we just stay here for a while?" He frowns a little, his voice confused. "I don't seem to be able to see any more."

"You really should be able to handle it better, you know. What with the divine blood and all."

The dark-haired boy rolls over, rests his head in the fair-haired boy's lap. "I don't want to be able to handle it better. I don't want to have divine blood." He sighs as the fair-haired boy begins to stroke his forehead with smooth white hands. "I just want…I don't know what I want. You know what I want. To make everything go away."

"Everything?" The fair-haired boy smiles down at him. Holds the bottle to the dark-haired boy's lips. "This helps, though, doesn't it?"

"Yes." The dark-haired boy sighs again, drinks again, reaches out to hold the fair-haired boy's hand. "It helps."

He lies for a while in silence, a sad smile on his face. The fair-haired boy watches him with pale, wide eyes.

"When I'm king," the dark-haired boy says slowly at last, his voice very far away, drifting into sleep, "when I'm king, I'll probably have to stop sleeping in the gutter. Kings very seldom sleep in the gutter, you know."

The fair-haired boy laughs. "Aralbarneth the Good did. Dressed as a beggar."

A long, possibly thoughtful pause. "That was to understand the cares of his people. Not because he was dead drunk."

"Well, you're not likely to end up being known as 'the Good' anyway, are you?"

"I'm not?"

The fair-haired boy strokes his friend's hair again, smoothing the dark curls, gently touching the flushed face. "No."

The dark-haired boy sits up again, drains the bottle and throws it across the street. It shatters in a shower of glass, spilling dregs of an oily liquid dark as blood. "You're probably right." He curls himself closer into the fair-haired boy's lap. "It does help. Thank you."

"For you, anything," the fair-haired boy says. He bends over to kiss the dark-haired boy's cheek. "We can go out again tomorrow, if you like. Other things I can think of, that might help more."

The dark-haired boy nods, half-asleep. His eyes are red rimmed and impossibly weary. "That would be nice," he says dreamily, clutching the fair-haired boy's hand.

The fair-haired boy runs his fingers through the dark-haired boy's shining curls. "Anything," he says.

Chapter Eighteen

I am the High Priestess of Great Tanis the Lord of Living and Dying. The center and meaning of my life is to kill for the God. For a thousand thousand years, the people of the Sekemleth Empire have offered themselves up to death beneath the knife.

The people of Tarboran built vast tombs to their dead, as high as watchtowers, gilded and carved and fragrant with cedar wood. The money they must have spent, the time they must have labored! A rich man's tomb was planned for him from the day he was born. Imagine it, going every day to supervise the construction of your own burial place, taking pride in it as the greatest achievement of your life. Looking forward to dying so that you can be buried and dead. And then the fire came down upon Tarboran, and the tombs were burned, and all the gold and glory lost. No one remembers their names, now, the tomb builders.

The people of Immier and Caltath, by contrast, feared death so intently and so absurdly that their kings became determined they should not die, and had themselves declared living gods who would rule forever. And, indeed, they did not die. But not dying is not a pleasant thing, in the end, and their rule was terrible, for they had no fear and no longing and no hope. And the people feared death the more, when they saw their kings living on and on without end, while they died. Immier fell in ruin, its king raving mad, its people mad likewise. They say plants grew up in the streets and the fields blackened with weeds, while the people sat in their houses praying for immortality. Caltath was taken by the sea, drowned by floods in the course of a single night. Its king alone survived, clinging to the very tip of the highest mountain, now an island in a churning sea. Some say he sits there still, immortal king of a barren rock.

Amrath wanted to kill the world. His banners were made of skin and bone. His watchword was "death." He mortared His fortresses with the blood of His enemies. He killed the people of His own cities, in the end. Then He died and there was no one left to bury Him, and the wild beasts gnawed His bones.

We are not like that. This is Sorlost, greatest of cities, that was old before Tarboran built her tombs, before the Godkings were even born. We live and we die. Not one without the other. Death is as natural as life, we say, and as great a blessing. No light without darkness. No joy without pain. Life is a glory. Death is a sweet release.

We lie, of course.

Chapter Nineteen

He'd missed Darath.

Three years, it had been. They'd sat and talked for a long time, after. Like they'd used to. Darath's golden-black hair had some gray around the temples that hadn't been there before, no longer quite the perfect creature he'd been. Only three years.

Starting something up again was a bad idea. Starting something up again now was a very bad idea. But Darath was right: nothing got a man's blood up like the prospect of someone else's imminent death. He and Darath understood each other. Fitted each other. Might even say they loved each other.

Bil would be upset. She'd been happier since things had fallen apart the last time. It must have been hard for her; Orhan wasn't callous enough not to realize that, nor not to feel guilty about it. She'd known, when she married him, but the difference between knowing and seeing had perhaps been greater than she'd realized. There had been evenings when the tension had leached into the walls.

Sex with another man or indeed relationship with another man, was not uncommon in Sorlost, as it was not uncommon anywhere. Better to say it was not looked down upon in Sorlost, as it could be elsewhere. Plenty of brothel boys and pretty young things who would be more than happy to spend some time with him.

Tam Rhyl kept a very lovely young man who accompanied him to banquets and parties, his own grandfather had had a slightly mysterious "secretary" whose role in the household Orhan had only fully understood years after both had died. But two men of equal status publicly acknowledging their relationship? When they were the heads of two great families it was considered almost dangerous. Even though the great families intermarried all the time. Even though the course of action they were currently embarking on had been planned and set in motion during the one period in the last ten years they hadn't been fucking. Even though he hadn't wanted Darath to get involved.

There was no way he could keep it from Bil, since Darath had stayed the night and most of the next morning. Quite a lot of Sorlost probably knew by now. Certainly everyone in his household unless they were blind and deaf. And if Bil somehow hadn't noticed, Celyse would delight in telling her. Her spies would have gone running before they'd even made it into the bedroom. He didn't want to upset his wife, in her condition. Should have waited until the baby was born.

Should have waited until the Emperor was dead, too. A few days, now, and everything would be so different.

The plan itself was painfully simple. Hire a troop of trained killers, smuggle them into the palace, let them kill everyone inside. Killing the Emperor alone was pointless. The Emperor was a figurehead. It was the Imperial Secretary, the Keeper of the Treasury, the clerk who noted down what the Emperor should be having for breakfast and whether the sun was shining today, that had to be got rid of. The bureaucrats would carry on regardless, whatever the foibles of the current incarnation of the Eternal Eminence, the Ever Living, the Lord of the Dawn Light. Kill the Emperor, in fact, and you ended up with a hapless child on the throne and power only further consolidated in the hands of his servants. To really make any changes, they all had to die. You had to get rid of everyone. Start again.

Tam Rhyl had wanted to do it with their own men at first, a

traditional assassination, argued that external help was too risky. But as far as Orhan could see, it was using your own men that was risky. Hiring a mercenary company kept it cleaner, more removed. Easier to bear.

The Sekemleth Empire was dying. A laughing stock. The Immish were arming and could walk across their borders and up to their walls and push them over like a boy kicking sand. It astonished him sometimes that it had not already happened. That the lure of their wealth and weakness hadn't drawn armies from across Irlast, trampling the Empire under their feet as they squabbled over its broken bones.

But something was coming. He knew it. Couldn't understand why the whole city didn't feel it, didn't awake screaming in fear in the night from the things crawling in the dark. The scent of blood in the air. The Immish arming was part of it, perhaps. Tensions rising. Thoughts of death. They'd never survive, as they were. But they didn't deserve to die. The people of Sorlost were just people living their lives. Looked at like that, he was a hero, a savior. Not a murderer and a traitor at all. Not—

"They seem a capable bunch, you'll be pleased to hear."

Darath appeared in the study doorway, followed by an anxious-looking door keep. Orhan started up from his thoughts, smiled at him and waved the servant away. Happiness sweet as candle-light. Darath came over to kiss him. Orhan clutched at him back, sliding his hands around Darath's waist. I'm dragging you into this squalor and I'm glad, he thought, because it means you're here with me. Three years. God's knives, I've missed you.

Perhaps Tam is right, he thought then with a sudden chill. Perhaps I'm only doing this because I needed something to keep me occupied without you. He kissed Darath in return. Began tugging at the fastenings of his clothes. Three years...

"Alas, no. We need to talk first." Darath pushed him off and pulled over a chair. Looked down with interest at the pile of papers on Orhan's desk. "Rewriting your will, Lord Emmereth?

That doesn't strike a particularly reassuring note given current circumstances."

Orhan sighed. "It seemed wise to take precautions."

"Really? If this goes wrong, they'll burn every last member of your household, then raze your estates to the ground and sow the ruins with salt. Whether or not you left a few thalers to the poor or remembered your second cousin's desire for a particular set of tea bowls will seem somewhat academic at that point, I'd have thought."

"No. But still…" He'd thought of sending Bil away somewhere, but there was nowhere she could go, and it would attract too much comment anyway. It was a curious sensation, that he held the lives of every servant, family member and sycophantic hanger-on balanced in the palm of his hand. Too huge and terrible to think about. Every life. His own and all the people linked to him.

"We'd best hope it doesn't go wrong then," Darath said cheerfully. He scanned the sheets of parchment. "Left me anything? A ring, a token, a lock of your hair?"

"You'll be as dead as I am." Orhan hurriedly swept the papers away into a box and closed the lid. "Which might explain why I hadn't wanted you to get involved. What do we need to talk about, then?"

"I just thought you'd like to know how events stand. I met with your friend Skie: he seems a sensible fellow, though one of his lieutenants clearly loathed me on sight. The date is confirmed by all, we just need to finalize the ways in with Tam. They have some money to buy equipment, seemed laughably impressed with the purses I gave them. One forgets how poor the Immish are. You could probably have offered them half what you did."

"Yes, well." Please, for the love of the God, don't suggest we ask for a discount at this point. "I shouldn't have let you meet them. You shouldn't have asked me."

"It was fun. I was careful."

"Were you?"

"Better than you would have been. You'd just have got their backs up, looking all guilty and ashamed. You know you would."

"Yes, probably, yes…" Orhan put the box of papers back in a cupboard under his desk, locked the door. "Seeing as you're here: I've found a couple of babies that seem suitable. The most promising mother is a congenital idiot, the grandmother likewise, apparently. The father is entirely unknown, but I can't imagine he was anything physically or intellectually exceptional, given what he was reduced to bedding. The child is due any day now. If it's a boy, it would be ideal."

"You have such a sense of Imperial dignity, Orhan."

They shared a wry smile. The Ever Living, the Eternal, the First and Last Ruler of the Sekemleth Empire, a mortal man who was immortal, who died and lived again a thousand times, reborn each time somewhere in what remained of his Empire. And so it could take years to find him. The current Emperor had been thirteen when he was finally recognized. Thirteen long, painful years of stalemate and stasis while everyone stared at every boy in the city in hope. Orhan was a rational man and had thought about things carefully. The only sensible solution was to identify the next incarnation before this one ended. A lot more efficient than years spent wandering around looking for a special sign of some sort or another to guide you. A flock of ravens cawing the word "emperor" had been the clue to this one's status. The sort of thing that gave the richest empire the world had ever known a bad name for superstitious idiocy, even among people who were credulous enough to believe their kings were descended from gods.

"And if the woman has the bad manners to have a girl? Or a corpse, come to that?"

"There are a couple of other likely candidates. A young whore down at the Weeping Docks, again due any time in the next few days now; another in Fair Flowers."

A wicked smile flashed across Darath's face: "If your timing had been better, you could have made your son Emperor. Want to delay things a few months?"

Had to laugh at that. "I think that would be a bit obvious, don't you? And I don't really feel like being executed just so my son can wear a black coat."

Darath smiled. "A slight disadvantage, I admit. I might even miss you."

Orhan sat in silence afterward. All he wanted, in the end. Perhaps Tam was right, he had simply been looking for something to occupy himself. If he and Darath had mended things sooner... or had not broken things off at all... Everything would go on unchanged, and there was no threat to Sorlost. He was dreaming, seeking fears, a mirror for his own unhappiness. Bored and rich and idealistic and wound-up enough to start planning murder, and then finding it had all got real and solid and too late to stop.

No, he thought then. Darath sees it. Fragments of it. He's not reckless enough to go into this without some cause. Just pretends he is. We can't explain our reasons, either of us. But he understands why. That it's necessary. We're too weak, the way we are, sitting on our piles of gold pretending nothing exists beyond our walls. We need to be ready. And yes, that does mean blood.

I need to hold on to that, he thought. That it's necessary. That Darath sees it too. If I was a bad person, he thought, doing this for bad reasons, I wouldn't keep questioning it.

That's so absurdly naïve, Orhan, he thought.

But something Darath had said remained nagging at him, uncomfortable in the back of his mind. He'd dined, Bil sitting opposite him in frozen silence, read for a while and was preparing to sleep when it suddenly came to him.

The penalty for high treason. Rarely enacted, in the long, faded centuries of the Empire's slow decline, but drummed into every nobleman as a child. He could remember his nurse telling it to him, his boyish confidence disbelieving, appalled and fascinated in equal measure. If one of the great families was found to have committed treason against the Empire or the Emperor, they were burned alive. Every member of their household was burned alive.

Women and children. Bondsmen. Servants. Errand boys. Regularly visited whores. Their holdings razed to the ground and destroyed utterly. The ruins sown with salt and ash.

It hadn't happened in his lifetime—yet—but he'd been taken to see the blackened wasteland that had once been the house of the Saddulae, an ancient line of petty kings with substantial holdings on the Chathean border who'd been absorbed into the Empire in a last sudden gasp of re-expansion a few centuries back. They were the last family to have been executed for treason against the Emperor, after they attempted to break free and ally again with Chathe. That had been fifty years ago, though it was remembered by the great families like it was yesterday. The Saddulae lands had been noted for the very high quality of their wine and oil. No longer, since the soil was now barren dead earth.

Wine. Old wine. A vintage fifty years old, an estate that no longer produced.

Rhyl was trying to warn him? Or threaten him? Why? For what?

Orhan sat up in bed, sick in his stomach, panic crushing him.

His death.

Bil, burning. His sister. His good-brother, stupid money-grabbing upstart that he was. Sterne. Amlis. The tiny unborn lump of Bil's child. His beautiful house. His books.

Darath. Oh, God's knives. Darath. If he hadn't given in to his wishes…

Too late to back out now. That might even be what Tam wanted. A warning hint, so he would step back, and Tam could play on alone. Take everything, after Orhan had done all the work. His money, his plans. His name. He'd only come to Tam with it because his position as Nithque to the Emperor meant he was more useful as an ally than an opponent. Necessary. Thought Tam understood. He should do, after all he'd seen and had done to him. Couldn't allow Tam to take it. And Darath would never forgive him for backing out now. He'd just have to keep alert.

As Tam had told him to be…

Signs and portents! Maybe it was just a coincidence. Maybe it was a nasty joke.

Orhan got up and paced his bedroom, walked out onto the balcony, looked down onto a courtyard thick with flowers. The moon shone very bright. The stars were bright too: he could see the Crescent, the White Lady, the great single red star of the Dragon's Mouth.

What to do, what to do...? Maybe it was simply an old cask of wine. Maybe it was from Chathe, or Immish, or across the Bitter bloody Sea.

There was a rustle of cloth behind him. He froze, no one could get in here, no one had any reason to get in here, but panic overcame him, "fifty years old, fifty years old, death for treason", a voice seemed to ring in his head, he could almost feel a knife in his back, he turned and Bil stood looking at him.

"What are you doing here?" She never came into his bedroom. He'd made it clear when he married her that she wasn't to go in there.

"I heard you walking about." She went over to him. In the moonlight, her scars were barely visible. In the moonlight, he thought, someone could have loved her. Until they touched her skin. She said: "You should have told me. About Darath."

"Why? What business is it of yours?" It came out harsher than he had meant it to, because he was so afraid.

"I'm going to have your heir. I live in this house. My father paid off the debts your father ran up on this house. It would have been polite. It was the same day we went to the Temple, Orhan. People are already beginning to laugh. Saying you finally managed to bed your wife and then went running straight back to Darath Vorley."

"You should be grateful they're saying the child is mine at all." She looked at him fiercely, her blue eyes pale in the silver light.

Orhan thought: that was cruel.

"You should come inside," he said. "You mustn't get cold, get sick." They sat down on low-backed wooden chairs placed by the balcony, smelling sweetly of resin and beeswax, the cushions stuffed with dried herbs. Bil looked at his bed for a moment then did not look at it again. Folded her hands in her lap. It was an odd sensation, being alone in his bedroom with a woman at night.

"I am happy about the baby," she said. "It will be nice for the house, too, to have a child in it. Make it lighter, full of noise. You will be a good father, Orhan. It's just...why does it have to be Darath, of all people? I used to play with Elis when I was little. He was horrible. My father seemed quite keen for me to marry him at one point. Before..."

"Well it's lucky for all of us it's not Elis I'm fucking then, I suppose." A great wave of tiredness swept over Orhan. He yawned. Not much sleep, the last couple of nights, and now this. "I'm sorry. That was crude. Go to bed, Bil. You need to sleep to keep the baby strong. I need to sleep."

"Good night, Orhan." She looked at him with her pale eyes and for a moment he thought she, too, knew something. Realized how much guilt he would feel, toward her and the tiny thing inside her, if the plan failed.

"Good night, Bil," he said.

Chapter Twenty

Shadows.

White light.

Everything falling. Like broken glass.

Moving and blurring together.

Lines of fire. Colored stars. His mouth tasted of blood and rot and honey. Sweet taste. Like water in the desert. Like the light of the sun.

Tasted of peace.

He licked his lips, trying to suck the last dried remnants into his mouth.

Gods, his head hurt.

Dug his hands into his pockets. Money. He had some money. Enough for more.

Tried to stand but his body was shaking and the room spun and he fell down. Tried to crawl but his legs wouldn't work and he lay staring at the wall. Moving. Things moving there.

Clutched the coins in his hands.

Hurting. Enough for more.

The thing's he'd done. Please. Please. Make it all go away.

Pretend the world's a good place.

"So you're awake, then?" Tobias's voice. Marith sat up dizzily. He seemed to be on the floor. The room was bright and a warm breeze drifted in through the open window. Tobias was standing in the doorway, carrying a tray with a jug and two cups. Marith stared in hopeful fascination at the jug.

"I've brought you some water. Thought you might be wanting some."

Water. He almost wanted to weep. "Water...yes...thank you..." It felt strange to speak, his voice hoarse, his throat dry and burning. Crashing in his head.

Tobias set the tray down on the table. Closed the door. Sat down at the table and looked at him with disgust. Not surprising: his lips would be stained blue-black, his hair and clothes were crusted with vomit and sweat. Carin had once told him he looked like something that had been buried for several days. "Looking like that, I'd be driven to drink," Carin had said, and they'd both laughed until he was sick.

"I've told the lads you were delirious," Tobias said shortly. "You were delirious, so it's hardly a lie. But I want a straight answer out of you. What you told me: it's true, isn't it? Who you are?"

Oh gods and demons. Marith tried to laugh. "I'd been drinking firewine for most of a day. I don't know what I told you I was. A god. A barrow-wraith. A stone."

Tobias poured him a cup of water. "No, boy. You know very well what you told me, and you know very well it's true. So who exactly are you, and what in all hells are you doing traipsing around penniless with the likes of us?"

Marith looked at him for a long time. The bright flickering lines of fire no longer flashed across his eyes, but Tobias's head had a lingering nimbus around it, like the crown of a god. Some people drank firewine to see visions. They were fools. He realized he was clutching a handful of coins and dropped them heavily onto the table. A metallic clink like sword blades. He closed his eyes in pain.

The truth, then. A relief, perhaps, to get it out. Stop lying and pretending, knowing they all stared at him unconvinced. *Plain as day you're high-born...* They might stop laughing at him if they knew. Or laugh at him all the more.

"My name is Marith Altrersyr," he said at last. "I am the eldest son of King Illyn Altrersyr of the White Isles, of the line of Amrath the Word Conqueror and of Serelethe who loosed Him on the world. My mother was Marissa of Ith, in whose veins flowed the blood of the Godkings of Immier and Caltath." He looked down at his hands and licked his lips again. A last fleeting taste of firewine. There was vomit on the sleeve of his jacket; he felt a maddening desire to lick it off. Like the alcohol-stinking blood he'd wiped off his hands a few days before, it seemed a terrible waste not to. He sighed and looked back up at Tobias. "Until a short time ago, I was heir to the White Isles, and fourth in line to the throne of Ith."

A long, strained silence. Finally Tobias said very faintly, "I see." Looked weary. "Marith Altrersyr. That makes you, what, one of the highest-ranking people in the whole of Irlast? So high pretty much everyone apart from the Yellow Emperor himself ought to be bowing and scraping to you. It also makes you dead, or so I heard."

"I am dead. Or hadn't you noticed?" Waves of pain shuddered across Marith's eyes. Picked up the cup to take a sip of water and his hands shook so much it splashed down his front, fell with a clatter and rolled across the floor.

"Who says I'm dead, then? My father?" He laughed mirthlessly. "The oldest and greatest lineage this side of the Bitter Sea. Even the Asekemlene Emperor is just a man, of a kind: the Altrersyr are descended from gods and monsters. And I am the first-born heir." Even now, it felt so good saying it. Good and terrible. Help me, Carin. Help me. Help me blot it out..."Or rather, I was. My father disowned and exiled me. I hadn't realized he was actually telling people I was dead. But as he's been wanting me dead for years now, it must have pleased him greatly to say it had finally happened."

Tobias's eyes bulged. "Disowned you?" he echoed dully. "Why?"

A scream welling up inside him. I can't say it, he thought. I can't. My mouth will turn to stone, my heart will crack and break. I'll choke on the words. Knives in his head, twisting and turning. You don't have a heart, though, Marith. You think you do but you don't. *You're vile! Vile!* A woman's voice, screaming, filled with hate.

"He had his reasons. Ones I'd have to be considerably drunker than I was last night to tell you." He smiled sweetly: "You can take that as an offer if you like."

Another silence. The tension in the room choking him. Tobias looked stupefied. Bent down, retrieved Marith's cup, refilled it, handed it back.

"I believe you," Tobias said finally. "Perhaps I'm a fool, but I believe you. I've seen things in you. Dark things. The others just think you're some stupid little lordling playing at living rough. But you've got enough death in you I can believe you're one of Amrath's kind. You're a dragon killer, after all. And if last night's anything to go by, I can believe your family's glad to see the back of you and call you dead, too."

They looked at one another, and for the first time Marith looked away first.

"So, Marith Altrersyr," Tobias said at last. "Or do you want me to call you Lord Prince, now? I think now perhaps we need to talk about some other things, too. What happened yesterday, for a start." Marith smiled encouragingly at him. Heard it all before, from his father, his stepmother, his brother, his father's friends. They'd even drafted in his old nursemaid to lecture him. Do you think I care? he'd laughed back at them. Do you think I don't know?

"Some lads in the troop liberated a keg of firewine a few years back. Didn't know what it was. Three of them, there were. Big, strong blokes, probably twice your size. One died, one went blind, one pissed blood and screamed he had insects crawling inside his head for two days. Skie had to slit his throat in the end to shut him up. You, on the other hand, seem to have drunk several bottles of the stuff and come out with shaking hands and a slightly green face."

Marith toyed with the coins on the table. "I can handle it better than most people, I suppose. Something in the blood. Minor benefit of my august and unpleasant ancestry. And a lot of practice." He looked down. "And I would appear to have ruined my new coat."

"Stop it." Tobias spoke very carefully. Anger radiating off him. He trusted me, Marith realized suddenly. For a little while, he trusted me. "Lad, if I'm to believe you, you're a prince with a lineage so high and mighty I shouldn't be able to look at you without someone locking me up for disrespect. Your family swims in gold. You've got a face so pretty, you're considerably better looking than most women I've met. You're clever, and you can just about use a sword. You killed a bloody dragon, for gods' sake. And yet last night I had to drag you unconscious and covered in vomit out of the most depressing hole I've ever had the misfortune to set foot in, after near drowning yourself in something that burned holes in the table-top. You're serving as a foot soldier in a rough mercenary troop a month's wages away from being brigands, on what's probably a suicide mission. You're about to be whipped for misconduct after stealing Company money. From the smell of you, at some point last night you pissed yourself. As far as I can see, you've fucked your life up more thoroughly and absolutely than anyone I've ever met. So whatever the hell is going on with you, I want to know. Prince of the line of Amrath you might be, but right now I'm your commanding officer. If you're inclined to go off on firewine binges, I'd quite like to know about it. Before you die, or get us all killed."

"I'm perfectly fine. As I said, I can handle it better than most people." Marith rubbed his face absently. His eyes were starting to itch again already. He realized Tobias was looking at him and forced himself to stop.

"We probably ought to talk about that, too, don't you think?" Tobias said in a cold voice. "Now I've been looking, I've seen a number of people round here with a habit of scratching their faces like they're bloody flea-ridden. Except it's not anything as wholesome as fleas, is it?"

Might as well tell him everything now. Everything except the one thing he couldn't say. "No. Unfortunately, it's not. Hatha root. Something else I'm inclined to go off on binges on. Lovely stuff, even more fun than firewine. Rips your mind apart for days at a time. Stop taking it, however..." His mouth was dry with longing: he took a long sip of water and tried to imagine it was something else.

Tobias looked thoughtful. "Skie knows, I assume?"

"That I'm an Altrersyr Prince, or that I'm a maudlin, hatha-addicted drunk? Why else do you think he let a green boy without a sword of his own join your select ranks? He didn't believe me at first. I'm not really surprised, given the state I was in at the time. Gave me a silver mark, I'm not sure whether out of pity or cruelty. Then told me that if I stayed alive for the next three days, he'd let me join the Company." The air shivered, cold as despair. Shadows moved on the walls, blocking out the light. Help me. Help me, Carin. Please. "Maybe I only lived to spite him. I crawled through the town on my hands and knees to get to your camp. I have absolutely no idea why joining up seemed quite so necessary, but it was apparently very important at the time that I did. So here I am. Traipsing around penniless with the likes of you. Fortunately, it turns out I quite like killing people."

The darkness faded. Beautiful lordly thing who got whatever he wanted without even having to raise his voice. Marith drained his cup. "Thank you for this, Tobias. Very thoughtful of you. And as you were also so kind as to remind me, I'm covered in vomit and look like hell. Do you think you could get a bath fetched for me?"

Chapter Twenty-One

Two young men, boys really, lie dozing side by side on a bed hung with red velvet, hands touching, smiling with tired eyes. One is slim and dark-haired, the other stockier and fair-blond. The room is bright with sunshine, light dances in through open windows bringing air that smells of salt and the sea.

"Good night," says the fair-haired boy.

"Was it?" The dark-haired boy rubs his eyes. "Where did we go in the end?"

"We didn't go anywhere. Stayed here in your room."

The dark-haired boy rubs his eyes again. He doesn't look entirely well. "Didn't we?"

"You didn't want to. Said you were perfectly happy where you were."

"Oh. Was I?"

"Hard to tell, really, what with you being mostly unconscious. But I think so, yes."

"Oh." The dark-haired boy thinks for a while. "Good."

The dark-haired boy gets up and goes over to the open window. Looks out over the sea that breaks on dark rocks below the room's walls. The sun sparkles on the water. Choppy, white-capped waves. Seals' heads bob about looking up at him. Spray blows up into his face.

"It is beautiful here," he says. "You're right. The most beautiful place in the world." He goes over to a table, pours himself a drink. "My head is killing me."

The fair-haired boy laughs. "I'm amazed."

The dark-haired boy picks up a small clay vial. "Some left." He contemplates the vial for a moment then drains it, washes it down with the drink.

The fair-haired boy shakes his head. "Gods, now that's making me nauseous. Kill or cure, is it?"

"I can hope." The dark-haired boy sits down on the bed again. Rubs his eyes. Blinks. Sighs. "You're kind to me," he says to the fair-haired boy. "Kind. It's so beautiful here. Thank you for showing me. We could go out riding tomorrow. Swimming." He takes his friend's hand. "Tomorrow. All those things. Don't you think?"

The sun shines in at the window. The water sparkles. The waves dance. Warm gentle afternoon sunlight. The smell of the sea.

The dark-haired boy sleeps again. A look of peace on his face.

The fair-haired boy sits and strokes his hair. Kisses him.

Weeps.

Chapter Twenty-Two

Thalia sat in her bedroom at the top of the Temple, hands clasped around her knees, trying to read. She had a book of old tales: Amarillia Swan Neck; the Golden Girl and the Silver Horses; the Butcher's Boy and the May Tree. It was an old book, taken from the Temple library, the gold leaf that curled around the great elaborate opening letters of each sentence worn and peeling, a couple of pages torn. The illustrations bright and vivid, lovely maidens and fearless peasant boys, black bulls with the heads of lions, horses with huge feathered wings. In her favorite picture, a beautiful girl with silvery hair sat by a stream of clear water waiting for her lover, whilst around her strange little man things with legs like chickens danced and tumbled, accompanying themselves on reed pipes and drums.

The door opened: the old priestess Samnel, light steps on the wooden floor, hard unsmiling eyes.

"My Lady." The relationship between them had become ever more formal, as Thalia had grown into her full role as High Priestess. When her predecessor had lived, Thalia had been Samnel's ally; now, she was Samnel's superior and the chosen vessel of her God. Special. Powerful, with powers and knowledge Samnel would never have and never know.

Will she befriend my successor when she comes? Thalia wondered of her. Make her an ally against myself? She had begun to suspect that it had not been the last High Priestess herself whom Samnel had hated but the office. The power. The fact that there was power there that she could not have.

"You should not read such books," Samnel said with a sniff, looking at the book lying on the floor. "Children's tales. Foreign nonsense. You should not fill your head with these nonsense things."

"There's no harm in them," said Thalia defensively. "Just stories."

"We need you to come down to the Large Hall. There is... trouble. Your judgment is sought on the matter."

Thalia stood up. "Wait," she said, and she carefully arranged the book on her table. She walked slowly down the stairs with Samnel beside her. "What is the trouble?" she asked.

The voice was half weary and half gloating. "Ausa. She made mistakes in the morning service, placed the things wrong on the Silver Altar. Then later she...she knocked over a candle. It went out."

"Ah." Fear came up inside Thalia. Grief.

In the large hall, Ausa was sitting on a low chair, her head bent. Two other priestesses stood across from her, watching. She raised her head and looked up at Thalia as she entered. Her skin was very dark, deep black with hair even blacker, but she looked ashen pale, all the blood drawn from her face. Her eyes were red and puffy with tears.

Tolneurn stood before her. His eyes moved to Thalia also. Bland light-brown eyes. One of the few men in the Temple. One of the few men she or any of the priestesses knew. He had a narrow face and white skin like he was always cold. He bowed, very slightly. Thalia suppressed a shiver and stood straight.

"What is the trouble here?" she said again, wanting to hear it from Tolneurn, make him speak in obedience to her. Ausa shifted in her seat.

"She has defiled the Altar." Old fat Ninia, voice hoarse and dry like dead leaves on dry earth.

Thalia said, "Ah" again. Trying to stall for time, perhaps, before what must be said was said.

"She must have her eyes cut out and her hands cut off." The more horrible, to hear it in Ninia's rasping quiet voice, her grandmotherly face remorseless as stones.

"She—" No mercy. No mercy, not before Tolneurn. If he had not been there, she would defy Ninia and Samnel and forgive. Without his presence, it would have been strength. But in front of him, the Imperial Presence, hand of the Emperor, it would seem weakness, a silly girl afraid of pain and hurt.

"Come, then," Thalia said. Ausa cowered back, hands clenched against the sides of the chair. Her eyes stared dumbly.

"Now?" asked Tolneurn. There was shock in his voice. Thalia thought: he did not think I would do it.

"Now." Get it done. Get it over. It must be done, so it must be done immediately. We all chose our lots, she thought. Ausa's yellow, mine red. What would we rather, that we had drawn the black or the white?

"I was tired," Ausa whispered. "I was tired, I haven't slept...I couldn't sleep, I didn't feel well. My hand...my hand slipped. I'm sorry. I didn't mean..."

Thalia said, "Be silent." Her hands trembled. "Come."

They walked together across the large hall, down a little cloistered walk giving onto the Temple gardens. "Look at the sun," Ausa said. "Look at the sun, Thalia." They walked very slowly. They entered one of the dark corridors that led to the Great Chamber. Ausa stopped in the dark, clutching the wall, shrank and crouched in the dead place. "Come," Thalia said. Her voice was very loud in the dark. They came out into the Great Chamber, into the brilliant blinding golden light. A choking noise came from Ausa. They crossed the Great Chamber. At the Silver Altar, Helase was kneeling, a hundred candles burning, one dead and cold. She looked up as they passed. They came to the curtain before the entrance to the Small Chamber. Thalia pushed it aside. Ausa followed her, a low moaning noise coming from her mouth like the noise of cattle. She is no longer alive, thought Thalia. She is no longer alive. Two slaves came forward out of the shadows where they crouched. Waiting. They lifted Ausa and placed her on her back on the altar stone, tied the ropes carefully around her to keep her from trying to move. Thalia watched until it was done. She is no longer alive, she thought, over and over. She is no longer alive. It took a very long time. Finally it was done. The slaves sank back into the shadows. Thalia bent down and drew up the knife in its bundle of cloth. Raised the blade. Don't look at her face, she thought, and immediately she looked and saw the black eyes looking back up at her wide and dry.

The words Caleste had taught her for this. Words she had never yet said. "Great Tanis, Lord of Living and Dying, Great Tanis Who Rules All Things, this one your servant has done a bad thing. She has brought darkness where there should be light. She has brought death where there should be life. We tremble before your anger, oh Lord. We bring her to you. We take her eyes, that she may see neither light nor dark. We take her hands, that she may use them for neither good nor evil. Take now this punishment and forgive her, oh Lord. From the fear of life and the fear of death, release us."

She brought the knife down. Again. Again. Again. Hands not stabbing but sawing, cutting at bone and sinew, almost beyond her strength. Ausa screamed until finally she stopped screaming. Thalia stood before her and raised her left arm. She cut herself from wrist to elbow, a shallow jagged cut over the course of her scars. The blood ran down, mingling with Ausa's blood. She stood for a moment, her arm shaking, the knife raised. Put down the knife and walked away, through the curtain, through the Great Chamber. The slaves came out of the shadows and carried Ausa away.

In a corridor she met Tolneurn. He had been waiting, perhaps. He looked at her, covered in Ausa's blood, her dress clinging to her body. His eyes flickered. Disgust and desire. Desire and disgust.

That was the secret, the thing Helase was too innocent to see. The reason poets clamored to write of the beauty of the High

Priestess. Disgust and desire. Desire and disgust. Samnel knew it: Thalia saw that in the older woman's face after every death, mocking and knowing. The thin face stared at her, pale man eyes, lust and loathing, jealousy of her power, revulsion at her act.

"It is done, then?" he asked, pointlessly.

"It is done."

"Is she—?"

"If she is unlucky, she will live." She would pace out her days doing what little useless things she could, a servant who could not serve, a priestess whom the God had abandoned. Better she had died under the knife. Better she had drawn a black lot. Better she had never been born. Thalia made herself stand very straight and tall as the man gazed at her. Why did he not move? Why did he not go, let her flee away and get clean? She was alive, she thought. She was my friend. So much life in her.

"She was your friend. Do you grieve for her?"

"She was a priestess who offended the God." Her legs felt as though they might buckle beneath her. The weight of Ausa's blood was crushing; her arm hurt where it bled. Still he looked at her.

"My Lady." Samnel. Come to rescue her. A kind act.

"They are waiting for you upstairs," said Samnel. Tolneurn bowed his head and left them, looking back for a moment as he went. Thalia let out a great sigh and almost fell against the older woman. Samnel flinched at the feel of her, the taint of her as they touched.

"I am sorry," Samnel said. "That it was Ausa. That it had to be done."

"It was needful," said Thalia in an empty voice. Not before Samnel, either. You worship Him with such ardor, she thought. This is what He wishes. What we must do. They went up the stairs together, the girl leaning on the woman's arm. In her bedroom, Thalia was washed and her wound treated, given a cup of warm water sweetened with honey. The servants who tended her were kind, though she could feel them drawing away from her. What she had done had not been done for a long time.

Ausa was somewhere down below, in the small infirmary with the old sick woman Calden who was too weak and senile to serve. Thalia could see the Temple in her mind as the God must see it, as though the roof had been taken off and the contents displayed like a toy. Ausa, in her bed, drugged and tied down. Thalia, standing at her window. She was so tired, she just wanted to sleep. She did not feel exhilarated, as she did after a sacrifice, only worn and trembling as if she had a fever. There was a service later she must officiate at.

She stood at the window, looking out at the bright sunlight and the flowers and the birds. Difficult to think of what she had done, bathed in the light and the warmth, a butterfly dancing on the sill. Guilt, crushing her. Shame. She did these things, for her God, for her pride. She could have defied Tolneurn. She could have defied them all. She could have defied the God. The weight of it, the pity of it. For herself, as much as for Ausa. That she came to these things. Blind and crippled, as Ausa was, trapped within the walls of life and death. Shedding blood. Killing. Locked away from the world. I bring life, she thought. But I will never see it.

The butterfly danced nearer and landed on her outstretched hand. Its wings were green and gold. A little child laughed somewhere down below in the garden, playing in the sun.

Chapter Twenty-Three

Tobias and Rate sat at a table in the Five Corners, arguing.

"We've got to go out and get the bloody gear," said Tobias. "Today. Now. We can't fuck everything up because of one bloody idiot boy."

"Emit's still missing," said Rate. "We ought to look for him again. He could be in trouble."

"Yeah? Well, where shall we look, then? Wander about and maybe another nice young lady will lead us to him?"

"I don't bloody know. He could be anywhere."

"He's dead," Tobias said flatly. "There's no point in looking for him. We don't have time to fuck around pointlessly looking for a corpse. He's dead and dumped outside the city walls by now."

Rate glared at him, stood up as if to walk out and start searching immediately right then. "How do you know that? Feel it in your bones? Known him so long you can tell when he snuffs it? Or are you such a good squad leader you'd feel the same for any of us? I know he's a shifty, grumpy bastard but we can't just leave him."

Oh for gods' sake. "How many men, exactly, do you think I've had to leave for dead in my time? He's dead, Rate. You know he is. Marith basically told us as much."

"I don't know that. You don't know. Marith—Oh. Fuck." Rate sat down again slowly. "You think Marith killed him?"

Tobias rolled his eyes. Maybe not as bright as he'd thought. Too trusting, underneath it all.

"But he...I mean...Why?"

Really not as bright as he'd thought. "Why do you bloody think, Rate?"

Rate still floundered. "But..." He frowned. "Oh gods. He didn't somehow end up in that hole drinking rat poison by mistake, did he?"

"No," Tobias said with a deep sigh. "He didn't. He very much didn't."

A look of realization in Rate's face, as if something had just been confirmed for him. "And the twitching...? He's a hatha addict as well, isn't he? I was half wondering, but he seemed so...so..."

A brief silence. Tobias felt his face go red with rage.

"What do you mean, you were half-wondering? Wondering what?"

"He...he has some of the symptoms. Of hatha cravings." Pause. Rate licked his lips. Embarrassed. You damn well should be embarrassed, Tobias thought. "He's good at hiding it, but...At first I thought you knew. And then, the trust you put in him, I thought I must be wrong..."

"You thought I knew? You didn't think to mention it? Gods and fucking demons, Rate!" Gods and demons and fuck. He'd thought the lad had some potential in him. Trusted him. Trusted Marith. What in all hells was bloody wrong with him suddenly? Put your life in your men's hands, and this is what happened. Idiots.

Rate said again, "I thought you knew. Then I thought, with the plan and everything, I thought I must be wrong...I was never sure...You didn't seem to think there was anything to worry about..."

"How many hatha addicts do you think I've met, exactly, the kind of life I live? And how do you even come to know about this stuff, come to that?"

More embarrassed. "My, uh...my cousin farms it. Alongside the cows. Most of the people in my part of Chathe do. It's not all rose trees and poets, Chathe. Several people in my village you'd think had bloody fleas, you didn't know they were just dying slowly of hatha poisoning."

Tobias sat with his mouth open. After a while he said faintly, "And you didn't think to maybe mention this earlier? Like, before I gave him a purse bulging with gold? No?"

"I thought you knew," Rate said yet again. "I thought I must be wrong. And I did try to say something. And it's none of my business anyway. You're in command, remember?"

"Yes... Yes." They'd all been mad and blind and wrong, these last few days. The city, maybe. The golden light and the golden dust and the strange air. Or something in the city. Marith killing. Him trusting. Rate being a stupid useless bastard. Emit being dead. Nothing felt quite right here. Get the job done and get out quick, he thought. Not good for the mind, this place.

Said exhaustedly, "I'm in command. Yes. Thank you for reminding me of that. It's my bloody fault, should have looked at him more closely." Skie should have told me, he thought savagely. Dangerous, keeping secrets like that from a man. You trusted your commander and he trusted you. Quickest way to die badly was to change that, in their line of work. "And now I apparently have a drug-addled, self-pitying drunk with the rarest bloodline in Irlast under my command. Or did you have your suspicions about that too?"

Rate stared at him. "Oh, come on. You actually believe him? That he's... he's... you know... All of that."

"Stupid as it sounds, I do." It sounded stupid even as Tobias said it. "We knew he was high-born: that's so bloody obvious he might as well be dressed in cloth of gold with a crown on his head. He speaks right, he looks right... There are some very odd stories about goings-on on the Whites. Headed for death, people keep saying about the Altrersyr Prince. Which he probably is, after what we saw last night. Don't tend to live long, firewine drinkers, one way or another. Somehow I'm guessing hatha eaters don't either. And after what we saw last night, I'd be tempted to throw him out and tell people he was dead too, if he was heir to my bloody kingdom. He says Skie knows, and Skie isn't fooled by things. And Skie's being cagey about something, wants to go to the Whites but doesn't want to talk about it, too. It all fits. Sort of..." He sighed. "You saw him last night. Do you think he was lying?"

"So...what are we going to do? What are you going to do?"

Run away screaming and hope I never see this place or any of you again in my bloody life. Hit something. Sit down, get drunk and have a good cry. "Nothing. Nothing I wouldn't be going to do anyway. We have a job to do, and we're doing it. Prince Marith signed up for this. A foot soldier under my command, that's what he is. Does as I say or he's punished for it. He's going out with us now to buy the gear, if he lives through to the end of the contract he'll be whipped for misconduct, then we decide what to do with him. Or Skie will, anyway. And until then we pretend we don't know about Emit. Makes things a whole lot easier that way."

"And Alxine?"

"We don't tell Alxine anything. Not who Marith is, not what he's done. If he works some of it out, fair enough. But otherwise, nothing. That makes things a whole lot easier too." Risky telling Rate. But he had to tell someone. It was the kind of thing you couldn't just not tell. Went round and round his head and he wasn't sure he wasn't mad for believing a word of it. Needed to talk it out, get some reassurance he wasn't. Say it.

He felt strangely humiliated, too, now he knew he'd had the descendant of Amrath the World Conqueror traipsing around after him digging the latrine trenches and making pots of near-on undrinkable tea.

Upstairs, Marith was thinking similar thoughts. He was a prisoner, now, he realized. They'd hardly let him go out without their supervision again. Whatever little freedom he had found was gone, he was caged in, now, by them and by himself. Tobias had taken back every last penny he'd had on him. And even if he had money, he couldn't leave: he'd signed something that he was dimly aware had said he couldn't leave on pain of death, and if he did, the only place to go was backward, to where Skie had found him. Revulsion rose up in him at the thought of that.

A tap on the door. One of the women, bringing back his clothes, miraculously clean and sweet-smelling, even the coat almost as good as new. She looked at him with a disgusted expression on her face as he stood shaking and shivering, still half out of his mind.

He dressed slowly, came slowly down the stairs. His steps sounded very loud on the smooth wood. The other men were lounging awkwardly in the little courtyard garden, trying to find something to do with themselves. Birds flitted about in the corner where a plate of crumbs had been set out for them. He could hear women chattering and laughing, the clanging of cooking pots as someone began preparing a meal.

Three pairs of eyes turned to look at him. He tried to smile, the way he'd always smiled at people who'd seen him as he really was, the smile of someone so high and lordly he could afford not to care. There was bread on the table, and honey and cheese. He sat down and helped himself. All the while the three men sat and looked at him silently. What did he expect them to do, he thought, get down and kneel? Men had groveled at his feet before now, prostrate in the dust when he told them his name. What would he do, how would he feel, if they did the same? Laugh, probably. He ate the bread in silence and felt better, though the taste was like ashes in his mouth.

Marith sat and looked at his plate and felt their eyes on him. Pity. Mockery. Disgust.

Memories came to him. Sunshine on high moorland. Gray rocks tumbling into a gray sea. Beech mast crunching beneath his horse's hooves, the light green and gold through the first new spring leaves. Men kneeling before him, women eyeing him with longing, a whole world at his feet. Gilded and pampered and lording it over everyone. Ruined and screaming and crawling blind in the dark.

Oh yes, he thought, I know what I am and what I've given up. Sometimes I even wonder why.

Rate said suddenly, "Remind me never, ever to get into any kind of drinking contest with you, Marith, boy."

It broke some of the tension. The others laughed. Marith laughed too. A sense of peace spread over him, sitting here in this pretty garden, breathing in the scent of honeysuckle, the other things seemed far away from him. He ate a little more bread and drank some water.

"We need to go out," Tobias said. "Get a few things. Think you can manage that without throwing up in the street?"

Marith nodded. Lines of fire flickering painfully across his vision. Probably. If he didn't have to think too hard or speak too much. "A drink would help," he almost said, then shut his mouth on it.

"You may not be surprised to hear we are all coming with you," Tobias went on.

Oh yes. Obviously. The cage door closing, so loud it rang in his head.

Alxine said, "What about Emit? Someone ought to stay here, case he comes back."

Three faces looked embarrassed. Alxine was simply too nice for his own good in some ways. A rather sad attribute in a professional killer.

Alxine scowled at them: "What? What?"

"If he comes back, he can cope on his own for a while," Tobias said carefully. "But I wouldn't pin my hopes on it, you get me, Alxine?"

"It's not hopes," said Alxine with a flush. "I never even really liked him. I just can't believe he'd just disappear. He's been with the Company for years. Where else has he got to go?"

"Where else have any of us got to go?" said Rate loudly. Marith almost choked on his cup of water.

"That's two of the men I shared a tent with," Alxine went on mournfully. "First Newlin gets flame-grilled by a dragon, now Emit just vanishes into thin air. It's like some bloody curse." He looked at Marith. "You'd better look out, you know." Marith almost choked again and Rate kicked him under the table. Tobias coughed loudly.

"It's like having a particularly dangerous job, is what it is," said

Rate. "You want a profound and total lack of people violently dying on you, try dairy farming instead."

"You can't just assume he's dead."

"If he turns up, he turns up," said Tobias firmly. "If he doesn't, he doesn't. But we can't waste any more time looking for him. And if everyone's ready, we'll go out now."

Swords. The crucial thing to buy was swords. One for Marith, one for Tobias, the blades they had had having been ruined by the dragon's blood, the metal corroded and desiccated, felt both too light and too heavy at the same time. Brittle like burned bone. The armorer's shop recommended to them was a long walk through prosperous, tree-lined streets busy with plump merchants and pretty women in fine silk. The stink of hot metal was crisp in the sunshine as they approached. Marith took a deep breath. Always liked the smell, scorched and sweet, a smell of his childhood, watching the forge at Malth Elelane, the leaping sparks, the crash of iron, the master smith drawing shapes in the molten bronze. Dragon smell. Closest thing to dragons, smiths and metal workers and bellows boys. Still worshipped, smiths, in some parts of the White Isles.

The goods on display here were plain and simply made but high quality. Lots of money involved in this thing. The whole company had strong suspicions of what they were likely to be doing, and the more money involved, the more obvious it was. Imperial assassination, thought Marith: his father would laugh until his sides ached if he knew what he was about.

Tobias nudged him in the small of his back. "Go on then, boy. Here we are. Just be yourself, yeah?"

Ah, ha-ha. Marith shot him a dark look and stepped into the armorer's. The other three followed him in. It was very gloomy inside, after the sunlight, and he blinked, his vision fading and twisting for a moment, his head spinning. He clutched at the doorframe to steady himself. Walked slowly forward. The armorer strode up to him, wiping his hands on his thick leather apron, taking in his fine coat, his face, his tired eyes.

"Can I help you, My Lord?" Respectful, head bowed in greeting. It seemed a long time since he had been addressed properly like this. Seen at once for what he was. He'd almost forgotten, already, the bright power of it.

"I need swords for my men. Something for myself, as well." Marith looked around haughtily, gazing with disdain at the merchandise on offer. He spoke in Literan, carefully better than the armorer's own. "I have been told that your products are not entirely badly made."

He'd had a sword, once, of course. A beautiful sword. Silver tracery on the hilt, and a single ruby the same black-red as his hair. A fine, thin blade, light as water, cruel as tears, the metal so dark it seemed to eat the light. A gift from his mother's kin. In a fit of intense, wine-sodden melancholy, he'd named it "Sorrow." Carin had laughed at him for days, but even after the drink had worn off the name had stuck irreparably. It just seemed to fit. The sword, and the way it felt in his hand.

Which was something of a joke in itself, given what he'd eventually done with it.

"If My Lord will see here, the grip?" the armorer was saying. Marith pulled his attention back to the shop. The man held a short sword out to him. The hilt was plain metal, worked at the pommel with the design of a star. The blade was long for its type, tapered, a ribbon of brilliant white bronze. The grip, on which the armorer's attention was focused, was bound round with red leather, cunningly wrought into the metal. A good sword. Marith took it and made a few strokes. It was bright in his hand. The blade made a very slight hiss as it moved through the air. A very good sword.

Also a very expensive sword. He looked quickly at Tobias, who looked back at him and made a tiny, almost imperceptible shake of his head. Marith sighed. He sheathed the sword lovingly and handed it back. "It is a beautiful thing. But I'm afraid to say I am in need of something a little cheaper." Tobias's hand flickered. "Quite a lot cheaper." Tight bastard, Marith thought.

The armorer looked disappointed. The sword was whipped away

and replaced in Marith's hands with a more standard piece. Marith made a few experimental strokes again. Much less interesting. The other had been special, this was just a bit of metal you might use to kill someone. A good metaphor for his own change of status, then. So perhaps fitting after all. He could call it "Ruin."

Tobias got one too, and a long thin-bladed knife. They bought half-helms as well, light smooth things like eggshell that pressed on the scalp. His father had a great helm, the metal tempered black, surmounted by a leather plume in the shape of a dragon. It looked like a diseased face. He'd been frightened of it, as a child, until he realized that it was just metal and cow skin shaped to the skull. His father was still his father inside it, hot with sweat dripping down his forehead. No magic in it. No horror. Just a lump of hammered bronze. But he hated it. The idea of being enclosed in it. Trapped.

Swords and helmets. Killing things. Marith paid carefully, the money shaking in his hand.

They were walking back down a large, crowded street in one of the wealthier areas of the town when Alxine suddenly raised a hand to Tobias's shoulder and said calmly, "Someone's following us."

"What?" Rate almost turned round before Tobias smacked him on his injured arm. He yelped in pain.

"A woman. Wealthy-looking, with guards."

Tobias frowned. "I haven't seen her."

"She's only been around a little while. We passed her as she was coming out of a shop a few streets back. She started after us a few moments later, she's quite far behind us still."

"Coincidence. She's just headed the same way we are."

"No. She's not even trying to conceal it. Turn round a moment, like you're looking at that girl back there. See?"

Tobias turned and caught a flash of expensive cloth, flanked by dark leather. The street was crowded, it was hard to see easily without being obvious. "If you say so," he said, confused and concerned. A woman. Why on earth would a woman be following them?

He thought for a moment. "We carry on a few paces, take the next turning, go into the nearest shop. She's still a good way behind us, so if we're quick she'll be confused and have to show herself. No point in us being subtle if she's not."

The nearest shop down the next turning turned out to be a jeweler's. A bell rang musically as Tobias opened the door, pretending to survey the wares inside. Gold and silver glittered on fat red cushions, illuminated by tall candles of yellow beeswax. Rate stared open-mouthed at the place. The shop-keeper bustled up from behind a curtained doorway, rubbing his hands as he caught sight of Marith.

"Anything in particular you are looking for, young sir?" he asked unctuously, waving his hand toward his display cases. "A ring for a special friend? A brooch for a cloak?"

Whatever Marith was about to say in reply was lost in the noise of the door being flung open, the bell ringing like mad. A woman's voice cried out. A young woman stood in the doorway, flanked by two men with swords. Short and fair-haired and plain. From the east, by her dress. High-born, by her dress, too. A high-born young woman from the east, staring at a high-born young man from the east with her face full of grief and pain and shock. Oh hell.

Marith stared back at her. Went pale, a look on his face that was both horrified and laughing. "Landra?" he said thickly. "What are you...? What are you doing here?"

"You..." Tears running down her face, her body trembling. "It is you...I thought...I was walking down the street...I saw...I saw you..." She spat at his feet suddenly. Her lips curling back like an animal. "You're dead! Dead! Your father swore...He swore on Carin's grave. That you were dead. He swore!"

A choking sound came from Marith's mouth. "He lied. The Altrersyr lie."

"He swore! He swore you were dead! Dead! I came out of a shop, you were there. In the street. I saw you! But your father swore! Swore you were dead!" She moved toward Marith, her arms raised. Tobias felt for a strange moment that she was going to embrace the boy. She struck him, screaming, cursing, spittle frothing at her lips. "Dead!" she screamed. "Dead! Dead! Dead!" The two guards with her drew their swords. They were both staring at Marith too, the same puzzled revolted faces. The taller of them stepped forward, raised his blade toward the boy, came at him. Rate responded almost instantly, leaping sideways with his knife already drawn. There was a crash as a display case fell over in a shower of gems. Marith stood still and blank, like he was waiting for the man to kill him. Gold bracelets rolled at his feet.

Death and damnation. Of all the squalid ways to die: cut down in a tasteless trinket shop by a glorified footman.

"Stop!" Tobias shouted hopelessly, just as the woman shouted "Hold!."

"Hold, Mandle." Mandle froze, sword halfway to Marith's chest, Rate's knife halfway to his guts. The woman stood before Marith, staring up at him, hatred roaring off her. "Dying here like this is too good for you. Now I know you're still alive, I want to plan your death. Do it properly. Not just see you die quickly now."

No answer. Marith's lips moved but nothing came out.

"This means war, Marith. Between our House and yours. You should be dead. Dead and rotting, like he is. When my father learns of this…War. You'll all be dead. We'll kill you all slowly. We will. Your father will regret his lies. You'll regret he didn't kill you as he said."

Marith finally came alive to her, and laughed.

"Kill them, then," he said. His voice was bitter and cold, worse than it had been the previous night. A dead voice. Empty. "You think I care? You think I ever cared? But you won't manage it. You'll be the ones to die. Like he was."

The woman crumpled. Like she might fall to the ground and break. She tried to say something but her voice faded away. "You're vile…" she whispered at last, breathing hard through her teeth. "Vile. Prince Ruin." Then she straightened herself and stumbled out of the shop, her men following her, still staring over their shoulders at Marith. Tobias stared back at them.

Silence. Rate bent down and began absentmindedly picking up the scattered jewelry. The shop-keeper gave a low moan and slumped to the floor. Marith stood immobile, eyes bright.

Tobias let out a long, pent-up breath. Turned to the shop-keeper, shrugged his shoulders apologetically. "No idea either, mate. Crazy bint." Desperately trying to sound casual. Or at least not like he was about to scream the place down and wring Marith's princely bloody neck. "But no harm done, eh?" Gestured at Rate: "My friend here's putting your shop back together, aren't you?"

Rate quickly dropped the last of the jewelry onto a display table, added the gold brooch he'd palmed a moment previously. "See? All right as rain again. Nothing broken. We probably ought to leave now, though, yes?"

They fled out of the door and away, Marith trailing behind them, face blank, needing the occasional nudge from Rate to keep him going in the right direction.

Navala was sweeping the front step when they arrived back at the Five Corners. She looked at them—at Marith—curiously. In the last three days, she'd seen him arrive back injured and covered in blood, passed out drunk and covered in vomit and now trembling and barely able to speak. To Tobias's profound irritation, she still cast him a long yearning smile when they came in.

"You," he barked at Marith as soon as they were alone in the hallway outside their rooms. "Go in there, shut the door and stay there. Okay? Don't even bloody move, for preference. You are confined there until given permission to leave. You," he turned to Rate, "go with him and make bloody certain he can't get out."

Marith stared at him for a moment, then slunk off like a boy after a beating, trailing his hand along the wall. Rate followed him, a snigger on his face.

Tobias pushed open his own door. A desperate need to sit down and close his eyes for a while, pretend none of this was happening.

Alxine followed him, shutting the door behind him. Oh not now, Tobias thought wearily. Not bloody now. Let me have just a few moments free of the bloody lot of you.

"So," Alxine said slowly, "care to tell me what exactly is going on here? The last couple of days have been a nightmare. And don't tell me you don't know, because you do."

"Don't speak to your commanding officer like that," Tobias growled back.

"Oh, come on, Tobias."

Tobias sank down onto his bed in exhaustion. "Okay. Okay." Things had gone beyond the point he could keep anyone in the dark now. And he probably owed it to Alxine, he'd known him long enough.

He was just finishing when Rate came back.

"He's shut in," Rate said cheerfully. "Windows shuttered, door locked. Just sitting there anyway, staring at the wall, laughs a bit occasionally. You're quite right, he's cracked as a smashed pot, that one, divine blood or no."

Alxine said, "Oh, come on. You don't believe that. How can he possibly be descended from some bogeyman? How can he possibly be related to a dragon? Does he look like a bloody dragon?"

Tobias and Rate exchanged glances. Easy to forget, having known Alxine for so long, that he wasn't from Irlast. Didn't know the tales they did, or not as anything more than tales, anyway.

"Let me tell you a story, then, Alxine," Tobias said. "A story about Marith's family. Then maybe you'll understand a bit."

Closed his eyes, seeing the wise woman in his village, the memory of her thin fingers like chicken bones moving as she spoke, the click of the bead necklace she wore, the younger children coughing and fidgeting, the smell of smoke from her hearth. Snot and greasy hair and her breath stank, but you forgot all that as she spoke, the magic of her words, the power of them, the images so clear in his mind and behind them the clatter of the loom as a rhythm, part of the story, part of the magic, weaving images like the cloth, so real he could see them. The great sacred stories, the god tales, the history of his world.

"It begins...It begins with a woman, a princess, a descendant of the old gods, and she lived in a country called Illyr, on the shores of the Bitter Sea, on the edge of the world.

"The kings of Illyr had been kings and more than kings since the world began. But the Salavene Wars came, the Godkings fighting, the ruin of Tarboran, the drowning of Caltath, and Illyr was brought low. And time passed, and it was a poor place, its land broken, and it was surrounded by enemies, with no strength left in its people to defend their homes. And the line of kings was weakening with the country, until all that was left was an old, sick man, and his young daughter, Serelethe.

"Now, the Kings of Illyr had been gods, once, and enchanters later, and Serelethe had the power of witchcraft in her. And she resolved to use her power to save Illyr and make it again a rich land, safe and prosperous, with no enemies and no fear. But what could she do, a young woman with a sick father? What could she do?

"What could she do? She called up the great powers, the dark powers, the things that live in the twilight, between day and night, between living and dying, that are neither alive nor dead.

"And something heard her, and answered her, and came at her call.

"Three days and three nights, Serelethe locked herself away in a high tower in her father's fortress. Three days and three nights, great mists hung around the fortress, so deep no man could see further than his own hand. And nine months later, Serelethe gave birth to three sons.

"The first to be born was a shadow, a demon, a formless thing of dark. And that had no name and no shape, and did not live. The second to be born was a dragon, red as blood, spouting flame. And that Serelethe locked away. And the last to be born was a man, or the semblance of a man, at least. And that was Amrath.

"Amrath grew tall and strong and handsome, and by the time He reached manhood, He was the greatest warrior and warleader the world had ever known. He led the armies of Illyr to victory after victory, until He had conquered all of Irlast, save only the city of Sorlost, for that city is unconquerable, and will be till the end of the world. At Amrath's word, the city of Elarne was burned, and every man, woman and child within it died. At Amrath's word, the palaces of Eralad were torn to dust and their lords buried alive in the ruins. At Amrath's word, the fields of Gallas were sown with corpses, and the grass that grows there is poisoned still. There was not a man living who did not fear Amrath.

"But at length the men of Illyr grew sated with gold and victory and blood, and they began to wonder what it was that they fought for. And the women of Illyr grew tired of seeing their sons and husbands and lovers go off to war. And the people of Illyr, men and women both, began to see that Amrath was a cruel man, and a bad king. For there was no justice in Illyr, no law and no mercy, only Amrath's will and Amrath's sword. So the people rose up and rebelled against Amrath, and sought to overthrow Him.

"Amrath's anger was woken, then, and He brought down fire and blood upon His own people, His own great city of Ethalden, whose very walls were built of gold. All of its people, He killed. Every one. And not a stone of its buildings did He leave standing.

"But the destruction set free the dragon, His brother, which Serelethe had imprisoned beneath the fortress Amrath had built, that had stood at the very heart of the city of Ethalden. Huge, it had grown, in the dark place where Serelethe had chained it. Huge, and wild, and filled with nothing but rage and hate against Serelethe and Amrath and all men. It came down upon the ruins of the city and burned Amrath's armies with its breath, and tore them to pieces with its claws, and swallowed them whole in its huge mouth. And when none were left living, it came for Amrath.

"Amrath fought the dragon for three days and three nights without ceasing. As the sun rose on the morning of the fourth day the dragon fell dying, bleeding from a thousand wounds. And Amrath fell dying also, His body broken in every bone and burned in every limb. And thus ended His reign, in blood and burning.

Thus ended the reign of Amrath, the World Conqueror, the greatest and the most terrible of the Lords of Irlast.

"The power of Illyr was ended, then and forever, for weeds now grow in her fields and nothing lives where Amrath's towers once stood. Amrath does not even have a grave, for no man dared to venture near to bury Him, but His body rotted away where it lay, and His bones were scattered by the birds.

"But Amrath had a wife, Eltheia of Ith, heir to the Godkings of Caltath and Immier. The most beautiful woman in the world, she was. Her hair was the color of summer evenings, and her smile was like the sun at dawn. And she had borne Amrath a son, Altrersys, still no more than a boy. And these two Serelethe took away from Illyr in a ship with sails of diamonds, and brought safely across the sea until they came to an island rich in timber and fruits and grains and herds. The people of the island were shepherds and wanderers, wild and simple, and when they saw Eltheia they were so overcome by her beauty and her brilliance that they made her their queen, and built for her the fortress of Malth Elelane, the Tower of Joy and Despair. And her son Altrersys was king after her.

"And he was the first of the Altrersyr, the heirs of Amrath, the World Conqueror, the Dragon Kin, the Demon Born."

Tobias bowed his head dramatically, opened his eyes. Rate pounded the table. Alxine blinked.

"I've heard the stories," said Alxine. "I just didn't think they were quite so...true."

"They're true all right," said Tobias. "The ruins of Ethalden stand proud in the sun, their stones rent and burned by dragon fire, in the plain of Illyr where no grass grows. I've been there, I've seen it. Seen a dragon, too. And seen Marith kill it."

"And his family are...proud of all that?"

"Extremely proud. Try very hard to live up to it, too. Hence our boy in the next room there." There was a low sound of sobbing through the wall as he spoke, like a fretful child.

"But it's...it's horrible," said Alxine weakly.

"Says the professional soldier and hired killer," said Rate.

"I haven't even touched on his mother's family," said Tobias with a grin. "Some of the stories about them, they make Amrath look like Aralbarneth the Good. Kept things in the family more, though, that lot. Never really went in for world conquest when they could be at home torturing each other."

"Marith Altrersyr," said Alxine. "Prince Marith. King Marith… Got a nice ring to it, that, don't you think? Kind of nice in the mouth."

"Nice in the mouth, eh?" said Rate. "Just his name, you mean, yeah?"

Alxine glared at him. "Prince Marith…What do you think he did, then? To that lady?"

"Abandoned her," said Tobias.

"Raped her," said Rate.

They were silent for a while.

"So what do we do now, then?" said Alxine.

Gods, why did they keep asking him that? Tobias said sharply, "We do what we're doing. What we're hired to bloody do. Who Marith is or isn't and what he has or hasn't done has got nothing to do with anything. After the job's over, then maybe we see. Prince Marith Altrersyr must be worth quite a bit, to the right people."

"Bit weird, though, isn't it?" said Alxine thoughtfully. "Now we know and all…"

"Bit weird 'cause you fancy him, you mean," said Rate.

Alxine shuddered. "Kind of puts you off a bit, things that have been going on recently. Not sure I really feel like fucking someone who's part god and part suicidal drunk, you know?"

PART TWO

THE BLADE

Chapter Twenty-Four

This morning, Demmy drew the red lot.

I had not even thought of it, after Ausa. She is alive, still, Helase says. Likely to heal, even, in as much as such wounds will heal. She bows her head and whispers dimly that it was her fault, that she was deserving of punishment, that she is blessed by Great Tanis Himself to have survived. She does not reproach me, she says.

But Demmy has drawn the red lot, and I will die in my turn. Ausa must be glad of it, deep down in her soul. I would be.

I went out into the garden, after I had been told. The children were playing there, running among the trees, chasing each other, shouting. Little fat Sissly skipping on sturdy short legs, fallen leaves caught in her curls. Corbele, much older than the rest and already in full training as a priestess, but wild and free and happiest in the company of little ones. Galana, shy and frightened and following her. Demmy the leader, making them run, setting the rules of the game. She does not know, yet, what any of this means.

I sat on the grass and watched them. The children shouted and ran and I felt...contented. At peace. As though some great labor has finished, and now I can rest a while. She is a pretty thing, of course, and clever, and sweet-natured. Beautiful slender hands. She will do well.

Helase came to me looking worried. Her eyes were swollen with tears. The last few days have been hard for her, for Ausa was her friend. I told her not to fear. She began to cry and I stopped her. I am still alive, I said. I will be alive for ten years yet. Unlike most who live, I can say the time of my death to the moment. For ten years I am safe. Doesn't that mean I am free of something? We watched the children play for a while in the sun.

There is a great rite, the dedication of the High Priestess-thatwill-be. It must be done immediately when the lot is drawn, so we must always be ready for whenever a child reaches the right age. It can come any day, or not for a hundred years. All the Temple was bustle and excitement, the news breaking out into the streets: there is a new High Priestess chosen! The red lot is drawn! The red lot is drawn! The people rejoice, for it means my succession is assured. A terrible thing it would be, if I were to grow old and die before another came to replace me, for there would be no sacrifice, perhaps no living and no dying in all the Sekemleth Empire, perhaps even in all the world. And so Demmy and I knelt side by side before the High Altar to be blessed, she looking so absurdly small beside me, grave and confused in a little golden dress too short at her legs. I thought, watching her, that I could remember my own dedication.

The Temple shone with candles, flames proud and tall and unwavering, smoke sweet as honey cakes. The priestesses sang for joy, where only a few days ago there was the heavy cloud of grief like vile air because of Ausa. Their voices rose in a great golden chant, the hymn to light and living, the song so beautiful it cannot be heard without weeping. I have done something so terrible to Ausa. I have seen the hour and the instrument of my death. But in the light and the singing and the glory I felt only happiness, great happiness like a warmth in my heart. There is no fear, there is no sorrow. There is life and there is dying, and we stand before them, lit by the sun.

After the ceremony, I went back to my bedroom, and sat for a long while alone. A servant brought me bread and cream and honey and I ate it gladly. Only a few days before I fast again, before the next killing time. It is one of the less sacred things I must tell Demmy, when she is older, that the High Priestess must enjoy eating when she can. These funny little things, like the trick of kneeling without leaving one's legs numb, or how to keep awake and thoughtful in the long night preceding a sacrifice, in the burning light before the High Altar in the candle heat. Odd details that Caleste taught me, and I must pass on to Demmy in my turn.

I lay down in my bed and thought how strange it is, that down below in another little room another girl is lying, and in ten years from now I will be dead and she will be sleeping in this room for the first time. Still it does not concern me as I thought. All I feel is peace, and the golden singing, and the understanding that we are alive.

I will go and watch the children play again tomorrow and every day for the next ten years. I will eat bread and cream and honey and read old tales of princesses. I will wear the golden dress on feast days and be as beautiful as Manora, and inspire terrible poetry about my hair and my skin.

I will live, and live, and live.

Chapter Twenty-Five

They kept Marith shut up alone in his room all night and most of the following day.

The night was the worst. He screamed and pleaded with them, but no one came. He sat in the dark and stared at the wall. It would not surprise him if they came to kill him. It would not surprise him if he died. He felt the dark close in around him, pressing on him, a great weight stifling him, smothering him. Go away. Make everything go away. Make the world a good place. Oh please. Oh please. "Carin," he cried out, but Carin would never come.

He awoke to shafts of bright sunlight streaming down on his face, and for a long time he lay still, uncertain as to where he was. The light moved slowly along the white wall; his eyes followed it, empty and tired. The door opened and Tobias came in with bread and water; he stared at it for a while then ate slowly, choking on the taste. His eyes hurt. His mind hurt. The light moved along the white wall, paler and weaker now. Wavering. Shadows began to grow and darkness to build in the sky. Things crawled across the walls, pressing on his skin. Good things. Things that hurt. He closed his eyes and opened them and the room was darker. The blades of light had faded away to ghosts.

The door opened again. Tobias came in.

"Get up," Tobias said shortly. "Navala's bringing a bath up for you. You get up, look presentable, explain to her you've been ill if she asks anything. Then you get washed and shaved and dressed and put this"—he dumped Marith's armor on the bed and covered it with the blanket—"on under your clothes. And then you come downstairs with a sweet smile on your face and do exactly what I tell you. Got it?"

Marith nodded slowly. He was going to go and kill people, he thought dully. Or get killed himself. He wasn't sure he particularly cared which. Navala brought up hot water for him and he smiled at her sweetly and said in a soft voice that he'd been ill.

He came down the stairs into the common room clean and shining and beautiful, a well-dressed young lord with sad eyes. Alyet smiled at him as she passed. His face was raw and itchy like it was being eaten away beneath the bones of his skull. His hands shook so badly he had to hold them clenched.

The others were sitting at the table, tense. He joined them, feeling himself falling with every step he took. Tobias looked at him for a moment and then shoved a cup over to him. He gulped it down, almost weeping with relief.

Tobias said, "Okay. We need to go now. Ready?" He followed them out slowly. Alyet waved at them as they went.

They walked through the dusk, long shadows falling around them. They passed two men in white silk fighting in silence, their shadows cast and recast in the torchlight, dancing on the walls. They passed a woman crouched in a doorway, her face a mass of sores. They passed a great red silk litter, lit from within, carried on the shoulders of dark-robed figures masked with hangman's hoods.

They came at last to the walls of the palace, and they stopped a moment, and stared.

It was beautiful, in the strange, grotesque way of Sorlostian architecture. In the twilight dark it seemed to glow, the great domes and towers shimmering gold and silver, the white walls beneath like a full moon. It looked like the crests of waves, or snow falling. Birds wheeling in the sky. Colored glass glittered across its surface, deep greens and blues and reds. Too beautiful and brilliant to be real. Like it would shatter if you touched it, or dissolve. Quicksilver poured from a jeweled cup, too bright, too liquid. The evening sun on clear water. A face reflected in tarnished bronze. Absurdly grand compared to his father's stronghold, so fragile-looking, also, as if it had been built out of sea foam. But Malth Elelane had been made to be defensible, hard gray stone above hard gray water, cold. This place had no need to repel invaders, for no invaders had ever made it through Sorlost's bronze walls.

His younger brother had been here. He'd come on a semi-official visit a few years ago, when he'd been the expendable one, the one no one cared about. Been received in the palace, knelt with just the right degree of near-respect before the great golden throne on which had sat what he had described as "a bored-looking man with a sour face." Couldn't remember a word of what they'd said to each other: the man's birth family had been fishmongers in a city in the desert, for gods' sake, what could he possibly have said that would be of interest to an Altrersyr? Tiothlyn had been more interested in the girls he'd met. Marith had envied the boy, at the time, that he'd been allowed to travel.

They approached the palace warily. No one around, no trouble so far. Too easy, thought Marith. Not right. Should be guards. People. But his head was pounding and he shook the thought away. He'd been thinking about home, he remembered. It would be nice to see it again, towers shining in the sun, reflecting back the swell of the sea at their feet. To sit before the fire in his bedchamber, listening to the crash of waves and the scream of seabirds. To ride down to the great wide expanse of Morr Bay and swim there. To lie on the warm sand afterward and let Carin stroke his hair.

Tobias said, "Here we are, then."

Marith blinked. Trying to remember. Get out of the memories. Here we are, then. Here.

He looked up. Stone faces, mouths open and screaming, framed all around with curling flowers.

"The Gate of Weeping." Where the Emperor was cut down with poisoned swords by his own bodyguards, bribed with the promise of immortal souls. The gateway fell to dust as the Emperor died and could not be rebuilt save with bricks mortared with the murderers' blood. But they got their reward: they were imprisoned inside the walls of the gatehouse, immortal but locked in stone, blind and dumb.

A particularly sick joke on somebody's part that it should be their chosen means of ingress.

"It should..." Tobias pushed cautiously. "Ah."

The gate swung open slowly on silent hinges. It gave onto a small courtyard, empty with an abandoned air. A dry fountain stood as its centerpiece, a woman with huge breasts carrying a water jar.

"Wonder if the water used to spurt out of her nipples?" said Rate.

The courtyard seemed to be used for storage. Wine and oil jars were stacked neatly against one corner, empty boxes piled in another. Rate unwrapped the bundle he was carrying and handed them their swords and helms.

So. Now they started killing people.

Two sides of the courtyard were high walls closing the palace complex off from the city beyond. A third was colonnaded, giving onto gardens rich in flowers. The fourth, immediately opposite the gate, had three doors, elaborately carved wood so heavily decorated they looked almost rotted. Tobias made for the middle door and gave it a push. Beyond it was a large near-empty storeroom. The walls were plain whitewash but the floor was a glorious jeweled mosaic of flowers and fruit trees, the ceiling richly molded plaster, its peaks and arabesques now dingy with cobwebs. Once a wealthy part of the palace, now obviously fallen into virtual disuse since the unfortunate incident at the gate. This room in turn opened onto another, slightly smaller chamber in a similar state of abandoned grandeur.

A door opened in front of them and a serving woman appeared. She dropped the box she was carrying and opened her mouth to scream. Tobias skewered her with his sword. She slumped over in a pool of blood.

"Everyone," he hissed through clenched teeth. "That's the orders. Everyone."

They went cautiously through the door the woman had come through, into a windowless hall lit with tall yellow candles.

Another doorway. Another hallway. Two guards in gold armor stood before a marble staircase, armed with long trident spears.

Tobias gestured silently to them, counting down on his fingers. They came round the corner hard, flying at the guards. Tobias took one of them in the neck before he'd even turned round. Marith barely had time to think before the other was on him, shouting in panic. He pulled his sword up and parried a stab of the trident. A stupid weapon for close quarters fighting. The blunt end of it clattered against a sconce in the wall, sending candles flying. Hot wax splashed on the floor. Rate was on the man now, angled his sword thrust in above the trident, but the guard brought the weapon up and knocked the blade away from him. Marith dived in low and slashed across the man's legs, drawing blood. Tobias finished it with a strike to the neck as the trident jerked down again in response. The gilded breastplate clattered loudly as it struck the marble floor.

Shouts came from further down the hallway. Two more guards appeared through an archway, this time armed with swords. They drew up short when they saw the chaos in front of them, then formed smartly into defensive positions, challenging the attackers to come at them first.

Tobias gestured to Alxine to watch the stairs and moved forward to engage the guards. Marith and Rate followed him. What the hell am I doing? Marith thought suddenly. Why don't I just surrender? Why didn't I just surrender and tell someone who I am and everything I know as soon as we first got here? Then one of the guards was on him and he parried and thrust and felt his sword bite hold and blood spurt up in his face and he remembered why. Fun. This was intensely, enjoyably fun. He hacked down violently and the guard fell dead at his feet.

"Up," Tobias indicated. "Up, up." They began to run up the stairs, Alxine shouting that something was coming down to meet them. Screams and shouts were beginning to ring out from across the palace now. Up, up. Up to where the important people were. Clattering footsteps on the stairs as three more men appeared, swords out already dripping blood. Their momentum almost brought them colliding with Alxine, who got a nasty slash on the arm and stumbled backward on the slippery marble steps. Rate howled and came at them while Tobias pulled Alxine to his feet. Marith whirled his sword, dancing across the stone, feeling wild laughter building up inside him. He threw off his helm and shook out his beautiful, shining hair; shouted "Amrath! Amrath! Amrath and the Altrersyr!" as he lunged at the man in front of him. The man grunted with astonishment as he died.

Behind the guards, a pair of wide-eyed, terrified serving boys were crouched against the wall. Marith cut them both down, stabbing one in the throat, slashing the other in the belly so that his innards spilled out like lacework, slippery and lustrous as pearls. Would be a long time dying, like that. To stop him attempting to crawl away, he struck the boy in the left leg at the knee joint, hearing bone and cartilage crack. Lie there! he thought. Lie there and die slowly, watching your life run out of you! Look at your own body shriveling and dying before your eyes. Nothing but meat and blood and muck, men are. Stripped you down to realizing that.

The stairs ended at a wide landing running off both left and right. Tobias led them right. Several doors opened off the landing: they went through them methodically, killing anyone they found. Another servant girl, her body already a mass of blood where she must have escaped from another squad of their men; two old men, petty court functionaries from the look of them, holding blunt swords in shaking hands. They killed and killed until Marith's head spun.

To fight in battle was exhilarating: he'd heard that often enough from his arms master and his father's warriors; he'd sat in his father's hall a thousand times listening to songs of Amrath's great victories, His battles, the glory and joy of a great host marshaled for conquest, the beauty of a duel between two heroes well matched in combat fighting to the death. As a child, he'd taken such pride in the deeds of his ancestors: Amrath, His vassal and good-brother Eltheri Calboride, Fylinn Dragonlord, Hilanis the Young King. Growing older, the stories repelled and fascinated him in equal measure. He understood them better, or perhaps he better understood himself. A shared comradeship of men, bound together by life and death, balanced bright as fire between the two but barely thinking of either, priding and measuring themselves and each other only by their prowess in killing, deliberately blind to anything deeper, more complex, more difficult to understand. He'd realized some measure of the truth of it, out there in the desert with the men around him. Found some comfort in it, even.

But this, this butchery of servant girls and old men, this was something else. Something that drove the pain in him, and fed on it, and fed it in turn. He tried to find ways of making his victims hurt before he killed them. It irritated him when Rate or Alxine or Tobias got to someone first. Mine, he thought angrily as he saw the others kill. That death should be mine.

Two men were slumped on the ground ahead of them, one half sitting, half lying, trying to hold his head on, skull cracked through to the bone and the brain matter beneath, the other crouching beside him, trying to help but horribly injured in his chest and arms, bloody and burned. They turned wild eyes toward the squad as they approached. Marith walked forward and killed them both, a slow sword thrust in the neck to one and a series of violent kicks to the head to the other, spilling gray pulp over the marble floor.

Tobias came up to join him. "You stupid bastard, Marith. They were two of ours."

Laughter. He looked down at the bodies. "It doesn't matter now, really, does it? Dead's dead."

They were in the state apartments of the palace now. The walls were lined with silk hangings, the air around them soft as breath. The floors were gold and gemstones, the ceilings carved perfumed wood. Every window shone illuminated as in midday sunlight, brilliant as diamond or with rich colors casting patterns on the walls. They were not lit from within or without. They were lit by themselves. Mage glass. Light glass. There was a piece of it set above the throne in the Great Hall at Malth Elelane, another in the chapel of Amrath, but they were small and clear, precious handspans of colorless glass. The extent of it here made Marith's eyes hurt to look.

They'd been through four or five more rooms before they encountered any further resistance. Five guards, swords already bloodied to the hilt, although two were injured. One badly, his face pale and clammy with pain. They came running down the corridor toward them, then pulled to a stop and came into a defensive formation.

Tobias pulled his men up in turn. There was a body lying on the floor, between them and the group of five. Marith looked at it absently. It was one of theirs, he vaguely recognized the face as someone Emit had talked to. The eyes were open, with an angry look to them.

The two groups eyed each other warily. Purely on numbers, the Sorlostians had the slight advantage, though the mercenaries were still virtually unharmed. The stand-off was broken when a young man came screaming down the corridor, pursued by two more mercenaries. The youth almost collided with the Sorlostians and suddenly the defenders were surrounded, four in front, two behind. Tobias roared to attack.

Bloody, struggling confusion. The corridor was narrower just here, decorative columns and big golden candle sconces making the space harder to negotiate. The presence of a dead body in a pool of blood didn't exactly help: Marith felt his feet slide nastily in the gore as he came forwards. His boots would be completely ruined, soon. Swords wheeled, difficult to fully control in the confined space. He had to pull himself sideways to avoid Rate's blade

as one of the Sorlostians parried it wide. Tobias swore loudly at
Rate and knocked the blade safely away.

"Bloody watch yourself, boy," Tobias grunted toward Marith.
Marith smiled sweetly back. Gods, this was so much fun. He
hacked viciously at the nearest opponent, almost catching Rate
in the hip when his blade went wide. Tobias grunted again but
didn't move to protect Rate the way he had Marith. Interesting.
He wondered what Tobias would do if he just turned and hacked
one of their own men down in front of him.

One of the Sorlostians managed to catch him on the shoulder, his
blade grating against Marith's armor, momentarily unbalancing him.
He lashed out but missed and struck the wall, his arm jarring as the
blade struck the stone with a screech. The impact sobered him a little,
jolted a bit of self-control back into him. He might sometimes think
he wanted to die, but he certainly didn't want to die here, hacked
up by hired guards who didn't even know who they were fighting.
"Amrath!" he shouted again and stabbed his adversary in the chest.

The man crumpled, hanging for a moment impaled on his blade
then collapsing at his feet. He was still just about alive, his eyes and
mouth moved like a fish, staring up at Marith. It looked like another
face: Marith saw the mouth open, the eyes searching him. He stared
back in horror, bile rising up in his throat. Fell back against the
wall, his sword clattering from his hand. Dying. Dying and dead
and gone. All the light running out of him, cracked away to nothing.
Empty. That's all living is, dying. But I was happy once, he thought
desperately. Happy. Alive. The room swam around him. He could
taste blood and raw alcohol in his mouth, thought he was going to
be sick or faint. "Marith!" someone shouted. The eyes gulped and
twitched. Dying. Dying. He fell to the floor and smashed his head
against the wall. Bright light flashed before his eyes. "Marith!" It
sounded like Carin's voice. Help me, Carin. Help me. Make everything go away. He screamed and screamed and screamed.

When he opened his eyes again, there was a small pile of corpses on
the floor in front of him. The man he'd killed was at the bottom,

face half hidden. Alxine was sitting leaning against the wall, his face a bloody mess; Rate was patching him up with a piece of torn cloth. "You're lucky," Tobias was saying. "Could have had your eye out."

Very slowly, Marith got to his feet, leaning heavily against the wall. All three men turned toward him. No, four—they seemed to have gained someone. Not Emit? No, Emit was dead. Hadn't he killed him somewhere? The other group of mercenaries, the ones who'd come down the corridor toward them. One of those. He blinked at the man, feeling as though he was looking up from under water.

"Back with us, then?" Tobias said coldly. He handed him a small leather bottle. "Drink?"

Marith took it and drank gratefully. His mouth was dry and parched, with the sharp tang of blood. Hadn't realized how thirsty he was. Their new companion regarded him warily. "Where's your friend?" he almost asked.

"You remember Riclin?" said Tobias. Marith didn't, but tried to smile at him like he did. The man flashed him a wide grin in return, showing two missing teeth. "Dragon killer. Didn't expect you to faint at the first sight of real blood."

"He's had a rough few days," said Rate, clapping Marith on the back so hard he almost fell over.

Tobias passed Marith a small hunk of dried meat and some dried fruit. He chewed cautiously, hungry but nauseous. He'd barely eaten anything in the last few days either, he realized. The food brought some strength back to him.

"Right." Tobias looked them over. "Now we've all got ourselves together again, everyone ready to get on? We've still got a bloody job to do."

They edged past the pile of bodies and carried on down the corridor. Screams and the clash of swords echoed toward them. And something else: faint, but increasingly obvious, the smell of smoke. The place was burning. An overturned candle, someone knocking over a lamp, wooden carvings and official paperwork and silk-hung walls...Tobias sniffed the air, a worried look on his face.

The next two rooms they came to were empty. The whole place was strangely empty. Marith's head felt slightly clearer and he began to think properly about certain things. He'd been born and bred in a royal fortress. Even in the middle of the night, it was quite difficult to go far without encountering a sometimes humiliatingly large number of people wandering around. Yet they'd been here a good while now, thirty armed men spread out across the building with orders to kill on sight, and met nothing like the resistance he would have expected. They should have been having to fight their way forwards at every step now.

Unless...

He turned to Tobias. "This is a set-up isn't it? They knew we were coming."

Rate froze. "What? Knew what? Who knew?" His face went white. "Oh gods and demons and all hells. No. No, Tobias."

Silence, then Tobias shook his head. "Sorry, lad. Thought you'd probably worked it out by now, to be honest."

"But...I mean...If it's a set-up...Oh fuck...I mean..." Rate started to shake violently, tears coming into his eyes. "We're getting out of here, aren't we? Aren't we?"

Idiot. Naïve, trusting idiot. Thought things would somehow be all right. Thought there was more than pain and killing and dying. We fight and we die, Rate, Marith thought. We fight and we die and that's the end of it. All there is. Death. Just death. That's what life is, Rate. Dying.

Marith laughed. "You still haven't understood yet, have you? There is no getting out. This really is a suicide mission. No one cares what happens to us, as long as the men we're aiming for die first. Suits whoever gets here with the defense to cut down as many nasty foreign invaders as possible. Makes them look more heroic that way. That's the basic idea, isn't it, Tobias? As long as you and Skie survive, the more casualties the better."

"Shut the fuck up!" shouted Rate. "Just bloody shut up!" Stared around, trying to find something to reassure him, panic like claustrophobia. "Why the fuck would Skie even be here, if that was true?"

"You think Skie's here? He's sitting in his lodgings somewhere, drinking good wine and waiting for you to die." Marith gestured at Alxine beside him. "You know all this, don't you, Alxine? Just waiting for death like I am, aren't you?"

"Shut up." Tobias hit him in the face. Marith staggered backward, licking blood from his lips. "Shut up, boy. Disease, you are. No wonder your father put it out you're dead." Turned to Rate. Looked almost sorry about it. Like he cared. "It's partly true, what he says, Rate. You're clever enough to have worked that out already if you'd really wanted to. Part of the deal—most of the men die here, it makes the eventual outcome look better for the people involved. But not us, okay? We get out. Alxine's done something like this before, he knows the drill." Alxine nodded. "The Company's mostly beaten down ex-soldiers and petty criminals now. You saw them get mashed by the dragon. Not much cop in a fight, not much use for anything really. Except dying in exchange for a bag of gold. We'll recruit again once we're back in Immish. Drum up some men, train them up a bit, do a few normal sellsword jobs until somebody needs something a bit more specialized. Always men running from something or someone who'll be more than happy to kill or be killed for a few marks and some company of an evening to keep their demons at bay, regular hot meals and the odd cask of strong drink." A grin. "Both of you two lads, for example."

There was a howl from Riclin, who'd been trailing along behind them. He flung himself at Tobias, bearing him down to the ground. Alxine contemplated the situation for a brief moment, then stabbed the man in the back of the neck. Riclin's arms and legs jerked frantically for a few heartbeats. Tobias shoved him off and pulled himself to his feet. His lip was split and he had a gash on his cheek to match Alxine's. He spat a large gobbet of blood at Marith.

"I take it he didn't know either, then?" said Rate savagely. Marith began to laugh uncontrollably at that, a wild, high-pitched laugh, until Tobias hit him again.

"You shut up now or I'll kill you too, whoever you are and whatever you're worth. Or I'll let Rate torture you first." Tobias sighed wearily. "I'm sorry, Rate. But you couldn't be allowed to know, could you? 'Sign up to the Free Company, two year contract, pay in arrears, we'll set you up to die badly before you make it through to get the cash.' You'd probably have been another corpse, to be honest with you, except that Geth's getting old and slow, and Alxine'd be bloody useless as a squad commander. But look, lad. I plan on getting you and Alxine out of here. And yes, it is probably a good idea to take the Lord Prince here with us, much as I'd like to slit his throat and piss on his corpse right now. So you need to do as I say, okay?"

Rate looked at him for a long moment. Then he nodded slowly. Not much else he could do. Trapped, as much as I am, Marith thought. Where have any of us got to go? They began to walk on down the corridor, treading over Riclin's corpse.

The next few hours were a long dark nightmare of fire and blood and smoke. They edged through the palace, killing as they went, the building slowly burning around them, the silk wall hangings going up like kindling, shrieking with flames that ran like liquid across the walls, and they walked into it, covered in blood, cutting down the men they met as they did so until their arms ached.

They came at last to a great pair of cedar wood doors, inlaid with gold, wider than a man's outstretched arms. A heap of bodies was piled before them. Some of the bodies were burned, their skin blackened, their armor soft and sweating, glowing with heat. The room in which they lay was itself on fire, the walls and ceiling burning and covering everything with ash and silk and tiny fragments of gold leaf. But it did not seem to Marith that these men had been burned by those flames. He thought again of the fire around the head of the statue in the Court of the Broken Knife, flames dancing in a ghostly wind.

"So, we...we go through there, then?" said Alxine slowly. They all looked at the great doorway. It looked like the doors of a tomb, or the doors to the city of the gods in a children's tale. There was something behind it that would hurt them.

The room they were standing in was on fire. There were shouts echoing through the chambers they had come through, men coming nearer. Could be friend, could be foe. If they turned to fight, they'd have their back to the doors. That might be worse.

"Oh, for gods' fucking sake." Tobias gave the doors a push. "I thought you were descended from bloody demons, boy. Scared of a man on a gold chair, are you?"

The doors opened. They stepped through.

There was indeed a gold chair. A huge gold chair, so vast it would swallow up any man who sat in it. It gaped like an open mouth. And a man was indeed sitting in the chair. A bored-looking man with a sour face. He was dressed all in black with a thin band of yellow silk round his head. He didn't look remotely dangerous. He looked half-terrified and convinced he was about to die.

Squad commander Gethen was lying on the floor in front of the throne. At least, it bore a passing resemblance to Gethen. His face was seared across with fire, one half perfectly smooth and untouched, the other charred down to the skull. Eyes and lips burned off. He still seemed to be vaguely alive. There were two other men lying with him. At least, they bore a passing resemblance to men. Mostly to cooked and gnawed bone. The air stank of roast meat.

Better than steak.

A troop of ten guards stood around the man on the throne. Their armor was not gold and their swords were not jeweled. They wore black armor that gleamed in the colored light streaming down from the mage glass windows behind them. They held long black swords, whose blades flickered with blue flames. Their helms covered their faces, so that only their eyes showed, dark and cold.

Two other men stood by the side of the throne. One was an

aging man with thin, gray hair framing a heavy, jowly face. He wore a long white robe, torn at the hem with a flash of blood down the front. The other was dressed in a simple robe of white cloth, his face ageless and impassive, smooth as obsidian. He was holding a long wooden staff.

They all looked at each other.

And then the world exploded in flames.

Chapter Twenty-Six

Blue fire licked and crackled around Marith's face. It tingled, like sea spray cold on the skin. He felt his face warm slightly. A faint smell of singeing from his hair and clothes.

Rate and Tobias and Alxine were burning. Screaming. He looked at them a moment. Their armor glowed red.

He took a slow step forward, pushing against air as thick and heavy as water. The heat on his face intensified, uncomfortable, stinging, scalding him. He took another step. His hands shook on the grip of his sword. The air was thick as honey. Like fighting against a strong current. The men behind him screamed and writhed. Burning. Dying. The room stank like a funeral pyre.

A third step. It was harder to keep upright now than it had ever been in his life. He felt pressure pounding on him, pushing him down, his back and knees buckling. His face was hot with pain. Breaking him. Ruining him. Crushing him like stone. Drowning him. The others were on the floor, thrashing about. They screamed like he had never heard anything scream before. He felt himself falling: with gritted teeth he took another step, half crawling, bent under a weight like the weight of death. Dying isn't easy, he thought. It's hard. It's so very hard. It hurts. He clung to his sword blindly, though the hilt was hot in his hands, stung him.

Blue flames filled his vision. Everything beyond them flickering shadow-dark. Another step. Another. Another.

The black-clad guards shifted toward him. The man on the throne cowered back. He took another step, his body howling with pain. Somewhere in the fires he could feel the mage staring at him. Angry. Frightened. Incredulous. Slowly, agonizingly, he raised his head.

The men behind him were probably dead by now. He was dying. Drowned in fire. Nothing left of him but the grip of his hands on the sword. Another step. Another. The guards were all around him, he could see them as black shapes moving beyond the flames. They held out their swords to him but did not strike him. His eyes filled with tears, the heat of the fire drying them as they poured down his cheeks. Another step.

He could see the mage through the fire, through the tears, see him even with closed eyes, a blazing light in the shape of a man. Raised his sword, holding it two-handed like the mage held his staff, trying to keep it from falling from his hands.

"I will not burn," he whispered through clenched teeth. His voice rasped in his throat. "I will not burn. I will not burn."

A crash like a clap of thunder, so loud it almost knocked him off his feet. He closed his eyes and clung on to the sword, willing his body not to collapse. I will not burn. I will not burn. I will not burn. Took another step forward, his eyes pressed shut against the pain.

I will not burn. I will not burn. I will not burn.

A great roar. Something howling in pain. So loud he could see it, white in the vision of his closed eyes. Pain. Fear.

The fire and the pressure broke off. Sudden, like a candle snuffed out, from light to dark with nothing in between. The lack of pain was so violent he almost fell forwards, gasping, half stunned. Deaf and blind and witless, conscious only that he still held his sword in his hands.

I won, he thought dimly.

The mage was crouched on the floor at Marith's feet, skin

bubbling and smoking, raw red burns opening up across his face and hands. Threw back his head and howled again, and Marith saw fire dancing in the back of the mage's throat. Flames began to flicker out from behind his eyes. Smoke and fire poured from his mouth and nose. Writhed and thrashed and screamed and spouted fire. Fire bursting out of him. Cracks of fire opening. Jerked and fell and lay still, smoke rising, black and charred through like a lump of burned wood.

Better than steak.

Marith took a long, shaky breath.

The man on the throne—the Emperor—was staring with a look of utter horror on his puffy face. The guards had formed a tight ring around the throne, swords pointing at Marith. Several of the blades shook. The man in white was backed up against the wall, also holding out a sword. Weakly and feebly, hardly knowing what to do with it. Rate, Tobias and Alxine stumbled slowly to their feet, faces grimacing with pain. Their skin was raw and red. But they were impressively otherwise unharmed. I saved them, Marith realized with a dizzy sensation of triumph. He laughed. His head swam and he almost fell over. He felt quite possibly worse than he'd ever done in his entire life.

"You...you killed him," the Emperor whispered hoarsely. "You...you didn't burn. You should have burned..." He started at his guards and began to shriek. "Kill him! Kill him now! Before he...he does anything else. Kill him!"

Five black-clad figures moved toward Marith, swords drawn on his heart. Dark blades, sharp as stars, burning blue. They could kill him as easily as thinking. He raised his own sword shakily. He'd felt more able to fight someone at the tail end of a four-day hatha binge. It almost didn't seem fair. Rate, Tobias and Alxine drew closer together behind him. There is no plan to get out, he thought. There never was. Not for any of us. We all just die. And perhaps he deserved it more than most. The five guards looked at him, expectant.

The guards came at them at a rush, flashing fire from their

blades. And they were good. Pressed them back, the four of them, fighting defensively, hardly attempting to do anything more than ward off the blows of the burning swords. They stung where they cut, hissing against the skin. I will not burn, Marith thought. I will not burn...Alxine stumbled backward, his sword falling useless from his wounded arm. I saved him from burning, Marith thought. His legs felt like they were made of lead; he tripped on Alxine's sword and almost fell himself. A sword struck him on the shoulder, drawing blood. Alxine was crying out as they trampled him, their own feet were killing him but they couldn't get him up because they'd be cut down in turn. Rate was wounded in the leg. The swords burned as they slashed them. Not fair.

Not fair.

I'm not going to die, Marith thought.

Blood everywhere. His whole body was covered in it. A voice was shouting: "Amrath! Amrath! Death and all demons! Amrath and the Altrersyr!" It came to him that it was his own. Four of the Imperial guards were dead. He had one of their swords in his hands, and the blue flames rushed over his hands, arching out from the blade, licking hungrily as he killed. He'd killed all four of the guards himself. He was still killing: he almost seemed to watch himself ward off two at once and then cut them down, severing one's head from its body. Everything he struck seemed tainted by oily smoke. Someone appeared in his vision and he swung round and almost struck them down, before realizing it was Rate. He probably shouldn't kill Rate. Not until he ran out of other people to kill. His mind was red. Everything was red. His head felt sodden with blood, spinning inside him, the one word "death" ringing in his ears. He would kill and kill and kill until the world was dead and empty. He didn't bother killing these men slowly. He simply killed them. Hungrily, joylessly. Nothing else in the world.

And so every one of the guards was dead. Not just dead: he seemed to have dismembered most of them. The Emperor was still sitting on his throne. He looked much the same, pale and puffy and stunned, except that he'd pissed and soiled himself. The man in white robes was still staring, with a strange expression on his face. He'd pissed and soiled himself too.

"I'll kill you, then." Marith turned to the Emperor on his stupid tasteless throne. The man squirmed and trembled before him. He switched to Literan, the absurd dead language of this absurd dead Empire. It made what he was saying even more gratifying. You can't shout in Literan, he remembered his tutor saying. Not made for it. Too weak and decadent to shout. And his accent was considerably more elegant than the Emperor's own. He shouted, "I'll kill you slowly and surely and you'll watch while I do it. You'll watch as I take your hands. Your feet. Your lips and your nose and your manhood. You'll watch and beg me to end it. Are you ready?"

He raised his sword. The man shrank back, moaning. Something in the man's whimpering caught Marith for a moment. Pity, almost. Sorrow and pain at what he was doing. At what he was. The death fires within him were beginning to fade; he felt drained and hollowed-out. Sticky with blood. His eyes were itching. He looked at the gore coating his hands and felt sick.

I could just leave, now, he thought. Walk back through the flames, curl up somewhere with a bottle of something and drink until he couldn't remember who he was to care. He could make it all go away. Go back somewhere that wasn't pain and dying and something screaming within him, struggling to get out.

Riding through a meadow when the hay was being cut. Riding through green summer trees. Reading a book by the fireside. Swimming in the sea.

Good things.

I know what I am. What I have given up.

Help me.

The man in white was still looking at him. Like he knew him. Like he hated him. Like he was dirt scraped off his shoe.

Help me.

He moved toward the Emperor, writhing on his throne with a face full of weak fear and a lap full of his own piss and shit.

Everything was red in his vision. "Death," he whispered. "Death!" The man in white let out a cry of terrified rage.

The doors of the throne room burst open. Ten men ran in, yelling, shouting, heading straight toward him.

And then Tobias rushed at him, and everything disappeared in a shower of broken glass.

Chapter Twenty-Seven

"You're getting fat."

Darath's body was bronze in the candlelight. The color of rich wood. Smooth, finely made, warm. Orhan ran his hand over Darath's chest.

"I'm not." Darath grabbed Orhan's hand before it reached his stomach.

"You are. I don't mind, though." Orhan kissed him lightly on the lips.

They lay tangled together in Darath's bed, dozing after sex. Darath had drawn down the shutters and filled the room with candles even in the sunshine of the afternoon, shutting out the world.

"Do you want something to eat? I could have some supper brought up."

"Not yet."

Darath sat up and poured himself a cup of iced water. "It's getting stuffy in here."

"Don't open the shutters." Didn't want to be reminded of anything beyond this room.

"What time do you think it is?"

"Too late."

"Hmm?"

"We have to leave at some point. This could be the last time we—"

Darath splashed him with water. "If I'm getting fat, you're getting morbid. It's a bad habit. Let's change the subject. Is the child really yours?"

"What?" Orhan sat up too and gestured for Darath to pass him a cup. "Why? Don't tell me you're jealous."

"Jealous? Surprised, more like. It's not yours, is it?"

"Darath, do you really think I'd tell you either way? You may be the desire of my life, but some things are private." Orhan smiled at him. "If it's a girl, I can betroth it to Elis, if you like."

"Elis?" Darath sounded genuinely astonished.

"He'd still be just under forty by the time she was ready for marriage. Then he'd get to be the Lord of the Rising Sun after me."

Darath burst out laughing. "That would make me your... Living and dying, no, that's just not right. I'm not bedding my little brother's good-father. Let's not even think about this. And I'm not marrying my brother to some serving boy's bastard, either."

"Now you're assuming it's not mine. You are jealous."

"I'm never jealous. How many men have you slept with, then, in the last few years? Describe them all, I won't even look upset, I swear."

"No one. You know that. No one but you."

Darath pulled a face at him. "Be still my heart, he loves me beyond reason... Come on, there must have been someone? Pretty curls and pouting lips? No? How disappointing. I've been through dozens..." He sipped his water thoughtfully, Orhan could see him purse his lips at the cold, sweet taste of it, sharp with lemon. "Speaking of such things, there seems to be a story spreading that the most beautiful boy in the world has been seen wandering around the city looking to buy swords, helmets and hatha root. Curious, don't you think?"

"I don't listen to stories. Even about beautiful boys."

"You should. It alarms me a little... I don't like people talking about someone buying weapons right now." Darath stretched and settled himself comfortably into Orhan's shoulder. "Oh, listen to me, now I'm being morbid. Are you sure you don't want a cup of wine, something to eat?"

Orhan shook his head. "I'm fine."

"So easy to please." Darath kissed him, wrapping his arms around him. Orhan's cup spilled and icy water poured over them, making them both cry out in surprise and then laugh. They fell back into the bed together, did not speak again for a long time.

"We really do need to get up now."

The candles had burned low and the room was gloomy, shadows dancing on the high walls. It must be getting on for evening. Time and more than time. Orhan's stomach roiled. *What are we about? Why don't we just stay here and fuck some more, and content ourselves with that?*

"You need to get up, Darath," he said.

Darath rolled over and groaned. "You've exhausted me…Lord of Living and Dying, just another moment dozing…" He sat up and rang the bell for a servant. "Come on then."

Body servants washed and dressed them in shirts and trousers, rich silk in bright colors, served them a light meal of bread and smoked meat. They drank a cup of wine afterward as a toast, eyes meeting silently. Then Darath dismissed the servants and they helped each other put on their armor. Orhan's fingers fumbled awkwardly with the fastenings. He'd had servants to do this, on the rare previous occasions he'd worn the stuff. They belted on their swords and took long knives also. No helms. No shields.

"Great Tanis, Lord of Living and Dying," Orhan murmured when they were finished, "we stand away from You now in the place between light and darkness, between life and death. Protect us, Lord Tanis, hear our prayers and give us life or death according to our due." Darath laughed shortly, but nodded. All things done as they ought. They ate a mouthful of salt and honey from a small white dish. Then they went down.

The men were waiting in the inner courtyard. Twenty of them, all the trained men of the House of the East and the House of

Flowers combined. Pitifully few, where once the High Lords of the Sekemleth Empire had kept private armies enough to overrun the world. But enough. They had been assembled apparently hastily, told that there was an emergency and that they were needed now. It must have stirred up the streets already, to see Orhan's men march out fully armed in their blue livery, faces confused and grim. But as they came out into the street they smelled smoke in the air, and heard screaming, and it was obvious that the city was alive with panic because the palace was on fire and men were dying in its halls. Voices were already beginning to cry of invasion and murder; as they went through the Court of the Broken Knife, a woman with blood on her clothes was screaming that she had escaped from the palace, where armed men with the look of Immish were slaughtering all that lived. Other lords would be assembling their men, word might even have reached the Imperial army outside the walls. They went on hurriedly, staring faces crying out in fear and reassurance as they went.

A man came running toward them, eyes very wide, a band of red silk tied around his chest. He nodded at Orhan and said simply, "It is done." The words were mechanical, as though he did not know what they meant. Which he probably didn't. Orhan smiled, astonishment and elation rising up within him, mixed with a deep shiver of horror at what he had just achieved. All was changed, now, whatever the outcome. He had changed the world...Only the hard part left. The part he feared with the practical, immediate fear for his own life. He was damned already now. Being cut to pieces was a more immediate concern.

From the direction of the palace came a great crash, like a roll of thunder. The sound hung in the air, almost deafening. Silence again, then a roar like a vast beast. The men started and stared at each other, Darath and Orhan with them. What in Great Tanis's name...? I must not be afraid, thought Orhan. This was my idea.

"What did you tell Elis?" he asked Darath.

Darath shook his head. "Nothing. I don't want him trying to work things out. What did you tell your wife?"

"Nothing, for the same reason." But he'd left her a letter among his papers, torturously trying to explain what he was doing and telling her that he was sorry. For what, he left unspoken. Marrying her, ignoring her, getting her killed, being born. If he'd lived, he wrote, he would have welcomed and cared for the child. Signed it with his full name and title, Orhan Emmereth, Lord of the Rising Sun, the Emperor's True Counselor and Friend, Warden of Immish and the Bitter Sea. Though Sorlost had not had suzerainty over Immish since the days of the Calboride Godkings, and had never had any interest in the Bitter Sea.

If he lived, he'd have to burn the wretched thing before Bil found it. If he died, it would probably be burned unopened when they torched the house and everyone he'd ever known. But it had felt necessary to pretend that Bil, at least, might survive until sunrise.

Tam Rhyl's men were waiting for them in the palace square. Ten men, well armed in good polished bronze. They blinked when they saw the numbers Orhan was leading but fell into line behind. Good. All set and waiting. They had mercenaries to kill.

A woman appeared at one of the shattered windows, her dress on fire, screaming. She seemed about to jump, but flames billowed up around her and she disappeared backward. Nobody can be alive in there, Orhan thought. Nobody. At least it made it easier for them, if everybody was already dead. Though it astonished him just how quickly the place had gone up. He thought of his sister's litter, enchanted against fire. And in a few paces, they'd be going in there. He drew a deep breath as they marched forwards. His hand brushed Darath's and they looked at each other. "I'm glad," he said quietly. Then they went through the great arch of the main entranceway that yawned open before them. In through the inner courtyard of the gate, where a fountain played, its water murky with blood. In through the first of the great audience rooms, floored and lined in gold, that led in and up to the throne room itself.

In and on, killing a handful of confused mercenaries as they went. In and on, until the doorways were choked with bodies and the walls ran with fire and blood. In and on, until they were too far to go back.

And then the doors closed on them. And then ten more men appeared, dressed in Tam Rhyl's colors, swords drawn. And then Tam Rhyl's men turned on them, cutting down several of their troops before they even had time to react.

Darath looked at them in utter confusion. Cursed as the realization took hold. Orhan didn't even wonder. Betrayed. He'd known all along, in the back of his mind. Nobody got away from something like this unbloodied. If Tam hadn't turned on him, he'd have had to turn on Tam. He raised his sword as the men came for him. I'm sorry, Darath, he thought. Really I am. But you did talk me into bringing you in on it. He'd almost suggested Darath didn't come at all, stayed safe at home waiting for news. No need for him to be here. No need for them both to die like this. Not when Darath could have lived a little longer and poisoned himself painlessly when he heard they'd failed.

There was another violent howl, nearer now and more terrible. Orhan shuddered. Too loud. No one should be able to cry out that loudly. Or as though they were in that much pain. The sound made the men squaring off against each other shudder, almost break off fighting to check that they were still alive.

Tam's men were fighting defensively, keeping together as a block, not trying anything too risky. They're trying to stall us, Orhan realized. They probably wanted him alive, to grovel and confess all before being horribly executed.

Orhan began to edge along the wall toward the further doors leading to the throne room. Gestured frantically to Darath to follow his lead, shouting an order to the men to push forward. Amlis was already dead, useless as he was. Sterne was down and dying. Might be best if he died, in some ways. Awkward, in an impossible future where they all survived, the four of them bending over the baby's cot. He signaled the men to press more aggressively, try to break through. If they only had orders to hold them...

Darath shouted and slumped over, and Orhan let out a cry of grief. No. No. No. He cut through a man to try and get to him. Couldn't see Darath die. Not like this. Tam's men's stance became more aggressive, no longer holding them back but trying to gain an advantage over them. The walls were beginning to burn. It was all going so wrong.

Several men from each side down, the fighting getting less organized, more spread out. A couple of Rhyl's men broke and ran. Orhan pushed forward again and found himself near the doors. Got one open and called to his men to rally through it. Couldn't see Darath any more. Couldn't wait and look for him, they'd all be dead anyway if he didn't finish this.

I'm sorry, he thought again as he ran.

In the next room, two servants were dead. In the room after that, he and Darath and Tam and the Emperor had sat together only a few days previously and pretended to discuss the affairs of Empire. Whoever survived would sit here in a few days' time and do the same. It's all just a bloody game, he thought. It doesn't matter to anyone outside this building. What does it matter who rules, as long as the gold keeps circulating? Nobody cares. Except those of us who live and die for it.

And then they were at the throne room itself, the doors crashing open, an utter catastrophe being played out inside. He'd planned for the Emperor to die, the whole damned point was for the Emperor to die, but it still struck him with astonished fear, to see a blood-soaked figure turning toward the throne, sword raised. Orhan shouted something incomprehensible. The men, his own and Tam's both, screamed with rage.

The bright figure lunged. I'm actually going to see it, Orhan thought wildly. I'm going to see the Emperor die. Whatever comes after, I've done it. I've brought down the throne. I've ended a reign that has lasted a thousand years.

It took him rather by surprise, therefore, when three of the men he'd paid to kill the Emperor pushed the fourth out of the window before he managed it, and then jumped out after him.

*   *   *

The men froze, swords pointing at each other, baffled mutters on their lips. The Emperor collapsed into a heap with eyes so wide with terror they looked like wild horses' eyes, shit spreading in his lap. Tam Rhyl and Orhan Emmereth faced each other, frowning, each daring the other to make the first move.

Orhan took the only course he could see open to him.

He stepped forward, stabbed Tam in the stomach and prostrated himself before the Imperial Throne.

Chapter Twenty-Eight

Thalia opened her eyes. Utter darkness, as always, the shutters of her bedroom closing out all light. And silence. The deep silence of the Temple at night, no one waking, the darkness of the God filling everything.

But something was wrong. She could feel something, pressing around her. A weight. Fear, flowing over her like water. An ache filling her head and her heart. Something was coming. Something was there.

She slid quietly out of bed and lit a candle. The tiny flame was like a jewel in her hand. Without thinking why, she changed from her night robe into a dress. Then she extinguished the candle again. Her eyes blinked for a moment, but the darkness was easy for her. She opened the door to her bedroom and stepped out. The corridor outside was faintly lit, moonlight and starlight filtering in from high windows. And another light. She started and peered out, almost needing to rise up on tip-toe to look. There was a red light in the sky, and smoke.

She crept further down the corridor, toward the stairs down to the rooms where the other priestesses slept. All the windows were shuttered, no one else would have seen. Fear filled the room.

The stairs creaked ahead of her. She stopped, drawing back. Not that way. There was another staircase, down from the back of her bedroom, leading straight to the heart of the Temple. She stole back into her bedroom and went down that way, creeping blind in the dark. She was not even sure how she knew something was seeking her, unless it was through the warning of her God. Demons, she thought. Death things. The ghosts of those she had killed. Then she took a deep breath of the dark air, drawing the dark into her, and knew better. Not demons. Men.

The stairs twisted and turned, the darkness like a living thing. She held her hand against the wall, but went on without hesitating, unafraid. She could see in the dark with her mind, as well as she could see in the light. She knew life and death and light and dark. But the men creeping down behind her would be afraid.

She came to the antechamber at the foot of the stairs. Now came the danger. The only way out led across the Great Chamber, blazing with light. No hiding place. No way to avoid being seen. But the light was her place also. Great Tanis would shield her there, as well and as safely as in the dark. And beyond that was the Small Chamber, the place of death absolute, where she would be safe. The place none would dare to go but herself.

The door opened silently at her touch and Thalia was in the Great Chamber. She gazed around her. Candles blazed, rich golden light; so much light there were no shadows on the floor. Only toward the great high ceiling did the shadows come. The air was warm and welcoming. The red light of the lamp on the High Altar gleamed.

Creaking and a muttered curse, quickly cut off, from the dark behind her. The men, coming down the stairs, frightened by the power of the God. Why did she not cry out, alert the others in the Temple? But the dark and the silence were inviolate. The God was here. The men following her were afraid. And she was the High Priestess, the greatest and holiest woman in the Sekemleth Empire. She would not shout out in fear.

She slid quickly across the Great Chamber, toward the heavy curtain and the room beyond. Slipped quickly behind it, into the Small Chamber that smelled always of blood. Her place. The High Priestess's place. She would be safe here, surely.

The two slaves crouched against the walls, as they always squatted, day and night, sleeping and waking, waiting for their mistress to bring a life for them to bind, waiting for their mistress to leave a corpse for them to remove. Thalia had never spoken to them. Did not know if they could speak. To hide and wait and watch was their purpose. They too were tools of her God and her duty, like the knife and the stone itself. In the pitch dark of the room their eyes regarded her with dumb curiosity. She stood before the stone, looking at the dim arch of the curtained doorway.

A long time seemed to pass. It was cold in the Small Chamber, despite the heat of the room beyond. Thalia shivered in her thin dress. Faint sounds from the Great Chamber, men creeping in the light, looking for her. There were three entrances through which she could have gone. And they would not dare this one. A voice, muffled, whispering something, agitated, afraid.

The curtain lifted. Not just moved aside but pulled away completely, flooding the Small Chamber with light and heat. Thalia almost cried out in anger. How dare they? How dare they? Four men with swords came toward her.

The two slaves rose to their feet, blinking in the light, confused. The fear of death take you! The fear of life take you! But they came toward her unfearing, undying, and she knew they had come to kill her. They killed the slaves who stood dumbly before them, the pattern of their lives so shattered they could do nothing but stare open-mouthed as the swords went through their hearts. In their long years of service in that room they had perhaps forgotten there was a world beyond the Small Chamber and the Great Chamber and the High Priestess and the knife.

She was frightened. Frightened down into her bones. They had come to kill. They had come to kill her. She thought of reaching down for the knife in its wrappings of cloth. But that would be pointless. She knew how to kill with a blade, not how to fight with one.

I am the High Priestess of the Lord of Living and Dying, she thought. The Beloved of Great Tanis. The most powerful woman in the Sekemleth Empire. She closed her eyes and took a deep breath. Darkness. The darkness of death. The darkness of living. Darkness and fear.

Power rushing through her.

Darkness and light. Life and death.

Every candle in the Great Chamber went out.

The men screamed in terror. The crushing power of the God coming down. Thalia darted in front of them and began to run.

She did not even know where she was running to. The great door of the Temple was closed but not locked. Never locked, day or night. She could not go back into the warren of corridors. There might be more men there, with more swords. And Ausa would be there, with no hands and no eyes. I will live, she thought. I will live, and live. She ran through the narrow passageway, finding its entrance by feel, by the strength of her desire for life. She pushed open the door, smooth on its hinges. She ran down the steps of the Great Temple, with people scattering before her in the night, and into the street beyond.

Chapter Twenty-Nine

Marith opened his eyes. He was in a garden, lying on soft grass. The air smelled of jasmine and lilac blossom. The honey-sweet perfume of roses. Damp leaves. A fountain plashed like children laughing. Birds called from the trees. The ground was cool and pleasant. Everything twinkled with tiny shards of colored mage glass, red and blue and green and white. Pieces were still falling, raining down on him. He watched them dance as they fell. Like jewels. Like snowflakes. Like eyes. Overhead, the great red star of the Dragon's Mouth burned down.

He had no idea how he'd got there, or even where he was. In the gardens of Malth Elelane, on a summer's night? Then Carin would be there beside him. He stared up at the Dragon's Mouth. Perhaps he ought to get up. His whole body seemed to be hurting. His mouth tasted of blood.

There was someone beside him, getting to his feet, groaning as he did so. Carin? It didn't look like Carin. And Carin wouldn't be holding a sword. Would he?

He was in the gardens of the Summer Palace of Sorlost, and Carin was long dead, and he'd just fallen out of a window.

Marith sat up. Tobias was leaning against a wall. Alxine was sitting next to him, his right arm a shattered mess of blood and bone, his face a mass of bruises. Rate was kneeling retching onto the grass.

"You...pushed me..." Marith's voice sounded weak and distant in his mouth. "I was going to kill him...You stopped me."

"I did." Tobias helped him get to his feet. "We ought to get moving. People will be looking for us."

"Why?"

"Because the other bloke paid more."

They began to walk slowly through the gardens. A silent pleasure ground of flowers, everything heavy with the scent of damp earth and soft petals, overlaid with the stink of death. A languid silence held. The palace burn behind them, the light of the flames making their shadows dance.

They came to a pool in which huge water lilies floated. Marith bent down and washed his face and hands. They were filthy with blood and ashes, the water that ran off them was black and vile. It glimmered with tiny fragments of mage glass.

"There's no one around," he said.

Tobias grunted. "All dead, probably."

"Where are we going, then?"

"Out of this accursed palace. Out of this accursed city. Back to the meeting place, like was agreed."

They came to a high wall of white porcelain, grown up with jasmine and wisteria and pale sweet peas. Too tall and smooth to climb. They followed it along a little and came to a colonnade giving onto a small courtyard. Marith laughed. The Gate of Weeping. They'd come full circle. They were back where they began.

Tobias sat down on the lip of the dry fountain, rubbing at his leg. He was limping badly. Not as badly as Rate, who was barely walking, he and Alxine supporting each other, their breath short and gasping with pain. The marble woman looked down on them, pouring out her empty vessel onto dry stone, a small shy smile on her face.

"The gate might be locked now," Tobias said slowly. "And gods only know what's behind it. Might be the whole Sorlostian army. Might be chaos. Might be nobody's even bloody noticed what's been going on here. The city gates are shut fast for the night, even if we make it that far. And we're so covered in filth nobody would let us out of them anyway. We've got maybe two, three hours till dawn. And when the light comes up we need to be somewhere where nobody can see us. Especially not you, Lord Prince. You look like..." He barked out a short, cold, harsh laugh. "You look like what you are, boy."

"So where are we going, then?"

"I wish I knew. Anyone got any ideas?"

Somewhere I can get enough drink and hatha to drown myself. Marith shrugged. "Not really, no."

They approached the gate. Tobias listened at it, then tried it carefully. It opened and the street beyond it was empty, though there was a sound of distant shouting and the occasional crash. They stood in the shadows by the high white wall.

"You didn't really think this bit through, did you?" said Marith. "Or did you just assume we'd all die before we got this far?"

"I've just laid waste to a palace, double-crossed a member of the Sorlostian high nobility and my commanding officer and walked out of it alive with all of my men still in possession of a head and four limbs each," said Tobias shortly. "I'm pretty impressed with myself, personally, thank you, boy. And getting out's always the hard bit. There's no point thinking it through. Whatever you plan turns to shit. They really weren't meant to turn up with a whole load of soldiers at the end though. The guys in black were all meant to die rather more easily and Lord White Robes was supposed to give us a hand, not just gawp at us."

"We could try the Five Corners." It was the first time Rate had spoken. His voice rasped painfully, as though he had too many teeth in his mouth. "They might...let us in...We've got clothes there..." He trailed off. No one on earth would let them in, looking the way they did. Not to let them out again, anyway.

Alxine said slowly, "We find a house to hide in and wait it out until they open the gates. Bit like we did in Telea."

Tobias shook his head. "That was a bloody siege. Half the houses were abandoned. Aren't many houses round here that aren't inhabited, as far as I've noticed."

A pause. Then Rate said, "There's a solution to that."

They all looked at Rate. Oh no. No, no. Not that. Not that.

Tobias laughed harshly. "You think? You can't hold a sword to fight, lad. You couldn't kill a new-born baby, state you're in. And you couldn't do it anyway, not when it came to it, could you?"

"True." Rate's eyes narrowed. "But Marith could."

They all looked at Marith. Oh no. No, no. He looked back at them. Rubbed his eyes wearily. All the joy had gone out of him. Replaced with shame. Disgust. He never wanted to see another drop of blood as long as he lived. He never wanted to hold a sword again. He couldn't do this. He couldn't. Just make it stop. Make it all stop. Make everything go away. Help me, he thought distantly. Help me. Please.

He sighed and rubbed his eyes again. "As long as I get the best bed afterward."

It was a small house, tucked next to a bookshop with an alley running off the other side. Quiet, so the neighbors wouldn't overhear.

He'd thought about it carefully. Not too run down: it had to have half-decent beds, a bath, food in the cupboards. Not much point doing what he was about to do for lice and rats and an empty larder. Not too wealthy either, that someone might be concerned about its inhabitants if they disappeared for a few days. Middling. Dull. Just a house. It was just bad luck for the people inside he happened to choose this particular one. It had gray and black beams on the outside that he rather liked, and a yellow door.

Hoped whoever lived there would be out gaping at the heart of the city burning down around them, or running like hell to get away from whatever foreign army rumor had it was invading. But they were all in bed fast asleep. And so Marith went through the house and killed everyone in it. There was in fact a new-born baby. He killed it. He killed three children, three women, two men, a dog and a cat. Then he found a bottle of what was probably wood alcohol and drank it as fast as he could. By the time he reached the bottom he'd almost blotted out the noise the baby had made before it died. Then he lay down in the best bed and slept for a long time.

Meat. Tea. Warm bread. Wood smoke.

Marith came cautiously down the stairs, following the smells and the sound of voices. He was still covered in blood and filth. Every part of his body hurt. His head was pounding so badly he could hardly see. The sound of the baby's crying rang in his ears. It was a triumph that he was alive at all.

A large, bright kitchen. Tobias was cooking salt meat and eggs. Rate and Alxine were sitting at a table eating bread and butter and drinking tea. There was a jug of milk on the table. Warm afternoon sunlight poured in through a small window looking onto a garden thick with fruit bushes.

"You haven't even taken your bloody armor off," Rate said almost cheerfully. Marith looked down. He hadn't. He'd woken to find he was still holding the sword as well. Luckily the blue flames had gone out. Alcohol, magic fire and bedclothes probably wouldn't have been the ideal combination for a restful sleep.

"I'd suggest you have a wash before you come another step closer," Rate continued. "You are possibly the most disgusting thing I've ever seen, right now. My Lord Prince. That smell is really putting me off my food."

Tobias drew him a bath and helped him peel off the layers of torn clothing and armor, scrub blood and ashes from his hair. Tiny pieces of mage glass streamed off him as he washed, leaving the filthy water twinkling. He'd seen the sea like that, once, alive with phosphorescent creatures. None of the clothes they could find for him fitted, but they were at least clean. Finally he sat beside Rate by the hearth, shivering despite the evening heat. Tobias served him bread and milk and tea and greasy fried meat. An uneasy calm seemed to have come over all of them. They crept around him without speaking of it; he did not speak of it either. But Rate's eyes strayed occasionally to a bolted door at the back of the kitchen, around which flies were beginning to buzz.

You look like what you are, boy.

"What's going on outside?" Marith asked at last.

Rate frowned. "A lot. We had a peek out earlier. Palace finally seems to have stopped burning, but now some other buildings have gone up as well. People on the streets with swords. Could almost be the beginnings of a civil war, by the look of it."

"Which would be a right pain," Alxine put in, "since they might keep the gates closed."

"Noble families fighting," said Tobias. "The ones as paid us to kill His Eminence, and the ones as paid us not to. And the ones as just feel they should probably get involved now everyone else is. Probably all good and happy. They'll get it all sorted in a few days and go back to just being rude to each other at parties."

Marith closed his eyes, trying to remember things. All he could see was blood. "That man, the man in white…Lord…Lord Rhyl. He paid us to…to kill everyone apart from the Emperor?"

Tobias nodded. "Yup. Anyone who'll pay a lot to have someone killed—like as not, someone else will always pay more to have them stay alive. Emperor's bloody grateful, calls him a hero, gives him full powers to appoint anyone he chooses to all those newly vacant Imperial jobs. And the men who actually did all the hard work die as traitors. Neat, eh? And he didn't pay us. He paid me."

Very neat. Except from the sounds of it things were getting out of control.

"How do you know who he is?" Tobias said suddenly. Looked laughably alarmed.

"How do you think? I've met him. He visited Malth Elelane the summer before last, around Sun's Height. My brother paid a visit here and spent most of it trailing around after his daughter, so he got the absurd idea he might be interested in marrying her." His father had laughed in the man's face, and Ti had personally laced the girl's food with abortifacient the day she left.

Pale eyes, staring at him, filled with loathing. Like he was nothing. Like he was filth scraped from the bottom of his shoe. Marith frowned. "He recognized me, I think."

"No offense, boy, but I'd be surprised if he'd been able to recognize you. While I'm sure your divine ancestry shines in your face and all that, you were probably looking a bit different the last time he saw you. Bit less covered in blood, for one thing."

From what the girl was reported to have gone through on the voyage home, the Altrersyr features must be engraved on the man's heart. And he had almost certainly made something of an impression personally at the feast on the last night, after Carin's dazzling suggestion he try mixing hatha with neat brandy as an aperitif. A memorable night for everyone else present, apparently. Marith nodded: "You're probably right."

"So, how do we go about getting the other half of the money, then?" said Rate. "This Lord Rhyl, we just turn up at his door or what?"

"What?" Tobias looked at him and laughed. "Gods, no. There is no other half of the money, lad. There never is, doing something like this. What we got up front is what we get. At least one lot of the people who contracted us should all be dead, and the others are really not going to want us hanging around."

"But..."

"Charge double and only expect to collect half. It's not that complicated." Tobias jangled a fat purse at his belt. "Ten thalers for killing the Emperor. And another fifteen thalers for not killing the Emperor. Quids in, we are." He handed a thaler and a silver dhol each to Rate and Alxine. "That's your share for now. Don't spend it all at once. Don't spend it at all until we're fifty leagues from here and still going, in fact, be my advice."

Marith looked at him. Tobias looked back and shook his head. Rate sniggered somewhere behind him.

Anger flashed over Marith. "You'd all be dead several times over if it wasn't for me."

"Indeed. And we're all very grateful, My Lord Prince. You're still not going anywhere out of my sight, though, and certainly not being allowed any money you might be tempted to spend on things, if you know what I mean. You're a valuable asset, boy. Would you trust you with so much as an iron mark, if you were me?"

Marith rubbed his face. His eyes itched horribly. A whole thaler's worth...Happiness. Peace. He sighed. "No, probably not." Yesterday, he'd have sworn to kill Tobias, for speaking to him like that. Maybe he would tomorrow, or the day after. I'm an Altrersyr prince, he thought bitterly. The heir to Amrath. I killed a dragon. I killed a mage. I killed more people than I can count. I could have killed the whole bloody lot of you. I still could. He stood up. "If you'll excuse me, then, I'm going back to bed. If I promise to be good and let you lock me in again, can I at least be permitted to take something to drink up with me?"

Tobias looked at him and laughed. They all laughed. He went upstairs and drank and lay in the dark in the best bed. Images of what he'd done floated up in his mind. Staring into the darkness, his eyes open, what he had done was terrible beyond thinking. But when he closed his eyes, he felt pride well up in him, a joy and a pleasure and a hope. The darkness pressed on him, heavy and soft like falling snow. *You look like what you are, boy.* It was all the same, he realized, whether he looked into the dark of the room or into the dark of his own mind.

Chapter Thirty

It didn't take long to get Tam Rhyl's men under control. Tam was down, Orhan was alive: they knew which way to turn if they wanted to live to see daybreak. The Emperor was so pathetically relieved to see Orhan take some kind of command of things that he almost collapsed in gratitude. The entire Imperial Guard had just been slaughtered and the palace set on fire. Someone had to be responsible, so it might as well be Tam Rhyl. Especially as Tam Rhyl was lying on the floor in a pool of blood in no state to argue back. The Emperor himself had been miraculously and inexplicably saved from being slaughtered or set on fire. Someone had to be responsible for that, too, so it might as well be Orhan Emmereth. Who was kneeling in front of him holding a sword, with a troop of armed men at his back. Any man with even half a brain usually believed what he was told in these particular circumstances.

Orhan had never thought so fast in his life.

Tam had betrayed him. The assassins had betrayed him. He'd lost, theoretically, since the Emperor was still alive and kicking with nervous fear. He'd just somehow won, at the same time. All the other important people in the palace seemed to be dead. Several bodies in suspiciously Immish-looking armor were lying around missing vital body parts, swords dripping with good honest Sorlostian blood.

The pressing thing now was to get the fires put out before the palace actually burned down completely. You live and learn, Orhan thought exhaustedly, looking at the smoke. If he ever arranged a massacre again, he'd ensure he had a bucket chain waiting alongside the swords. But, to be fair, he thought, it seemed basically impossible that the palace could burn. It was the Imperial Palace of the Asekemlene Emperor of Sorlost the Golden, the only mortal man to escape the finality of death. It had stood beyond cities. Beyond empires. Beyond gods. Constant in his life, and in all human lives. It would stand when the waters rose and life ceased and the world was drowned. It couldn't just burn down.

So he'd better get people going with buckets to stop it before it did.

What to do with the Asekemlene Emperor himself was also something of a problem, since His Eternal Eminence couldn't leave the palace except to visit the Great Temple and even then he had to go by palanquin, his feet never touching the ground. Hadn't really planned for this either, seeing as he was supposed to be dead. In the end, Orhan remembered the bathing house in the gardens, isolated from the main building by stone colonnades and running water and with space and comfort enough for the Emperor to feel just about at home. Space for Orhan himself, too: he wasn't going to leave the Emperor's side until everything was settled and his personal candidates had been selected as Imperial Secretary, Imperial Presence in the Temple and every other post down to the girl who washed the Imperial chamber pot. The Emperor, for his part, was still so terrified he'd make more fuss if Orhan left him alone than he would if he got into bed with him.

Orhan divided the men around him into two, one larger party to begin work putting out the fires and gathering the bodies, the other to accompany the Emperor to the bathing house. The great families would be bringing men up to the palace, the Imperial army would be beginning to stir. Needed to consolidate, have things clearly and securely in hand before anyone else arrived.

He came out into the great audience chamber where they had originally fought Tam's men. Found Darath slumped on the ground.

Wounded. Oh God's knives. He'd forgotten in everything that had happened since.

"Let me see," he said urgently, running over. Darath frowned at him, then nodded reluctantly. Proud bastard. Seen him in the depths of passion, in a towering rage, asleep, drunk, taking a piss, in bed with flu, kneeling before him begging to suck his cock, but the God forbid Orhan should see him wincing in pain after someone stuck a sword in his gut. He gently helped Darath roll onto his side. The wound was long, scoring across from the right hipbone up toward the navel, but not deep. A deeper wound there was inevitably fatal, though a man could live for days fevered and screaming first. He closed his eyes for a moment and murmured a little prayer of thanks.

"I'll live, then?" Darath said, trying to sound as if he'd never been worried. He smiled at the Emperor, surrounded by Emmereth and Vorley men and staring wide-eyed at the two of them. "We... we didn't quite pull things off the way we'd intended we would, I assume?"

"The Emperor is alive, praise Great Tanis the Lord of Living and Dying, and his enemies have been vanquished," said Orhan loudly. "The palace is secured and peace restored." He looked around at the bodies scattered on the ground around them, men beginning to sort them into piles. His men. Darath's men. Tam Rhyl's men. Palace guards. Invading assassins. The Sorlostians would be buried quickly, before they began to stink. But the murderers must be displayed in full gory detail in the Gray Square.

Darath got up slowly, wincing with pain. Orhan supported him over to where the Emperor was standing ringed with Emmereth men.

"My Lord Eminence, light of the world," said Darath, hissing in pain through clenched teeth, "my heart rejoices that I have been injured doing service to you and your Empire. I will look upon my scars with pleasure, that they were incurred to save your immortal life. My only regret is that I could have suffered greater pain to spare you greater suffering." He bowed awkwardly and blinked at Orhan: I would prostrate myself, but I fear I would offend My Lord's eyes by collapsing in agony if I did.

They got the Emperor settled in the bathing house with relative ease, cleaned up and changed into a half-decent robe salvaged from the Imperial bedroom; sent a man to the kitchens for food and wine. The gates and entrances were all secured by Emmereth and Vorley men, and most of the fires were out. Silk and carved wood paneling burned quickly and savagely but not deep. Might even have the Emperor back on his throne by the morning, if they could get the bloodstains scraped off the floor. Finally, exhaustedly, Orhan was able to attend to Darath, cleaning and binding his wound and kissing him with deep and passionate relief.

Then the other lords began to arrive, and the real work started. March Verneth with twenty armed men, Holt Amdelle with fifteen. Lesser families too, the city's leading merchants, ranking officers from the Imperial army, all crowding around shouting and arguing, the Emperor sitting dazed and exhausted, Orhan by his side watching it all. Holt and Mannelin Aviced could see which way the wind was blowing and leaped at it delightedly. March looked profoundly skeptical.

"Tamlath Rhyl attempting to assassinate the Emperor?" His eyes bored into Orhan and Darath.

"Tamlath Rhyl is unconscious and under guard," said Orhan smoothly. A sword in the stomach and a dose of hatha syrup tended to have that effect. "Should he recover, he will be subjected to careful questioning to ascertain the truth of what has happened here." The knowledge of what he would have to do sickened him.

"But that's about what it looks like," Darath followed up brightly.

March grunted and nodded at Holt and Mannelin. "Can't argue with the four of you, I suppose."

"Five," said Darath, as Elis entered the room with ten men at his back. "We would appear to have the advantage on numbers, My Lord Verneth." Most of the High Council, now Tam was dying.

March's gaze moved from Orhan to Darath to Holt to the Emperor. Holt shifted but remained standing near Orhan. A long pause, their weary eyes watching each other. Orhan's hand itched for the hilt of the sword he still wore at his hip. Now we see. Now we see if we can hold them, even for a little while.

And...No. Of course we can't. March turned and strode out of the room, shouting orders to his men as he went. Cammor Tardein followed him; after a moment, Samn Magreth did likewise, as did a couple of the more minor lords. So it begins, thought Orhan wearily. He'd hoped for a brief while that the Verneths' long-standing quarrels with the House of the Sun in Shadow would swing them toward him. But there'd be looters on the streets by now too, he shouldn't wonder. And any moment now—

And any moment now, one of his men burst into the bathhouse, face cut and bloodied, to report that the Great Temple had been attacked, several women and temple slaves were dead, the High Priestess herself was missing.

Chapter Thirty-One

God's knives.

The Emperor turned paler than ever, a choking sound coming from his mouth. Gasps of horrified astonishment from several of the men present.

God's knives.

"This...This..." Orhan struggled to regain control of his mind. "This goes far deeper than I had...had feared. I knew...I knew Lord Rhyl intended harm to the Emperor, but I did not suspect... I did not suspect...I..." Great Tanis. God's knives. Questioning Tam would be worse even than he had thought, if he had this to worm out of the man too. Still a halfway decent man, are you, Orhan? a voice whispered in his heart.

God's knives.

And so more orders were drawn up, disposition organized, Amdelle men sent to the Temple, Aviced men sent to take charge of Tam's house and household, soldiers called out and sent to patrol the streets. March Verneth to worry about. Most people were keeping indoors but armed men were out searching for invaders and looters were emerging; a fight breaking out near the Temple; fighting in the streets near the House of the Sun in Shadow between Tam's men and his own.

God's knives. God's knives.

It had been a long night. Going to be a long day ahead too.

"You should get some sleep," Darath said gently. "There's nothing more anyone can do tonight."

Orhan shook his head. He knew exactly what would happen if he released his control on things. And if Tam woke when he was sleeping..."Later," he said dimly. "You sleep, Darath. You need to heal."

Darath nodded. "I'll leave Elis here with you."

Wonderful. The man seemed to have come straight from a brothel. Hadn't even managed to get his shirt done up properly. What use he'd be, Orhan couldn't imagine.

Darath drew him into a corner, away from the guards and the sleeping Emperor on his couch. "Then maybe you can explain to me what exactly you've done at the Temple, when I wake up again. Unless you still don't trust me to know."

Oh for Great Tanis' sake..."What did you think we were going to do," Orhan replied tetchily, "bribe the High Priestess to identify the right baby? It was the only way." He almost laughed. "And I never told you, or anyone, because you might try to stop it. Even most of the men we hired didn't know about it, the man Skie was bound to strict secrecy, too." Rumors that Lord Emmereth was responsible for an attempt on the Emperor would be one thing. The slightest hint he or Darath had been involved in an attack on the Temple, however...If he was to be damned, he'd be damned in private, without Darath being dragged into it. "And so Tam never knew to stop it. And so we now have this absurd situation to resolve, on top of everything else." The sheer cost of arranging for the red lot to be drawn had been crippling, and for little apparent purpose if the woman was simply missing and then turned up again. And so more things to do. More pain. More damnation. More death.

The gray hour before dawn was the worst. Not as ill-fated as dusk, but still a perilous time, a time of passing and change, neither living nor dead. Things had settled down, exhaustion finally overcoming excitement. Elis and Holt stayed in the bathing house, curled up on chairs and dozed. Everything calm, sleep pulling at Orhan, but a sense of fear hung over him, like birds screaming overhead. A sound of weeping. A scent of blood in the air. So much still to do, so much still so open to collapse. He felt like the palace itself, shaken and burned. Why did I do this? he kept thinking. Why?

Orhan was dozing himself when a man shook him violently awake again. Tam Rhyl had recovered consciousness. He went quickly to the small storeroom where they were holding the dying man, giving strict instructions to be fetched if anything happened or anyone came.

Tam lay on the floor covered in a bloody cloak, his face clammy, his breath rasping in pain. Orhan was half surprised he was still alive at all. Don't you dare die on me now, he thought with shame. Not until the Emperor and March Verneth have heard your confession. He knelt down and carefully untied the bandage he'd wrapped around the man's flabby belly. The wound underneath was beginning to stink.

"You...won, then?" Tam whispered. His lips were very dry. Orhan gave him a little water from a jewel-encrusted cup.

"Just about. We're both on the border between living and dying, Tam. You'll die soon whatever. I need you to save me. You know what I'll pay if you do."

Tam nodded slowly. "I tried to make it too complicated." Speaking to himself as much as to Orhan. "I tried to play everyone... But you shouldn't have won..."

"Where's the High Priestess?" Orhan pressed his hands down hard on the wound, breaking the clots and feeling hot blood well up.

A gasp of pain. Tam's face white. "What...are you talking about?"

Orhan pressed harder, feeling sick to his core. "I won't save her, Tam. I'll let them all burn alive. Your wife. Your son. Your daughter. Your boy. Where is she?"

"Who?" Despair in Tam's eyes. "Who? You can't let Liseen die. Please, Orhan...Not after...what I made her do. That vile boy, Tiothlyn Altrersyr...He crippled her. She was pregnant, Orhan, and he...I made her bed him...My own daughter...She loathed him...But I wanted...You can't let her die, Orhan."

Don't tell me, thought Orhan. I don't want to hear this. I can't bear to hear any more pain. "Where is the High Priestess, Tam?" he asked. "Where?"

"I...I don't know what you're talking about. Liseen, Orhan... Please, save Liseen..."

"Where?"

"I don't know...Please...Please...I'll tell the Emperor. Please..."

Orhan removed his hands and retied the bandage. "You can have some more hatha, if you want. Keeps the pain away, though it will kill you quicker. I'll bring the Emperor to you later. You confess all, that you plotted to kill him, that those men were acting on your orders, that they were about to kill him when I stepped in to save the day. As soon as that's done, I'll get them away to safety. Your daughter, your wife, your son."

Tam nodded again. "The Emperor? He's...still alive?" He smiled weakly. "I won, then. You'll appoint...good men. The kind of men I would have chosen...You'll do as I...would have done." His face was blurred with pain but he shook his head when Orhan offered him the vial of hatha syrup. "No. No more. I'll see him...as I am... Lie to him as I am." A spasm of pain tore through him and he gasped and writhed, clutching at his stomach. Grasped Orhan's arm and muttered something, his face pallid, his voice harsh and urgent, not his voice at all. "Alive...He's...still alive. Shouldn't be alive... What have we done? What have you done? He'll kill us, Orhan!"

"I've done what was needful," Orhan said as he left. Speaking to himself as much as to Tam. He went out into the gardens, where dawn was breaking and birds were singing in the trees. He washed his hands in the lake, and was sick, and wept at what he was reduced to doing. There is never any need for these things, he thought. We could just have got on with our lives.

Tam Rhyl confessed to everything a few hours later, the Emperor and everyone and anyone Orhan could drum up in attendance.

March Verneth was not among them, his men engaged in minor skirmishes with Orhan's in the Gray Square, ostensibly over the best way of shoring up the smoldering Great Temple buildings. Cammor Tardein was present, his support for March wavering after Elis, in an uncharacteristic display of cunning, started dropping suggestive hints regarding a possible marriage proposal to the youngest Tardein girl. That Darath was making the same hints to March about Elis and a possible marriage proposal to the oldest Verneth girl was possibly unfortunate, but not unpredictable if any of them thought about it. By mid-afternoon, the Emperor was back on his slightly smoke-stained throne in the charred shell of his palace, appointing Orhan the Emperor's Nithque in Tam's place and filling the Imperial Bureaucracy with Emmereth and Vorley placemen. The Imperial army, sworn solely and absolutely to the person of Emperor, patrolled the streets glaring at people to stop panicking and get back to normal life. By late afternoon, Orhan was sitting in an office off the throne room, half dead from exhaustion, trying to focus his smoke-sore eyes on a list of the identifiable casualties and what their jobs had been.

"A very effective coup, Orhan. I should congratulate you. Very novel, I must say."

Orhan spun round. His sister stood looking at him. She seemed almost pleased.

"Holt is thrilled. Good-brother to the Emperor's personal savior! He finally sees a reason in having married me. Forgave me my last dress bill, even. You did it all for that, I'm sure."

Orhan sighed. "I'm tired. I'm busy. Go away."

"I thought you might want someone to watch over you while you slept. Stop someone else sticking a knife in your heart. Although Darath seems to have done that several times over already."

"Indeed. Go away. I can't sleep now anyway."

Celyse sat down next to him. "You need to sleep, Orhan. Really. Even Darath is worrying about you. You can't do this alone, not all of it."

"I have so far. We're all still a heartbeat from dying if I let go now."

"Oh, March will come around. Eloise knows which way things are going. She's not as stupid as her son. He's just piqued none of this occurred to him first."

"None of what, Celyse? I had the privilege of saving His Eternal Eminence from Tamlath Rhyl's fiendishly cunning attempt at his life, an attempt possibly but not definitively planned with support from Immish. Nothing 'occurred' to me."

"Oh, yes, yes. Well, March is piqued he didn't do the saving first, then. He's making his big stand now to feel he's a free agent, then he'll come back to see what he can get out of this. A Vorley marriage and a couple of men he trusts in lucrative positions, assurance this all means what we all know it means, I believe is the likely current price."

She was good at this, his sister. "So what does it all mean?" Orhan asked. Interesting to find out what they were saying about his reasons for all this.

"Restored glory to the Empire. Better counsel to the Emperor. Greater strength through greater wisdom. A big army recruitment drive. Oh, don't worry, brother dear, everybody knows your motives for everything were purer than pure. Far more so than March Verneth's would have been, if any of this had occurred to him first."

Orhan rubbed his eyes. "And as a result I have a lot of work to do. Do your sources also say whether the current price is acceptable to everyone?" It would be nice to get this all over before blood had to start flying in the Gray Square. March had a wonderworker of some kind, he thought vaguely. The litter-maker. Didn't Celyse say Eloise had kept him on? They'd do all this, and end up blasted to ashes by someone originally hired to flash up a party...

"I couldn't possibly say at this stage. If Elis gets a better haircut, that might help. But what will you do about Cam Tardein's girl? Or is poor Elis going to have to commit bigamy?"

The woman knew everything, she really did. He should probably be profoundly relieved she hadn't known about his plans. Or at least hadn't told anyone about them if she had.

Celyse looked thoughtful for a moment. "No, wait, of course: there's my own dear son, isn't there? Better hope Bil has a girl, brother dearest, he'll be a much more attractive prospect with the Emmereth titles attached as well. Zoa Tardein's pretty-faced enough, if a bit old for him really. I expect he'll be content. Whether she will…But her father will make her, of course." She laughed. "We're all as subtle as blunt blades, in the end, aren't we? It's only Darath I wonder about. Did he really do all this out of lust for you?"

Despite everything, Orhan couldn't help but laugh too. "I'm not that good a lover, Celyse." He'd wondered about Darath's reasons himself on occasion. The thrill of the game? The chance to be something more than he was? The need to find something new to spend his money on? Or perhaps he really did share Orhan's vision of a renewed Empire, better governed, stronger, more disciplined, kinder to its people.

Kinder! He almost wept thinking that. A few hours ago he'd been torturing an old friend and he was still trying to believe it was for a greater good.

But it would be. It would be. Things had to change. They had to. If he had to make every change himself.

People, he thought wearily. Not "things." People. No euphemisms. The bone-white truth, as he'd given Tam. People had to be changed. A whole lot of people. We killed people, in order that others may live. We soaked the city in blood, to make it clean. It's for the best. One day people will see that. Yes?

He sighed again, and left Celyse in charge while he had a bath and a sleep. She would have managed to pull it off properly, he thought sourly. Probably at a lower cost, in coin and lives.

Chapter Thirty-Two

If Skie was still alive, Tobias would have to kill him.

Tobias had reached this conclusion before everything had even started. Been contemplating it for a year or more, indeed, before this job came up and offered the ideal opportunity. Skie and Geth were good comrades. Skie was an excellent commander. But... Couldn't really put it into words. He'd just outgrown them. Needed to be his own man. And Skie had bloody shafted him, not telling him about Lord Prince Marith bloody Altrersyr. "*Not much for us there, I'd have thought*"! Fed up with splitting the rewards of his labor three ways, seeing Skie pocket most of it "for the Company." The money from Lord Rhyl was all his. They'd agreed, him and Skie, that Geth was becoming expendable. Getting old. Making mistakes. Never been the same since he took a spear in his arm the winter before last. Betraying Skie as well was just a logical extension of that.

So now he was on his own with a good haul of money and two half-decent men to build on. Things looked like they might be getting rather more unstable all over the place, what with conspiracy in Sorlost, deeping fever in Chathe and whatever the hell was going on in the Whites. Could only be to the good for a man in his line of work.

And then on top of that there was poor lost little Prince Marith.

Currently passed out in a pool of vomit in the best bedroom, apparently now entirely dependent on Tobias for everything in his sorry excuse for a life. The gratitude he'd shown when Tobias had given him a bottle of spirits from the house's larder had been almost touching. Gone upstairs quiet as a lamb, smiled sadly when Tobias had locked the door on him. Could probably butcher all three of them in a heartbeat. Instead, he'd just looked at them with tired eyes. Worth a lot of money to the right people. Showed almost frightening promise as a hired killer, too.

Prince Marith. Marith wasn't passed out in a pool of vomit in the best bedroom, he'd be sitting in an impregnable fortress at his father's right hand learning how to be a king. How to command people. Lead armies. Wield power. Make people grovel. All that crap.

Tobias would have pissed himself laughing just thinking about that, not long ago. Pretty new boy Marith, who dug the latrines.

Descendant of Amrath. Demon born, dragon kin. All that crap.

His face, killing people.

Somehow it made the skin crawl.

Skie has been a fool there too, Tobias thought then, not to have kept a closer check on the boy. Cost them Emit. Emit would have died anyway, so it hadn't been the worst thing ever to have happened in Irlast. But it was still bloody dangerous, having something like that around without knowing it.

Oh, yes, Skie was getting old and making mistakes. Misjudged how to handle Marith. Got too complacent with Tobias. Secrets and firewine drunks and betrayal—if Skie'd not been getting rusty he would have seen the danger in one of them, at least.

Even going to Sorlost at all. An unreal city. A dream. They killed children here to ensure that old men were able to die. What did Skie think, that they could come here and not be changed by something?

Rate's leg was recovered enough the next morning that he was able to stand to cook breakfast. Fast healing, he was, he said proudly. But Alxine was still shaky and in pain, his arm heavily bandaged. Tobias didn't feel particularly good himself, his leg aching like an old man, slightly feverish. Could do with another few days in bed. They'd have to move on soon, though. Someone was bound to start wondering where whoever had lived in the house had disappeared to. And the smell coming out of the cellar was becoming frankly vile.

The streets outside were still empty. There had been men out at first, some armed and shouting about invasion, some obviously taking the opportunity to engage in a little light looting while no one really knew what was going on. The shop next door had been ignored, fortunately. Bringing down an empire and then being killed in the subsequent petty violence when someone did over a bookshop would have been a particularly pathetic way to go. But now everything was quiet, the occasional figure scurrying from one house to another but nothing more.

"We ought to be leaving," Tobias said to Rate and Alxine over a breakfast of stale bread and stale meat. Marith sat silently in the corner, nursing a cup of water with his head in his hands. Really didn't look well. The only reason he was there at all was because they'd dragged him downstairs. If he was awake, Tobias wanted him firmly where he could see him.

"You need to eat something, boy," Tobias said encouragingly at him. "Get some strength up. The bread's not that bad."

Marith shook his head, blinked red-rimmed eyes.

"Suit yourself." Tobias surveyed his men. "I'm going to send Rate out for a look round. If the gates are open, we'll head out after lunch. Try to get up into the hills before dusk. Be slow-going, but I'll feel a lot better once we're out of here for good and all."

With a nagging feeling that he was repeating a previous mistake, Tobias gave Rate a handful of dhol for some more new clothes and supplies.

"You sure there'll be shops open to buy from?" Rate asked.

Alxine rolled his eyes. "This is the heart of an empire built on trade, Rate, not a village of cow herds. Course everything'll be open. A couple of buildings burning down and some big nobs being dead doesn't stop people wanting bread and novelty goods."

Rate looked at the coins and grinned. "Fine. In that case, I'll see you all in a firewine pit around sundown, then. Or shall I just be extra generous and give it all to a dying street whore straight off?"

"Don't even bloody joke about it, you bastard. And don't be so cruel as to mention the f-word in My Lord Prince's presence, either. Look at his poor little face. Looks like he's going to cry."

To Tobias's intense relief, Rate returned just after midday with clothes, fresh bread, dried meat and raisins, and a lot of news.

"The gates are open. The main ones, the Gate of Dust and the Gate of the Evening, anyway. Lots of soldiers around, but I don't think they're looking for people, just on edge generally. I spoke to a few people while I was shopping: nobody's quite sure what happened but the general view seems to be that the Immish attempted some kind of armed attack. The Emperor is said to be alive: or, at least, nobody's saying he's dead. A couple of the nobles started skirmishing but that all seems to have faded out too. Several Immish families got it in the neck, though. Mob went through and torched a couple of Immish merchants' houses and shops. 'Death to the murdering foreigners', usual sort of thing. The Street of the Money-lenders was quite badly hit. Several of the blokes lynched there may not actually have been Immish, in the bright light of a new day and all, but you know how these things can go. The big thing they're all talking about is that their Great Temple was desecrated. Very unlucky, obviously. Several of the priestesses are dead. Including the High Priestess. The one who…you know… children and everything…"

"Good riddance," said Alxine with a shudder. "Hardly a great loss to the world."

"Oh, they're all terribly upset. Some of them seem to believe their dead will stop dying if the High Priestess isn't around to, um, encourage things along. Point out enough people must have died in the last few days to rather obviously disprove that, and they just look at you funny. Point out people not dying sounds quite good too and they get really antsy and start muttering under their breath."

"First rule of success in our line of work is not to bate the locals, Rate," said Alxine. "Especially not when you've just butchered half their government."

Curious. More than curious. "Odd thing to happen the same night, don't you think? Unless…" Tobias frowned. "Do they say who did it?"

"They seem quite convinced it was the Immish. Got a couple of dead Immish blokes they're waving around with their heads chopped off." Rate looked up suddenly. "Fuck. We did it?"

Alxine whistled. "Nobody mentioned that. Thank all the gods Skie didn't give us that to do. I wouldn't have gone in there for any money."

Which is presumably why he didn't tell anyone, Tobias thought. Far less risky in practice, killing a load of women, but…Hired soldiers could combine profane rationality with a superstition that would cripple most hedge witches. He'd probably have thought twice about doing it, if he'd been asked. So Skie had taken a couple of particularly unlucky buggers and done it himself. And been unlucky himself, hopefully.

"Well, they certainly got value for money out of us lot," Tobias said.

Have a quick lunch of odds and ends left in the house larder and then just try and get out. The city was alive with fear; the air was seething around them, there was a smell of smoke and burning, ash from the palace was still blowing on the wind. Small knots of armed men occasionally marched past, staring at them suspiciously as men out walking in a group, but asking no questions. People hurried about their tasks with wary faces. In the smaller streets children played hesitantly, unsure why their parents were afraid but feeling it and responding to it in kind. Even the street whores and the hatha addicts kept silent and resentful in the shadows, frightened and sullen that this trouble had come and disturbed their painful little lives.

They skirted wide round the Great Temple, agreeing without speaking that it was not worth going too close. Soldiers do not believe in gods until they do something to offend them. A place best avoided at the best of times by those not born in the Empire, the Temple. Decorated now by Skie's head.

The streets became busier as they neared the gate. People were moving toward it with bundles, foreigners, Immish especially, frightened for what had happened, trying to get away. It's all over now, Marith wanted to shout. There's not much point you leaving now, is there? Everything's settling down again and you can just get on with your lives. The Emperor's on his throne and the city is saved from chaos. I know: the man walking next to me made me leave him there.

In a narrow street leading down to the Gate of Dust, they stopped for a moment, sitting to rest on a carved bench outside a wine shop with shuttered windows and a broken door. The roofs of the buildings almost met above them, reducing the sky to a thin high ribbon, shining colorless bright. The air was soft and cool with a smell of stone. It is a beautiful city, Marith thought, looking around him at the carved flowers decorating the building opposite. Alxine was tired out already, his face pale and sweaty; he was struggling to keep going. If he was anyone else, Marith thought, Tobias would have killed him by now and had done with it. Should have let him do it in the palace and saved Alxine several days of pain. Tobias looked drawn and weary too. Only Rate seemed even half alive.

A movement, a flash of something golden and shining, made Marith stand up and step away from the other men. A woman was pressed up against the wall of a narrow alleyway across the street, four men in a circle around her, leering at her, one holding a knife. Nothing to concern himself with, except that the woman was rather more attractive than most. He almost turned away again.

And then the woman raised her face toward him, and he almost fell to his knees in the street.

Light. A light in her, a light radiating out of her, that shone in

Marith's face and almost blinded him with its warmth. The sun rising. The sun on bright water. The sun through green leaves. Stabbed in his heart and his mind. Brought tears into his eyes and made his body tremble. The air screamed around him, hateful and cold.

Living and dying. Fear and pain.

Joy. Desire. Forgiveness. Love.

Marith stepped toward her. The four men turned, shouting at him. He came toward them and even though his eyes never left the woman's face something in him made them run from him. Then suddenly he was alone with her in the lip of a filthy alleyway, the light pouring from her, her face filling his vision with light.

She almost fell into his arms, weeping. The light died out of her face and he saw that she was exhausted, her clothes dirty and torn. Her skin was dark rich brown, like sweet chestnuts, her hair long and black as night. Her eyes as she stared at him were brilliant deep twilight blue. The blue of oceans and storms at evening. The blue of the sky before dawn. The blue of weeping, and of joy.

Emmna therelen, mesereth meterelethem
Isthereuneth lei
Isthereuneth hethelenmei lei.
Interethne memestheone memkabest
Sesesmen hethelenmei lei.
In the midst of the desert,
You came to me like water,
Your face gazing, like water.
So quickly my love came, like flowers.

"Are you hurt?" he asked dully. His head spinning as he looked at her. She shied back, fear in her eyes. Oh, no. No, no, no. She couldn't fear him. She couldn't leave. He clutched her hand, afraid to stop touching her. A sudden horror filled him, that if he saw light in her face, she saw darkness in his.

"I am Prince Marith Altrersyr," he said hurriedly. "I can help you." He saw her start at his name. Curse it. Curse himself. He had spoken in Pernish at first, unthinking, but switched to Literan, hoping it might reassure her. "I...I can help you. I want to help you. Are you hurt?"

"They did not hurt me." She spoke Pernish back to him. Her voice soft and sweet with a heavy accent like thick honey. It made him shiver from head to foot. He held fast to her hand, warmth running into him from her skin, the light rising through her onto him. Everything was silent in his mind. Somewhere far away, things beat like wings.

"I would have killed them, if they had." If she were harmed, he would search the city and kill everything living until he found them. But she did not seem to have been harmed.

Marith led her away from the alleyway down the street. A few people about, watching. A troop of soldiers went past and gave them a quick glance. She flinched from the watching eyes. She moved her body awkwardly, and he saw that her left arm was covered in scabs and scars from wrist to elbow, ugly and vile against her perfect skin.

"You are hurt," he said, anger in his voice. Old wounds, slabby things that festered and did not heal, like his own hand. But it horrified him, that she should ever have been hurt. Linked them, both marked like that, and in almost the same place.

He was glad of his hurts, if it linked him to her. Almost glad of hers, if it gave him another moment to speak to her.

She cried out "No!" and twisted away from him, trying to hide her arm. Her thin sleeveless gray dress was no cover at all for her, she could only try to tuck her arm behind her in such a way that it was more visible, for her trying to hide it. Her dress was dirty and ripped at the hem. Almost without thinking, Marith took off the cloak he was wearing and wrapped it around her, folding it over her to cover her arm.

The fear in her was clearing a little. She looked him up and down, taking in the pack on his shoulder and the water-skin at his belt. "You are leaving the city?" she asked slowly.

Marith nodded. Rate was coming toward him, his face full of anger. They'd drag him away any moment now.

She looked hesitant. "If you are leaving the city, may I...may I accompany you? I..." She blushed, looked at the ground. "I have nowhere to go and I...I need to get away. This is not a good place. And you...you have been kind..."

"It would be my honor," he said, falling self-consciously into the court speak of his upbringing. A brave prince rescuing a lady, like a hero from a song. That was what he was, too. What he could be.

He turned to Rate and Alxine and Tobias, gathered around him grumbling. He smiled and he was a prince again and they would do as he commanded because he could not imagine they could do otherwise. "She will come with us," he said. "Come with me. Or I will kill you all. I swear it. On my blood and my name."

A long pause. The girl stood looking from one to another, no longer afraid but with the light back in her face. She herself seemed now unsurprised that they would help her, four strange men with knives in their eyes. There was power in her. It radiated from her like the light. They would do as she wanted because she could not imagine they could do otherwise. She smiled at them.

"This is insane," said Alxine. But he nodded. He had a kind heart, to help a woman in distress.

Rate didn't say anything, but he looked at the girl's face and her slender body in her thin dress.

And Tobias? Tobias didn't have the strength left to argue.

The lordly voice, the voice that got in your head and made you obey it before you realized what you were even doing. Things in Marith's face that said it probably wasn't a good idea to argue. People were beginning to watch them with interest. Causing a scene. We really don't want to cause a scene just now, Tobias thought. Just get out. Get out, and sort everything out later, when we're safely away.

The girl was, he had to admit, almost breathtakingly beautiful. You could do a lot, a shameful part of him whispered, with a girl like that in tow. There was something in her face, too, that made him feel frightened of not helping her.

"She is entirely your responsibility," Tobias hissed. "We don't lift a finger to help her. She's yours, you're ours. Got it? You follow my orders, she follows you. And you don't speak a word to each other that isn't said loudly, and in Pernish. You even look at her like you're plotting things, I kill her."

Marith gave him a look, something unreadable, then turned his eyes back to the girl.

"Come on then," Tobias said slowly. "Let's get going."

They walked on to the gates, the woman nervous, gazing about her and ahead of her. She flinched as they came to the soldiers waiting there. The gates were open, the city trying to pretend things were as normal. Things were as normal, almost. The Emperor hadn't been murdered. Not in anybody's interests to catch the men who hadn't done it. Blame the Immish. Blame the dead. Blame the bloke who annoyed you a week last Lanethday by talking too loud. Blame demons and the dark. Just don't even think to blame the men now running everything, and don't even think to ask what anyone knows. The soldiers contemplated them uninterestedly and let them through.

And so Alxine and Rate and Tobias and the descendant of Amrath and the High Priestess of the Lord of Living and Dying walked together through the city gates into the desert, and nobody in all Sorlost even noticed them as they went.

Chapter Thirty-Three

They walked all day in the heat, slowly, two of the men limping, the third clutching his arm, stopping often to rest or drink. Only the dark-haired boy, Marith, did not seem tired. He walked close by her side, watching her with sidelong glances, his beautiful terrible eyes flickering over her face.

Thalia gazed at the country around her with disappointed awe. The vastness of it, the sprawl and stink and ugliness of it. The huge sky hazy blue overhead, the farmlands and villages spreading around. Sorlost had been terrifying beyond her imaginings, a chaos of shouting, dangerous, outside anything she could understand. The country she walked through now was worse, even, for she had never seen wide spaces, barren hills, empty sky. Her world had walls and boundaries and doors.

"We'll stop here awhile," the man Tobias, the man who seemed to be the leader, said gruffly. He was exhausted, angry and in pain: she could see and feel it radiating off him, even more than the others. Older, weaker, filled with a sense of failure that bit at him.

They reached a small copse of scrubby trees, set back a little from the track they were following. They had left the road almost immediately, heading up slowly toward the hills before them where settlements were fewer. Best not to meet people just yet, Tobias had said. Thalia did not understand why he said it, but she was glad. She did not want to meet people just yet.

The trees gave a little shelter from a warm wind that blew grit into Thalia's eyes and mouth and made her hair whip around her. She sat quietly while the men checked over the area then unpacked meager supplies of food. She looked at the small trees, pale wood with pale, fine leaves that shivered in the wind, flashing silver undersides. The ground was half barren, thin yellow grass crowned here and there with brilliant pink flowers. Looking up into the sky, she saw for a moment a bird hovering away to the east, wings beating frantically to hold still in the wind, before it shot downwards and disappeared into the tawny landscape. A hawk, she thought. She had read of hawks, but never seen one. She had never seen a goat before she watched a flock of them meander across their path. She had never seen houses, or carts, or dried meat, or a horse. She had never seen the trees she was sitting under, or the scrubby yellow grass with pink flowers, or the afternoon sunlight filling the vast expanse of the sky. She had never seen running water.

The three men, the other three as she thought of them, ignored her. They ate their food, talking among themselves of small things. Marith and Thalia sat a little apart, though she was conscious that the others watched them—no, watched him—continually, as though afraid. Marith himself barely spoke to her, seemed to want to avoid her looking at him fully, but gave her his food and water, until she had to make him eat and drink himself, not give it all to her. "I don't feel hungry," he said in a quiet voice, but when she made him eat some bread he ate quickly, like someone who had not eaten for a long time. She still wore his cloak; he had removed his jacket and spread it carefully for her to sit on. His eyes sought hers. She met them and he rubbed his face painfully, blinked and looked away.

After they had rested a little, Tobias made them get up and continue walking, for all that it was getting toward evening now. After a while a village came into view in a low valley ahead of them: Tobias made them turn aside, track back into the scrub. The ground was becoming barren scree. No trees. The desert came very close here; he was leading them into it, away from anything that lived. What are you so afraid of? Thalia wondered. She felt fear in all of them.

Past dusk when Tobias allowed them to stop again. That they had walked through the dusk was stranger than anything to her. Dusk was the time of terror, the time that was neither light nor dark, the time everything in her world stopped. She had stopped walking as she felt the twilight fall, staring around her, her voice stammering out the words of her prayer. Here in the desert the dusk was horrifying, an abyss swallowing her up, a physical pain. So huge. So hungry. The other three men muttered angrily, Tobias barking at her to be silent, to keep walking. Marith reached out and touched her hand, then drew back. He kept trying to touch her, like a child trying to touch a flame. She could feel him, strong and vivid like the hawk in the sky.

Tobias had chosen a good place. Trees. A small stream. Thalia liked the stream, only the third stream she had ever encountered, the water trickling over stones. In the firelight she could just see the water reflecting the flames, its surface smooth as skin. The fire itself was small, the dry sticks spitting as they burned, giving off a sweet-scented smoke. The youngest of the other three, the fair-blond one, Rate, made tea over the fire. The man with the copper-colored skin, Alxine, sat against a tree and Tobias rebandaged his arm.

Thalia got up and walked a little way away from them, into the dark beyond the circle of the fire, toward the stream. Marith got up and walked a little way away from them too, toward her. She heard Tobias call out to him sharply, Marith's voice mutter something low and sad in reply. This seemed to satisfy them: Tobias grunted and she heard Rate laugh.

He came to sit beside her, his presence strong and clear in the dark. Even in the dark, even with his terrible eyes and his downcast face, she could see how beautiful he was. His face when he had first appeared before her, driving the men attacking her away, brilliant as cold light. The touch of his hand as he raised her to her feet, scalding her.

"You are really...one of the Altrersyr? A descendant of Amrath?" Thalia said hesitantly.

She felt him flinch, in the dark. "I shouldn't have told you that," he said. His voice was very sad and very hesitant. He rubbed at his eyes. It was something about him that irritated her. The only thing about him that was not perfectly beautiful. He picked up a small stone and threw it into the water of the stream, and he told her who he was, and what had befallen him.

Thalia sat looking ahead of her into the dark. She saw the moon emerge from behind a cloud, a bright thin waxing crescent, and she realized she should have been fasting and kneeling in prayer before the High Altar, waiting to kill a man. She laughed, and he started at the sound, and in a sudden rush she told him who she was in answer. And then he laughed too, a wild sad laugh, and threw another stone into the stream.

"I knew it," he said after a while. He dared look at her a little more, now. As though her knowing who he was gave him a confidence in himself. "I didn't know you were...were that, of course." Child killer, her mind whispered. Child killer, murderer, as she was called across Irlast and even to the other side of the Bitter Sea. "But I knew you were something beyond...beyond everything. I can't explain..." He shook his head and sighed. "You must not tell the other men," he said then. "They...they won't understand. They will fear you. You made them take you along with us. Or I did, I don't know. But what they would do, if they found out what you are, I know that."

They sat in silence a while longer, side by side with the water running before them. Thalia shivered with cold despite the cloak wrapped around her. A great, intense tiredness came over her, her eyes grew heavy, she yawned. She had not slept for a long time, another lifetime ago; all had changed since she had last slept.

"Why have you come to me?" Marith asked her.

She wondered at the question, as though she had fled her Temple and abandoned everything because he wanted her to. "I wanted to live," she said sleepily, as though that explained it all.

Marith made a sound that might have been a laugh or a sigh. He must have heard the exhaustion in her voice, for he carefully helped her to her feet and led her back to the low campfire flames where the three men sat. They had been watching them, she thought.

Marith took off his jacket, laid it on the ground for her. "You'll be too cold," she said faintly, but she was so tired. She lay down on his jacket wrapped in his cloak and fell asleep, even with the cold and the hard ground and the men sitting around her. Marith lay down a little way away from her, face turned to the dark.

Gray dawn light, pink and gold streaking the sky in the east. Birds calling, a desert fox shrieking with a harsh cry, the scream of a hawk high in the thin air.

Thalia woke from fitful sleep to noises she had never known, cold like she had never felt. Not the death cold of the Small Chamber, but the cold of a world alive and living and brilliant with life. She sat up, pulling Marith's cloak about her shoulders. Her eyes were dirty and gritty, her hair an itchy tangle, her throat dry, her body stiff and sore. But the beauty of the world awakening caught in her throat and made her gaze around her with wide, astonished eyes.

Marith was sitting staring into the ashes of the fire. His face was pinched, his lips almost blue from cold. His body in his rough shirt looked thin and crushed. He must be half-frozen, Thalia realized, dressed only in his shirt. He looked up at her as she sat up and his face brightened, the weariness and the cold going out of it. He smiled softly at her.

"I've never heard birdsong like this," Thalia said awkwardly, wanting something to say between them. It seemed half-natural as breathing, half-fearful as facing the men in the Temple come to kill her, looking at him and talking to him. "I've never...I've never seen dawn light like this. It's so beautiful."

"You should see the sun rise over the winter sea," Marith said.

"Or over a meadow in hoarfrost. You should hear birdsong in an oak forest on a midsummer morning." He smiled again. "You should see your face with the sun catching in your eyes."

Thalia blushed and looked away.

"I'll build up the fire," he said. "The…the others will be waking. They'll want to get on." He shivered in the cold. Thalia started up, handed him his jacket, trying to shake the dust out of it. He took it carefully, thanking her almost reverentially. How strange he is, she thought. He walked a little way beneath the trees, gathering up more sticks. He rubbed at his face as he did so, and she saw his body shake again, twitching as if in pain. So men had twitched beneath the point of her knife.

"Lord Prince!" A hoarse, angry voice: Tobias was standing watching Marith. Marith started, his shoulders slumping. Tobias waved at him. "Don't go too far, remember, boy? Not where I can't see you."

He is their prisoner, perhaps, Thalia thought. But then if he was their prisoner why had they allowed him to bring her with them? What was going on between these four men was a mystery to her which she understood clearly she could not ask any of them to explain.

Marith returned with an armful of sticks and built up the fire.

"Too much smoke," Tobias muttered, but he saw Marith shivering and said nothing more. Rate made tea again, offered Thalia a cup though it meant going without himself. She thanked him as she took it, the first words she had exchanged with him. He smiled at her kindly enough. Tobias snorted at the exchange.

There was hard bread again, and dried meat, and dried fruit. Marith divided his carefully with Thalia, offering her far more than he kept for himself. She pressed food back on him, and his face shone. He, a prince, a descendant of the World Conqueror, a man with a sword at his hip and the marks of battle on his hands and face, he seemed to feel the thanks of the woman he had rescued from a dirty alley were so far above him he must tremble if she looked at him.

Rate rolled his eyes at the way Marith was with her, and she felt something unspoken pass between the four men. Marith did not speak to her again for a while, sitting hunched in silence eating the bread she had given back to him, eyes down in the dust.

After they had eaten and washed themselves in the stream they set off again, walking slowly through the scrub. The men were more tired than they had been the day before, their faces grayer, more creased with pain. Tobias and Rate's limps were worse, Alxine's left arm held stiffly by his side. Thalia felt it also, the ache in her body from sleeping on cold, hard ground, the weariness and hunger after the long day's walk and knowing there was no resting. Her feet were sore and blistered in her thin soft shoes and she, too, began to limp. It began to occur to her, in her new-born naïvety, to wonder where they had got their injuries, and why they carried swords, and why they were leaving the city for the wilds.

Marith saw her limping and came over to her. His face was haggard, scratches around his eyes. And yet there was a brightness in him that grew as he walked, so that he seemed stronger than the others, healthier, happier. He took her arm; after a while, as she was tired, he put his arm around her to take her weight onto him, half carrying her along.

"Tobias has...has some money he owes me," he said after a while. "We'll have to go into a village today, we need proper supplies. We can buy you clothes and shoes and things there, perhaps. Horses even. It's too long a journey on foot. Wherever it is."

Thalia nodded, intent on the walking. The other men were watching and listening; she did not like it. She had tried to talk to him in Literan, so they could not overhear, but he had glanced at Tobias before answering her in Pernish, more loudly than before.

"Why are you leaving?" she asked. "Where are you going?" Why are you here? she almost said. But she could not ask him that, the words dried on her tongue.

A silence. The rough tramp of their footsteps on the grit and pebbles they walked on, the labored sound of her breathing, weary in the heat.

"We...did things," Marith said at last. "I don't want to talk about it...I...We..."

"You were part of the attack on the palace. Weren't you?"

"You know?" He frowned. "Of course you know. I saw that, when you looked at me, when we first met. I didn't...I mean..."

How could I possibly have known that? she thought. Just a sudden terrible frightened guess. The panic in the city, running out into the dark and thinking she was free of something, and instead the streets were filled with shouts and torches, voices screaming that the Immish were invading, the Emperor dead. Men with knives. A troop of soldiers. A building going up in flames. It had struck her dumb. Left her reeling in fear. But it was death for a priestess to leave the Great Temple. For the High Priestess above all. The Small Chamber and the knife. Demmy's little white hands—Demmy had only drawn the lot so recently, she thought suddenly. The God, then, had known what she would do? Demmy would have to kill her. And so she could not go back. She would not go back. And the city had been terrible and terrifying. So much noise, crashing over her like water, surging like a storm about her head. He had seemed to offer some kind of safety: a man with a sword, who was offering to help her.

"I didn't kill him," said Marith. "Your Emperor. I wouldn't— I'd never—I mean...I would never have harmed you. He"—he gestured to Tobias—"he was paid to do it. I was doing...what he told me to do." He sighed deeply, rubbed at his face. "That's not true. You know that, too. I wanted to do it. I—" He rubbed at his face harder, wincing at the pain.

"I'm sorry," he said. "You must hate me now, I suppose. If you didn't before. And you'd probably be right to. What I am." In the bright brilliant white light of the desert, shadows beat in his eyes like wings.

Thalia walked on beside him, weary in the heat.

Finally, in the afternoon, Tobias decided it was probably safe to turn down out of the wilds to try to find a town. Bloody knackering, trudging along in the heat with his whole body aching, nothing to think about but the nagging sense of terror someone was pursuing them and the profoundly irritating sight of Marith edging around the girl. The boy was so bloody jumpy it made Tobias's teeth ache. It was weird and unpleasant having a woman around at the best of times. Really awkward trying to sleep on a bit of hard rough ground next to one that looked the way she did. They needed to find an inn. A hot meal. Someone to have a proper look at Alxine's arm. Some way to ditch the damn girl.

Maybe an hour's walk on the road brought them to a small crumbling town with a large crumbling caravanserai. "The Seeker After Wisdom", it was called, its sign showing a dead man hanging suspended from a dead tree. Rooms were four dhol apiece, demand being high given the number of Immish or potentially Immish people currently running like hell out of Sorlost. Nobody asked particular questions about who they were or where they were headed. Or why they were all injured and unkempt. At a table in the common room, a drunk man with a strong Immish accent was bemoaning at length that he'd lost everything he'd ever owned. From the way he was being profoundly ignored, he'd been saying it for most of the day.

Marith came up to him with a pleasingly needy look in his face. "I need—He frowned. "I want some of the money you owe me. Now, if you please." The lordly voice, and then a resigned sigh. "It's highly unlikely I'd be able to find someone selling hatha in a place like this at a few hours' notice even if there wasn't a plague in Chathe affecting the supply, and I solemnly swear on my name and my blood not to spend it on anything…interesting, anyway. Thalia needs clothes, new shoes." He rubbed his eyes. "Please, Tobias." The effort that particular word must have cost him.

"Thalia does, does she? Quite the hero, you are, boy. Two silver dhol, and the rooms and tonight all come out of your share, if I ever decide to give it to you. Agreed?"

A long pause, then Marith nodded.

"And I do the purchasing."

"Oh, come on."

Looking forward to taking the girl out on a little shopping trip, were you? Trying to impress her by flashing some money around? "The Altrersyr lie, I seem to remember someone saying recently. You killed a friend of mine for drug money a few days ago, you degenerate little shit. You really telling me you wouldn't leave a defenseless girl wearing a dirty dress if temptation came your way? You'd probably whore her out in the street, if someone offered you a bottle of something in return."

"No! No. I—" Marith sighed again. "A clean dress or two, preferably with long sleeves, a cloak, a blanket if we're going to be sleeping outdoors again. Shoes."

"I'll see what I can do, then. But this isn't exactly a bustling metropolis with souk." Long sleeves, eh?

Had to admit, though, Thalia looked even more astonishing scrubbed clean in a simple brown dress, her hair loosely tied back. Rate almost drooled as she joined them nervously at a table at the back of the common room. Marith even looked up from the cup of watered wine Tobias had generously allowed him to buy himself. She sat down next to Marith, staring around the room like she'd never been in an inn before. With uncharacteristic generosity, Rate offered to fetch her a drink. She looked half astonished and asked for a cup of water. The water round here tasting like goat shit, he brought her a cup of wine instead.

A serving girl brought over bowls of stew, heavily spiced to disguise the rotten meat. The bread wasn't bad either, after several days of Rate's cooking and hard tack. They ate in near silence, the four men made awkward by the woman's presence and by the changed relationships between them. Tobias listened with interest to the conversation around them instead. All the talk, of course, was with what had happened in Sorlost. The Emperor, he gathered, did indeed still seem to be alive, according to official proclamations, anyway, and the latest rumors had someone called the Emperor's Nithque responsible. The bloke who'd paid them not to do it: ironic, that. Or possibly just cruelly predictable. The desecration of the

Temple occupied most minds: they knew nothing of the Emperor and the government, and cared less, but what had happened to the religious heart of their world clearly troubled them. As Rate had said, would have thought they'd be pleased if people stopped dying, but there you go. No accounting for people's beliefs.

The twilight bell tolled out. Silence. The girl bit her lip and looked around.

"Should have been a sacrifice night," one of the men at the next table said loudly after the bell had tolled again. His companion hushed him, several men muttered into their drinks and spat for luck. The girl shivered. Marith looked at her oddly. She stared at him and he looked away.

Gods, they were setting Tobias's teeth on edge.

After a long strained pause the noise in the inn started up a bit. Rate and Alxine tried to have some kind of conversation about something. Marith kept picking his cup up and putting it down again until Tobias wanted to hit him.

The girl sat silent, watching everything. Watching Marith. Marith kept trying not to look at her. She kept trying to look at him.

That is not a good idea, girl, Tobias wanted to shout. Really not. And that's not just sour grapes on my part 'cause you'd not look at me like that if I was begging you for it on my hands and knees.

Just get it over with and get a room, another part of him wanted to shout. This is getting embarrassing here. I've already got you a room, in fact.

Whatever you decide to do, he wanted to shout, just do it. This is making my teeth ache. Come on. You killed a dragon, Marith boy. You're a sodding prince. She's whistling for you. Your life can't be that bad.

The girl looked straight at Marith. Marith looked back. She smiled. They got up together. Walked out of the room and up the stairs. A couple of people hooted approval.

Marith hadn't even stopped to finish his drink.

"Bugger," said Rate. "That's my chances blown, then."

"We should have warned her," said Alxine.

"Your chances too. So you're jealous of her, you mean." Rate tried to look nasty and witty: "Actually, on second thoughts, she'll come round to me pretty quick. Just have to wait for him to puke on her or do that thing where he cries and bangs his head against the wall."

"Exactly. We should have warned her," said Alxine again.

Tobias nodded, guilty. We should. And it was going to be considerably harder to ditch her now, too.

"Why?" said Rate irritably. "Why should we have warned her? Why is she even here? Lord Prince there says she's coming with us, doesn't even know her name at that point, she's standing there with dirt in her hair and eyes like a scared kitten, and we just somehow go along with it. The city's burning around us so we take a bloody woman along when we decide to escape it, just because he says so. Why? That's the question, isn't it? None of us can answer it. We brought her along because... None of us know why. Because the boy would have shouted and cried otherwise. Because we're bloody idiots. Because she's got a truly amazing behind. Witchcraft, maybe." He got up. He and Marith were supposed to be sharing a room. "Well, I might as well get another jug of beer. I assume I'm on your floor tonight, unless our fair lovers are feeling particularly generous with their affections."

Thalia lay awake for a long time, afterward. Marith slept curled into a ball, his hands clenched. Occasionally he would moan or whisper, shaking his head, his face contorted with pain. Even in his sleep he sometimes rubbed at his eyes; when this happened his whole body would shudder and tense. After he had done this a couple of times, Thalia reached out tentatively and stroked his face. Marith sighed gently, the weariness around his eyes relaxing for a moment, his hands releasing. He looked very young and very beautiful, her hands were black against his moon-white skin. This, more even than what had gone before, was strange and mysterious to Thalia. Her hands had killed men, and women, and children.

They had dripped with blood. They had cut her own body, over and over until the scabs would never heal. Now they smoothed a man's face and he sighed and slipped deeper and more comfortably into sleep for a little while, his expression eased, a faint sad smile on his lips.

After a time he tensed again, twitching and whimpering, clawing weakly at his mouth. She stroked his face again and his eyes opened. They stared at each other. Then Marith's eyes closed and he rolled over away from her, mumbled something. Thalia sat up, unsure whether to leave. It was so hard to sleep, with someone else beside her. She had not slept with anyone else in the same room as her since she was five years old and drew the red lot. The sound of Marith's breathing was loud and almost hypnotic: she could not stop listening to it, following its patterns, trying to find words in it. Simply the sense of someone else present was haunting. Frightening. The inn itself was noisy, the night outside noisy. She was used to silence and utter darkness, the great weight of her God blotting out all sound. Marith twitched again and cried out.

Not a bad choice, she thought almost in amusement. If the High Priestess of Great Tanis Who Rules All Things was to abandon her allotted calling, it was only fitting it should be in the company of a high-born prince and one of her God's enemies. Then the boy whimpered in his sleep again, twisting his hands, and it seemed absurd he should be either.

She slept, and suddenly there was soft gray light filling the room and the sound of voices in the road outside. A dog barked, a voice called out to it to come to heel; goats bleated; a cock crowed. Marith was sitting up, watching her. He smiled when he saw she was awake. He looked so perfect her breath caught and a stab of pain darted through her body like bright water, the dawn sun picking out the fine high bones of his face, the muscles of his shoulders, the hollow at the base of his throat. His eyes were soft and amused, cool gray like rain clouds. He blinked as she gazed at him, his eyelashes brushing the blue shadows beneath his eyes.

He had long eyelashes, long as a girl's or a child's, deep black and almost shot with gold.

His face was slightly marred, she saw now that she was so close to him in the bright morning light. Fine silver lines, like faint traceries of lace, curled outwards from around his eyes, almost imperceptible against the creamy white skin.

"You're beautiful," she said without thinking, then blushed.

He laughed and lay back on the rough pillow. "Not as beautiful as you. Good morning."

Thalia sat up in confusion, pulling the blanket around her. She was naked, and he was looking at her. "You don't...you don't mind that I'm still here?" she said.

"Well, I suppose theoretically I've wasted the money I spent on a room for you." He reached over and kissed her mouth, pulling her down into his arms. "I don't mind in the least. Certainly not compared to some of the ways I've woken up..." His eyes glittered. "So: in the last month I have killed a dragon, burned a sorcerer alive with his own spells and deflowered the High Priestess of the Great Temple of Sorlost. I don't think even Amrath Himself could make that claim."

Thalia twisted away from him. "Don't...don't say it like that." Disgust and desire. Desire and disgust.

"I'm sorry." He took her hand and rolled her back toward him. "I didn't mean it like that." She frowned at him and he smiled ruefully, his eyes alight and sparkling. Why had she thought there was darkness in him? He shone with bright clear light. He looked so young, so full of pride in himself. "Well, no, actually, I probably did. But really, as drinking boasts go, bedding the holiest woman in the Sekemleth Empire is pretty impressive, you know."

Am I the holiest woman in the Sekemleth Empire any more? Thalia thought. Am I anything more than a woman with nothing of her own at all? But she smiled back at him. "As impressive as bedding an outcast Altrersyr Prince?"

He rubbed his eyes and stretched lazily, folding his arms around her. He seemed so different to the sad figure afraid to look at her, afraid of the men with him. So confident and careless. So utterly at ease with himself and the world. Certain of himself. Certain of her. The grief that had woken in her faded away again as quickly as it had come. He is so very beautiful, she thought. And not just beautiful. A feeling of peace in her looking at him, as she felt standing at dawn in her Temple listening to the Great Hymn, her hands damp and scented with flowers. Joy and certainty and clear calm.

"Let's just stay here all day. Have some food brought up to us, and a couple of bottles of something sweet to drink. Bread and honey and wine, ripe yellow peaches I can taste in your mouth when I kiss you. Get deliciously drunk and fuck for hours. We can just stay here together, the descendant of Amrath and the High Priestess of Sorlost, making love in a lumpy bed to the sound of goats bleating. In bright sunlight, and in the evening shadows, and in the dark by candlelight. And tomorrow we can wake up and do it all over again. It would make a change from killing people, anyway, which is all I seem to have been doing recently. And then the day after tomorrow..." Marith smiled brilliantly, an idea suddenly catching him, lighting up his face. "And then the day after tomorrow we'll start out for Ith. You'll be the most beautiful woman at the court of Malth Tyrenae. I'll have them dress you in gold and silver, with diamonds in your hair, and make them prostrate themselves at your feet." He kissed her again, full of joy and excitement. "And then after that..."

"How did you get that scar?"

They lay curled together, the rich warm light of full morning bathing them both, making Marith's body white silver and Thalia's dark bronze. She traced her fingers over the mass of heavy scabs on the back of his left hand.

"I told you, I killed a dragon..."

"No!" She laughed. "That's too absurdly romantic to speak of."

"It wasn't at the time." He laughed too. "And then some... other things happened. Mostly involving swords. Mine and other people's. Stopped it ever healing."

She leaned over and kissed his face. "What about the marks around your eyes, then? Did you kill a manticore? Or a cockatrice?"

"No. No!" She started back from him. He kissed her face in turn, filled with guilt and shame. "Don't ask me about that. Please."

She said, "A woman?" But then she looked into his eyes, and her own eyes widened a little as if in fear, and she was silent.

"Nothing interesting." He kissed the scars of her left arm and then her mouth. Her breasts. Her throat. The dark things receded. He kissed her stomach. The smooth soft curve of her hip.

And then there was a loud knocking on the door, and Rate shouting that they needed to get up, and that he knew exactly what they were doing in there but didn't expect it would take Marith very long so he might as well get it over with, he just hoped Marith could properly rise to the occasion, if they knew what he meant. Thalia sat up with a cry. Curse Rate. Curse him and kill him and let the dogs eat his corpse. He should have died back in Sorlost.

"It's all right." Marith stroked Thalia's face, helping her to pull her dress on and comb out her hair. He kissed her hands as she did so. Long, slim fingers, dark in her black hair...Utterly distracting. Mesmerizing, like everything else about her. Desire for her burned in him like nothing he'd ever known. Even when he closed his eyes, he saw her face, shining, brilliant with light. "He's just jealous. He's not an outcast Altrersyr Prince making love to the holiest woman in the Sekemleth Empire. And also the entire inn must know what we're doing." He pulled on his own clothes. He'd ripped his shirt taking it off last night, he discovered. Thalia laughed at that. "We should go down to breakfast," he said, "before Rate breaks the door down trying to see you naked."

Chapter Thirty-Four

Ith, with its forests and meadows and mountains rich in gold and quicksilver, where the old gods had walked before the world was changed.

Why it had not occurred to him to go there, now seemed a mystery to Marith. He was their kin, the only child of the king's own sister. He was fourth in line to the throne, for gods' sake! They would take him in and make him again what he was. He would be a prince in exile, building a court around him, claiming his rights as heir to the White Isles. But it somehow hadn't crossed his mind, when the ship carrying him into exile dumped him unceremoniously on the quayside of a run down Immish fishing port and sailed straight away again, leaving him with nothing but the clothes he stood up in and twelve gold marks to his name, entirely and utterly alone for perhaps the first time in his life.

The fact that his father's men had fed him enough hatha to poison a small town during the journey had possibly had something to do with it, it occurred to him. He might not have been thinking particularly clearly by the time they left him at the Skerneheh docks. Remembering how to stand up had been about the limit of his intellectual capabilities. And then... They'd given him enough money to break himself with and he'd more than obliged them, failing only to actually just drop dead in a gutter one night. Until

Skie found him, and somehow death in battle had seemed marginally less unappealing than death choking on his own vomit. Everything after that had been happenstance. Chaos and confusion and still half-hoping he could just die on them. Blot it out. Make it all go away. And now here he was, somehow not only alive, but bedding the holiest and most beautiful woman in Irlast. That was probably worth something, in the balance of things.

They came down to breakfast hand in hand, to leers from Rate and several of the other guests. Marith smiled back at them. He held his head with a confidence he hadn't felt for a long time, easy in himself, cheerful, almost without pain. The light shone in Thalia's face, warming him. He was surprised the other men couldn't see it. Or perhaps they did, for they watched her softly and their leers died away.

He sat down opposite Tobias, poured himself a bowl of smoky-scented tea. He was hungry and thirsty. Normal feelings. Even the physical pain of his hatha cravings seemed to have subsided for the moment.

"We're going to Ith," he said cheerfully.

Tobias looked at him. "We are, are we?"

Marith flashed him a smile. A new feeling was coming, bright and warm, a remembrance of things a long time ago. "Oh, don't worry, I'm sure my uncle will be pleased enough with you for escorting me there. See you're rewarded according to your due. When I come into my own, I might even give you all something myself. Minor titles, maybe. A small estate and a large pile of gold."

A long pause. Tobias seemed to be contemplating things. "Can't say it hadn't occurred to me, boy. Obvious choice. But it's a long way…" And I don't trust you a hair's breadth, his face said, clear as day.

"So is everywhere. We have money for transport."

Tobias looked at him. "We do, do we?"

Stubborn, wretched, suspicious bastard. Marith tried to keep his voice calm, though his hand went to his belt where his knife was. "Forgive me, Tobias, I misspoke. You have money for transport.

Money I will repay you in triple once I am back where I belong, swimming in gold and dripping in diamonds or however it goes. Money you wouldn't be here to hold if I hadn't done your dirty work for you when it mattered. I'm tired of all this. We're buying horses, better equipment, better food. I'm ordering you."

Alxine muttered something inaudible. Rate stared at him.

"You've changed your tune, boy," Tobias said after a moment. Still trying to beat him down. Not seeing what he should see. "Must be good between the sheets, your girl there. Thought all you wanted was an unpleasant death."

Their eyes met again. *You look like what you are, boy . . .* Tobias shuddered and looked at the floor.

Beat you, Marith thought with a grin. Beat you. He went over to the innkeep, ordered wine, demanded someone fetch anyone who might have a horse they might be persuaded to sell him, demanded the village women be summoned to find better clothes for himself and Thalia. The three other men sat dumb.

They left that afternoon, a very different group from the four who had walked down out of the hills. Marith was dressed in a silk shirt and leggings, a green coat with embroidered sleeves meant for the local big man's favorite son's wedding; Thalia in a yellow dress meant for the local big man's favorite son's bride. Both had been hastily adjusted while a messenger was sent around the farms looking for horses and a cart or carriage. Thalia, Marith had realized, had absolutely no idea how to ride. She needed shade and comfort. And a carriage would be a better place for the two of them to sleep than a tent.

Any thought of returning to the meeting place with Skie and digging out the stuff they had left behind was long gone: they were not members of The Free Company of the Sword now but a high noble, his lady and their escort. They had white bread and water and wine and fresh fruit stored in the carriage, grain for the horses, blankets, pillows for Thalia. Marith wore the black sword at his hip, the blue flames almost visible along its blade.

The people of the town bowed down before him, not knowing who he was but sensing the power in him; Rate and Alxine and Tobias seemed to diminish before him, finally, truly seeing him. Thalia watched him silently with dazzled eyes.

It was only a farmer's wagon, covered over in plain brown canvas; the horses farm horses, unattractive and cheaply saddled; the clothes shoddy and rough. But it would all suffice for now, until they reached Immish and could get something far, far better. The whole lot had cost four talents; Tobias had paid it out like a man in a nightmare. How all this had happened, he could not seem to understand. Marith, in truth, could barely understand it either. He felt as he had felt when he killed the Imperial Guard. He felt as he had felt when he killed the dragon. He felt as he had felt as a child. He rode his horse at the head of the group, his head held high, forcing the horse to run and buck and plunge and shy up so that he could feel the giddy power he had over it, making it do as he willed it, breaking it to him. I am myself again, he thought. But that thought sobered him, and he rode back and came alongside the carriage, looking at Thalia, and something of the fear he had felt before came back into him.

He ordered the party to stop for the night a little before dusk. Thalia should not be made to travel during the dusk. *Seserenthelae aus perhalish*: Night comes. We survive. A strange time. A time of nothingness. He found himself looking forward to seeing it with her beside him.

They were taking the old abandoned desert road, the road they had flanked on their way in, riding out into the great wild places where nothing lived. Only a few hours' ride from the town, and the world was empty. Dust and rock underfoot, scrub trees, delft grass, carrion birds. The Dragon's Mouth overhead, already visible in the twilight, blazing red. A fire was made up, food prepared and eaten and cleaned away: Marith did not help with the work but sat apart, a lord watching his servants, sipping wine, gazing east into the night.

Thalia helped them, helplessly, for she had never even thought of these kinds of chores. She fetched water from the stream that had drawn them to camp there, delighting again in the rush of water, the feel of the wet sand of its shallow bed beneath her feet. Rate grunted thanks at her when she gave him the filled pail, then turned his back on her, his shoulders set and tense. She stood for a moment then walked over to Marith.

"May I join you?" It was almost the first time they had spoken since they had left his bedroom that morning, everything since then a bustle of preparations and Marith lording it over everyone. She hadn't been sure how he wanted her to treat him. Whether he expected her to kneel at his feet as the farmers selling him the cart almost had. But his face brightened to a warm smile as he saw her.

"You don't...you don't need to ask that." Sorrow in his eyes for a moment: he is afraid I might no longer want him, Thalia realized in confusion. She sat down beside him and he kissed her gently, a faint sigh of something like relief on his lips. "This is better, isn't it? Wine and cushions and treated as befits you. And all as nothing compared to what I'll give you soon enough. All the gold in my kingdom, I'll lay at your feet."

She looked into the dark sky, following his eyes. "What are you looking at?"

"What am I looking at? The sky. The stars. My home. Going to Ith makes me think of things...And what I'll do after that...A few days ago all I wanted was to drink till I was dead. Now..." He kissed her again. "What are you looking at?"

Thalia paused for a moment, then said in a rush, "I should have been killing a man, yesterday evening."

"Now that's an interesting thought...Not entirely an unpleasant one, either." He drew her closer toward him. Disgust and desire. Desire and disgust. Would that be all it ever came to? He saw her frown. Grew serious. "We've both killed men and women and children, beautiful girl. You with far more reason than I have, and far less choice."

Another silence, gazing side by side into the dark.

Thalia gestured to the three men by the fire. "They hate you, now, you know."

"They always hated me. But now they fear me. And that's better too, don't you think?"

"Why? Why should you want to be feared? Or hated?" Thalia frowned. "You almost sound as though you enjoy it."

"I don't enjoy it. I just don't care. Everyone fears and hates me. Or rather, everyone fears and hates my name. What I am. You feared me too, a little, at first. Admit it. I saw your face when I told you who I am." He sighed, rubbed hard at his eyes. "I've read something about your Temple. I know what it means, your Lord of Living and Dying. Why you do what you do. Did what you did. I don't understand it, but I know what it means. You make things live. Keep the balance. You bring life to the living, and death to those who need to die. Which is not something anyone can say about many members of my family." He closed his eyes and murmured, half to himself, half to Thalia:

"Like rainfall, like storms in the desert, drowning, engendering,
Soaking the parched earth and washing away all that survives
there.

Is that how it goes? I never understood Gyste's obsession with rain until I saw it rain in the desert, drowning one half of the world and giving new life to the other."

"You've read *The Song of the Red Year*?"

"Oh, I've read most things worth reading. Occasionally even whilst sober. Particularly when they're about impossibly beautiful women. I always preferred *The Silver Tree*, though, until I met you, which I'm told is very bad taste."

"I've never read it. *The Silver Tree*."

"No? Good. Far too filthy for your holy mind to comprehend." Marith stretched himself out on the hard ground, his head in her lap. "I'll demonstrate bits of it later, if you like."

They were still for a while, Thalia stroking her fingers through his beautiful shining hair, looking down at his face and then up at the stars. She had never seen so many stars. The Dragon's Mouth winked at her. His star, she thought. A bat flew past overhead, squeaking faintly, almost inaudible. What did it eat, out here? A fox called and made her start. The men at the fire started too, then laughed.

"What if they kill us in our sleep?" Thalia said suddenly.

Marith, who had been half-asleep, dozing and almost purring like a cat, opened his eyes in confusion. "What? Who? Why?"

"The...the men. Your...companions." She didn't like using their names. They frightened her, more now than ever. "They could just kill us both and ride off and no one would ever know."

"Them? They wouldn't kill me, beautiful girl. They wouldn't dare." Marith sat up and shook dust from his coat. "They know I would kill them first. Selling me back to my uncle is about the only thing they can do to salvage anything and start afresh."

He stood up, pulling her up with him. "We should go to bed. We have a very long ride ahead of us tomorrow. And I have some poetry to enlighten you about first, beautiful girl."

The next day passed in similar fashion, and the next, and the next, on and on into a blur of dry barren hills and vast dusty skies. Thalia's fear of the men accompanying them subsided, as they all seemed to relax in each other's company again, relationships shifting and changing. After his first cold hauteur, Marith softened a little, helping with some of the work, exchanging brief words with the other men. He was happier for it, Thalia could see, less preoccupied with the idea of what he was or what he should be, more contented in himself as a man doing and being, alive beneath the great curve of the sky.

He even seemed to enjoy gathering scrub for the fire or fetching water, gazing around at the wide landscape with something like peace in his eyes. Riding his horse he loved. He would sometimes give the horse its head and ride it as fast as it could go into the dun hills, wheeling back in a great circle to rejoin them, shouting and waving his sword.

"You'll ride it to death," Tobias muttered at him, "it's a bloody farm horse, not a war charger. And there's not enough water for you to go tearing off and making it thirstier than it needs to be."

Marith spurred the horse into a gallop and brought it back in a cloud of dust, made it rear up and snort. "She's a lovely horse," he said. "She enjoys it. I think I might call her Fire." He smiled at Thalia, switching to Literan. "Or God's Knife."

He tried to teach Thalia to ride it, one evening when they stopped early because they had found a good-sized stream, flowing over rocks with clean water free of dust, bordered with low trees and delft grass blooming pink. She laughed and almost fell off several times and he gave up, promising her a pretty white palfrey when they reached Ith.

The number of things he'd promised her when they reached Ith, Thalia thought, she'd need a palace of her own to house them in.

As his manner softened he seemed, curiously, more of a lord than ever, treating the other men with the easy confidence of a man unafraid of them or himself. At night, weary after a long day riding in the heat, he sat under the stars and told her about Ith, which he had visited before several times as a boy, and his home on the White Isles, where it rained half the summer and snowed white and pure in the wintertime. He described the high moors, like and unalike to the wastes they were riding through, barren yet filled with life; the forests, which seemed to her to be like vast gardens; the sea, which she could not begin to understand no matter how he tried to evoke it for her. Like the idea of snow, and frost, and bitter cold rain, it was a mystery to her that he could not unravel, and he could only smile and say, "You'll see, beautiful girl." They made love in the cramped bed in the back of the little carriage, giggling and trying to be silent as Rate, Tobias and Alxine snored outside. He recited the whole of *The Silver Tree* to her in solemn whispers, and *The Song of the Red Year*, cupping her face in his hand and telling her she was far more beautiful than Manora. He even knew a couple of the poems written about Thalia herself, which he intoned half mocking, half overcome with astonishment that he held the subject in his arms as he spoke. The darkness Thalia had first seen in him retreated, leaving him clean and pure and cold.

He did not talk of Sorlost, and nor did she ask. And in his sleep he whimpered, and thrashed about, and tore at his eyes and his mouth.

And then one night, when they had been journeying for twenty days and were in the midst of the great desert, she summoned up her courage and asked him the thing she must know.

"Why did your father disinherit you?" she said simply. "Why are you here? What did you do?"

Marith had been lying with his head in her lap, letting her stroke his hair. He sat up and looked at her. It had been a very hot day riding: his face was tired and drawn. Perhaps this wasn't a good time to ask, she thought. But she had to know, and she had waited long enough. She had a right to know. The night air was still and harsh; she felt something in it approaching, some fear, and the words burst out of her.

"Ah." He sighed. "So we come to it. Nobody has yet dared ask. Whether I want to tell you...What could I have done that was so very terrible my father would cast out his son and heir? All the things my family have ever done, and what offense could I have committed that was so terrible it couldn't be forgiven?" He frowned. "I'm rambling. I'm sorry. You truly want to know?"

Thalia nodded, slowly. Marith drained his wine cup. He closed his eyes, and when he opened them they seemed darker. "I killed someone. A man. The heir to the richest and most powerful of my father's nobles. Carin Relast, his name was." He shut his eyes again, his hand gripping the cup in his hand so tightly his knuckles went white. "My best and only friend."

Chapter Thirty-Five

Two young men, boys really, stand looking at each other against the backdrop of a crowded room. One is slim and dark-haired, the other stockier and fair-blond. They stand in the common room of an expensive, bustling inn, brightly lit glass and polished tables, windows open to a walled garden filled with the scent of summer flowers. A gathering silence spreads around them, eating away at the very walls.

The dark-haired boy holds a sword clutched in his hand. The blade of the sword is covered in blood. The fair-haired boy staggers backward, sways on his feet, crumples slowly to the ground at the dark-haired boy's feet. There is a great wound in his chest where his heart is. His eyes stare in confusion. The dark-haired boy stares back. The look on his face is impossible to describe.

The room is utterly silent now, save for the drip of blood from the sword. The few other people in the room sit frozen. The dark-haired boy stares and stares. Then he throws back his head and screams. The sound he makes is like the noise an animal might make as it is ripped apart. It echoes round the room. There is another silence. The dark-haired boy looks down at the blood on his hands, the blood that has burst out from the fair-haired boy's heart. He raises his hands to his mouth and licks it off. Then he sinks down to the ground beside the fair-haired boy and begins to laugh. He is still laughing when men in green-tinted armor come to take him away. He does not resist, does not even look at them. Other men carefully lift the fair-haired boy's body and carry it out into the sunlight. A woman's voice rings out, wailing in pain. The men turn back to the room. Slowly, carefully, they kill every person there.

Chapter Thirty-Six

"Why?" Thalia asked after a long while.

Marith rubbed roughly at his face. "Because of what he was doing to me. Because otherwise he would have ended up killing me. Because I loved him. Because he knew me." I don't know why, he thought. I don't know why. I'll never know.

Why do we do anything? he thought.

"And your father banished you for it?"

"My father couldn't give a damn." Marith drained his cup again, his fingers hovering over the wine skin resting beside him. He refilled his cup, took a few sips then pushed it roughly away, so that it fell and the wine spilled out dark as blood in the dust. He watched the pool of wine spreading for a moment. "Carin's father, however..."

He retrieved his cup, filled it again, drank again, scratched his face again. "My father would have ignored it, but the Relasts made too much trouble. They're distant kin of ours, hold the island of Third, the nearest to the mainland. Powerful and rich. Lord Relast, in particular, is not a man even my father would want to cross. And I think...I think now he hated me even before. Lord Relast, I mean. I don't need to think to know my father hates me. That all the kindness and generosity he showed me as Carin's friend was part of the game. Sometimes...sometimes I think he put Carin up to it. Made him love me. Made him destroy me. Thought he could control me, through him. So then when I killed him…He played his most precious piece, and lost. And so he was angry. And my father had to appease him. And my father loathes me anyway, so he threw me away. He has another son, after all. One without my…problems. Nobody ever wagered hard coin on whether Ti would make it through the next half year alive and with his mind still intact. The odds of my surviving much longer, however, were so low it was barely worthwhile making the wager. My father just cut his losses early. Ended it."

Silence. "Ended what?" Thalia asked at last in a quiet, confused voice. "Why should he loathe you? Why shouldn't you stay alive? Why should people wager on it? I don't understand. Any of this."

Beautiful, and proud, and certain, and full of joy. Somewhere far away Marith could hear something screaming. His voice. Screaming.

"You haven't realized?" He laughed harshly. "But then you wouldn't, of course. Ask Tobias. Ask him about how Carin ruined me. I'm sure he'd love to tell you everything about me and my secrets."

She stood up, and Marith thought she was going to walk away. All gone, he thought. All lost. Sorrow and ruin. A dead man and a living woman, both too far beyond him to come back. For a moment he saw, not the woman, but Carin standing before him. There was dust where Carin's heart should have been. "I'm sorry," he whispered, but his lips were too dry to speak.

Carin had known what he was. What he could be. What was inside him, clawing at him to get out. Help me, Carin, he'd begged over and over. Help me blot it out. I love you. Help me. And Carin had helped him. Oh, he had. Drink and drugs and ruin and all done out of such love. Kind.

Perhaps he'd killed Carin to spare him. So Carin didn't have to see what he would become.

You must hate me now, I suppose, he'd said to Thalia. If you didn't before. And you'd probably be right to. Everyone hates and fears me. What I am.

What I will be.

It's better, he thought. If she walks away. Then she won't have to see, either.

And then Thalia knelt down beside him, and placed her arms around him, and kissed his forehead that was hot and dizzy with pain. He shuddered at her touch: she held him and there was light in her, and the light burned. He did not want the light. He wanted to go back into the dark and stay there, where nothing could hurt him, where he belonged. I'll kill you too, he thought. Keep away from me. She was silent, holding him. Her skin smelled sweet and warm. He was half unsure who she was, Thalia or Carin, but he clutched at her, burying his face in her hair.

She began murmuring something in Literan under her breath. Praying for him. Praying to her cursed God.

"Dear Lord, Great Tanis Who Rules All Things, from the fear of life and the fear of death, release us. Dear Lord, Great Tanis Who Rules All Things, from the fear of life and the fear of death, release us. Dear Lord, Great Tanis Who Rules All Things, from the fear of life and the fear of death, release us. We live. We die. For these things, we are grateful. Dear Lord, Great Tanis Who Rules All Things—"

Marith twisted in her arms. Don't pray for me. Don't you dare pray for me. Don't you know what I am, by now? Things screamed in the distance. Shadows crawling in his eyes and in his skin. I'll kill you. I'll kill you. I'll kill us all. But she held him and murmured her prayers in a voice like candle flames.

Seserenthelae aus perhalish. Night comes. We survive. Her voice, and her heart, and the light, no longer burning. The light, shining out of her. He began to weep. Long, gentle sobs, like a child.

Chapter Thirty-Seven

You will say I am a fool.

He is beautiful. God's knives, he is beautiful. Beautiful like nothing else in the world. And because of that, you will think me a fool, an innocent running from a prison, throwing herself into his arms because he is a man and a prince and as beautiful as the moon. You think me a stupid girl, love-struck and love-blind, clinging to poems and dreams.

I want to live, I decided after Ausa. I want to live and I will live. I would have lived in the Temple, I suppose, as much as I was able. It had a peace of a kind, and a power of a kind for me. Lived with gardens of flowers, and little children playing, and a thousand candles burning and the Great Hymn to the rising sun. Lived with the knife, and the Small Chamber, and the slaves waiting there with no names and no voices left to speak. Lived with Ausa, and Tolneurn, and Demmy. My guilt. My demons. Are they any worse than his? But as I conjured up the fear and the dark I saw something, a chance, a freedom, a world beyond.

So many dead men I have seen. And the Temple slaves, the priestesses, the worshippers, those who claim to serve the Temple and its God but who prostrate themselves before the fear of death and the fear of life. He need have no fear, of living or dying. He need fear nothing. He is so beautiful. So living. So filled with life.

He blazes with it, sharp and terrible and alive. He is like the knife in the Temple, the blade shining in the dark.

I can see us both, in the dark, shining. Crowned in silver. Throned in gold. Radiant with light. Not a bad thing to see, surely?

But still, you will say I am a fool.

Chapter Thirty-Eight

They arrived at last at a small village, the last tiny forgotten vestige of Empire trade routes before the desert gave way slowly to the plains of Immish. Another five or six days' hard ride, Tobias reckoned, and they should be safely across the border. The road they had taken was more direct than the route in, but no less empty and inhospitable. They had passed a few scattered dwellings, even the occasional ruined caravan inn. They had not stopped at any of them, Tobias urging caution. He seemed almost to flinch at the wind, now.

That afternoon, however, they had come upon the village, clustered around a small brackish oasis, caught up in the midst of some local celebration. Tobias, again, advised that they hurry on past, but the smell of food and wine, the sounds of laughter, music and song, made the other men pause. Thalia looked frightened, and wanted to go on, but Marith for once ignored her. She'd have to get used to noise and company and crowds.

Rooms were engaged, the horses stabled, dusty water heated for baths. Thalia put on the yellow dress, tight fitted to her body with full, swirling skirts, vulgar and cheap but pretty enough on her and flattering her luminous dark skin. It left her arms bare, so she wore a scarf of fine pale silk, embroidered in gold and pink flowers like a summer meadow, wrapped around her left forearm.

Her hair hung down her back, long and straight like a fall of dark water. Her dress was cut low. Her eyes were nervous and brilliant. No one would look at her arms.

In the village square crowds had gathered in the sunset, hot and noisy with shouts and singing, pitch-soaked torches making shadows dance. Music struck up, couples dancing. Thalia had never seen dancing, was at first frightened by the whirling bodies and stamping feet. She looked around her, wide-eyed at the chaos swirling around them. The dancers leaped in circles, spinning and running, bending arms and heads in suddenly jagged twists and turns. They understand the brevity of life, here, Marith thought. How alone we all are beneath the vastness of the desert sky. He had been born and bred on an island, spent his life among men who sailed out on the pitiless sea. The same desperate clinging to life, knowing it was nothing, could be crushed out at any moment, nothing left. So they danced it out in the dust.

The music was stamping feet and drums and piping flutes that rose and fell in coils. It was familiar to Thalia, he felt her body sway a little to the rhythms, recognizing the beats and counter-beats, the pauses and sudden changes in tempo that sounded strange to his ears. Deliciously erotic, but something under it frightened him. How foreign she was to him. Knowing things he did not. One song within which he could just about make out the words "sun" and "darkness" made her shiver in his arms. "It is like—" she began, then stopped and closed her mouth on the words. Marith shivered in turn. Like a song from her Temple. He had not thought, though he should have, that she would feel any regret at the leaving of it. He loved her. She had no right to feel nostalgia, or regret.

"We should go back to the inn," he said in a little while. The air was heavy with the smell of drink; it was searing hot from the torches but also bitterly cold. The atmosphere growing thicker and wilder. Men leered at Thalia; Marith stared at them and they drew back. This was all a mistake, he thought. We shouldn't have stopped here. This isn't her place, or mine. She was so far above this mummery, whilst he...He watched the weaving figures, twisting in a long spiraling pattern of stamping feet around the square, dancing and shouting and singing while the darkness ate at them. You will all die, his mind whispered. This brightness is only the surface. Beneath is the darkness: you will all die.

"Come and dance with me," Thalia said suddenly.

Marith started. "Dance?"

"Yes, dance. I'd like to. That's why we stopped here, isn't it? I thought you probably enjoyed this sort of thing." She smiled at him almost archly. "From what little I know, most young men seem to."

"I do...I did...I mean..."

"Rate seems to be." Rate was holding a large mug of something in one hand and a kebab in the other, eyeing a remarkably well-built young woman dancing in front of him. His face was lit with a vast grin.

"Rate doesn't..." He stopped. "Come on then." Took her hand and whirled her into the twisting mass of figures. The dance was a fast one, half running, stepping out patterns as they crossed and re-crossed the beaten ground. The ribbon of dancers traced in and out of the torches, the light casting Marith's face in crimson, Thalia's deep gold. He began to laugh giddily, his breath fast as they went. Their feet pounded out the rhythm of his heart.

They danced for hours, not the descendant of Amrath and the High Priestess of Great Tanis but only a man and a woman enjoying themselves, swirling and stamping and jumping to the music's roar. Marith drank strong, sour wine and local spirits that burned the throat until he was stumbling on his feet and tripping over his words and Thalia was laughing at him. The shadows were just shadows cast by torches. The people were just dancers, wild and alive.

Finally, Thalia was exhausted and Marith's head was spinning and the torches were beginning to burn down. The celebrants were yawning, drunk and weary with aching feet. In the east, the sky was beginning to turn gray. Rate had disappeared on the arm of the woman he'd been leering at. Alxine and Tobias were nowhere to be seen. They went back to the inn, where Thalia helped Marith up the stairs, laughed pitilessly as she watched his fuddled attempts to remove his boots. They fell into bed laughing, Marith dimly aware it was him they were laughing at. He pressed his face into her hair and she kissed his forehead, her lips cool on his flushed skin. "That's nice," he whispered muzzily. "Nice. Carin used to do that." His voice drifted. "We'll have dances like that at Malth Elelane, when I'm crowned. When I make you queen."

He fell asleep immediately, a deep calm sleep, his face soft and weary. Thalia lay a little while listening to his breathing, watching him in the faint light.

Nobody in the village woke early the next morning. It was almost noon by the time Marith wandered downstairs, to find Thalia sitting talking with Alxine at a table in the inn's courtyard. He frowned at the sight of Alxine speaking to her, her face animated and smiling, honey and bread crumbs on her lips.

"Marith!" She turned to him and his heart leaped at the way she spoke his name. She offered him bread, poured him a cup of water from a stone jug. Brackish and dusty, warm in the sun. He sat down on the wooden bench next to her. Put his arm possessively around her waist.

"You came down without me," he said stiffly.

"I didn't want to wake you. You looked so peaceful." She giggled at Alxine. "And I needed some fresh air. My Lord Prince reeked of stale alcohol and was snoring fit to wake the dead."

Marith frowned. "Where is everyone?" he asked. Didn't like it, her talking to Alxine like this. Sour in his head. And something else pulling at him, a vague disquiet at the back of his mind, blurred by sleep and alcohol. There was a strong desire in him just to start drinking again and not stop for the rest of the day.

Alxine said, "Tobias is seeing to the horses. Rate is..." He and Thalia both laughed. "Rate is upstairs, trying to avoid last night's remarkably well-built conquest's remarkably well-built husband."

Their laughter softened him. He kissed Thalia, leaned his head on her shoulder. "Some things, you'll have to get used to, Thalia, my beloved. *You have possessed my heart and my soul, my love, but even for you, oh most beautiful, the sun will not rise again at dusk.* Although that may in fact refer to something else. And don't ever suggest I snore."

"The Altrersyr do not snore, then?" said Thalia in a very solemn voice.

Marith laughed himself. "Be grateful my aching head is soothed by your sweet voice, my lady. I think you forget to whom you speak. The Altrersyr do not take such insults lightly. My father has killed men for less. No, we certainly do not snore."

Thalia glanced around her and then said sweetly in his ear in Literan, "The High Priestess of the Lord of Living and Dying may insult whosoever she chooses. Especially when they still smell like a distillery."

"I'm sure I do, oh, most beautiful." Marith closed his eyes. "Drink, dance, enjoy yourself, you bade me. Can you be so cruel as to condemn a poor slave for obeying his mistress's every command? And how you come to know what a distillery smells like, I shall refrain from enquiring." The world behind his eyelids was golden in the sun. Her hair tickled his face. He could almost hear her heartbeat and the blood pumping in her veins. She began to sing one of the songs from the previous night, very low and quiet, so gentle he could not make out the words, only the dull soft drone of the tune. Her voice was like honey. He dozed on her shoulder, his whole world her scent and her voice and the sunlight on his upturned face.

They discovered what the festival had been for the following afternoon.

The village was quiet and oddly strained, a strange hesitancy hanging over the place, as though the carnival of the previous night had been a beginning, not an end. "They are waiting for something," Alxine said thoughtfully. Thalia only shook her head. "Nothing like this is done in Sorlost," she said when Alxine suggested it must be some part of the festival. "It is like...It is like the moment of twilight. I don't like it."

It is like the moment before I kill a man, Thalia thought. It was not that the people were not about: they bustled in the main square, clearing away the rubbish, setting things straight, sweeping the ground clean. Children danced around, tired-eyed and still overexcited, running and shouting and getting underfoot. But there was a feeling in the air like a gathering storm, faces raised sometimes to the sky, muttering something only to be told to hush.

Tobias came in after a while, dusty from attending to the horses. The stable boy, Thalia gathered from his mutterings, had also enjoyed the festivities rather too much. Tobias stamped his hand down heavily on the table when he sat down, calling out loudly for more food. The noise woke Marith, who sat up groggily and almost fell off the bench.

"Good morning, Tobias."

"It's well after noon," said Tobias coldly.

Marith shrugged. "Ah, well. Nothing important happened this morning anyway."

The innkeep's wife came in with fresh tea, more drinking bowls, a plate of bread and curd cheese. Tobias ate hungrily. The woman smiled broadly at Marith, who smiled back at her, sighed, and poured himself a bowl of tea.

"Today, is it, you're leaving?" the woman asked Marith. She glanced up at the brilliant blue sky. "Good day for it."

"Today, and as soon as possible," Tobias said shortly.

Marith winced.

Alxine came to join them again, having gone off for a wander around the village.

"We're going," Tobias told him as he sat down. "Get Rate while I sort out the supplies."

They met a short while later outside the stables. Marith saddled up his horse then helped Thalia carefully into the covered back of the cart, arranging cushions and blankets for her. She yawned widely.

"Oh, I'm so tired. I should be used to staying awake all night."

He wrapped a light blanket carefully over her, even though it was hot. A caring thing, he thought vaguely. "Sleep for a while. I'd join you, if I could."

"You've been sleeping all morning."

"And I could sleep all afternoon, pillowed in your arms. I am not looking forward to several hours' ride in the sun, either."

"That's your own fault, Lord Prince." She looked longingly at the inn, with its beds and bathtub. "We could stay until tomorrow…"

"No. I…" He hesitated. "We need to get on. We shouldn't stay here any longer. Maybe we shouldn't have stopped at all. There's something…"

"Yes." She felt it too. Of course she did. But he couldn't put it into words. Last night had been a bright, unlooked-for happiness, but there was something here that troubled him. Thalia curled up in the back of the cart, closing her eyes against the sun. "And I won't have to put up with you snoring in my ear."

He grinned his boy's grin. "The Altrersyr do not snore. Not now I'm disappointingly sober again, anyway."

The horses, at least, were well rested after the late start, and trotted forward eagerly enough. The land about quickly emptied, high desert with only a few stunted thorn trees clinging on desperately in the parched sand. It was hot as a furnace, a scalding wind blowing dust. After a while, the three riders took turns sitting beside Rate in the scant shade of the cart front, their horse led on a long rein. Thalia dozed in the back, tossing and turning in the heat. They had had a few days like this, finding no shade, no water, but this seemed the worst. A heavy, dead sense over everything.

The sun was beginning to sink in the sky when Alxine, who was sitting beside Rate, pointed suddenly out at something off to their left, on the top of a small incline. "A horse!"

Wild horses were not uncommon out here. Or horses grown wild after their owners had died of thirst. Marith, dozing miserably in the saddle, looked with little interest, then stared. Rate and Tobias were staring too. A very beautiful horse, with a strong slender neck and a glossy roan coat, liveried in fine green leather, its head decked with gold ornaments. Not a wild horse. Not a farm horse even. Expensive. Well cared for. Hobbled and saddled and abandoned in the middle of the desert. It whinnied pitifully when it saw them, tried to rear up despite the rope around its legs. Its eyes rolled, showing the whites all round.

Marith dismounted and edged carefully toward it. The horse whinnied again, snorted and stamped. He held out his hand, began to talk quietly in a nonsense babble of languages. It flared its nostrils. Stamped.

"It's all right. It's all right. Lovely horse. Fine horse." He caught the bridle. Stroked the lathered head and neck. It pulled and tried to buck, then settled a little and sniffed at him.

"Good horse. Good horse. Calm down, then I can give you some water and grain." The horse flicked its ears at the word "water." Snorted loud. He'd been speaking Pernish, so that told him almost nothing, except that it must have been out in the sun like this for a while. He led it back down to the track and gave it water. It drank gratefully, blowing through its nose. He stroked its neck lovingly.

Tobias and Rate came to look. "Allene," said Tobias. "That's where its owner's from. You see those buckles on the head straps? And the stirrups? Southern work, that. No saddlebag, though. Any sign of the rider, up there?"

Marith shook his head. "Not that I could see. Just the horse."

"Tracks?"

Marith shrugged. Still three parts hung-over. Had about three hours' sleep. The wind blowing the sand around and the horse had been trampling and pissing up there. "I have absolutely no idea."

Tobias rolled his eyes at him, stomped off to look. Marith ordered Rate to fetch some grain and a few raisins, a cloth to rub the horse down. Thalia came up to him looking almost jealous. The horse snorted and tossed its head and she stepped back nervously.

"It's all right," he said again. "It will be fine in a moment. It's just skittish." He fed it a handful of dried fruit and it nosed at his shoulder more comfortably.

Marith was rubbing the horse down when Tobias returned. "There's tracks," Tobias said wearily. "Leading away to the east. One man, alone. Then something else."

Oh gods. You know what's coming, a voice whispered in Marith's mind. You know. You've known since you came back into the desert. Tobias knew too, he could see it in the defeat in the man's face. Three parts hung-over and three hours' sleep and this. He rubbed his eyes painfully, the first time in days.

"Stay here," Marith ordered Thalia. "Sit in the cart." He looked at Tobias's face. "Alxine, stay with her. Keep your sword out."

The incline fell away steeply into a flat plain. It was very hot, the air very close. No trees or grasses, just sand and jagged rocks that caught at the foot. But ahead of them, a few crows circled, cawing raggedly.

The body was sprawled on its back in a circle of blackened sand, arms thrown out to the sides. Ripped to pieces. The blood was clotted and black with flies. Crows had torn out its innards. A man, possibly dressed in a brown shirt and brown leggings. A few strands of hair and a graying beard.

A long wooden staff, as tall as the man himself and broader than his forearm, lay in the dust next to him. It was broken jaggedly in two.

A silence.

"Oh fuck," Rate said at last.

Tobias frowned. "It's the mage. The wonder worker. From the square in Sorlost. You remember, with the fire and the colored lights?"

"It's missing half its face," said Rate. "How can you tell that?"

"No, he's right," Marith said slowly. "That's a mage's staff, anyway. And those marks in the dust are from mage fire."

Rate whistled softly through his teeth. "We should probably leave here as quickly as bloody well possible, then?"

The blood drained from Marith's face. He turned and looked back toward the cart and horses, hidden behind the incline.

"Haven't heard her scream, yet," said Tobias. "But you're right, the pair of you. We should go. Now." He bent down, rifled quickly through the man's pockets, retrieving a handful of coins and an ornately handled knife. "Wonder where his saddlebags went. He must have had water, food…"

"There." Rate pointed to a dark heap in the sand away to the right. He went cautiously toward it. Returned carrying a large travel sack. "Looks like a camp. Gods know why he left his horse up there behind him."

"I don't think he did," said Tobias. "I think the horse got up there on its own. Even hobbled. There are some odd marks in the sand back there."

Another silence.

"Oh fuck," said Rate.

They rode the horses hard, pressing on as late as they could into the night. You know what's coming, a voice whispered in Marith's mind. You know. You've known since you came back into the desert. They were fleeing, but they could just as easily be fleeing toward it.

I will not burn, he thought bitterly. He traced his hand over the hilt of the black sword.

On the next morning, riding into the rising sun. The Fire Star burned beside it. The desert shimmered like liquid gold: Marith looked back and saw Thalia's face glowing as she sat next to Rate in the cart. Her hair and eyes blazed, reflecting the sun. As beautiful as the dawn. I don't want to die, he thought. It grew hotter than ever, the sun remorseless, still no running water and no shade. They sat for lunch in the small shadow of the cart, dried meat warm and rancid in the heat, drinking warm rancid water from their water-skins.

Thalia pointed, shielding her eyes against the bright sun. "There's something flying up there. Circling us."

Alxine looked up too. The sun was right in his face, blazing. He squinted. "There's something…a bird, I think. No, wait…it's too big. Too big…"

Thalia screamed then, for a great dark shape came down out of the sky, blotting out the light. A stink of hot iron. The beating of vast wings.

The dragon was gray, a deep, storm-cloud gray in which all the colors of the world flickered. Its eyes were green, the green of trees and leaves. Eyes that knew things men could never know. The other dragon, the little dragon, had been an animal. A creature. This dragon was something else.

It settled in the road in front of them. Perfect and beautiful. A wonder. Utterly real. Everything else around it ceased and fell to nothing beside it. It sat and watched them, perfectly still, only its eyes moving, and the flames beating and smoking in its nostrils as it breathed.

Its eyes flickered as it looked at Marith. Something that might have been a frown or a smile came across its face. Its black tongue came out, twitching in the air. It lashed its tail twice.

Ah gods. Amrath and Eltheia. Be kind. Be kind. I don't want... I don't want to die.

Marith stepped forward. The dragon hissed, showing white teeth as long as a man's arm, cruel and sharp. It beat its tail, sending up a cloud of dust. Another step. Another. He stopped perhaps ten paces from the cavernous mouth. He drew his sword and raised it aloft, staring back at the dragon with great dark eyes. Blue fire crackled down the length of the blade. When he spoke his voice shook.

"I am of your blood, and the blood of she that loosed you. I am of your blood, and the blood of He that slew you. You will not attack me, or my companions. I command it. By my name and my blood and my sword, I command it. Else I will kill you."

The dragon looked down at him. For a long moment the two stood facing each other, eyes locked. There was absolute silence. Tobias, Thalia, Alxine and Rate crouched in the dust, trembling. The horses rolled their eyes but stood still.

The dragon could snap a man in two, grind him into nothing, burn him to ashes. Not a human thing. Like bidding a rock to move, or water to flow uphill. Like bidding the sun not to set.

But slowly it bowed its head, and blinked its vast green eyes.

Marith laughed then, a wild laugh that was barely human. The same sound he had made that night in Sorlost when he had killed Emit and drunk firewine and laughed like something rotted and dead.

The dragon hissed long and angry, and then it spoke, its voice clear and ringing, the deep music of a great old bell. Its breath was hot like a furnace, flame riding on its words. Its voice seemed to echo beyond language, deep into the mind. Itheralik, the Old Tongue, the tongue of Amrath, the tongue of the Godkings of Caltath. What other language would dragons speak, save that spoken by dead gods?

Studied it. Struggled over it. Hated it. And now it came clear in Marith's thoughts, the words and the answers, like he was born to it.

"*Amrath Tiameneke emnek geklam. Kel Altrersnanet kel imrahnei Amrathek?*" Amrath died fighting a dragon. Do you think you are greater than Amrath, little Altrersyr boy? It shifted itself up, beating open its great wings. The skin of them was deep red. Dried blood red. Firewine red. Almost the same black-red as Marith's hair. "*Ren nanel ykelesti Altrersnanet. Ren se kel memrak. Kekelmen enoheles arelasivs. Keneken na ylik nekast. Kekelmen bek malis.*" You are far from home, little Altrersyr boy. Very far. And you have weakness in you. I can taste it, when I look at you. You run from your own shadow.

Marith said quietly, "*Kekeme hast i kane, Tiamenekil?*" I am not running from you though, am I, dragon?

The dragon snorted fire, growling and flexing its wings again, vast and gleaming, like a wave breaking on the shore. "You killed one of my sons, little Altrersyr boy."

"I killed my best friend, dragon. Do you think I care about your son?" Marith gripped his sword more tightly, trying to keep his gaze fixed on the dragon's eyes. He could control it. He could perhaps even kill it. He held it bound to him on a thin tight leash of his will.

So much power, he thought. In it. In him.

The dragon moved its head a little, surveying the four figures behind him.

"Curious company you keep, little Altrersyr boy. Your woman, is she? And your servants?"

"You do not look at her!" He raised his sword again and the dragon jerked and hissed and laughed.

"I see her, too, little Altrersyr boy. An interesting choice of woman for you. For the path you take."

"Leave here. Leave us in peace. Go back into the wilds and do not follow us. Swear it." The blue fire on the sword flickered. "*Ahmeniket!*" Swear it!

The great green eyes stared down. "But I am hungry and angry, little Altrersyr boy. I long to kill. I hunger to kill. The men of the desert offered up prayers and chants and dances to me, then sent out a fool man to kill me. But all it did was stir up my desire. The man burned me, little Altrersyr boy." It spread open its wings again, and Marith saw a jagged dark tear in the skin of the left wingspan. The wings closed, like a fan closing, the body lowered, like a dog coming into a crouch or a horse kneeling to be ridden. "*Ahmenieken ekliket Ansikanderakesis. Ansikanderakesis Amrakane.*" Marith jerked his head and the dragon snorted. "If I was stronger, I would kill you now. Better that I did. You know that as well as I, little Altrersyr boy." Another laugh. "*Ahmenieken ekliket.* I swear it. But I must be revenged on something. For what the little mage thing did. For what you will do. And then I will leave you be." The great head twisted, the long neck sinuous, snaking round to view the four figures crouching defenseless in the sand. "Not your woman, no. Though it would be kindness to her, perhaps. But—"

Fire burst from the dragon's throat. It roared and leaped forward, knocking Marith to one side. He stumbled, dropping the sword. The blue flames died. The dragon mounted into the sky, wings blocking the light. It shone in the sun like heat haze. Clouds of dust stirred up and falling, sand grains sparkling gold. Like broken glass falling. Like colored stars.

Thalia screamed. Rate screamed. Tobias cursed.

Alxine lay in the dust, torn to pieces, his head ripped from his body, limbs crushed and bent.

Chapter Thirty-Nine

The next weeks were...interesting. Orhan was effectively the ruler of the Sekemleth Empire. It was almost enjoyable.

When he awoke the morning after the morning after he'd failed to assassinate the Emperor, the light was bright and he must have been asleep for a long time. He felt groggy and headachy, but slightly less weary. And he seemed to still be alive, and not under arrest, so things were likely to have remained somewhat under his control. Or his sister's, rather. He'd commandeered a room in the palace (one of the surviving servants, with grim inevitability, had tried to put him in Tam's old room). The air was fresh under the smoke stink, the walls were soothing cool pale peaceful green.

Hope!

He bathed and dressed, his mind busy with all the tasks he had still to do. The High Priestess. That was the next big thing. Find a way of ensuring she was confirmed dead. Which meant he'd have to produce a body. Then there was Tam's family, that he somehow had to save from the fire. Others would have to die in their place, of course. Couldn't tip his scales too far toward the good. Too late to try for redemption. Just expediency, and saving the life of a crippled girl and a woman he'd known since he was born.

It suddenly occurred to him that he was being dressed in his own clothes. Some of his best, too, a fine shirt of blue silk, dark gray leggings, a belt with an ornate gold buckle, a richly embroidered green jacket, a silver cloak. Celyse. She must have had them sent for while he slept. God's knives, she was efficient. Thought of all the details.

The door opened and Darath walked in, smiling broadly at him. Orhan's heart jolted.

"They said you were awake. Looking rather better than the last time I saw you, too." Darath put his arms around Orhan's neck and kissed him, then began tugging at the fastenings on his clothes. "I very much like your new titles. Perhaps you can recite them to me."

"What's been happening?" Orhan asked him firmly. Focus. Things to sort out. People to kill. "Has March come round yet? Is there still fighting anywhere? How's the city holding generally?"

"Do we really have to talk business right now?" Darath sat down on the bed. Pulled Orhan over next to him.

"Yes. We do. If we want to live, anyway."

"Yes, yes, I suppose…We're fine. The city is fairly calm. March is in a rage because Elis has somehow managed to contract himself to two different women in three hours, only one of whom has the misfortune to be a Verneth, but he's pulled his men back. He can see which way things are going. Some more buildings burned down last night, but the fires are out now. Money-lenders, mostly, you may be interested to hear. You didn't set all this in motion just to burn your banking house down to the ground, did you?"

"Tempting, but no. I'm not that devious. Also I'd have borrowed more first, if I had. Anything else? How's the Emperor? And stop that…"

"You really are boring this morning. I seem to remember we were doing this the other way round a few days ago, you couldn't keep your hands off me…The Emperor's still weak at the knees and white-faced with terror. Still clinging to you as the greatest hero the Empire has ever seen. Seems rather taken with your sister, too. Furious with March for any suggestion of suspicious conduct he may harbor against you. Or me. Relax, Orhan. Things are going well. We're safe. Ish. Can I please take your clothes off you now? We can get straight back to business afterward."

A servant brought a light meal later, bread and sweet-cured meat and soft cheese. Lemon-scented water, ice cold; flowery tea; sweet, dark wine. Cimma fruit, crusted with honey and spices, its rancid smell drifting over the room like the smoke. The tea bowls were a porcelain so thin and pale that their hands showed through it. Orhan stretched back in his chair, looking down at the palace gardens beneath them, the sun sparkling on the bathing pool, lilac flowers nodding in the breeze. The city rose behind them, the towers and domes of the great houses jumbled elegantly, the House of Silver flashing in the light.

"This is all rather glorious, isn't it?"

"You're richer than the Emperor, Darath. Your house is better furnished. You drink better wine and eat better food."

"'Tis true." Darath chewed a piece of fruit lazily. "But it's more fun doing it here. The view's better, too. Some thoughtless bastard put a palace in the way of my balcony."

A tap at the door. A functionary in the Imperial uniform of dark gray and gold appeared. A nervous look on his face. One of the few survivors, who now leaped out of his skin whenever someone entered the same room as him.

"His Eminence wishes you see you, My Lord Nithque," he said meekly. What does he think is going to happen? Orhan wondered. We'll cut him down where he stands? Having a new reputation as an Imperial hero seemed to be something of a mixed blessing when he was dealing with palace servants. Unless the man had just assumed he and Darath were still right in the middle of things.

"Work." Darath helped himself to another piece of cimma fruit, the juice running down his chin in sticky rivulets. "The one great disadvantage of power. I'll see you later. Dinner? Here?"

Orhan followed the functionary down the Imperial Chambers. A palace to redecorate. A Treasury to manage. Trade and defense to reorganize. Alliances to reconsider. An Empire to rebuild. Oh, yes, work. Darath was the perfect co-conspirator, leaving it all to him to manage.

* * *

Slaves worked day and night to get the palace and the Great Temple in some kind of order. The latter had not been seriously damaged: the Great Chamber had been knocked about a bit, several slaves and three priestesses were dead. One foreign assassin had been found alive if terrified out of his wits drooling profanities, but had been swiftly torn to pieces by a screaming mob. Every candle in the place had gone out, even the red lamp on the High Altar. It would need some kind of formal ceremony of rededication and thanks; Orhan had Celyse planning it already. Glory to the Empire, the Emperor, and the Emmereths. Lots of gold splashed around the city on new clothing and jewelry and food. Fountains running with wine and honey; bread for the masses; whores dancing in the streets offering kisses for free; certain substances suddenly available surprisingly cheaply to those interested in such filthy things. He'd have to temporarily rescind the edict against travelers from Chathe to achieve the last, but it was probably worth the risk. Everybody had to be happy and glad to see the new regime, even the street scum.

Orhan was beginning to suspect that Tam had been right, too: keeping the Emperor alive and bowed down with gratitude was a far more effective way of seizing power than killing him would have been. That the Emperor must, deep down, be aware Orhan had come fairly close to assassinating him whilst at the same time saving him from being brutally killed by the very assassins he'd hired was, quite possibly, an accidental masterstroke. Holt Amdelle seemed genuinely to believe Orhan's version of events, but pretty much everyone else who mattered was quite obviously vaguely aware how things had fallen, but were just under the impression he had somehow controlled it all from first to last. Perhaps he had: been playing a game so complex even he hadn't understood the moves he was making, the twists of the pieces as his failure led to victory.

In which case, he was possibly the most brilliant strategic genius

Irlast had ever known. Which seemed a truly horrifying thing to think. You got lucky, Orhan, he told himself sternly. You're only able to think that because you got so lucky that you're not now dead.

The day of the ceremony dawned very hot. The priestesses had been gathered in the Temple all night, keeping vigil, praying in the dark of the Great Chamber. As dawn broke, the candles were relit on the altars and the red lamp blazed a brilliant crimson, bright as rubies and fresh blood. The Great Hymn resounded around the huge room, the candles flared up one after another in a long sigh like a wave. At the moment the red lamp was lit, the sun caught the small high windows in the east and turned them pure and perfect gold. The priestesses threw up their arms, their gray robes shining, their masks glittering with the dark eyes behind; before the High Altar, the tiny figure of a child knelt, clothed in silver, the lamp casting a red tinge to her hair and eyes. She had beautiful hands, slender and long and very white.

The common people of the city had been permitted into the Temple to see this great moment: Orhan had been clear on this, and the old priestess Ninia had agreed with him. They needed to witness the light returning, the Temple and the city made whole and healed, the power of the God and the Empire blazing up. Literally. Arguably a bit over-symbolic, but Orhan rather liked the theatrics. Some things weren't meant to be subtle.

He watched from the back of the room, filled again with an astonished sense of wonder at what he had achieved. Darath hadn't wanted him to go: there was a part of him that had agreed, drawn back, shuddered at it. A buried fear that the candles would refuse to light, that the child at the altar would rise up and scream out in the voice of the God that he was damned. In the dark before the dawn came the jeweled masks had been dimly visible, nodding and floating like birds, and he had felt horror seeing them. A rational man, but a guilty one. But he was glad, now, that he had come. The joy of it, the candles and the singing, the gasp of wonder and beauty as the darkness burst into life. He felt cleaner, perhaps more at peace with what he'd done. Glory to the Empire. Glory to the city. Glory to the God.

The great ceremony itself took place in the afternoon. The entire city seemed to smell of cooking and perfume. The great families bustled about in fine clothes and glittering jewels, drawing up before the Temple in litters radiant with light. Orhan and Bil traveled together in a new litter of cool green silk. Bil was dressed in silver, her lovely hair falling loose about her waist, caught back from her face with a net of tiny diamonds. Her face and body had a plumpness to them, the swell of the baby was beginning to show. A new fashion for long sleeves and concealing gauzes, Orhan thought. Or artificial scars molded in wax and clay. Though she'd perhaps care less now anyway, now that she had power and glory and a coming child.

Bil fidgeted with her rings. "I read your letter," she said.

"I meant to burn it."

"I did."

A silence. The litter jolted to a halt. They mounted the steps, stopped for a moment before the great closed door. The wood stared at them, an ancient thing, alive, the knots eyes, the grain rippling fur. The great gashes stood out starkly. As in the morning, Orhan felt fear settle on him, waiting for the doorway to seal itself before him with a crash. Bil stepped forward, pushed the door. It opened.

The dark of the narrow corridor seemed less terrible, this time. Less crushing. Bil gripped his hand but did not seem to feel the same fear either, walking behind him with her head raised. The Great Chamber beyond blazed like a furnace: again, less frightening, less terrible. It was already crowded with the nobles and the wealthiest of the merchants, the priestesses, the Imperial officials, the few foreign somebodies who still happened to be around. Orhan and Bil took their places at the very front of the chamber, staring up at the High Altar and the tiny figure enthroned beside it. She wore gold and silver, hastily fashioned to fit her child's frame.

Finally, trumpets, a voice shouting, "The Emperor! All kneel for the Ever Living Emperor! Avert your eyes and kneel and be thankful! We live and we die! The Emperor comes! The Emperor comes!" The assembled congregation knelt carefully. All but the child in gold who sat stiffly on her throne, her face all eyes, fidgeting with the hem of her dress. The Emperor entered slowly, cautiously walking the length of the chamber, flanked by two guards in black armor with drawn swords. That, the Emperor himself had insisted upon, though Orhan hated it and Celyse thought it vulgar in the extreme.

The Emperor seated himself carefully on a gilt chair next to and a little in front of Orhan's own. The new High Priestess stared at him. She was obviously scared out of her wits. No trouble there, either. She'd do as she was bid. She came back from the killing trembling, clutching the arm of the old priestess Ninia who had had to help and accompany her. Too weak to wield a knife. Such beautiful little white hands. Orhan felt sick at it. But it was the only way.

I shouldn't have come, he thought. I shouldn't have seen this. Her.

There was a great banquet after, in the vast, hastily redecorated festival chamber of the palace. Celyse had placed Orhan and Darath next to each other, Bil away on the other side of the Emperor's dais so she could not see them, but in a grand place with various Verneth and Amdelle women somehow quite obviously beneath her. Darath reached out from his couch and touched Orhan's arm.

After the banquet he traveled with Bil back to the House of the East in the new green litter, quiet and tired in the dark. The city swirled around them, people singing and dancing and fucking in the streets. In the Court of the Fountain two men fought, white silks blossoming with blood. In the Court of the Broken Knife a woman wept beneath the faceless statue, a tiny candle flickering at her side. Bil pulled the curtains closed, and the figures became ghosts, their shouts far off.

"It was kind of you," she said. "To come home with me."

"I—" I might go on to Darath's house, Orhan almost said, but didn't. Taken over an Empire, stabbed and then tortured a man he'd known since he was a child, but still couldn't manage the full and exhausting complications of his wretched personal life. If he could just bring himself to really dislike Bil, it would be so much easier.

"I'm sorry Sterne's dead," Orhan said suddenly.

"It doesn't matter."

"Truly?"

Bil drew herself more upright, folding her hands over her belly where the tiny child lay. "No. Truly, it's horrible and I miss him. Truly, I feel utter grief at his death, and I can't even mourn him properly, because then people will know. Truly, I hate you for getting him into things that killed him. Your lover knew what was happening and survived, and you get to sit next to him at dinner and smile at him. You sent mine to his death."

"Yes."

"But now I'm the wife of the Nithque to the Emperor, and my child will inherit wealth unbounded, and my father has finally stopped looking at me as though he wants to weep with apology every moment."

"Again, yes."

The litter halted as a great crowd of revelers surged past them in the narrow street, their shapes moving like shadow puppets on the silk walls of the litter. Voices called, drunk and singing: "Who's inside?"

When they heard it was Lord Emmereth, the voices took up a cheer. Bil squeaked as the litter rocked a little, people crowding close. Their guards shouted and threatened, the people cheered again and moved on.

Orhan smiled wryly. "I wonder how long that will last?"

He slept late the next day, like everyone else in the city apart from the wretches clearing up the mess. From the look of the crowds last night, that would be work worthy of a poem. *The Song of the Red Morning*, in which the poet's hopeless love for a woman is compared to the never-ending task of shoveling filth from the city's streets. Orhan bathed and dressed, smiling at the memory of the ragged cheers for the Emmereth name. That hadn't been heard in Sorlost for centuries.

Back to the palace after lunch, things to arrange and rearrange. Would this get boring, turn to a yearning for his quiet life of refined pointlessness? He'd barely had a chance to read a book since that night, only endless reports. Must have been the only sober man in the city last night too.

He sat down at his desk, unrolled the map of Irlast and looked at it yet again. The Sekemleth Empire, edged in gold leaf, Sorlost a gilt blob at its center. So pathetically small! A badly drawn dragon flapped to the east of the city, Chathe and Theme hemming them in to the west and north. Immish very large and bright, her borders already redrawn. Little room to maneuver, Orhan thought gloomily. The great Treasury ledgers were no better, a long list of debts, deficits and uncollected revenues exquisitely written in golden ink. Orhan's hands traced carefully over the beautiful embossed leather of the covers: the books were reportedly bound in human skin. He opened one, took up a pen and slashed through a number of annual payments, one apparently made to himself, two to Darath. March's stipend, for his role as "First Lord and Viceroy of Riva", had better stay as it was for the moment. Orhan didn't even know where Riva had been.

Costs, costs, more costs…How could it be so expensive to run a palace effectively inhabited by one person? Builders' bills coming in; a load more furniture to purchase; a large number of widows' pensions to put into payment now too. Best to keep the newly-bereaved on-side. Darath's joke about the money-lenders came back to him: a really clever man would have got rid of all the paperwork as well as the bureaucracy, and started again with a literally blank page.

A quiet tap on the door: one of the palace secretaries, a youngish man with a narrow dark face and black hair flecked with gold, holding a large scroll.

"My Lord Nithque."

"Gallus." Orhan couldn't help liking the man. Efficient, helpful, bright, good-looking, cynical.

"The letter to the Immish High Council, My Lord."

Orhan took the scroll and unrolled it. Beautifully written, the seal of the Empire set in gold on the bottom, so heavy it almost tore at the silver tissue it was written on. "That was quick work," he said approvingly. Scanned over the text. All correct, and the man had tidied up his syntax in a couple of places where he'd struggled to find the right words.

"I'll get the Emperor to sign it as soon as he's awake." Which wouldn't be for hours. "No, wait, I'll sign it myself." A clear signal of a new regime, changes. Strength. "Then it needs to go by fast courier to Alborn."

It was a letter of formal apology. The Sekemleth Empire held Immish in no way responsible for the recent outrageous events against the life of the Eternal and Ever Living Emperor and the High Priestess of the Lord of Living and Dying, Great Tanis Who Rules All Things, and had been assured the High Council was doing all it could to root out the conspirators clearly active within her borders. Any hostilities expressed by the subjects of the Sekemleth Empire against Immish persons or their property were purely the private actions of a people grieving and enraged by the attempt on the life of their beloved Emperor and the attack on the Temple of their God, and should in no way be taken as suggesting an official hardening of the Empire's relations with Immish. No compensation would therefore be payable. The Ever Living Emperor did, however, express sorrow for any individual's losses. As no official action had or was being taken against any citizen of Immish, any goods and possessions left abandoned in the city of Sorlost or its environs were considered forfeit and rendered the possession of the Imperial Treasury.

"It's quite…strong," Gallus said as he took the letter and sealed it.

Orhan stamped it with the Imperial crest of a winged lion. "It's meant to be strong. But if you read it carefully, there's nothing Immish can actually object to. Their assassins did try to kill our

Emperor and bring down our city." The scope of that lie in itself, he hoped, sent some kind of a signal: the Sekemleth Empire was tired of petty games and internal intrigues.

Gallus nodded thoughtfully. "I'll send two couriers, My Lord. Good horses. I know the men to choose."

Orhan smiled. "Good."

Gallus's eyes flicked to the books on the table. "The Treasury ledgers, My Lord?"

"Indeed. Remarkably depressing reading. The recent entries have seen a marked decline in the quality of the handwriting, too."

Gallus paused for a moment, then said quietly, "If My Lord wishes... I can help him with where the money is going. Who some of the payments are to. Which are more necessary than others."

Orhan smiled again. "Can you, now? Not receiving one yourself, then?"

"Several, My Lord." Gallus ran his finger down a list of payments, raising his eyebrows slightly as he came to the scored-through Vorley and Emmereth entries. "This... and this... and this... come to me." His eyes met Orhan's. "One of them might, perhaps, be considered to continue to remain necessary? For the moment, at least..."

"It might." Sensible man. Quick and dynamic. Took his chances but didn't push it. Could go far, Orhan thought. He'd have to look into promoting him. Though Darath might not like it. Knew he'd always had a weakness for gold hair.

Chapter Forty

They left Alxine where he lay, scattering a little sand over him but otherwise abandoning his body to the crows. They had no real choice: they had nothing to bury him with, and none of them wished to linger. As he was Aelish, from the uncharted territories on the other side of the Bitter Sea, none of them knew even what god he had worshipped, or what he had believed would happen to him now that he had died. Eternal feasting with his kin in the afterlife, Tobias said vaguely. Or possibly a big nasty toothy tentacled thing came and ate your soul. Ten years, he said, he'd known Alxine, and Alxine never really mentioned it, so it couldn't have been particularly important.

"Not among the useless things they teach princes, then?" asked Rate.

Tobias shook his head at him. "Don't bother the boy, now, lad." Marith was sitting on the sand, staring up into the sky, his eyes following where the dragon had gone. He scratched heavily at his face, looking gray and drawn.

Tobias poured a libation of wine beside the body. "Wherever your soul ends up, peace," he said awkwardly. "Whether that's the beer halls of your ancestors or the digestive system of a squid." He poured three cups and passed them to the others.

Marith smiled at him bitterly as he took his. "Should let more people get killed more often," he said harshly as he drank.

Thalia did not join them, standing apart. A male thing, she judged. Men who had fought and killed together. Alxine was dead. That was the end of it. She went up to Marith afterward and placed her hand on his arm. He shrugged her off and walked away. Anger in him. And fear.

Ansikanderakesis Amrakane.

Sikandemethemis. That word she knew. An obscure honorific, barely used outside of a few old hymns, the words of an ancient chant. It meant "lord." "Master." "King."

Not a Literan word. Itheralik.

"Marith." She followed him. "It wasn't your fault. You saved the rest of us. Life and death have to be balanced. People have to die."

" 'We live. We die. For these things, we are grateful'?" Bitterness and dark in his eyes. "I'm a dragonlord now, I suppose. Two dragons I've met, two I've mastered. Almost." He rubbed at his face again. "Just leave me alone a while, Thalia."

They rode on, Tobias glancing behind him once at the dark heap in the distance, upon which the crows were now descending. He threw a stone and they scattered but returned in a moment, calling. Followed the dragon, perhaps.

Again, they rode as long as they could, well into the darkness. "It did say it would leave us alone?" asked Rate anxiously as they finally drew up to make camp. "It won't come while we sleep?"

"Not a lot we could do if it did," Tobias grunted.

"It said it would leave us untroubled," Marith said slowly. He rode close beside the cart, slumped in the saddle, all the life gone out of him. Dismounted slowly and stiffly, like an old man, walked a few paces and sat down in the sand. "It should keep its word. If not…If not, I suppose I'll have to kill it. But as I'm planning to drink everything we have left and then sleep like the dead, we'll just all have to hope everything is fine until the morning."

Shadows in the dark. Things calling him. She saw it, as she

watched him. *Ansikanderakesis. Ansikanderakesis Amrakane.* Lord. Master. King.

It was a barren place they had stopped in, a flat depression in a long slope of shifting gravel that moved under the horses' hooves. A tiny pool of muddy dirty water, a few insects buzzing wearily over its surface. A couple of scrub bushes, half-dead and desiccated, clinging on in the scree. But they were so tired now.

Thalia helped Tobias manage the horses, something she was beginning to find she was good at, trying to overcome her fear of them. The size of the creatures still unnerved her.

"You've just seen a bloody dragon," Tobias muttered at her. "How can a horse seem big to you?"

"That was a dragon," she said simply. "It's not a human thing. These are. They're so big, but they do what we tell them."

"He did what I told him, for a while. You've just got to treat them right. Break them, then make them your friend."

She looked at him.

"You're a fool, girl," Tobias said shortly. "Can't you see that? Look, when we get to Immish...I could give you some money. A couple of talents. One of the horses, even. You don't...You don't have to stay with us. With him."

Thalia gave the roan horse some grain and said nothing.

"We're running out of supplies," Tobias said after a while. "Better hope we get down to the grasslands soon. Got two spare horses now, of course. Shame horses can't eat horsemeat."

He was trying to frighten her. Shock her. "How long will it be?" This was the longest Thalia had ever spoken to him.

"Till the Immish border? Four or five days, still, I should think. Unless we're lost, of course. Look, girl. Thalia. Listen: I mean it about the money and the horse. Think about it, yeah? Face like yours, you don't seem stupid, either...you really don't need to stay with him. You're better than him. You don't know him like I do. Believe me on that."

Thalia dug her nails into her palms. I am the Chosen of the Lord of Living and Dying, she thought. The words of life and death are written on my skin. Child killer. Bringer of light. The holiest woman in Irlast.

You think I don't know what he is?

"I don't have to stay with him, no. I know that. I do have some power of my own, you know."

He snorted. "Just think about it, yeah?"

Marith appeared beside them. His face was bone-weary, but he smiled gently and took the roan horse's rein from her hands. "You shouldn't be doing that, beautiful girl," he said softly. "You sit and eat and go to sleep. I'll manage what needs doing here."

"Thank you."

He smiled sadly. "You don't need to thank me, Thalia."

She flashed a smile almost of triumph at Tobias.

Tobias shook his head and went to join Rate.

They made a small fire, a little huddle of a few sticks that smoked and gave off a pungent, bitter smell. Horribly exposed, it looked out there in the night, a beacon to great green eyes. But it seemed horrible too not to have a fire, to sit cold and blind. They did not bother to cook food or make tea, but sat edgily around the tiny flames eating hard, stale bread.

"He did say he thought he was cursed," said Rate. "Newlin, Emit, now him."

Tobias rolled his eyes. "That's not cursed. Or only in a manner of speaking."

Marith made a coughing sound. "Just bad luck," he said.

The fire crackled and spat. The moon was vast in the sky, the stars broken silver. So many. She would not have thought, in the lights and shelter of the city, looking at the little patch of sky above the Temple, that there could be so many. That they could be so frightening. I should be killing a man again tonight, Thalia thought suddenly.

She pressed closer to Marith and he kissed her and they went off to sleep held tight in each other's arms, like children rather than lovers beneath the abyssal sky. He had done the work that needed doing, drunk only water, cared for Thalia as though she were the one who had done something great and wonderful. He muttered in his sleep, and scratched at his face, and sighed.

When Thalia awoke next morning, she smelled food cooking. It was already light, the pale white light of morning. A bird seemed to be singing, which confused her. They were in the midst of the desert, surely? The dead place. Yet a bird was singing, and she heard a human voice answer it, trying and failing to whistle.

Marith was gone. She got down from the cart, pulling her cloak around her in the chill of the morning. The sky was pink and golden, still deep blue in the far west but washed over with light. She drew in a deep, long breath of air that was sweet in her mouth. Marith was sitting by the fire, poking a pan in which dried meat was frying. The kettle was boiling for tea. He had his back to her, didn't see she was watching him. As she watched, the meat sizzled and some of the fat caught, sending up a burst of flame and smoke and a charred smell. He cursed, then laughed, then noticed her.

"Thalia!" His face was clean in the clean light. "I'm making breakfast! Meat and fried bread. Come and have some."

Thalia sat down by the fire. Marith solemnly served her burned fried dried meat and burned fried stale bread. It stuck to the pan as he scraped it off. Poured her a cup of very strongly brewed tea. She ate carefully and equally solemnly.

"You can't cook," she said at last.

"I know." He grinned. "But since I can command dragons now, I thought I might try it. You would probably have said I couldn't do either, yesterday morning." He took a few sips of tea, then grimaced and poured it away. "I won't be offended. I really cannot seem to learn tea-making. It looks so easy, too."

Thalia frowned. "You shouldn't waste water. Or food. Tobias will—"

"I'm not. Look." He gestured to the north-east, and Thalia saw, then, the dim shape of trees far away low in the distance.

"Immish?"

He nodded. "Trees. Woods. Fields. Rain. Still a while to them, of course. The whole day, perhaps two. But I'd guess we're closer than Tobias thought. Once we're in Immish, there are proper roads, good ones. We can make good time, get better horses. Then one of the eastern ports, Skerneheh or somewhere—" a look of distaste momentarily crossed his face "—and a fast ship up the coast to Ith. And then—"

He broke off. Raised his head, his eyes widening. Thalia looked up too as a great shadow passed above them. The fire flared up in the wind from the beat of vast wings.

The dragon passed overhead, low enough that they saw its scales and the curl of its claws. It spouted flame, but upward, into the sky. It turned and flew back into the west, gleaming rose-gold in the sun. They saw flame spout again. And then it was no bigger than a bird. And then it was gone.

Thalia let out a long, shaky breath. Marith laughed. "And then I'll make you a queen," he said, as if they had not both nearly died.

Birds came increasingly, snapping at little flies. The grass began to appear again, scrub bushes and thorns, lizards and spiders and life. Running water. Only a few days, it had been, but they all leaped at the water, bathing and washing the dust out of their clothes as though it had been years. Marith thought of the other stream, where he had killed a dragon, of the men bathing in the rainwater while Alxine watched. Now he bathed with Thalia, and saw the water run like jewels as she shook out her hair.

"It's not fair," Rate muttered. "That Alxine got so close. Bloody stupid." But somehow they didn't really talk about Alxine, and it didn't really seem to matter. Yesterday he'd been alive, and the world had been dead. Now he was dead, and the world was coming alive. They were alive, where they might also have been dead.

And he had been killed by a dragon. It was an astonishing way to go. Marith brooded a little, rankled by his own failure to completely control the creature, but also wondered.

After another day Tobias decreed that they were in Immish now, or on the borders at least. Reneneth, the nearest town, couldn't be more than a few days' ride away. A different place, different land and sky. Different air, moister, cooler. Different trees from those Thalia knew, taller, thicker, finer leaved; Marith could see wonder in her eyes as she gazed about her, her face confused and delighted by the gradual reawakening of the world around them after the desert. More birds; more flowers; a pair of deer, a mother and child, glimpsed among the trees ahead of them in the gold of the afternoon. The leaves were beginning to turn faint brown and russet: autumn was drawing in, he realized, here where seasons passed and changed and time did not seem to stand still. It would be almost winter by the time they reached Ith. A good season to begin himself anew, when the wind scoured the world clean to begin itself again. He had not liked the unchanging nature of Sorlost.

And then winter...Thalia had never seen winter. He would take her out in a sleigh, racing across the snow wrapped in thick furs. Riding fast over the frost and hearing it crunch underfoot. Skating on the ice of a frozen field. The great feast of Sunreturn, which she did not even know by its right name, when one feasted and danced for a day and a night and day to welcome back the light.

There'd been a very heavy cold three winters back, so long and hard even the great river Emdell had frozen thick enough to stand on and they'd held the feast there on the ice, skating in the dark with the moon making the ice shine, all the ladies of the court whirling around him in fur cloaks, showing only their eyes. He and Carin had ridden upriver together that night; it had snowed again and they had been briefly, utterly alone, the two of them lost in a world of pure and silent white.

He hadn't thought about Carin for days now, he realized. It shocked him. But the memories were fainter in his mind. So quickly, now...Only a few months it had been. He wondered for a moment which of them he would choose, if somehow he could have a choice.

Then she called out to him, pointing out a hawk hovering utterly still save the wild beating of its wings, a dragon in miniature, dropping down like a thunderbolt, and he did not think of these things.

They stopped early the next afternoon, by a thick stream of sweet water, almost a river. It was banked with willow trees. Fish swam in the shallow water, glistening over smooth pebbles. Tobias tried to catch them but gave up, then Rate somehow got one, fat and brown with rainbow shadows. There was a smell of thyme and wild garlic from the green banks. A good place.

Thalia went off alone to the water. She still found the sight of running water a marvel: Marith liked to watch her, gazing enchanted into the swirling eddies, feeling the play of the current on her hands or feet. But this evening he left her alone to her thoughts and stretched out on the scrubby grass beneath one of the willows, staring up into its leaves as the evening drew in. Rate and Tobias were arguing over how to cook the fish; he half-listened to their voices, thinking vaguely of his own woods and rivers, riding through them fast on a chestnut horse, taking Thalia walking in green hills, laying her down on moss and leaf litter that would tangle in her hair...

A shadow. Tobias was standing over him. Marith sat up and Tobias squatted beside him.

"Didn't wake you, did I?" Tobias said gruffly.

"Just daydreaming. It's good here."

"Is it?" Tobias looked around him. A smile crossed his face. "It is, at that, isn't it? You forget, just looking at places for their strategic value. Simple pleasure in simple things. You look well, boy. Lord Prince. The girl suits you. Didn't think you had it in you, to be honest with you."

Marith looked at him curiously. "Thank you. I think."

"Happy, then, are you? Content?"

"I... Yes." He hadn't even thought it in those terms. "Yes."

"That's good then, I suppose. Shame it took so many people dying. But probably good, yes?"

"Yes..." Content. He hadn't felt content for a long time. There was a sudden waft of sweet, pungent smoke as Rate started cooking the fish. A bird called loudly in the tree above him. Content. Yes. He was content. Happy, even.

Tobias held out his hand. "So I suppose you won't be wanting this, then?"

A small clay vial, its neck sealed with wax.

Oh gods. Oh gods. No. Oh, please, no.

"That's...That's..."

"Interesting, the things you can pick up once you know what to look for, when everyone else is busy running around getting supplies fit for a prince." Tobias tried to smile at him. Eyes shifted guiltily away. Had the decency to look ashamed.

Oh gods.

Please. Please. Please.

Help me.

I don't need it, Marith tried to think. Not now. These last few days...Like he'd been through all the fires of a forge and been remade, burned away and scalded clean. She knows me, he thought, she knows me and she is still so bright with light, she's known darkness and death as I have and she is so radiant and so alive. I could be like that, he thought. I could just...just be alive. Happy. Content.

Tobias was frowning at him. Trying to look hard and strong. "You killed Emit for stuff like this not that long ago. Come on, then. Here it is."

"Why?" His whole body trembling. Help me help me help me. "We're going to Ith and you'll be rewarded...I told you...Why?"

"Why what? Maybe I just saw it and thought of you...A reward, like. For seeing off the dragon and that. Saving us all from burning. Killing a baby. Killing Emit. Killing all those men and women and children you killed." Tobias spat in the dust. "A reward."

I can't...I don't need it...I promised her I'd help her. She was kind to me.

Blot it out, he thought. Make it all go away.

But I don't...I don't...

"Don't worry about the girl," said Tobias. "She's better off with me and Rate. I've seen you, boy, remember. Seen what you do to people. Seen what you are. She's too good for you."

"No...No..." Marith bowed his head. "Please..." Don't say it. Don't say it. I know she is. She's radiant with light and I...I know what I am. But I can hope. Pretend. "Don't say it. Please."

"It's good stuff, the bloke selling it told me." Tobias's voice lowered. "Your face, when you were killing people...I saw you, boy. Filth. Murderer. Monster. Demon. Disease. That's what you are. You terrify me. I can't let you go to Ith, boy. You know that. Can't let you have power and command. I know what you are. What you'd do. Think of this as a kindness, like. 'Cause it is. To you and her and us."

He dropped the vial into Marith's hand.

There suddenly in Marith's mind the image of a statue, its face so corrupted as to be unrecognizable, holding aloft a burden too damaged to be seen. In its other hand, a broken knife. A woman sitting weeping at its feet. Black fire, burning, running over it all. Faceless and broken and ruined and empty of anything. The Court of the Broken Knife, the square the statue stood in was called. A sad, hateful, ill-fated place.

A kindness, he thought. Oh, yes.

Chapter Forty-One

Thalia came back up from the river, where she had found a little beach of pale sand, her feet wet and muddy. She stopped. Rate and Tobias were sitting by the fire. They rose up when she approached and came toward her. Fear gripped suddenly at her heart. Tobias held a sword. Marith's sword.

"Where is he?" she cried out. He was dead. They'd killed him. She'd left him alone and they'd killed him.

"He's alive, don't worry." Tobias gestured to the wagon. "We're not going to harm him. Or you."

"Fish's ready," said Rate. "If you want some."

She'd told him they were dangerous. She'd told him.

"Look, girl," said Tobias, "there are two ways we can do this. I don't want to harm you. I told you, I want to help you. I mean it. Yeah? So you can sit down here with us, eat some fish, ride along to Reneneth where I'll give you some money, like I offered to. Immish is a good place. Actually, to be honest with you, Reneneth's a shithole, but Immish in general is a good place. Or, hell, given Reneneth's a shithole, you can ride along with us all the way to Alborn if you like, or anywhere else we feel like going. Alborn... now that is a good place. A face like yours and a sword like mine and the bit of cash we're making, we could do pretty well there." He waved the sword. "Or I could tie you up and dump you in there beside him, and you can end up dead or whatever happens to him. Or I could kill you now."

"You've known him for a few days," said Rate. "Fucked him a few times. And he's really not quite what you think he is. You've got your whole life ahead of you. Come and sit down and have some fish."

The fire and the dark and the power in her. She braced herself, closed her eyes, summoned up her strength. She had defeated armed men in her Temple. She was the knife of God, the holiest woman in Irlast. She had no fear of them. She could destroy them. There was nobody in all the world she need fear. She understood that, looking at them, two men who thought they could harm her, she, she who was the Chosen of the God. She had kept life and death balanced. The most powerful woman in the world.

The campfire flickered. Darkness growing around them. Tobias's face looked strained. Rate whimpered and took a step back. Fear in the air, alive, licking at them. Thalia raised her hands.

The campfire flickered. She sat down.

She was in the midst of a wilderness. She'd die anyway, or worse, without them. All kinds of power lay in her. But she had absolutely no idea how to survive in the wilds.

"Clever girl," said Tobias.

Thalia stared at him. He paled. Looked away.

"I want to see him."

"Not a good idea," said Rate.

"I want to see him. Now." The High Priestess of Great Tanis. Rate and Tobias nodded, led her round to the wagon. She noticed Tobias kept his hand on the hilt of his sword.

Marith sat slumped, propped up against the canvas of the wall, his hands bound behind his back. His eyes were open, staring blankly at things she could not see. His mouth moved silently, shaping the same meaningless sound over and over. Spittle trickled over his lips.

"Hatha," Rate said. "I wouldn't waste your breath trying to talk to him. The amount he's taken, he wouldn't understand a word you were saying. Tobias did try to warn you. Really not worth you caring about, see?"

Thalia bent down beside her lover. Hopeless. His face did not respond, not even a flicker of his eyes. Cautiously, she reached out and touched him. He didn't move. "Marith," she whispered. No response. "Marith." Louder. Nothing.

"Told you it wasn't a good idea," said Rate. "The fish is getting cold. Come and eat."

"I—" The way his face had shone, looking at her. The way he'd been so afraid of her, then smiled, then laughed in her arms.

Marith made a mumbling sound. Spittle trickled down his face. No, she thought. She certainly didn't need to stay with him.

She went back and sat down by the campfire and ate fish with Rate and Tobias. His presence blazed behind her in the wagon, grating on her mind. They felt it too, she saw, jumping at shadows every time the fire crackled, their eyes sliding away reluctant to look at her. Stinking of guilt.

That night, she dreamed again of herself and Marith crowned in silver, seated on golden thrones. A beautiful dream. Woke groggy and frightened, to hear Rate and Tobias still awake, talking about him.

"...could just kill him," Rate was saying.

"Oh, I'm tempted, lad. Very tempted indeed." The fire crackled and she missed whatever else Tobias said.

"...pay to do it for us," Tobias was saying when she could hear clearly again. "Feels...cleaner, don't you think?"

"More profitable, that means, then, does it?"

A kind of sigh. "Yeah. That too."

"So how much?"

"Ten talents. She gave me two already, when I met her in Sorlost."

"Gods, Tobias. There anyone in your life you've not screwed over for coin?"

"Coin never stabbed a man in the back, Rate, lad. Or the front or the gut or the head, come to that. It wasn't a definite thing, anyway. Just...if things went one way and not another, be good to know where she was and how to contact her. That we might be coming this way. Take advantage of opportunities when they present themselves to you screaming and obviously wealthy. Find out who they are, where they're lodged. Let them know you might be interested in discussing certain things. Very pleased, she was, thinking of ways to kill him, once she'd got over the shock of him being alive."

Thalia curled up tighter, tried not to hear them. Guilt. Guilt. Shame. He had been their prisoner all the time, then, she thought.

The next morning Rate and Tobias smiled at her like nothing had happened, and spoke to her kindly and cheerfully, and she helped with the horses and preparing breakfast, and they rode on. Silence from the wagon. Just don't look, she thought. Don't look. The sunlight was golden on the grasslands, the trees were bronze and green and gold. Rate found some ripe plums and gave her one, it was sweet and tart and the juice ran down her chin. A herd of deer ran on ahead of them. Tobias pointed out a kestrel on the wing.

PART THREE

THE LIGHT OF THE SUN

Chapter Forty-Two

It was raining in Sorlost.

Rain was a rare occurrence. A beautiful thing. The smell of it rolled off the ground, sweet and heavy, exhilarating. Dust and ashes were churned into thick black mud, richly fertile, staining the city's stones. Dust into earth. Growing things. Children splashed naked in the puddles, shrieking. The corpses of drowned vermin floated on the water. Everything clean.

Lord Tanis lives in a palace soaked with water, whose gardens smell always of damp and growth. But we men must live in the dry places. Until it rains, and we think we see, for a moment, what it must mean to be God. Or so Maran Gyste had once written, anyway. But he wasn't half as good a poet as everyone said.

At the edge of the Court of the Fountain, Orhan stood in the rain. It always made him think of his childhood, watching the children dance in it. The brilliance of the memories. The scent of it, evoking pain like prodding a sore tooth. Raindrops bounced off the marble of the fountain, beating down the jets of water. The paving stones ran a thumb's height deep with water pitted like hammered tin. A lake, shining where a city had been drowned. The whores and hatha addicts and beggars picked through it as carefully as wading birds, fishing for treasures, rainwater streaming off them and all the colors of their clothes and skin running and blurring and staining the ground.

Something of a holiday, rainfall. Not many people about in it other than to enjoy it. Commerce ground to a halt as street sellers rushed to get their goods under cover, shop owners pulled closed their shutters, shoppers and errand boys ran for shelter or threw back their heads to dance. A spice merchant swore and screamed as a sack of saffron overturned, tiny red threads floating like worms and the water swirling yellow. A litter lurched by, its canopy cascading water, the bearers' hands slipping on its waxed poles. Two women squeaked and squealed and almost fell over on high jeweled shoes, while the man with them struggled to wrap a great bale of silk in his cloak. A merchant selling garlands laughed like a madman as his lovely paper offerings dissolved into mush on his brass tray.

And then it stopped again, and the sun came out, and the steam rose from the soaked ground. The sky was filled with birds and butterflies and everything blossomed, drinking up the water, sucking it up, holding on to it, eddies swirling in the corners of the streets, rivers rushing down steps and across courtyards depositing fallen leaves and crushed petals and dead animals and a thousand pieces of the detritus of the human world. Orhan watched them float together down the Street of Flowers. He waded through the dirty waters, his guards picking their way behind him. Three street children ran past shouting and the spray spattered his clothes. Waves, they made, as they ran. The youngest, a girl, turned to laugh at Orhan, soaked and bespattered with mud. A bag of sweetmeats drifted past, rocking on the water like a boat. She bent to pick it up, stared at Orhan in challenge and triumph, disappeared off down the street.

He walked on into the Gray Square where the Temple squatted in a pool of silver, its reflection staring back at it, wondering, lost in contemplation of itself and what it was and what it had been. Its knowledge of him beat off it like the rain.

Filthy and soaking with the smell of steam rising from his clothes, he went up the steps and through the high narrow door. The dark was the more terrible, for the lush smell of the world outside. Suddenly cut out, replaced by metal and stone and candle wax and fire. Blood. Under everything, always and forever, blood. The light burned his eyes as he stepped through into the Great Chamber. He knelt a moment before an altar. There was a hush, supplicants and priestesses looking at him, knowing who he was. Our savior, some of they still thought of him. The man who saved the city from something, though no one quite seemed certain any more from what.

"Please tell the Imperial Presence that the Lord of the Rising Sun is here to see him," Orhan commanded a priestess when she approached him. She nodded mutely. He stood and waited, pretending to ignore everyone around him, looking at the walls.

"This way, My Lord," the priestess said. Orhan recognized her as one of those who had arranged the candles he had purchased. A young woman's face beneath her mask, plump and bright-eyed. She directed him to a Temple slave who led him out of the Great Chamber through the small doorway in the east wall that he had often stared at wondering about as a child. Dark and narrow, like the main entrance. Another half-closed mouth. Life and death crushed at him, gnashing silent teeth. How can they stand it to live here? he thought. But they must be used to it, I suppose.

Beyond the dark were antechambers and offices and all the dull, fascinating bureaucracy of the place. Initiated into the secrets of its heart. A little courtyard to provide light and air, with a pool of blue water upon which lilies floated, its tiled floor gleaming, shiny with rain. A short, windowless corridor. A silver gilt door. The slave tapped and opened it and Orhan went in.

"The Lord of the Rising Sun, My Lord."

Tolneurn looked up from his desk. He was a short man, fat around his middle but with a thin face and thin hair; his neck looked too thick for his head. He stood and bowed low to Orhan.

"Lord Emmereth."

Orhan blinked, tried to draw his attention back to the office and the mundane things in hand. God's knives, he was tired. On edge, his mind wandering.

The slave seated himself carefully in the corner, drew out paper and pen and inkstone. Tolneurn stood and waited. Orhan sat with a sigh.

"The new High Priestess—" he began.

"Demerele is learning quickly. As one would expect. Though she still finds some aspects of her role...more difficult than others. She will learn, I am sure." Tolneurn smiled wearily. "The situation is not without precedent. The High Priestess Liseel died of deeping fever before her successor had even been born. The High Priestess Mar—" Tolneurn raised his eyes to Orhan a moment "—the High Priestess Mar fled the Temple in the company of a slave, leaving a girl of twelve to replace her. In both cases, the Temple managed and the world did not end." Tolneurn paused. "After six years here, it sometimes surprises me that such things have happened so rarely."

You've been rehearsing this, haven't you? Orhan thought. Marshaling your arguments, cueing up your lines. Refuse to make this easy for me, just to see me driven to say it. "Indeed. But she cried again, I'm told, after the last sacrifice. Worse than before."

Tolneurn's pale eyes flickered. "She's a child of five."

You bastard. Orhan took a deep breath. "She's the High Priestess of the Lord of Living and Dying. She who brings death to the dying and life to those who wait to be born. People heard her. What do you think they are starting to say?"

"She's a child of five," Tolneurn said again.

Yes. Yes, she is. A child of five. "The city is unsettled enough as it is, with everything that has happened. We cannot afford for people to get alarmed by a child crying. Rumors will start. Have started already. Omens of misfortune. She must be controlled. The crying must stop." His voice sounded mercilessly in his ears. "Will stop, do you understand? Immediately."

Tolneurn picked at things on his desk, looked at his hands. He said slowly, "If people are alarmed, if they see omens of misfortune...Let me be frank with you, My Lord. We had peace, as far as I am aware, before certain things occurred. We had a

High Priestess, and her successor had just been chosen; there was nothing to concern us save the quality of the next grape harvest. I hear the things the people pray for, Lord Emmereth. Every day, I hear them. They do not ask for change. They do not ask for the great days of Empire returned. None of them, not even the High Lords. They do not ask for blood on the streets. If they believe in misfortunes, it is up to the Emperor to reassure them. We are concerned with life and death in this place, not the mundane frivolities that lie between. As the Emperor and the Palace and the Nithque have made abundantly and repeatedly clear. Omens of misfortune are your business, not ours."

The mundane frivolities that lie between! Say that to me again, when the Temple's burning and the Immish are cutting your throat open with a blunt knife. It's blood on the streets I'm trying to prevent. Orhan banged the table, perhaps more violently than he'd intended. "The crying must be stopped! She must learn. As you keep saying, she's a child. A child should be controllable." He sighed and rubbed his hands through his hair. "I know this is difficult. I cannot think what it must be like for her. I do not enjoy this. But I have no other choice. We have no other choice. You must make her learn. Make her understand."

"She wakes screaming every night!" Tolneurn shouted back. "Every single night! Refuses to go to bed! Wets herself! She's a child of five! You cannot make this go on! What do you expect me to do?" He stared at Orhan. "She will go mad soon, Lord Emmereth. She is breaking under this. As any child would. We had to give her keleth seed, the last time, and still she cried and screamed in fear. The medica gives her milk spiked with brandy at night, to try to get her to sleep. So what do you suggest I do, My Lord? Dose her with hatha? Beat her? Promise her a new doll if she can kill a man without crying?"

I don't know. God's knives, I don't know. Hadn't thought of any of this when he was planning it all. Who would? "The High Priestess-that-was—" he began hesitantly.

"The High Priestess-that-was had ten years to prepare herself!

She was a young woman, not a child. And she was half maddened with it herself. And she—" Tolneurn broke off, silence falling in the room, the slave shifting in his seat.

"And she?"

"She...is dead," said Tolneurn.

There was a silence. The slave twitched in his chair.

"You are the Imperial Presence in the Temple," Orhan said. "The hand of the Emperor before God. As you say, such things have happened before. There must be ways to manage this. There are women here who are used to dealing with children, are there not? They must be able to do something."

Tolneurn threw up his hands in despair. "I say again, we have tried everything. I say again, she is five years old."

Orhan rose to his feet. So futile. His anger had come too quickly and now there was nothing he could say. Defeated, as he expected to have been. She's five years old. But he hadn't thought...What did he know about children?

"Your wife is pregnant, I believe," Tolneurn said. "When you are a father, Lord Emmereth, perhaps you will think on this conversation and on what you are expecting a child to do."

Orhan thought: I am expecting a child to do what our God bids us. I am expecting a child to uphold the role for which she was born. I am expecting you to sacrifice one child in order that the city will go on untroubled. One child I do not know and have barely seen.

Orhan thought: at least she's not being burned alive.

Orhan thought: of course it would be different if it was my child.

This whole part of his plan had been a mistake. A disaster, every bit of it. So logical and necessary it had seemed back then. Kill the High Priestess, ensure a child successor weak enough to be controlled. If Great Tanis chose His Beloved through the granting of the red lot, then it was not even impiety, if the red lot was drawn. He'd instructed the old priestess Samnel to place one black lot in the box with the red ones. Great Tanis could have steered the child's hand, if He truly didn't want her.

Though he hadn't told Darath about that detail, for fear he'd reopen his wound with laughing.

You are an Imperial functionary and a man of power, he thought to the image of Tolneurn's pallid, thin face. I know about you: you rose from comparatively little and your father from even less. You've reached dizzy heights, for someone of your background. So there's blood there under your nails somewhere, blood and betrayal and a blind eye. We both know this is grotesque. But that's power. The best either of us can do is feel guilty about it. She's a five-year-old girl. Yes. And how many five-year-old girls die of hunger? Sell themselves for a few coppers? Beg on the streets? What will happen to all these five-year-old girls if the Immish come? Great minds have debated for centuries whether one life ruined is worth half a hundred saved. Far greater minds than yours or mine.

When he left the Temple the rainwater had all but evaporated, leaving dark lines in the cracks between flagstones, muddy detritus in the corners of the streets. The dust was coming back into the air. For a short brief while after a rainstorm everything was clear and brilliant with the sharp bright quality of fresh water. Then the dust came again and the world was softened again, like a woman looking through a gauze veil. *I see you through silk and dreaming*, some poet had written of Sorlost in the driest years. The dust of silk and dreaming, crumbled stone and dried shit. The dust blown in from the desert, golden as pollen, making the city glitter like a seam of quartz in dry rock. Abrading the skin and the heart.

Chapter Forty-Three

Reneneth. The first and last town in Immish, clinging to the scraps of Imperial trade and the needs of those remaining travelers mad or money-crazed enough to risk the old road. Huge, ruined caravanserai lined its streets, the last remnants of its days as a part of the Sekemleth Empire, in the times long since past when Sorlost had been the center of all things, Immish a grassland of barbarians desperate for its briefest glance. Its newer buildings clung to the ruins, short squat houses with sloping roofs and small windows, aping some of the old Sorlostian fashions in their courtyard gardens and broken fountains. But colder and damper, built against the cold and the damp, the stonework less elaborate, the colors more muted, the air heavier, dirtier, without the languid murmur of self-pleasuring decay. An empty place. Unkempt. Sorlost had its dreams of splendor, Alborn its new gaudy flush of power. Reneneth sat deaf and dumb and crippled, like a beggar punished for theft.

Tobias left Rate and Thalia with the wagon, hidden in a knot of trees just outside the walls, and went off to investigate, taking the mage's horse. Thalia sat quietly beside Rate, watching him sharpening his sword. He was tense. She was tense. Guilt burned in her heart.

"You knew him for a few days. Fucked him a few times," said Rate again. "You're better off without him, really you are. Really you are."

"He's going to die," said Thalia. "Isn't he?"

Rate didn't say anything.

"He saved your life," said Thalia.

Rate didn't say anything. Carried on sharpening and sharpening his sword. Stinking of guilt.

"What will happen to him?" asked Thalia.

Rate put down the sword. "Look, just stop thinking about him, girl."

They sat in silence.

"We're selling him to a woman called Landra," said Rate. "Lady Landra Relast, daughter of Denethlen Relast, Lord of Third. Third's one of the Whites, girl. The White Isles? That place he said he'd make you queen of? Yeah? There. I can't say I'm thrilled about it, in some ways, to be entirely honest with you. But...you know..."

Relast...Marith's friend, Thalia remembered, had been called Carin Relast. The friend he'd killed. She shivered. No, she thought. I don't know. I hope I never do.

"She'll kill him," said Rate. "Seems, um, very keen on seeing him dead. Paying us a great deal for him. Awful lot of money, people keep paying us to see people dead. If only I had that much money I could waste it on paying people to kill people for me..."

Silence.

"I didn't know about it," Rate said. Defensive. Raw with guilt. "Tobias didn't tell me. Not until...Until it was done..." He trailed off, started sharpening his sword again. "It's better this way, girl. We all said at the time you were a fool. I should have warned you before you got tangled up with him. You're worth twenty of him. Me and Tobias will look after you, yeah?"

Thalia said nothing. Watched Rate sharpening the sword.

"I'll go and check on him," said Rate awkwardly. "See how he's doing. Get him ready to go." He got up, stamped around to the back of the wagon. Thalia went with him. See him again one last time, she thought. Say good-bye.

Marith was semi-conscious. He attempted to say something,

blinking at them, when he saw Thalia she almost thought that his eyes lit up. But all that came out was an incoherent babble that trailed away into silence. His eyes left her, stared desperately at Rate.

"I haven't got any more," said Rate shortly.

Marith blinked and closed his eyes.

Thalia ducked her head back out of the wagon, shaking. Sick. Guilt. Guilt. Guilt.

"As I said, better off without him," said Rate. He sat down again beside her. "Gods…Stupid boy! What I could have done, in his place…Looks! Wealth! Power! Women like you throwing yourselves at his feet! And he just pissed and puked it all away. Prince Ruin, that Lady Landra called him. Good name, hey?"

"Tobias gave it to him," said Thalia.

"He took it," Rate said.

His face, frightened of her. His face, alight with laughter, bending to kiss her, whispering her name. His face, when the dragon spoke to him, and he had the power in him to rule the world. He had helped her. He had been kind to her. Loved her, even, perhaps.

I know what he is, she thought. But he's a better man, she thought, a better man than he knows. Beautiful. Kind. Powerful. My lover. A king.

Thalia looked at Rate. Rate looked at her. Looked away. Looked back.

Thalia stood up.

The sunlight dimmed. Shadows. The air hissed. She could feel them, the shadows, crawling and calling around the wagon, in the cracks of things, around him.

"Kneel," she said to Rate.

Rate laughed uncertainly.

"Kneel," she said.

Rate laughed again. "I'm not…not…"

"Kneel."

The horses snorted and nickered and stamped, frightened. Clouds over the sun. Something in the air screaming. The shadows, screaming. Triumphant. From the wagon, Marith made a choking weeping sound.

Rate knelt on the ground before her. His face was white. "Don't...Don't...I'm not...Please, girl...Thalia...I didn't want to do it...I didn't know...You're better off..."

The abyss opening beneath him. Death. And life, as terrible. Futile. Darkness. Light. All fear. Fear of living. Fear of dying. Shadows. Death.

Rate whimpered and shivered and buried his face in the ground.

Thalia went round to the back of the wagon. Her lover sat where she had left him, his face lost.

"Marith."

No answer. She fumbled at the rope binding him, got it untied.

"Marith. Get up. Get up."

He raised his head. Blinked at her.

"Get up!"

"Thalia?" His voice was heavy and slurred. "What's...what's happening? My head...hurts..."

"Just get up." She pulled Marith awkwardly to his feet. He almost fell over again, clutching at her for support. "Come on."

"I can't see," Marith said weakly. "I don't...I can't see."

"Just come on. Please." She pushed him violently down the steps of the cart. He fell face first into the grass, lay there mumbling something. Thalia climbed out after him.

Rate was pulling himself to his feet. He saw Marith and shouted. Thalia turned to him, caught between the two. Get Marith upright. Rate's hands went to his sword.

"Get up!" she screamed at Marith.

Rate had his sword out. The blade flashed. He was going to kill them, she thought. Marith was crawling across the ground toward the sword.

She screamed in rage.

Rate froze, his eyes wide as the cartwheels. Terror in his face.

"Kneel," Thalia said to Rate.

He knelt.

"Put the sword down."

He dropped it. Thalia picked it up. She looked at him a long moment.

"I'm sorry," she said to Rate. She stuck the sword into him. He fell down dead in a heap.

I'm sorry, she thought.

She turned to Marith. "Get up."

Marith stared at her.

Why? she thought. Why any of this? Why do they all have to do this to each other? Hurt each other? Fight? What is it they all think they need?

So what to do now? she thought. Looking around. What to do? Get the horses. But Marith was hardly in a fit state to ride a horse. Just walk. Get somewhere. Find some cover. Rest. She began to search through the wagon. Water. Food. Blankets. Had to get going. Tobias could be back any minute. She gathered up a round loaf of dry bread, a water-skin, a blanket. Maybe she could lead a horse? No: Tobias would see. You couldn't hide a horse. She hesitated, then carefully picked up the sword again. He'd need it, surely? If...if they met with trouble. If Tobias found them. If the dragon came back. She held it like a snake, far out in front of her, afraid of it. Its blade was filthy with Rate's blood.

"Come on, Marith." She looked at him, crawling feebly across the ground toward her. He barely knew who she was. Barely knew who he was. And she was going to give him a sword? Water. She should give him water. She knelt down beside him and offered him the water-skin. He drank it gratefully, then coughed and was almost sick. The water seemed to help a little: he managed to get to his feet, looked at her almost coherently, blinking and shaking his head. Looked at Rate's body, then back at her.

Is this really a good idea? she thought. Just leave him. Look at him! Worthless. Pitiful. Damaged. I knew him for a few days and slept with him a couple of times. That's all. I've given him a chance. Now leave him and go.

She could go into the town...Send someone to find him. She could tell people he was sick, needed help. There must be money, in the packs somewhere, she could sell the horses, the sword, get a room in an inn...Her hands were sticky with blood.

Leave him. Go.

Then the sound of horses in the road, coming toward them.

"Run!" Thalia cried out, and then the horsemen were on them. So quick. Everything so quick. So many. They could just be people passing, she thought desperately. Travelers. They might even help them. She could say Marith was sick, that they'd been attacked by bandits, that—

The horses slowed and stopped. Seven. Big, heavy and dark, far larger than the horses they had bought outside Sorlost. Six dark, and one roan.

A woman stared down at them. Elegant, authoritative. Cold. She was dressed in a long blue dress, her hair yellow, framing a square, plain face. She could only be a few years older than Thalia herself, but her face looked terribly weary, as though she had worn and wept herself older than she was. There was anger there, too. Deep, real anger. Hatred. Grief. A keen, bitter joy.

"Prince Ruin," the woman said brightly. "Surround them. Swords." Five dark-colored horses formed a circle, the men mounted on them drawing out long blades. Tobias sat on the roan horse watching it all. He might even look sad.

Caught. Thalia slumped on her feet.

"Landra?" Marith was gazing at the woman, blinking heavily, swaying on his feet. "You were...you were in that city...the one...the one I was just in...or...Are we back home? This isn't home, though..." He rubbed his eyes. Giggled at her. "What are you doing here? You were in that city...that city...We're not at home, are we? I saw you in that city. But we're not in that city... not any more..." He trailed off pathetically, still rubbing at his face. "You were in...that city..."

The woman snorted. "Gods, you're disgusting. Tie him up. And the woman."

One of the men moved to dismount, grinning. There was a shout from Tobias: "No! Not the girl! You said you'd let her go!"

"I have five men at my back," Landra said smoothly. "I'll pay you for them both, don't worry."

"You said you'd let her go!" Tobias shouted again. His hand was on the hilt of his sword. Thalia raised the sword she was holding, her hands trembling. She heard Marith laugh, very far off. The horses nickered and stamped, twisting backward away from her.

"I've already killed Rate," Thalia said, trying to make her voice firm.

"Oh gods." The woman Landra let out a peal of laughter. "Let's all just kill each other, shall we? Put down the sword, girl."

"I'll kill you," Thalia cried out desperately.

"Put it down, Thalia, girl," Tobias said with a sigh. "Five men on horseback. They'd cut you both to pieces before you could move. And I wouldn't help you. Not for him."

Marith stumbled next to her, staring confusedly from one blade to another, trying to make sense of anything.

Tobias was right. No point. No point at all.

Thalia dropped the sword at the woman's feet. A man stepped forward and bound her arms, then swung her up onto one of the horses. Thalia watched blankly as they did the same with Marith, draping him across the saddle like a sack. His head lolled horribly.

"When he's sober enough to walk," Landra said coldly, "he can be led behind." She spurred her horse and the men followed her, riding fast across the flat ground, hooves drumming up the dust. Tobias watched them go. Cold, hard-faced.

She'd killed Rate. For this.

Chapter Forty-Four

We ride through into Reneneth. No one looks at us, even at the two of us bound as prisoners, Marith staggering behind Landra's horse. The streets are filthy and full of rubbish. The air smells of rubbish. A hateful place. Sad and cold. We are taken through into a courtyard that smells of sewage. Taken upstairs to a room that smells the same. He lies on the floor unconscious. Moaning and itching at his face.

I am the Chosen of the Lord of Living and Dying, Great Tanis Who Rules All Things. The holiest woman in the Sekemleth Empire. The holiest woman in all Irlast. I have strength and power and the light within me. I have killed men and women and children. I have seen eyes pure with fear and hope as they look at my face. I have watched them die. I know what death means. What it is. Thus I thought I understood the world. Life and death. The desire to live. Then I ran out into the city and found it was a cruel place. That life is a cruel thing. Then he took me into the world, and showed me it could be beautiful beyond anything I had imagined. Crueler. Sadder. Richer and more alive with hope.

And now it is all taken away.

Great Tanis, Lord of All Things, help me. Please.

Why?

Why must men do these things?

Chapter Forty-Five

"Wakey, wakey. Breakfast fit for a king. Don't say Her Ladyship isn't generous to you." A man. Holding a knife in one hand, a tray in the other. Marith sat up groggily. The smell of warm bread made his stomach roil. He bent forwards and was sick. At least his head didn't seem to be hurting quite so much.

"Charming," the man snarled at him. "Your woman can clean that up for you, Lord Prince. I'm bloody not." He slopped the tray down amusingly close to the pool of vomit. Liquid flashed over the sides of a small jug. Marith stared at it dully. Hopefully.

"Water," the man said.

Thirsty. Dry mouth. Nasty taste like blood. Marith reached over and poured himself a cup of water, gulped it down with shaking hands. The door slammed shut. Creak of a lock. The room was dark again. Closed shutters. Thin veins of gold light shining on the floor. He held out his hand and one shone onto his scabs. A thin crack of sunshine. He moved his hand away. A gold crack on the floor. Dust motes. He moved his hand back.

Your woman? he thought. Looked around him.

The woman sat in the corner, watching him.

"Thalia?" That was her name. Yes. Thalia. She had put her hands on him once, and filled him with warmth and hope.

She came over to him slowly, only a few steps but it seemed

to take forever. She looked like a long-legged bird, a crane or a heron, taking slow awkward steps in an element that was not her own. Sat down beside him, regarded him gravely in the dark. Utter shame filled him. But I had to, he thought. Don't you see? I had to. It's better this way. I thought it would be better for you.

"It's too dark," he said. "I wish...I wish I could see you more clearly. Your face."

She laughed. The room grew darker, shapes looming, darkness pressing at his eyes. Then light flickered. A lamp, high up out of reach on a hook on the wall. Brilliant and alight.

Her face shone in the light. So it had shone once when he first met her. Once? Only so little time ago. An eternity. He stared at her.

"You...how did you do that?" he asked. His voice felt strange from lack of use. His words were still slurred and echoing, as though coming from somewhere deep underground.

A faint smile crossed her face. In the light she was drawn, broken, her eyes exhausted, red with pain. "I have some power of my own, you know."

Marith reached toward her and she drew back from him, her eyes wide as an untamed horse. Everything so awkward between them, the room heavy with tension. Ruined. Like Carin before her. Ruined.

I feel disgusting, Marith thought. I probably look worse than I feel. We were better off in the dark.

Thalia's face shifted as she watched him; she clapped her hands over her mouth and a wild high-pitched laugh burst out of her. She reached out and stroked his matted hair.

I'm sorry, he thought. He had a dull, confused memory of her trying to help him.

"Marith," she said.

"Thank you," he said afterward, looking at the lamp. "For the light." Days, he'd been in the dark. The light anchored him, like a sun. The dark is all there is, he thought. The dark is all that's real. But the illusion of light is beautiful.

Silence. The lamplight flickering.

"I killed Rate," said Thalia. "I killed him. Stabbed him. And now we're here. What are we going to do?"

Marith sighed. Not think about it. Fuck some more. Sleep and hope his hangover went away.

He poured himself another cup of water, surveyed the room. Small. Empty. The windows shuttered and he'd guess high up anyway from the way the sounds drifted in. The door locked and guarded: he could hear the tread of feet outside, never moving far beyond the edges of the doorframe. Boring job, though the sounds of them at it had possibly livened things up a bit. An inn, probably, some kind of lodging house, a stop-over on the way back home to die.

"Very little we can do," he said at last. Thalia looked at him sharply. "What did you expect, beautiful girl? That I'd cut our way out of here? Whistle up a dragon? I haven't even got a sword. And even if I did, my hands are shaking too much to hold one. I'm sorry," he said.

Unanswerable. He pressed his face into her hair. It still had a sweet scent to it, faint and fragile, like dried roses. He nuzzled his head into her shoulder. His head ached.

"Some day soon, we'll sleep in a silver bed with silk curtains, and you'll wear dresses of gold. You can hear the sound of the sea, from my chambers in Malth Elelane. The seabirds calling. The windows face east. Into the rising sun. Into the sea. You'll like the sea."

"Some day soon, we'll be dead."

Marith said nothing, staring up at the light.

"I'm sorry," he said.

A little time later. He'd perhaps been asleep. Footsteps in the corridor, a woman's voice barking out commands.

"Someone's coming," said Thalia. The flame of the lamp flared then died.

The door opened. Landra Relast, accompanied by two men armed with knives. She stood facing them, her eyes cold and sad.

"Prince Ruin."

Marith tried to smile at her. "Hello, Landra."

Her face wrinkled at the vomit on the floor, the filthy state of Marith's clothes. "Your father swore you were dead. If I hadn't been walking down that street and seen you, if I'd been looking the other way... Your father must have been laughing, lying to us about you! Filth and liars, you are. You and your kin. But now I'll kill you as you deserve. The old ways. Slow and painful. So now perhaps I'm glad he lied."

So strained. Trying so, so hard to seem as cruel as she wanted to allow herself to be. You always hated me, thought Marith. The gods only know why. I never did anything to hurt you. As though you hated me because I let Carin ruin me as your father wanted. That's your guilt. If you'd been blind to it. If you'd been looking the other way.

He almost laughed.

Landra said, "We leave in a little while. You"—a glance at Thalia—"will be mounted with one of my guards. You"—another scowl at Marith—"will ride on your own. If your horse moves out of line for anything, the man will cut her throat. Then we'll cut you down. I have five armed men with me. So don't even think it. When we stop for the night, you'll be taken straight upstairs again. If you make any noise, she dies. If you make one move I don't like, she dies. We'll be in Skerneheh soon enough. Then a ship home to Malth Salene. Then you die."

"Going to cut my throat on Carin's grave, are you? Libations to the dead?" A pain stabbing through him as he spoke Carin's name. He scratched angrily at his face. "He understood why I killed him, you know. I saw it in his eyes."

Landra spat at his feet and went out.

Silence.

Thalia said suddenly, "Was she your lover?"

"What?" Marith looked at her in astonishment. "Landra? Gods, no."

"The way you...the way you spoke to her..."

"Jealous?" He tried to laugh. "I've known her since we were children, that's all. The sister of my best and dearest friend. She hates me. Always has. As you may have guessed."

I should have begged her to let Thalia go, he thought.

The door opened again. Two armed men entered, followed by a frightened looking maidservant and then two more men carrying a bathtub.

"You're to be washed and dressed," one of the men said gruffly.

Servants brought cold water in large, heavy buckets. One bucket seemed to have pond weed still floating in it. Charming of Landra to go to so much trouble.

"Strip," the man commanded them once the bath was filled. "Both of you." Thalia went pale. Her hand clutching at Marith's arm.

"Strip." Anger in the man's voice. Hands jerking on swords.

Marith slipped off his filthy shirt. "Better just do as he says." I'll cut his eyes out and make him eat them in front of you, one day, he thought. I swear it. On my name and my blood, I swear it. He stepped into the cold water, shivering. The maidservant scrubbed them both down with lye soap while the men leered at Thalia.

The least erotic bath with a woman he could possibly imagine.

"Now walk." They walked together down the corridor, Thalia in front of him. He tried to take her hand but the men pulled him away from her. And she flinched away from him, too, her face fixed on the floor.

Ruined.

In the courtyard of the inn people bustled around loading baggage onto packhorses. A dog ran underfoot and was kicked away, a small child peeped through a doorway, eyes wide. A guardsman pulled Thalia roughly toward him, lifted her up into the saddle. She looked so fragile, twisted awkwardly between the horse's head and the body of the man who held her. A wounded child or a captive bird.

You did this, a voice echoed in Marith's mind. You. You.

A man led a horse toward him. Marith vaguely recognized him. Mandle. The man's name was Mandle. Landra's man. Carin's, once.

"My Lord Prince." The man's voice gray and icy. "Your horse." His eyes laughed cruelly. Marith turned and saw a broken-down packhorse.

Mandle had seen him crawl out of enough squalor in his time. The man couldn't really think he'd feel insulted by a piss poor horse? He swung himself up into the saddle, which creaked alarmingly under his weight. Mandle mounted up too, moved his own horse until it was pressed up so close Marith could feel the heat coming off it. The packhorse snorted and shied back. Marith struggled to control it, cursing as he ended up scraping his left leg against the stable wall. The dog yelped.

"Keep that bloody horse under control," Mandle shouted at him. "We ride shoulder to shoulder like this all the way to Skerneheh, Prince Ruin. So your bloody horse better get to bloody like it. You too. Horse does that too many times, it dies and you're walking on the end of its rein."

Marith sighed and shifted himself around, trying to get comfortable. The horse snorted again.

Landra swept into the courtyard, her face set hard. She glanced over at Marith, still struggling with the horse, and her lips curled. Her own horse was black, beautifully saddled in rich dark colors, its mane tied with ribbons, bronze ornaments on its head. Her cloak was the brilliant deep green and gold of her family, embroidered in a pattern of swirling flowers. The colors stood out vivid against the glossy black. Beneath it, she wore a traveling dress of dark gray velvet, gold thread work snaking around her breasts and waist.

Thalia should wear a dress like that, a cloak like that.

Marith's horse snorted, the saddle shifting nastily. The party began to move forwards, two armed men in front, then Landra and her two women, three servants leading packhorses, then another three men, Marith in their midst. Thalia let out a cry of terror as the horse she was on started moving. The man she was mounted with cursed and struck her and she cried out again, making the horse shy.

"You shut your mouth," the man shouted. He yanked the bridle hard: the horse shied again, skittered sideways. Thalia swayed in the saddle, crying out and weeping; the man let loose his grip on her and she almost fell, screaming in fear.

"Whoopsa!" Pulled her upright, repeated the trick to the other side. The horse reared up, its hooves treading air, then kicked back, and he almost let go of her again. The men around them cheered. Landra watched impassively, her eyes far away.

"Don't you go falling off there then, girl." The man squeezed her breasts and Marith heard her choke out a cry. "Want me to hold you nice and tight now, do you?"

Mandle grinned at Marith, closing his hand on his arm, nudging the horses ever closer together. "He'll do worse than kill her, Prince Ruin. So you do as you're told." He raised his voice. "That's enough, Jaerl. Don't want your horse wearing itself out."

They rode out through the streets of Reneneth, stinking of rot and rubbish, heavy with flies and filth. The crumbled buildings looked leprous, raddled and eaten away, green and rank with mold. Walls bulged like abscessed wounds. Sickness and death. Sickness and death. I looked forward to reaching this place, Marith thought slowly, trotting on his broken-down horse. I thought there would be freedom here.

Let the fires come. Let the fires come to burn it clean. Faces watched as they passed, this procession of wealth and power and pain. Die, he thought. Every single one of you. Every single one of you who sees me here like this. I'll kill you all. Kill you all and hang your corpses up for the crows, I swear it. On my name and my blood, I swear it. He rubbed at his eyes and wished he was back in the wagon, drugged and uncaring and at peace.

All morning they rode in the hot sunshine. Cooler than the desert, no longer the same dry, desiccating air, but hot and wearing, on a bad horse with no water. The guards passed water-skins among themselves but did not offer them to Marith or Thalia.

The landscape was richer than the country around Sorlost, trees and flowers, fields of crops, orchards growing small wizened apples and glossy black cimma fruit. Goats ran everywhere, bells on their necks clanking; there were cows too, thin and dark-eyed with great heavy horns and grotesquely dangling throats. Little shrines at the roadside: they had left the rule of Great Tanis and come into the domain of smaller deities, the old bitter blind gods of the human world. Jaerl spat for luck as they passed one, a gray hump of rock, formless, but with a gaping mouth like a frog. Flowers had been laid before it, withered now and skeletal.

Around noon they stopped, the women sliding off their horses, chattering excitedly, the servants hurrying to spread rugs, prepare drinks and food. The land around was scrubby woodland, no houses or even chimney smoke visible; they had stopped at the bottom of a shallow incline, where a stream flowed lazily among willow trees. There was a scent of mint, and a brackishness from the water over it, rancid-sweet. Marith looked at the water and the willow trees and saw Thalia looking back at him, eyes filled with pain.

One brief moment of his life, brilliant as birdsong. Only a few days, since he had last sat beneath a willow tree beside a stream.

Mandle jerked his arm, pointing at a patch of rough ground away from the women, where the men sat with drawn swords. "Dismount, Prince Ruin. Sit down on that stone and don't move." He fingered the hilt of his own sword, a shining thing of yellowed metal, green enamel on the hilt. "Don't speak, either."

Jaerl pulled Thalia down and pushed her to sitting a little way away from him. She moved stiffly, hunched and bent over, shaking. She looked like the little gray hump of rock they had passed that was a god. Formless. Worn to nothing. Empty.

"I said, want a drink, Prince Ruin?" Marith blinked, the sunlight hurting his eyes. Mandle's face swam before him. He reached up gratefully, took the skin the man offered, taking a long drink.

Not water. Spirits of some kind, strong and harsh. He gulped it down, tears streaming down his face. When they came to remount he staggered, barely able to stand, fell in the dust and lay there dizzy until they hauled him up. Sat slumped in his saddle, face lolling forward into the horse's filthy, matted mane. The men laughed at him, the sound swirling around him like bells.

By the time they stopped again he had sobered a bit, his mouth tasting filthy, bile in his throat. He almost fell from his horse, begged for water in a cracked voice, then begged for more of whatever they'd given him before. They laughed at him again and refused. And then he was remounted, and they were going on, and evening was coming, the first stars visible in the deep blue of the sky.

They stopped for the night in another caravan inn, smaller than that in Reneneth but better kept, cleaner with a smell of warm brick and horse manure rather than decay and rotted stone. Lamps flickered in the doorway. A plump young innkeep's wife, pinkcheeked and smiling, her smile fading as Marith and Thalia were hurried past her up creaking stairs into a room at the very top of the house.

"Don't want no trouble," Marith heard her protest in the strong, ugly accent of Immish.

"And you'll get none, you shut your mouth and close your eyes," someone growled back. Then Mandle's voice, kinder and softer, lilting with its Whites accent that made Marith almost weep: "They'll be no trouble, mistress. A bad thing, he is. Just leave him be. Leave them both be."

Another small room. Another locked door. No shutters, this time, just a window too small and high up to climb out of. Water, and bread, and cheese. A tiny candle in a clay dish. Not the dark again. He was grateful for that, at least. Not having to see her light. He didn't want to see her light. It would burn him, now. His eyes could no longer bear it.

"Marith?" Thalia sat on the bed and looked at him. Pity, and anger, and something else. She placed her hands on his forehead. Cool hands. Soft. Carin used to do that, too. It helped, sometimes.

Take things away. Things he didn't want. Things he couldn't stop. Good things, that hurt him.

"I could try..." She looked so weary. "I could try to put the fear on them. When they come next with water, or to check. If you...If you killed them. We could maybe run..."

"Run where? There's nowhere to go. I can't kill everyone in the place."

Maybe I could, he thought. Maybe it would be fun to try... Kill them all and burn the inn down around them, feeding the flames with human fat. His mouth still tasted of dust. His head hurt like he was dying. He was so tired. Not tonight. Tonight he would sleep. He put his arms around Thalia and kissed her. She shuddered and then embraced him back. Their shadows danced on the wall behind them. Moonlight came in at the window, silver and clean. Even when the candle died, there was a little light.

The next day the same, riding slumped in the saddle, jerking uncomfortably on the broken-down horse. They didn't give him alcohol again, just warmish water and dry bread. He ate and drank mechanically, rode mechanically, hoped against hope every time they gave him water that it was something else. In the night, locked together in a bedroom, he drew Thalia into his arms and felt briefly that there might be some kindness in the world. She made the light, once or twice, but it burned him so that he cried out and hid his eyes from her. They did not speak.

Only ten days, it was, he realized later. Only ten days, from Reneneth to Skerneheh. It felt like an eternity. And like no time at all. No rhythm, no sense, no awareness of anything. Just light, too bright to bear, and dark again, and Thalia's hands on his face.

They had come to a stretch of forest, ash and elm and holm oak, the land rising into hills that met the sea coast in a jumble of black cliffs. A few hours outside Skerneheh, but wild country, the woods dank and untouched. Too steep for habitation, hard rock jutting up through the soil. Few birds but crows.

The horses drew close together, nickering edgily. Mandle called out to the men to keep wary, told Landra and the other women to keep close. Hands rested on sword hilts. Going slowly, uphill. Hanging silence.

A scream of animal pain. A horse reared up, treading the air, its eyes wild. An arrow in the curved lines of its throat. White feathers crawling with lice. The horse staggered and fell sideways with a crash, bringing its rider down with it.

Another arrow grazed Mandle's shoulder. Another, from the other side of the road, struck one of the servants in the neck. He fell forwards slowly, clawing at Landra's horse as he died.

"Bandits!" Mandle shouted. One of the women screamed, her mount rearing as she let go of its reins. Marith's horse shrieked and collided with the one next to it, almost knocking both riders to the ground.

Ten armed men burst out of the trees on either side of them.

The guardsmen moved forward. Trying to surround the women. Landra pulled her horse around. She drew out a long knife. Mandle's gaze flicked from Marith to Landra and back again. Thalia was seated on Jaerl's horse, in front of Jaerl's body like a shield, getting in the way of his sword arm. Marith looked back at Mandle for a moment, their eyes meeting.

Keep her alive. Please.

Then the killing began.

Everything was hacking and stabbing, the packhorses frantic in the middle of it, one of the women still screaming on and on. Marith kicked wildly at one of the bandits coming toward him, missing entirely, wrestling to get his horse to move. They should have such an advantage, mounted men defending against foot, but the road here was narrow, rough, pot-holed, sloping steeply up. Everything a confusion, nowhere to move, no space, men ducking under the horses' heads, the injured horse kicking and dying, two servants dead and underfoot, attackers, defenders, defended all caught up together. And he was unarmed, against a heavy broadsword that lashed out at his horse's flanks.

Mandle skewered one, twisted round to block another coming up on Landra. Landra's knife was bloody: a large dark-bearded man grabbed at her bridle and she stabbed his hand, hard and vicious, pulled her horse back round to crash into him as he leaped back. Two closed in on Jaerl. Jaerl's horse reared, he brought it forward a few paces, swinging with his sword, missing one. The other jumped out of the way of kicking hooves, came in again on Jaerl's left where Thalia was between him and Jaerl's blade. Oh gods and demons, Thalia! Thalia! Jaerl wheeled the horse, kicked at his attacker, then pushed Thalia from the saddle. She screamed as she fell, the horse's hooves stamping around her. Jaerl's sword coming down at the bandit almost on top of her.

Marith charged toward them, riding down another bandit who turned too late to avoid the horse crashing into him. His horse pulled up at the impact, putting its left foreleg into a hole and jerking so hard Marith was nearly thrown off. He half fell, half slid from the saddle, shoving his way through the chaos of bodies, stumbling toward her. Everything was roaring in his ears and his eyes.

Thalia was already pulling herself to her feet when he reached her. "Get behind me," he shouted to her, though there was no in front or behind, just men and horses turning and turning at each other. Jaerl's horse almost struck them. Thalia had to pull him backward as a sword stroke came down at him. The sword came again and he tried to strike it away with his hand. Mandle plunged toward them, smashing into the man's arm with his own sword. The bandit reeled backward, his arm hanging limp and useless, stumbled and crashed down into Marith. The feel of the blood on his skin, beautiful as water. Like the rain in the desert. Like the sea on a hot summer day. Another bandit came at them, Landra seemed to be shouting something, Thalia dragged at his arm.

Then suddenly the road was empty. Five bandits dead in the fallen leaves and dirt. Marith sank down exhaustedly. His head rang like fire.

"Gods and demons." Mandle was staring around at the ruins.

Two dead horses. Two dead servants. One dead guardsman. "Were they bloody demented?"

"Starving," said Jaerl. "They were bloody starving. Poor country, round here." He gestured at the dark trees. "Can't really grow much."

"Could have just waited a while longer and died of hunger, then."

"Really?" Jaerl spat at one of corpses. "That what you'd do, is it? You'll see Skerneheh later, you'll understand."

Mandle shrugged. "Get the bodies covered over and we'll be out of here. Quickly, mind."

Jaerl looked over at the body of his fellow guardsman, and for a moment Marith wondered if he was going to object, demand a proper burial for the man. That sort of thing seemed to matter to these hardened killing types. Got so misty-eyed and miserable over a bloody corpse. Although, if it was about the only thing one had to look forward to...

Not entirely fair. He'd felt moved himself, by Alxine's death. Burying him had seemed necessary. It was hardly this man's fault, if the only thing he'd had in the world to live by had been a good sword arm. Now he was going to end up dumped behind a tree with a handful of leaf mold over him until foxes and wildcats ripped him apart. Nobody would know he'd lived at all.

The best way to avoid dying, he thought then, is not to live.

"You can help move the bodies, Prince Ruin," Mandle said gruffly at him. Marith almost jumped, his hands shaking again. Scratched painfully at his face.

"I—"

"You nothing. Get moving and drag them. That tree there'll do."

Marith bent and pulled awkwardly at one of the bandit's ankles. Hard, heavy work, pulling the corpse over the rough road and into the undergrowth. Dead eyes looked up at him. Was this the one who had died almost in his arms? His whole body was shaking by the time he returned.

"Clearing up the mess is harder than making it, you see, Prince Ruin?"

I see, he thought dully. His shirt was filthy with blood. The feel of it. The look in the eyes as men died.

It was dusk when they arrived in Skerneheh. A small city or a large town, hugging the mouth of the River Skaer, set within a steep valley so that it seemed hemmed in with dank hills, black cliffs rising sharply from either side of the harbor. A poor city, as Reneneth had been a poor town. Left behind by Immish's growing power and glory. The men traded in salt fish and ambergris, bred with the things living in the cold waters, seemed half fish themselves with bulging eyes and thick mouths that closed on their words.

He'd spent several months here, dead drunk and tearing himself apart with hatha, Carin's blood still ground in under his nails. He wondered if he could find the inn. Very near the harbor wall: he'd been just about able to make it that far, when they threw him off the ship. It had stunk of dog shit. The innkeep had let him sleep in the doorway, when he ran out of coin for a room.

At the gates, the same questions, the same answers, the same bored soldiers, three days' stubble, breath reeking of stale food. Marith had wondered if there might be trouble, questioning, eyebrows raised at him and at Thalia, so obviously prisoners. I could shout, he thought. Protest that they're holding me captive. Beg them to help me…Landra smiled her cold smile at them, rich and plain, shining with gold, and they waved them through untroubled, into narrow cobbled streets leading down toward the sea. The air smelled of salt and fish and seaweed; Marith sighed as he breathed it in. The water was a thin dark line, white crests just visible, a few boats tiny on the horizon. It came to him suddenly that Thalia had never before seen the sea, that he'd told her he'd show it to her, show her how beautiful it was, how terrible, ever changing yet ever the same. After the empty pain of the last few days, he felt a brilliant, glittering joy at the thought of it.

They rode through the gates down narrow streets. Turned away from the sea.

Back again up to a room in an inn, a locked door, the smell

of alcohol maddening as it drifted up. Seagulls began to scream outside their window, fighting over something. Thalia jumped at the sound. He'd always liked it, painful and harsh and lonely. Lonely things, seagulls. Vicious. And then to see them fly...Almost like dragons, they were, soaring out over the sea.

The next morning broke damp and sluggish. A mist rolling in. Tiny droplets of water beaded Thalia's hair. Her eyes radiantly blue against a gray world. She looked around her curiously, shivering. She'd never seen drizzle and mist and damp before, Marith realized. Her face frowned like a wet cat. Perhaps she wouldn't like the sea, after all. It occurred to him that she might get seasick.

They rode slowly down to the harbor in the pale dawn light, the streets still largely silent. The gulls wheeled and screamed overhead. Toward the harbor, the streets became busier, night fishing boats coming in with their catch, trades being made. A whaling ship had arrived in the night, the vast carcass floating alongside it, belly-up. Blood still eddied from the wounds hacked in its sides. Ambergris and oil and blubber and baleen and flesh and bone. A fortune in its hulking corpse.

A man was waiting on the quayside, well-dressed but weather-stained. Their ship's captain. Dark red hair, a red beard grizzled with damp, his leather jerkin bright red and yellow, the flashy colors such men seemed to like. Landra drew forwards, Mandle a few paces behind her. They dismounted and walked up to him. He bowed his head.

"My Lady. The ship's ready, set to sail." The captain spoke in Pernish, with the Islands accent. From Third. One of Lord Relast's ships, probably, abandoning whatever had been its business at Landra's command.

"Her name?"

"*Brightwatch*, My Lady. Yonder." He gestured at the small ship bobbing out beyond the breakwater, yellow sails gleaming.

"A good name," Landra said. Marith, craning his head, saw

that the figurehead was a woman holding a sunburst, golden hair and golden rays. He frowned.

The captain shifted, looked at Marith. "That him, then, is it? The one who—" He broke off. "Him? But—That's—He's—" His face went white and puffy, grub-like. "Gods and demons, my lady. I'm not taking him, like that. He's dead...And the king..." He drew himself up a little, trying to look anything less than terrified. "Whatever is going on here, My Lady, I want no part in it."

"The king will never know," Landra said savagely. "And you do not serve the king. You serve me. And whoever he might resemble, he is a nameless peasant boy you never saw before and will never see again. Understand?"

"I don't serve you, My Lady, I serve your Lord father. And he serves the king." The captain bowed his head weakly. "If you're sure and certain, My Lady..."

"Sure and certain," Landra said in a bitter voice. "Now get him on board."

Down narrow slippery steps into a rowing boat, out across to the *Brightwatch*. Only Mandle and the two women remained with them. The remaining servant and the guardsmen, hired men, had been paid off and left at the inn. Marith feared for a moment that Thalia would scream again, feeling the motion of the boat under her, but she sat immobile, her eyes blank. He trailed his hand over the side, then licked the salt water. Harsh and stinging in his mouth. A reminder that he was alive.

The seagulls screamed overhead, circling the boat.

Chapter Forty-Six

That fucking poisonous bastard Marith. That sick, vile, diseased, degenerate fucking bastard shit. Gods and demons, he should have knifed him when he had the chance. Gods and demons and piss, he should have stuck with him and held out for the money the boy had offered him.

In an inn near the harbor where the air stank of rotten fish and whale's blood, Tobias sat at a table in the furthest corner and watched from the window as the *Brightwatch* set sail.

The inn wasn't a bad one, as such places went. The bedding wasn't too filthy, the food was passably edible and the beer was watered down but not actually rancid. He'd stayed in worse, just about. Could have stayed in a lot better, talents and thalers burning a hole in the leather pouch at his waist. It was greasy from where he kept grasping it to check it was still there.

A lot of gold. An awful lot of gold. You could buy a village with that much gold. He felt almost too frightened to spend it.

The serving girl brought him barley flatcakes and some smoked fish. Not bad, actually. When he had finished, he walked out to the quayside, stood for a while watching the ships on the water. The sun was beginning to break through the clouds, burning off the sea mist, making the sea sparkle far out beyond the harbor wall. White caps on the waves. Tobias walked down among the men busy and groaning on the wet stones, hauling great boxes of silver-green fish.

"I'm looking for a ship going to the Whites," he said.

One of the men blinked at him with bulbous eyes, silver-green like the fish. "The Whites? You missed one." He shrugged in the direction of the open sea. "Gone." The man's voice was hoarse, harsh as the sea grating on pebbles. Echoing underneath. His hands were crabbed and too dry-looking. Soaked too long in the water. Thick yellow nails split and softened like wet wood.

"Another likely?"

"Always another likely."

"Soon?"

"Soon enough, I should think."

Bet you're a barrel of laughs after a few drinks. "Where," Tobias said carefully, "is the next ship that's going to the Whites?"

"That one." The man pointed slowly to a low, dark-colored ship lying out in the water, its mast hung with a brilliant green sail. "*Glasswater*, she's called. Come from Morr Town. Going back to Morr Town. Brought tin and brightstone. Bringing back gods know what."

Tobias nodded. Odd things, Illyn Altrersyr was said to like. Well, but the last ship to have left here for the White bore as its cargo a dead man. Couldn't be any stranger. He thanked the man, gave him a copper penny and walked back down the quayside toward his inn.

"*Glasswater*," he said to the serving girl. "Know any of her crew?"

The girl looked thoughtful. "No. Can't say I do."

Tobias wandered out again onto the quay, watched men hauling boxes and coiling great twists of pitch-stained rope. An utter mystery to him, the ways of sailors and seafarers. The whaling ship was a mass of activity, figures crawling over the vast corpse, comically tiny in comparison, stained and greasy with blood and fat. A lovely image of human frailty and deathlust: it's fucking huge, so let's fucking kill it. They used long-hooked poles to drag the body toward a slipway, grunting and gasping, a chorus of curses as the tail slipped sideways in a great spray of bloody water, a howl of pain and panic as a pole jerked and knocked one of the men off balance. He teetered for a moment, then fell heavily, thrashing in the water between the dead whale and the wall of the quay. One of his colleagues hauled him out, swearing. The rest ignored him, straining at their work, inching the corpse painfully up the smooth stone. Tobias stared at it amazed as it emerged. Bigger than a house. Bigger than a bloody dragon. The blank dead eyes glossy, like dark polished bronze. The vast mouth slightly open. Scar tissue whorled on its flanks. Stranger than a bloody dragon too, he thought. The whalers set at it with saws, hacking and cleaving. Like it was nothing unusual. The whole harbor stank of blood and flesh. Men taking a city. Men storming a fortress. The head section came away to cheers. They were crawling inside it, cutting it to pieces from the inside out. The smell of its body, innards and fat. What the fuck do you do with several miles of whale intestine? A drill for the head, to get at the oil inside. Something that might be the liver, dark red, velvety, a sheen on it like a woman's lips.

Enough watching. Mesmerizing though the spectacle was, he needed to get on.

Tobias moved up the quay, eyeing the men milling around. The whale had attracted quite a crowd of onlookers. He stopped next to a tall man with a ragged black beard.

"Quite a sight." The man nodded. "Know any of the crew from the *Glasswater*?" The direct approach.

"The *Glasswater*?" Another thoughtful pause. You're going to say no, aren't you? Tobias thought gloomily. "From her meself, as it happens. Looking for passage to the Whites, are you?"

"Could be."

"The captain's over yonder, seeing to supplies. Out of the stink. It'll cost you, mind."

"Assumed as much." He probably had enough money to buy the bloody boat. Tobias followed the sailor toward a more expensive inn, set back from the seafront, looking away from the sea up toward the town. Houses. Shops. Taverns. Dogs and horses and pigeons and even the odd woman. Last thing a rich sailor wants is a sea view. Probably breathed in the smell of horse shit from the stables and felt jubilation that it wasn't fish and salt.

Two hours later, Tobias was packing up his gear in preparation to sail. He'd not been on a ship in a long time. Several years. Really didn't trust boats, there being nowhere to run to if and when things went to shit.

He carefully touched the purse of money secured inside his shirt. Talents and thalers clinked. You don't need to do this, he thought. The amount of money he had, he could just head off to Alborn, live a quiet life with a couple of rooms and a girl to clean them. Eat fried pig every morning and drink beer in the afternoon with the sun setting warm on his face. Never do anything again, apart from get fat and lazy and pleasantly weak in the arms and legs. Wear soft cloth and sandals. Buy the girl a pretty dress and a necklace to match.

Marith had made that decision, for about five heartbeats, a thousand years ago and more by a riverbank. He'd seen it in the boy's face, that one moment. Just be alive. Just live, and feel contented in it. Sunshine. Trees. Birdsong. The lovely way a woman's hips moved as she walked. Not much else one needed in life. A lot more than most people had.

'Cause that had all worked out so bloody well, hadn't it?

He paid the innkeep and went to meet his ship. The tide had come in: they'd brought the *Glasswater* into the harbor, moored up on the quay as far as possible from the collapsing bulk of the whale, now a ruined mass like the skeleton of a burned building. The water and the air churned with gulls and fish come to glut themselves.

The dark-bearded sailor was standing on the quay beside the walkway—plank, wasn't it?—onto the ship. "Astonishing, don't you think?" he said conversationally, watching Tobias's eyes on the butchery.

"It's...impressive, I'll grant you."

The sailor grinned. "But lucrative. Whale's our return cargo, tasty delicacies for the rich folk of Morr Town. Cost what we brought and more besides, and weighs less. Stinks worse, though. You'll be Tobias, then?"

Tobias nodded.

"Yartek." The man nodded in turn. "Set? We sail as soon as the tide turns. Get away from this."

He had the soft, feathery Pernish of the Whites. Tobias could almost imagine him reciting poetry alongside Prince Fucking Bastard and Corruption and Ruin. Mustn't tar a whole kingdom with assumptions though. Just because their ruling family were all sick in the head. The ship looked clean and well-kept, probably fast from her shape and large sail, funny smell hanging about her from the cargo but the last sea journey he'd made had been far worse. Felt almost hopeful as they sailed out into the light and the water, leaving the dead and betrayed and backstabbed behind.

Paying through the nose for passage turned out to mean almost getting his throat cut the first night. Two of them, big men with short ragged beards like Yartek's. One clamped his hand over Tobias's mouth, the other stuck a knife blade over his windpipe. Tobias, awake and half expecting it, slapped his arms up and got the knife wielder in the chest. Clearly could tar a whole kingdom. His assailant jerked and whacked his head on the ceiling of the tiny cubbyhole thing serving as Tobias's berth. What did they take him for, an idiot?

The thump and Tobias's enraged roar must have woken half the ship. Which could be either very good or very, very bad. Tobias followed up by punching knifeman hard in the face before sliding hurriedly out of the bunk. Extremely fortuitously, he landed on knifeman's bare foot. Handclamper seemed to be trying to retreat in a hurry. In the light of a rancid lantern, it appeared to be Yartek. Tobias contemplated going after him too, but settled on punching knifeman in the face again. There was a satisfying crunch of nose. A warm, sticky feeling on Tobias's hand.

Two other sailors appeared, drawn by the noise.

"What the fuck?" someone started shouting. Knifeman was reeling around, clutching his face. Tobias kicked him between the legs, whereupon he collapsed in a heap. Weak as piss, these boys. Weak as bloody piss.

"Tried to fucking knife me," he explained to no one and everyone. "Yartek and this guy."

The crew looked down at their fallen comrade, rolling around on the floor clutching his manhood, blood running out of his nose.

"Didn't do it very well," the shorter one said.

"No." Tobias tried to look heroically shocked and wounded. "They didn't."

"Excitement over then," the short sailor said. "Back to bed, lads. Including you, Leg. Try not to get too much blood on the deck."

Gods, this lot made Skie look overemotional. Tobias lay awake in his cubbyhole fingering his sword and listening to the sounds of the ship moving around him.

A strange piping sound woke him from a fitful dream about shadowy creatures with toothless, bulbous mouths. Morning roll-call, he realized after a moment. The night crew giving way to the day. Crawled groggily out of his bunk, strapped his sword back onto his belt then scrambled out onto the deck. It was early morning, gray and cold, rot-colored clouds massing ominously on the horizon before them. That feel in the air of held calm before a storm. Pressure, like he'd last felt staring into Marith's ruined burned-out eyes. Mercenaries were almost as good weather readers as sailors, for similar although perhaps slightly less urgent reasons. Tobias shivered. He'd rather have had his throat cut quietly than drown.

Thinking of which, there was Yartek, eyeing him nervously, a bruise on his cheek. I don't even remember hitting him, Tobias thought. Oh, no, wait, I think he whacked his head on something running away. He waved cheerfully. Yartek looked hastily away and then back at him with a humiliated face.

"Leg" was about, too, his nose a glorious mass of black, blue and crimson looking rather like embroidery on a woman's dress. He and Yartek seemed to be avoiding each other. Tobias sauntered over to him.

"Make a habit of trying to kill your passengers, do you?"

"Piss off and fuck yourself." The comic sound of the voice through the broken nose was most pleasing.

"Try it again, I'll kill you." Tobias touched the hilt of his sword.

Leg jerked his head at the clouds. "To be honest, if she's as bad as she looks, in a few hours' time you'll be wishing I'd managed it."

Tobias looked at the clouds again, and at the sheer bare cliffs of the Immish coastline looming away on their left. We've been at sea less than a full day. Overnight, basically. And we're possibly about to die within sight of land. Like a pitched battle against impossible and overwhelming odds, only without the ever-appealing option of desertion. Curse Marith-damned-Altrersyr for the thousand-and-first time.

The storm hit sometime after midday. Not that it was possible to judge midday, the sky being so dark by then that it might as well have been twilight. *Sesere*-whateveritis, thought Tobias. Night comes. We survive. It had always struck him as a particularly low-aspiration credo, as beliefs went.

The waves were getting bigger and bigger. The wind was rising, cracking in the sails, hurting the eyes. No rain, but you could see it moving in, a dark curtain in front of them, the sound of it beating on the sea loud as a living thing. Sailors scrambled around the deck and rigging, shouting. Tobias and the two other passengers watched them from the pitiful lack of shelter provided by the bunk huts on the deck. The only other place to go was down below into the hold, which would be worse, an utter surrender of control to the elements. I could have been killed by a dragon, Tobias thought. I will not die already underwater in a coffin stinking of rotted whale fat.

"Get out of the bloody way!" Yartek screamed at them, running past with a coil of rope. He seemed to be instrumental in doing something to the sail, so Tobias felt some relief he hadn't had it in him to draw his sword last night.

"One day out," the woman beside him, Raeta, he thought her name was, muttered. "Captain should just have turned back at first light."

"Can't just turn back," the third and richest-looking passenger said darkly. "If merchant ships turned back every time the weather got up, nothing would ever sail."

Acceptable added cost of trade goods. Until it was your fucking ship.

The rain hit, then, sudden and painful, a great roar of noise as it struck the deck and the canvas of the sail. The sea seemed to boil under the force of it.

"I think we should get under cover," the rich man said. The ship juddered violently. Huge waves, their surface pitted from the raindrops, churning up the ship; the sky now dark as coal fires, dull lights flickering across the clouds. Lightning and storm spirits shrieking and riding the winds. Green-white fingers traced through the rigging, whipping and probing at rope and canvas and men's hands. Frantic blowing of a whistle. A man screamed and fell. Blood on his mouth like fine long claws. The snap of a rope, more screams as the released tension caused it to rebound and strike like a snake. More men falling. Men rushing across the deck, calling out orders, the whistle blowing.

"We should go below," said the woman Raeta. "Shelter in the hold."

I'm not going down there, thought Tobias. I'm not dying in the bloody dark in a bloody box. I'm not breathing in whale rot and bilge water as my last breath of air before my lungs give out.

"Below," Raeta said, pulling his hand. "Come on, you fool." He could almost see the figures in the air, circling and dancing, tearing with teeth and nails. Beautiful, they were said to be.

"Get out of the fucking way!" a sailor shouted at them. Possibly Yartek. The deck tipped suddenly, sending Tobias staggering. Salt water hit him in the face hard as a punch, tasting like blood, like a shock going through him. Raeta lurched into his arms, their heads bashing together. He grabbed at her as the ship tilted again in the other direction, riding up on a wave, spinning in the wind. The sail screamed as they ripped around. Another rope broke, lashing across the deck. Green-white hands snapping it like a whip. A wave crashed onto the deck and suddenly Tobias was half-floating in hissing foam. Gods it was so fucking cold. Things like long, long fingers pulled at his legs, tangled him, wrapped themselves in knots around him, sank into his skin through his clothes.

"Just get below!" Tobias found himself crashing through the hatch into the hold. Raeta fell on top of him. They slithered down the ladder and ended up in a soaked heap on the floor. It was very dark, water running in rivulets around them. Rats running around them too.

"Close the hatch!" someone yelled. Tobias, half-stunned, dragged himself back up the ladder. Another surge of water hit him in the face as he struggled and finally pulled it shut. He fell down again gasping. Never felt so bloody useless. Like some knock-kneed recruit dropping his sword and bearing his neck for a kill stroke when he bent to pick it up.

"Thank you," he grunted at Raeta. In the dark she was nothing more than a shape. He remembered yellow hair around a clear face.

"We'll probably still drown," she said brightly.

"No." Soaking wet and humiliated, he felt more confident. Couldn't hear the wind screaming, see the things in the sky. Just a storm. Just weather. Ships sailed through wind and rain all the time. "Blow out soon enough."

The ship tipped and jerked. Thrashing on the water. It reminded Tobias of a body shuddering as it died. He crawled a little way and found a large barrel to lean against. The woman crawled next to him.

"You think?" She was speaking Immish, but her accent and her dress were from the Whites. So might be able to tell him something useful about Morr Town and Seneth. Unusual, a woman traveling alone. And as a passenger on a merchant ship. Interested him as a result, despite himself.

"Going to Morr Town?" he asked her.

"Just sit in the dark and chat until we die, shall we?" Raeta laughed. "I'm going to Turn, on Fealene Isle. But fewer boats go there."

An awkward pause, the ship lurching. Crash of water dripping in through the cracks in the deck.

"This is the worst place to encounter a storm," Raeta said. "Our bad luck. Even half a day further on, we could have put in at Lanth or Immerlas. Polle Island, even. But here...If we're driven onto the cliffs, we'll be smashed apart."

"Know the journey well, then?"

"Done it once or twice. Been through storms once or twice."

"Had the crew try to slit your throat once or twice?"

"Hah. No." Tobias could hear her grin in the dark. "I'm the captain's sister."

That was...interesting. "Know if they're going to try to slit mine again, then?"

"If we survive this, good chance of it." She sucked in a breath, knocked against Tobias as the ship rolled. "You did maybe help me a bit when we were slipping all over the place up there. And gave Leg a good walloping. Tell you what, you give me one of those nice big gold coins you've got there, I'll tell my brother to leave you alone."

"You don't think if you let me live I might start telling people all over Morr Town what it is you get up to on this ship of an evening?"

Tobias heard her grin again, wider. Somehow saw her mouth with gleaming smiling teeth. "And who's going to believe you? My brother sells cheap, buys expensive. Makes a bit extra in creative ways. Good for everyone. You know all that anyway. Wouldn't bother trying to tell. And it's nothing to do with me, either. I'm just hitching a lift to visit our old mother back home on Fealene."

"How about you tell your brother to have our fellow passenger knifed instead, I tell him to rest easy tonight and then forget I ever met him, then we all enjoy the rest of the voyage in peace?"

"I'll think about it." Raeta stretched in the dark. "You've got the smell of money about you, Tobias. Look of hate about you, too. Blood on your hands. What you going to Seneth for, then, with no baggage but a sword and a bag of gold round your neck?"

"Witch woman, now, are you?"

"Ha." She snorted through her nose like a horse. "I can smell blood and gold on a man. See it in his face. Your future's a nasty thing, Tobias. Don't need to be a witch to see that."

"My past's been a nasty thing. My present's not looking particularly great right now either. And blood and gold smells a hell of a lot better than whale shit and salt."

"Indeed and so." She kissed his cheek. Not sexual: like a mother kissing a clever child. Her lips were hot and dry on Tobias's skin. He shivered. "I will tell my brother to let you live, I think."

They lapsed into silence, the storm rising to such a pitch their voices would have been lost had they tried to talk. The ship creaked and shifted, rose and fell. Thank all the gods the cargo seemed securely tied down. Occasional sounds like something scraping against the hull. Hours, it seemed, there in the dark. No longer any idea whether it was day or night, how much time had passed. We could be dead and drowned and in an afterlife, Tobias thought. Ghosts or something, floating on a ghost sea.

You're going as mad as the boy, he thought then. What the fuck are you thinking? There isn't a bloody afterlife. Not for Amrath, not for Marith and certainly not for you. We're just lumps of meat. We just die. And we're not dead.

He really needed a piss and a crap, in fact. That proved he was still alive in itself: in no religion or folk-tale, anywhere, ever, did the dead need a crap. His legs were feeling nasty and cramped too. If he crawled to the other side of the hold behind some more barrels, would Raeta somehow not notice? Between the roar of the storm and the stink of whale, probably not...

"Gods, that smells disgusting!" Raeta shouted a very short while later. "Amrath and Eltheia, man, couldn't you just wait?"

"No." Tobias made his way back to her, face blazing with humiliation. "I bloody couldn't."

"You'll have to clean it up as soon as the weather drops."

"What do you think I am?" A soldier never soiled a camp. Knew too well the consequences of uncleanliness.

"A man who shits on the floor?" Raeta said sweetly.

The ship lurched again, with an ominous creak of rope as the cargo shifted. We'll be buggered if the barrels start moving, Tobias thought. Crushed to death by whale excretion and my own shit. Poetic, like. Another shower of water streamed down through the closed hatchway. We seem to be losing, Tobias thought. Tapping on the hull, scratching like hard, long fingernails. Things in the air. Things in the water. And those black cliffs somewhere off the port bow, running straight down into the sea sharp as knapped flint.

He was hungry, too. Thirsty. Scared. Bored. It was strange, not being part of it. Sitting down there with no idea what was going on or whether things were swinging their way whilst others fought the great fight. So many years of being in charge, sending out orders, knowing how things were falling, seeing it all in his mind. This powerlessness was so...dull. Didn't feel like himself. Didn't feel like any of this was really happening. Maybe that's what fucks the high lords so badly, he thought. They just sit there, not really a part of anything. So powerful they're kind of powerless, 'cause they don't actually do any of it. Nothing's real. They're not real. Everything's shadows to them, themselves included. Don't really exist like we do, in the solid world of shit and piss and blood that means you're alive. No action on the world.

"Got anything to drink?" he asked Raeta.

"Should be water in some of the barrels," she said. "No idea which, without light, so you'd have to chance it and hope it isn't whale oil..."

Oh, they thought they did things. Thought they changed the world, trampled on it, built great works and tore them down. Thought they pissed on the common folk and then made them smile in gratitude. But they were ghosts, in the end. Didn't do anything with their own hands, not so as they could say "that was me." Just words, they were. Like gods indeed, in that respect: all their power depended on someone else to do all the heavy lifting. If someone some day said "no", they'd be buggered. Just be left to shout louder and end up either begging or sticking them with a knife.

"Got anything to eat?" he asked Raeta.

"Should be hard tack and salt meat in some of the barrels," she said.

The motion of the ship began to calm, the roar of wind and rain and waves to lessen. Don't tell me we've actually survived? Tobias thought. Bloody hell, surprises never cease.

Of course, that means I've now got to scrape my own shit off the hold floor...

"Think we can probably risk going above," Raeta said. They crawled up the ladder and gingerly opened the hatch. The deck above reminded Tobias of a fortress following an unsuccessful assault. Bloody chaos, literally and figuratively, but with an air of exhausted, crazed relief. Half the rigging seemed to be in pieces, but the sail had held. Sailors were already scaling the mast with great coils of rope over their arms. The bunk huts were smashed up, and they were missing the rowing boat thing. Still raining, but far less furiously. Just rain, from a sky that was just gray. Just wind, blowing his lungs clear of the stench of the hold. Waves foam-capped, no longer monsters, sending up spray as they struck the prow.

Being alive is bloody wonderful, Tobias thought. Gods and demons and fuck, the world's a beautiful place.

Three of the crew were drowned, ripped overboard from the mast. Another two were injured. Really not such a bad butcher's bill. Nothing damaged so bad they couldn't continue. Not a very bad storm, it seemed, all noise and bluster and comparatively little force.

"Yeah," Tobias said, "met plenty of blokes like that." Green-white fingers tearing and tapping. Hands like ropes pulling at his legs in the swirl of the water. Imagination and paranoia, a trick of light and currents...

He sat eating with Raeta, cross-legged on the deck. Golden evening light illuminated the flecks of gray in her hair. Not that he was interested, but he couldn't help noticing. Shitting in front of someone whilst contemplating the shared prospect of cold slow death made a bond like that. Probably worse things to see as the last image of your existence than long yellow hair floating in the water you were drowning in. And a hell of a lot better to look at now than the food, which was hard tack already suggestively wormy and dried beef. Another deep truth known to all soldiers and sailors: food does not taste any better for being garnished with relief at still being alive and in possession of all four limbs. Arguably, it actually tasted kind of worse. I survived hell and high water, for this?

"Should be better weather for a while now," said Raeta.

"And what makes you say that?"

"Optimism," she said cheerfully. "Also the fact that there are plenty of places to put in to harbor and wait it out now we're past the Sker coast. With your luck, we won't meet another storm till we need to go into open water for the last run into the Whites."

"With my luck?"

"Actually, you know, you're bloody lucky, Tobias. In that you survive everything. It's just those around you that don't."

Thalia's blue eyes, guilty and ashamed. Marith's white dead face, broken with surrender, knowing he'd just taken every last chance of hope away. Yeah.

And Rate and Alxine and Skie and Geth and Emit and...

"Stop it," he said savagely.

"Stop what?" she said with a smile and a shrug.

So the journey went on. Almost enjoyable, at times, when the autumn sunshine was warm on the deck and the sea sparkled and the land to their left was low and dark and filled with safe harbors. A few clear nights when the stars were bright. A group of dolphins appeared one evening, dancing and leaping, seemingly trying to race the boat. The third passenger disappeared the night after the storm, and Raeta had a nice new cloak, thick wool with a double weave. She appeared quite happy to spend time with Tobias, explaining some of the detail about ships and sailing, equally interested in the carefully selected stories he told of life as a hired sword.

She was also happy to talk about the Whites, Morr Town and Malth Elelane.

"My brother's seen the king," she said, "tall man, he said he was, dark-haired like they all are, very stern. Rode a huge horse and dripped with jewels. And the queen: beautiful, he said she was, all golden and pink and sparkling. He married her for love, after all. But stern too. Didn't see them very close, mind. And it was years ago, too. He doesn't leave Malth Elelane much, now, King Illyn."

"No?"

"Not been a happy place, they say, the court, these last few years. And San says the mood in Morr Town's bitter as knives, since the prince died. The story is the king's quicker to anger than ever, now, and even the court fears him. Not that it was unexpected," she went on, "the stories that went round about him. The prince, I mean. San had it on good authority that—"

"Yes, yes." The last thing he wanted was to sit here being told gossip about bloody Marith.

"Most people are interested," said Raeta irritably. "Kind of thing you have to take pride in."

Tobias shook his head. Suppose you did, in a strange kind of way.

"But he's dead now." She sighed almost wistfully. "My mother met the last king, Nevethlyn. Claims he stuck his hand up her dress, in fact, which really isn't the kind of thing a woman wants to hear from her aged mum."

Tobias must have looked disbelieving, because she frowned at him and went on, "My mother was a maidservant to Lord Reven before she married. When King Nevethlyn paid a visit to Fealene, she brought his bath water every night."

"Charming man."

"You wouldn't do that, of course, you were king?"

"Course I bloody would. Can still hold it against someone else for having the power to do it, though, can't I?" Tobias thought a moment. "Nevethlyn's the one who...you know?"

"Opened his own throat on the eve of the current king's eighteenth birthday, five days after his army had been routed in Illyr? Bled to death slowly over the course of the next three months, rot setting into the wound and making it ooze black pus? Oh yes. That's him. My mother wasn't exactly upset, as you can imagine."

One of those hilarious military debacles a professional never heard about without shuddering. The most recent of the long line of attempts by Amrath's descendants to take back Amrath's kingdom. Or the blasted wasteland of barely civilized sheep-shaggers it now consists of, anyway. Assembles a crack army, a couple of mages, warships, the works. In the face of all evidence to the contrary, sails off kind of expecting said sheep-shaggers to either fall to their knees in rejoicing at the return of their rightful king or at least just give in and die horribly. Kind of ends up totally wrong, like always. Nobody could ever really say what the fault was, even. The army just...didn't win. Somehow ended up penned in between a cliff top and a swamp with half the soldiers dying of marshfever. And, curiously enough, being penned in between a cliff top and a swamp with half your soldiers dying of marshfever turns out to be a really bad place from which to attempt a panicked midnight retreat.

And the king, heart-broken and alone with his failure, shamed in the eyes of his people and his ancestors, but cursed with the Altrersyr propensity not to die easily...

Got a couple of good ballads out of the mess, at least, same as the last four times they tried it. The kind that made you either weep copiously or piss yourself laughing. Hadn't really clicked it was Marith's grandpa.

Raeta nodded at the darkening sky. "It's getting late. I'm turning in. We'll pass Third, tomorrow, if the wind holds. Could reach Seneth by next dawn. Night."

"Night." He sometimes wondered if she'd be interested in fucking him. Had concluded almost certainly not.

Tobias sat up a little longer, looking at the sky. It still felt strange, having no role on the ship, no jobs to attend to. No men looking to him for orders or reassurance or a good bollocking when they fucked something up. No need to keep looking out himself for someone in need of a good bollocking for fucking something up. Just sitting around, waiting. Waiting, with Prince Marith and King Illyn ahead of him. Gods only knew what that would bring. Gods only knew why he was doing all this.

A nice little house in the sunshine, a nice little girl to clean it, beer every evening, a fat soft bloated gut...

Gods only knew what he'd been doing getting into any of this. It had all seemed so easy, at the time. Neat and clever and give yourself a big pat on the back for initiative. Now he was fucked and fucked and fucked again. Revenge. Futility. Prince Marith. The ultimate pointlessness of everything in his life, that he'd come through near-on twenty years of war and killing and ended up like this. Absolutely nothing to do to take his mind off it all, either, apart from chat away to a pretty woman who quite obviously had no interest in sleeping with him and was just as bored as he was. He rolled himself up and went to sleep, still with his sword next to him and his knife under his pillow in case Raeta decided she'd got bored of talking to him.

Three days later the ship docked at Morr Town, and he set off slowly up the hill to Malth Elelane, the Tower of Joy and Despair, to see the king.

Chapter Forty-Seven

Orhan walked across the Court of the Fountain, watching the water dance. No one was fighting there tonight. Very few people about. A street seller was offering candied rose petals; he bought a bag and ate them slowly. Pale pink, like the dawn. The crystals of sugar crunched in his mouth. He'd walked here with Darath, meat fat dripping nastily down his chin, sighing at his beloved's elaborate overdramatics. He wondered if their desire would wane again, now Darath no longer had the game to play with him. Building up was always less erotic than tearing down.

He rested against the lip of the fountain, his guards stopping puzzled around him. He had more, now, six large men, hard-faced, who had cost him a huge amount to hire in order to cost him a huge amount more to keep. Cold, like metal. He couldn't imagine Bil bedding any of them. They had been taken on at short notice: he felt nervous around them, in a way he never had with Amlis or Sterne.

Would this, too, become tedious, having to be flanked everywhere by armed men, trapped by the idea of others doing to him what he had done to others? He had raised the possibility in people's minds again, after these long years of peace. Conspiracy and murder.

The twilight bell sounded. A sacrifice night again. That poor child. The city held rigid, breathing in the silence of a man's death. Then the spell broke, the moment of danger passed. Across the square a sudden commotion: a woman, young and ragged, falling into the dust, not rising again. Someone shouting. Orhan's men drew closer around him, swords out. Orhan sent one over to investigate. He came back shaking his head: just another street girl, dropping dead of something vile. Unlucky omen, Orhan thought, for her to have fallen there. It was the Court of the Broken Knife that usually claimed them. A better place to die. The Court of the Fountain was for the living, and those who died for glory.

I'd better take care not to die there, then, he thought.

"Send someone to clear away the body," Orhan ordered. No one else would bother, not a corpse with nothing worth taking to make it worth the while. He did not like to see it there, in the beautiful square with the fountain playing and the lamplight bright.

When he got home, Bil was sitting in the inner courtyard, eating grapes and watching the ferfews chasing moths. In the gloom her hair blazed. She was dressed in yellow and green, like flowers, a loose dress to cover her growing belly.

"You're working too hard," she said. "You'll be worn out."

"I enjoy it."

She sat up, almost took his arm. She'd heard what he had had proclaimed today, then. Of course she had. But he had somehow hoped she might not have heard. Closed herself off into baby things. It repelled him, her swelling belly and her knowing this.

She said, "Will you really burn Samerna Rhyl alive?"

"It has to be done."

"Burn Samerna? Burn the children alive?"

Even to his own wife, he could not risk telling the truth. Even to his own wife, he would be the man who killed them, who burned them. No one could ever know he'd spared them. Of all the things he had done and all the reasons for doing them, those around him would condemn him for this above all. And he wouldn't even have actually done it.

Just killed someone else's family instead, to make his own

conscience slightly easier to bear. Nothing important, on top of all the rest. But bitter.

"It would have been me," Bil said. "If you'd failed."

"It still could be."

"You can't...you can't pardon them?"

Wearily: "No."

"But they didn't do anything. It's cruel."

Wearily: "Yes."

She looked at the walls. "When?"

"Next week. Tearday. You'll need to be there. We all will."

She seemed about to speak, then nodded silently.

A servant called them in to a late dinner. Roasted lamb dressed with honey, warm bread, cold greens cooked with onions. Orhan ate absently, planning the work he needed to do tomorrow. Letters to Chathe and Tarboran. Ith. The White Isles. Elis's wedding. That needed doing fast, to bind March to them. Before Elis mucked it up and the girl refused him. And his nephew: pity the poor bride there, too.

After they had eaten, Orhan wondered about going to see Darath. Or even going back to the palace, work again at the endless tasks. He went out into the gardens, looked up at the sky. Ferfews called around him. Ghost birds. Souls of the dead. The dead had no souls. But if they did, they were here, with him, calling in sweet low voices. The scent of jasmine was very strong. He'd finally got the stink of blood and burning out of his mind. Smell it again, in a few days' time, when women and children and a roomful of servants died.

I did it for the good of the Empire, he thought heavily. One day everything will rise again, the people happy and triumphant, the gold pennants of the city catching the wind, the kings of Irlast bowing down before us. Hope and power and new purpose. I will remake the world, or a small part of it at least. I will be praised, afterward.

Clouds came again, blotting out the moon. No stars apart from the red gleam of the Fire Star. The call of the birds in sweet low voices. Ghosts.

Orhan went into the house and up into his bedroom, and tried to sleep. All he could think of was the proclamation he had had made and the next things he needed to do. He woke early, went down to the palace and sat with the maps and the ledgers and the letters, planning changes, planning improvements. Fewer children starving. Fewer women dying unmourned in the street. Hope and power and new purpose. The good of the Empire. Written down in gold ink in books bound with human skin.

Chapter Forty-Eight

They were dragged up on deck, blinking at the light. Marith stared around him shakily. The great golden cliffs of Third loomed before them, crested at the top with the brown of raw, turned earth. The morning sun blazed on the peak of Calen Mon, picking out the birds circling it. A jagged ravine broke the line of the cliffs below the mountain, darker rocks running with water and deep green vegetation, goats picking over the sheer falls. To the north of the peak, woodland, sweeping down to meet the sea in low cliffs and a little shingle beach. The trees were almost bare now. Like bones. Seals lay on the beach, their dogs' heads raised, watching. A few fishing boats bobbed on the choppy water, sails red or pale blue.

Landra appeared on deck, wrapped in a heavy fur-trimmed cloak against the cold wind. Her hair was braided with gold, though her clothes were creased and crumpled after weeks at sea. Her eyes looked tired as she gazed out at the land rising before them.

"Home. I thought you might like to see it, Prince Ruin."

Marith nodded slowly. The most beautiful place in the world. He felt Thalia shiver beside him, staring at the water and the cliffs. The first time they'd been allowed out of a filthy compartment in the hold for two weeks. The sky and the light were painful, the air stank of sweet cleanliness. She looked half-frozen in her thin dirty gown. The wind whipped her hair, made it fly out around her. Black fire, burning. Bare branches tearing at the sky. I said I'd show you my home, he thought. And so we'll die there. Better than living, perhaps, knowing what will come to me. And better here than anywhere else.

"Where are we making land?" he asked Landra. "Escral? Or Toreth?" To see Malth Salene again, rising above the dark waters of Torlan Bay, its walls painted green and gold, apple trees crowning the headland upon which it stood…

"Neither." Her hands gripped the rails of the ship. "We make land here, Prince Ruin. Go across country. Honored guests disembark from their ships at Toreth Harbor and ride the golden road to Malth Salene. Murderers and outcasts and dead men take the lich way, come in through the back gates where the middens are piled."

The old roads. Older than Malth Salene. Older than the Relasts, or the Altrersyr. Nothing more than a thin line in the earth, leading from the tumbled rocks below Calen Mon in winding paths over the moors toward the fortress three days' walk away. Ended as they began, nowhere anyone went to, nowhere anyone needed to go. Such roads ran all across the island, leading from nowhere to nowhere, ending blank and pointless at the cliff edge and the sea. Roads one could walk to kill oneself, pockets filled with yellow stones. Roads the dead might walk, if they cared to walk in the wild places. He'd ridden them with Carin, trying to understand them. Found only that there was nothing to understand. Landra was such a romantic, to think of it.

Couldn't have anyone recognizing him, either, Marith thought. That was the real reason why, of course: you could hardly take the heir to the kingdom into a major port town and not have someone notice. People would recognize him, in Toreth. Predominantly tavern keepers, hatha merchants and the men employed to sweep the gutters, in point of fact, but still, people who would recognize him.

They came ashore in another rowing boat, splashing out into the shallows, cold waves breaking around their legs. Gods, it was sweet. The sound of the water breaking on pebbles was perfect music. Gulls again, wilder than most in this wild place, angry at being disturbed. The seals looked at them with eyes as dark and smooth and uncomprehending as the shingle. A rough scramble up into the woods behind the beach, Landra's eyes fierce and laughing as Thalia struggled and stared, haunted by the sea and the stone and the earth and the sky, cold and frightened, seeing this land only as something terrible, cruel and empty as the desert had been. The old gods must lie heavy on her, she who was sworn to another god. And her eyes widened, when they came to the lich road. She felt it, Marith saw. Felt it as he had done, once.

Marith and Thalia walked bound, led on long ropes. Landra strode ahead, Mandle beside her grim-faced, holding the ropes like leading reins. Just the four of them: Landra's women, all Landra's things, had been left on the ship. It was madness, to do this. Landra would be punishing herself more than she could possibly humiliate him.

He'd promised Carin he'd marry Landra, once. The closest he could come to giving Carin his crown. Carin had wanted it. Or rather, Carin's father had wanted it. Made Carin ask him. *Marry my sister, Marith. Marry her and make her queen.* Their fingers curled round each other. Carin's plain face smiling down at him. Everything fractured and bright behind his eyes. *You have to marry her, you know. Anyone else will be jealous. But she loves me almost as much as she loathes you.* Neither of them cared, really. But it had been good, to give something Carin could give to his father without pain.

They walked on, into the wind. Cold. He could still hear the sea behind them, pounding on the stones of the shore.

After a short while, Thalia was shaking, seemed ready to collapse. Her hair whipped around her face in tendrils that blocked her vision, her lips and face and hands looked blue and dead. Marith stopped walking as she stumbled and gasped, her ankle catching in a hole and making her trip awkwardly.

"She needs help. She can't walk." He turned to Landra, striding angrily back to him. "Please. Please, Landra."

Pale blue eyes flicked between his face and Thalia's. "Help her, then." The voice cold and bitter. You're jealous, Marith thought. Jealous for Carin, that I love her. That I could love anyone other than Carin. He came over to Thalia and she fell into him, gasping. Her body shook with cold.

"Untie me," he said slowly to Landra. "Please, Landra. I..." He paused, licked his lips, steeled himself. "I swear I won't try to run. I swear I won't try to fight. On my name and my blood, I swear it."

"The Altrersyr lie," Landra said.

Of course we do. You don't hold a kingdom and a legend as the vilest family in Irlast without lying occasionally. "Yes," he said wearily, "we lie. My father lied to you. I've lied to you. I've lied to Carin. I'm a worthless lying drunk and a murderer. But in Amrath's name, I swear. I—" He went down carefully on his knees. "Just let me help her, Landra. Please. Please."

Landra snorted. She looked confused, to see him at her feet. A long pause; he could see her thinking, weighing up everything in her mind, her anger at his love for Thalia, her anger at his humility to her, the danger of him running, balancing them with the suffering of this poor woman whom she was killing as surely as he'd killed Carin.

"Untie his hands. He can hold her."

Mandle twisted uncomfortably. "My Lady—"

"Untie him. We won't get much further, if the girl can't walk." Landra raised her hand impatiently at the man's muttering. "Place the rope around his neck. If he tries to run, tighten it."

Mandle grinned as he changed over the bindings, making a lengthy show of knotting the rope so that it hung heavily at the point on Marith's throat where the pulse beat between his collarbones. The man had carried him drunk and sobbing out of a tavern somewhere in Toreth, once. Seemed a nice enough bloke then, a good steady shoulder to lean on.

They walked on, Thalia clutched in Marith's arms, shaking with cold and exhaustion. He almost felt the pain in her, the weight of this land pressing on her, like shouting in the head or the roar of water in the ears. So much walking. All he ever seemed to have done was walk, through desert and wasteland and heat and cold, thinking and changing and feeling and trying to hide from things. Toward it. Always and forever, he had been walking toward it.

"I love you," he whispered to Thalia. For you, he thought. All for you. You'll see what I'll give you, soon enough. The rope jerked tighter at his neck and Mandle laughed. Landra laughed too, but too harshly, as though she was trying to find some comfort in what she knew was only pointless and cruel. They walked on, over the lich road, in the cold wind, across the moor.

When Thalia awoke the next morning, the landscape was silver with frost.

Marith had tried to explain it to her, in the desert outside Sorlost, his eyes closed as he spoke. Trying to shape into words the beauty of it, the breath-taking sense of purity and hope and pain it brought. She had not been able to comprehend it, she who had lived all her life in the walls of her Temple, in the heat. The dawn in the desert had been astonishing, joyous, perfect with life. This was different, more terrifying, so beautiful it tore her heart from her breast, so remorseless it brought tears to her eyes. The trees furred thick with ice, ice crusting the ground, picking out every blade of grass, turning it into something like nothing she could imagine, a world made of glass and diamond where nothing could live. In the strange pale light the bare trees were even darker, against the new whiteness of the ground. A stream showed black and gold, reflecting the first sun, a gaping scar of light, heavy and solid as skin. And cold. Cold as the Small Chamber. Cold as Marith's eyes.

God is here, she thought, looking at the frost. God is here in this place, but not my God. Not Great Tanis, who is the Lord of Living and Dying, who is hungry and fierce and loving and strong and burns with light and dark. Other gods, gods of silence. Gods like the taste of cold salt water. Gods of the living world. No power, save the power to astonish and make one weep at the beauty of them, and the knowledge that they are deadly and terrible and beautiful and nothing, and have no care for man or sunlight or hope or despair. Gods that simply are.

A bird broke the stillness, its wings beating up, loud as trumpets in the frozen air. The spell was broken: the people around her began moving about, talking, tending the fire. So futile, their actions seemed, against the frozen world.

They had camped in a small stone hut built low down in a valley nestled between the sweep of the moors. Very old and tumbledown, one side open to the air and looking out over mossy grass, a hearth in one corner and stone shelf beds raised up from a stone floor. Birds had nested in the roof, but were flown for the winter, leaving only thick trails of green-white filth down the walls and onto the floor.

Not a good place. Thalia felt it with a shudder as she entered. A smell of blood, old and faint. But not the blood of dying. She saw Marith twitch as he crossed the threshold, his face lit for a moment. He shook his head, wearily, as she had seen him do once or twice when he had been drinking and a shadow came over him and made him sigh. He sat down quietly in the corner, the rope still around his neck, wrapped her in his arms as she sat beside him. Landra sat in the further corner from them, by the hearth, as Mandle began to build up a fire and prepare a camp. All she had known, Thalia thought, of life beyond the walls of the Temple: campfires and camp cookery and hard-faced men who set about their work whilst looking at her with bitter eyes.

She was left free, but with wrists bound behind her back. Marith, Mandle bound hand and foot, then tied the rope to a stone standing just outside the threshold of the hut.

"I swore I wouldn't run," Marith said, the first words he had spoken since he had knelt on the ground at Landra's feet. "I swore, and I do still swear."

"You've lied and you do still lie," Landra said shortly. Marith laughed. The fire sputtered into life with a crackle and a pungent burst of smoke.

"Let's get the tea on, then," Mandle said. "Bloody freezing, I am."

In the light from the fire the night outside was suddenly darker, the stone at the entranceway more clearly picked out. Not a good thing, it was, squatting there, god-charmed and blood-reeking, half as tall as a man and with the look of a man to it. It did not seem well omened, that Marith was bound to it.

"What is this place?" she asked him, taken with fear.

"A way house," he answered, before Mandle jerked the rope and shouted, "No talking." And then they unbound her to eat, and bound her again, and she was asleep huddled next to Marith in the cold, shivering even as she slept but too exhausted not to sleep dreamlessly and wake wishing she could sleep longer. And the frost was there before her, cruel and beautiful and utterly unknown to her, like a language she had never before heard chanting out a song of prayer.

Marith whimpered in his sleep beside her, his body twitching. Pity, it moved her to. Why, she thought, why could he find no peace? She'd thought herself so much more worn down than him, so much more broken and driven to exhaustion and pain. But she saw now that he had been living on nothing, going on and going on crushed down to dust. She watched him wake as weary as he had been before he slept, eat hard bread and hot tea in the ice-cold morning light, his hair rumpled, his face pinched with a look of pain now always around his eyes. He gasped with relief when they unbound his hands, rubbed madly at his face. He must be in agony, she realized, unable to claw at the itching that ate at him.

"Come on then. Up." Mandle jerked her roughly to her feet, then took up the rope that haltered Marith like an animal. Landra looked worn out, tired and pained, dirty and crumpled, but her face was set with grim determination. She seemed so endlessly resolved to torture them. Were they all like this, in the east? Hard and remorseless and cruel? Savage, Thalia thought. Savages. Her own body felt exhausted beyond exhaustion, the cold so deep in her bones she would surely never be warm again. No gain could come of this, no benefit to Landra or her kin, only more grief. No joy. No purpose.

Their footsteps crunched on the icy grass, still almost the only sound; their breath puffed out in white clouds. Thalia thought again of the dragon, breathing smoke and steam. She had seen her breath condense like this in the desert, in the night and the dawn; yet it was different here, in full morning sunlight, in a white silent world. She could see why Marith had spoken of it with yearning.

They walked for hours. The sun melted the frost. The road took them over a great high curve of barren hillside, brown with dry heather, down a steep incline into a narrow pass verdant with grass and moss. Pebbles slipped and clattered underfoot, very loud in the silence of the place. The walls closed in, gray stone rearing up out of the green earth. A stream coursed down the rocks, staining them black, running off across the ground clear as bright glass. The pebbles of the path gleamed brown beneath the water when they crossed.

Then up again, the land rising back up to tawny moorland and great outcroppings of dark rock. No one else walked the path, they saw nothing living. An empty land, as empty as the sea. And yet beautiful. Marith's face shone as he looked around him.

Ansikanderakesis, she thought. A king in his kingdom indeed.

Mandle stopped suddenly, holding up his hand.

"What is it?" Landra said. She sounded almost nervous. Marith caught it too, looked ahead curiously.

"Horses." They could all hear them now, thundering hooves like that terrible day outside Reneneth.

"Horses?" Landra frowned. "From Malth Salene, it must be. Nobody else would be out here."

"Unless it's brigands, My Lady," said Mandle.

"Not brigands," said Landra. She sounded frightened. "Not so close to Malth Salene. Someone must have brought word."

Marith had raised his head, staring into the distance at the riders coming closer. Green and gold pennants fluttering, that put Thalia in mind of the kites she had seen sometimes in the square of sky above the Temple that had been her world. Green and gold, that Marith had said were the Relast colors. A flush rose in Landra's face, her throat worked and her lips moved.

As they had once before, the horses rode down upon them and stopped almost in a circle, great dark things and one white. Armed men, in heavy bronze helmets. Three horses, led on long reins, saddled and harnessed in scarlet leather. An older man, perhaps forty, graying, heavy-faced, in plainer clothes but wrapped around in power.

"Uncle—" Landra began. The older man turned his face to her, then dismounted and came toward Marith. The whole group stiffened, an indrawn breath held as sharp as the frost.

The man bowed his head awkwardly, then went down slowly on one knee. "My Lord Prince," he said.

"Aris." Marith looked at him. Confused.

"You will forgive…What has been done here," the man said in a strained voice. "My Lord Prince. Lord Relast did not countenance this."

"Deneth…" Marith still seemed utterly lost.

"We are here to escort you to Malth Salene, My Lord Prince." The man turned to the other men, gesturing for them to dismount. "Attend to them. Cloaks, and wine."

Marith gazed dully at the gray-haired man. As if none of this was entirely unexpected yet also as unreal as a dream.

Landra argued and shouted, stamping her foot and almost spitting.

"He killed my brother! Your future Lord! He deserves nothing but pain."

"He is the rightful heir to the White Isles," the gray-haired man said. "A Prince of the Altrersyr."

"He's an exile and a murderer! A dead man! When my father hears of this—"

"Your father sent me, you fool. We lathered the horses half senseless to get to you."

"He killed Carin!" Landra cried again.

"Yes." The faces locked; Thalia could see familial resemblance in the square jaws and the pale blue eyes. "Have some wine, Landra. You look half dead yourself." He came over to Marith and Thalia. "Are you fit to ride, My Lord? We have horses for you and...and the lady."

"Lady Thalia." Marith's arm tightened on Thalia's waist. "You will accord her every courtesy you accord me. Treat her as you would an Altrersyr princess." He must have seen Thalia glance nervously at the horses. "She will ride with me, on my horse." Laughed dryly. "Tempted as I am to make Landra walk, we'll make better time if she rides. Mandle, however..." He shook his head, rubbed his eyes wearily. "No. He can have the other horse."

Marith swung up easily into the saddle, lifting Thalia and helping her arrange herself before him. He pressed his face into her hair for a moment, sighing with pleasure or pain, then commanded the horse forward at a rush, breathing out with a little "ha" sound as it leaped at his words and ran the bare landscape into the wind, its mane flying, Thalia's hair flying, her eyes watering, the air suddenly brighter around them, the sky pale with light. Birds, for the first time in this place, black against the pale sky. The first sign of life here. Everything felt more alive. "Ha," said Marith again. He slowed the horse a little, waiting for the rest to catch them.

"Not afraid, are you?" he asked. The wind caught his words.

"No," Thalia said in reply, half-lying.

"Good." He whipped up the horse again and made it run faster. Distant voices behind them shouted. A thunder of hooves as a couple of the men raced to follow them, Marith laughing, then pulling the horse in to allow them to catch up.

"I swore I wouldn't run," he said. The old man, Aris, snorted and muttered something under his breath.

"Who is he?" Thalia asked after a little while. Her shock and confusion was wearing off, the numb feeling in her mind easing a little.

"He? Oh. Yes. I never actually introduced you, did I? Aris Relast. Some kin of Deneth's. A servant, though he pretends otherwise."

"Deneth?"

He sighed. "Gods, I forget. Denethlen Relast. Lord Relast. Landra's father. And Carin's. My enemy, or so I thought. Curious, that he should send all this. Almost a hero's welcome." She could hear the amusement in his voice for the first time in many days, wry and self-mocking. "Well, we shall see in a while, now. He may just think it entertaining, to wrap me in status and then kill me. It entertained him no end to see the state to which he and his son reduced me, I'm sure."

A pause, and then, more seriously but still with mockery, "You are the only woman I've ever knelt for, you know. To you, and for you. All this, for you, Thalia."

It was full night when they reached the great fortress of Malth Salene, their horses lathered and worn. Thalia saw it approaching, rising up dark against a darker sky, yellow firelights glowing in narrow window slits. Rough and angular, so different from Sorlost with its domes and towers of gold. It had no houses around it, rose up sheer and sudden, a rock jutting from the thin soil like the rocks on the moor. The land narrowed, a track like a neck with the sea far below. Cold, and the sea was trying to swallow it, batter down the cliffs, reach up its claws to them. The air smelled of salt. Marith had said it was a beautiful place. The most beautiful place in all his kingdom.

Gates were thrown open: they had come, she saw, to an outer wall, high as the walls of her Temple, giving onto a courtyard aflame with torchlight. Marith spurred the horse forward, racing in through the gates in a great clatter of hooves. A voice behind them shouted "The Prince! The Prince comes! Amrath! Amrath and the Altrersyr!" Marith threw back the hood of his cloak and wheeled the horse about.

Every person present in the courtyard fell to their knees, heads bent.

They hung for a moment frozen, the two of them on the great horse, the people kneeling. The courtyard was very much like the courtyard of the caravan inns that were all Thalia really knew of the world of men. It seemed to her, therefore, disappointing as the entrance to a great noble's fortress, dirty and crowded, not much larger than the courtyard at the inn in Reneneth, straw on the ground, horse shit, dogs, small doorways and narrow windows with metal bars. The back entranceway, the stables and service areas, though she did not know it then.

The other riders came in after them and the gate was closed. Aris Relast swung down and knelt again at Marith's feet.

"My Lord Prince. Welcome to Malth Salene. On My Lord Relast's behalf, I bid you enter and be welcome here."

Chapter Forty-Nine

Marith looked around the courtyard slowly, then dismounted and helped Thalia slide down into his arms. She shivered at his embrace, then pressed herself against him. I don't know, she thought, I don't know what to do. Do I even want to stay with him, now? She yawned in exhaustion. The warm windows looked so inviting. There was a smell of wood smoke in the air. Tonight, she thought, I do.

"Deneth not coming to greet me in person, then?" Marith said with his boy's grin. "No, no, it's late, no one knew quite when I'd arrive, he would hardly be waiting out here half the night in the cold by the midden heap. Of course I understand, he'll see me in the morning when I'm clean and presentable, and spare us both the indignity of having to talk to me in the rags his daughter dressed me in."

"We have your chamber prepared—" Aris Relast looked for a moment at Thalia, his eyebrows raised, something questioning between him and Marith "—baths, food, hot wine will be ready shortly. If you will follow me, My Lord?"

"I think I probably know where I'm going. Could get there blind. Have done repeatedly, in fact." Marith took Thalia's arm and led her through a small doorway into the bulk of the building itself, down a small corridor which opened out into a wide hall, brightly lit with torches, and then up a wide flight of stairs. Aris Relast followed behind them, flicking wide-eyed, panicked servants out of their way with a frown and a wave of his hand. Thalia gazed at it all in exhausted confusion. A world so different to her own. Bare polished stone on the floor, green and gold panels on the walls painted with a blazon of suns. Wall sconces of verdigrised copper. Oppressive, she found it.

At the top of the stairs, another hallway, stone walls hung with tapestries depicting pastoral scenes, lords and ladies in shining dresses hunting or dancing in green woodlands, a feast spread in a meadow carpeted with flowers. Marith stopped and looked at one for a moment. It showed a group of young men out hunting, counting up their kills. Two men rode slightly apart, their faces turned away from the rest, the necks of their horses close together like swans' necks.

More stairs, a spiral staircase with a banister of carved wood. Marith laughed a little as they climbed it. Another hallway, a carved door. "This one, I assume?" he said lightly. Avis Relast nodded. Marith reached out to open the door, his hand pausing a moment then the door pushing open. He made a noise that might have been a laugh, or a sigh, or a murmur of pain.

A grand suite of rooms. Richly furnished. The bedroom itself was large and striking, dominated by a great bed hung with red cloth. Marith strode over to a painted chest and threw it open, revealing a mass of dark clothing neatly folded, smelling of herbs.

"Still here." He laughed again. "You didn't burn them, then? Everything as I left it, my clothes, my chamber, even after I've been dead all these months."

He looked around the room again, his eyes very wide, and Thalia looked and saw the ghosts of two young men looking back at him. She shuddered, and he shuddered too, and shook his head.

"I need a drink. Something to eat. A hot bath." He gestured to Aris. "See to it."

Aris left, bowing his head and muttering "My Lord Prince" again as he went. So strange, it sounded. Marith sat down on the bed and Thalia joined him. Soft. Comfortable. She hadn't slept in a comfortable bed for a long time. Tiredness overwhelmed her, thundering in her eyes. She sank into Marith's shoulder, exhausted. Hard even to understand what they said, in their fast soft lilting Pernish, her mind so stunned with it all.

"Don't fall asleep yet, beautiful girl," Marith said softly in Literan. Safe and familiar. Thalia smiled half-asleep.

"All I want is to sleep," she whispered back.

Too tired to eat or drink, when servants brought pastries and fruit and cold meat and hot, spiced wine. But she stirred herself when they were escorted down the hallway to a room equipped for bathing. The hot water made her even sleepier: she collapsed into bed afterward, clean and warm and sweet-scented, safe in Marith's arms. In the silence as she fell asleep she could hear the sea, far off. And another sound, that might have been two young men talking together quietly.

She saw the next day, in the light, the size and glory of the place, that Marith had not been wrong to call it beautiful, though it was a beauty strange to her. It was a high, windswept tower, carved in white-gray stone. Outside, a wall enclosed a wide area of gardens and orchards and meadow grass, running in places right to the edge of a cliff falling off sheer into the sea. The wall was painted green and gold, the Relast colors. A well-made road, paved in the same pale stone as the keep, ran down to the town below that sat hugging the water, a jumble of dark roofs. Ships floated in the harbor in a blaze of sails: one, she guessed, must be the ship they had sailed in, whose captain had spared them several more days' pain by running as fast as he could for Malth Salene and its lord.

"What does the name mean?" she asked Marith over what passed for breakfast, eaten well after noon when they had finally woken from exhausted sleep. "Malth Salene? I've never heard the word Salene before. It doesn't sound Pernish. But it's not Literan or Immish."

He frowned a little. He had not looked happy since he woke,

for all he seemed more rested and comfortable. "It's Itheralik. Saleiot means 'to shine' or 'to sparkle.' 'To dance like the sunlight on fast-flowing water', perhaps. So Malth Salene: the Tower of the Shining Sea. It's an old word. An old name. Older than the Relast family, as the tower is older than they are. As old as the lich roads." A look of pain again in his face that she could not understand; he itched at his eyes impatiently, turned his face away from the water that did indeed shine beyond the walls.

"The lich roads... The dead do indeed walk there, I think," said Thalia. "It is good that they came for us, took us away. I would not have wanted to stay longer on that road."

Marith raised his head sharply. "The dead...?" He frowned again. "It is not only the dead who walk there, beautiful girl. The things that walk there—"

Yes, she thought. I know what walks there. It is good indeed, that someone came.

"A seamstress is coming," Marith said suddenly, to change the subject. So much tension still between them. It does not occur to him, she thought, that I might feel anger, or pain. Disappointment, even, perhaps, in him. I saw him abased and abject. He knows what I saw. Yet it does not occur to him that I might no longer want him. That I might wish to leave. Marith looked awkwardly at her, then smiled bright and innocent, his eyes caressing her face. "She's to dress you as a queen. I told you I'd adorn you as the most beautiful woman in Malth Tyrenae; you'll have to settle for being the most beautiful woman on Third, which is far less of a compliment. She's to bring everything she has."

"A new pair of shoes would be more useful," Thalia said brightly in reply. Don't think of it. Don't think of it. This is what he is, also. Beautiful and sad and full of pride in himself. A shining prince in a shining tower. That was a better thought.

"Oh, I'm sure you can have every pair in Toreth. I'll have some made in solid gold for you, or sewn from rose petals sent in a fast ship from Chathe." He smiled like a boy and she tried to smile back.

The seamstress came a short while later with gowns for her,

and she forgot her discomfort and her anger in the glorious game of trying things on. A cloak of black velvet, edged and lined with fur, clasped with silver roses. A dress of deep golden-green silk, embroidered at the neck with flowers and leaves in bronze and brown. Another in apricot, embroidered all over with tiny gold stars. Gray velvet, soft as breathing, trimmed in silver and dark twilight blue. Satin green and blue and gold like a peacock's tail, the pattern shifting as the dress moved. White silk, sewn with green and pink like blossom. Slippers and boots, in fine leather, with buckles of silver and gold. Thalia gazed at them all in astonishment. Marith looked at her with hopeful eyes.

"A goldsmith will come later, too. Bring you jewels to match. Sapphires, like your eyes. Diamonds. Rubies, of course." He stroked her face, light in his eyes. "The dresses will have to be altered. You're far too tall and slender for most of the women here. But that can be done quickly." He shot a hard glance at the seamstress. "Very quickly."

"You don't have any money," Thalia said at last. Money was something else she was slowly becoming aware of, realizing the advantages of its possession, the consequences of its lack. All her power and her status, and she had been stripped to nothing, within a few moments of walking out from her Temple with nothing of her own. "How are you paying for all this?"

"I don't have any money now. But one day I'll have everything. And I want you to look like I already do." He sighed and rubbed his face, laughed shortly. So unhappy again. Ashamed. She shouldn't have said it, Thalia thought. Should have let him pretend all was as it had been when he last stood in this room dressed in these clothes. "I can borrow money. I've got drinking debts I can't possibly ever meet now anyway, beautiful girl. A few dresses and some diamonds are neither here nor there."

Thalia ran her hand over the gray velvet dress. Soft as skin, smooth to the touch.

"Try it on," Marith said eagerly. "No, try the gold one first."

"You're enjoying this, aren't you?"

He laughed, more happily this time. "Of course."

She put on the dress, a maidservant helping her. The bodice was low and tight-fitted, the skirt slim, swirling around her legs. It was heavy and strange on her, after the loose light dresses she was used to. Like the dresses for the great ceremonies of the Temple. Like the liveries of the servants scurrying around the keep with their heads bowed.

Marith gazed at her with a song in his eyes and she forgot that, too. His fingers closed on her hair and pulled at her gown and sent the seamstress running, shining fabric piled in her arms.

"I'll see Lord Relast, now, I suppose."

Aris Relast looked entirely nonplussed: "His Lordship…uh… is indeed eager to meet with you, My Lord Prince."

"Kept him waiting, have we?" Marith stretched and yawned. Aris Relast stood in the doorway, his face sour. Marith smiled at him sweetly. "I suppose I'd better let him attend, then." He stood up, feeling the room lurch around him. Several hours of drinking and fucking possibly not the best preparation for what he was about to have to do. He'd been aware of knocking at the door earlier, Lord Relast presumably wanting it confirmed to his own face that his son's murderer really was still alive. It might have been politic to seem at least vaguely grateful for his hospitality, rather than ignore it entirely and open another bottle of wine.

Two things, Deneth Relast could want of him. He had genuinely no idea which it would be.

In either case, he'd have one perfect afternoon to hold to himself first.

Marith pulled on his coat, the rich dark Altrersyr red, slightly obvious perhaps. Thalia wore the gray dress. It made his coat look brighter and more vibrant beside her. His queen. He'd have a red dress made for her, too. Blood and firewine and her mouth.

Back down the long corridors, the wide staircases. Memory choked him for a moment. So many times, he'd walked here with Carin. His hands felt suddenly sticky, still covered in Carin's blood. The way skin felt after touching something unclean. Knowing it was there, not visible to the naked eye but throbbing so that he could almost hear it. He rubbed his hand on Thalia's dress, trying to think himself back to the glorious afternoon. She mistook his gesture, smiled and stroked his hand back, her face still bright with pleasure. She seemed easier in herself also, things mended between them, the haunted look fading from her eyes. Far easier to apologize appropriately, half-drunk and in ecstasy.

I love you, he thought. I love you. I'm sorry. You know I am.

Dusk was already pressing at the windows. He'd forgotten, somehow, after months spent in the changeless seasonless dream of the Sekemleth Empire, that night came in earlier here. All day, Deneth Relast must have been waiting, to receive his son's murderer. He looked at Thalia a moment, looking at the dusk, whispering words. Should it be a killing night for her? She must count the days still, mark it in her mind. The moon would be different in Sorlost. A man? A woman? A child?

A pulse beat in his ears. Disgust and desire. Desire and disgust.

They stopped outside the heavy door of Lord Relast's private chambers. Aris knocked. The door opened. They went in. Deneth Relast rose from his desk as they entered. A handsome enough man, in his youth, gray-haired and gray-bearded now, his stocky body going a little to fat. Sad for Landra and Carin both, that they'd inherited their father's body and their mother's face.

"My Lord Prince."

Marith inclined his head very slightly. "Lord Relast."

"You will sit?" Deneth Relast indicated chairs, poured cups of heavy-scented wine. Seabirds screamed outside the window: the fishing ships must be coming in, in Toreth Harbor. In the corner of the room, a little figurine of Amrath squatted on a shelf, a candle burning next to it. The motion of the door closing made the flame dance and the figurine itself seemed to move.

Curious thing, to worship one's own kin. Marith nodded at it.

"Landra said that you were alive," Deneth Relast began crisply, without formality. "I did not believe her, at first—"

And Landra had accused him of lying! "Of course you knew I

was alive. You wouldn't believe a word my father told you, without proof." He felt utterly confident and powerful, suddenly, sitting here talking with this man whose son he had loved and killed. Twist the knife. Harder. In my heart, and yours. "My father didn't care about Carin. Not enough to stain himself so far as to actually kill me. Neither did you, in the end. Punished him for it, but not that far. You were angry at the time, but now . . . You and he have both probably been getting word of me since I left the Whites."

Deneth lowered his eyes. "Indeed. My wife and children needed to believe it, though. Landra in particular is naïve. Almost as naïve as my son was."

Don't speak about him! Don't mention his name! Nobody can mention his name but me. The little Amrath figurine moved as the candle flickered. Thalia tensed, sensing it. Deneth shifted in his seat, but plowed on.

"Tiothlyn is heir now, of course," he said slowly. "Seems . . . capable, if unimaginative and inclined to the coarse."

"Don't speak about Ti."

"Tiothlyn is the only reason you are still alive," Deneth said sharply. "Rather than nameless and faceless and dead on a spike, as you should be."

Guessed right, then. "Shouldn't have demanded my head yourself, then, should you?"

A silence, the candlelight flickering. The ghost of a boy with fair hair. Marith could almost feel him, hands cool on his forehead, warm on his shoulder. Side by side, their heads touching, fingers entwined.

Deneth glanced at Thalia. "And what would you have done in my place, My Lord Prince? Forgiven? Laughed it away?"

"You put him up to it! You made him do it! He hurt me first! It wasn't my fault!" So weak and petulant, his voice sounded. Marith drained his cup, his hands shaking. "What did you think would happen? Father's wanted Ti to take my place for years. Must have thanked you for finally getting rid of me for him. You walked into that one, didn't you? All your plans for me fall through and

Carin's dead and you're so angry, and then the anger wears off and you realize Ti and the queen and her family are all smiling and you've lost everything and made it worse. Gods, they must have laughed at you."

Deneth blinked. His face was white. "Your father—" Shrugged. "This is not a good time, I think, My Lord Prince. Let us go and eat. We can talk again afterward, when we are refreshed."

Dinner was served in a small dining room instead of the Great Hall. Not a formal banquet, just Deneth and his wife Jora and Landra and little Savane, and Aris at the far end. Marith was seated at Deneth's right hand, the place of honor. Almost like old times. Landra sat across from him, her face hard as stone. She looked so much like Carin. He could see all their eyes watching him. Shocked and hating. Pressure on his back, scrabbling at his skull. Gods only knew what they saw, when they looked at him. Make it stop, he thought. Make it go away. Make everything go away. I'd tell you I was sorry, but you wouldn't believe me anyway.

Servants served little pies of pickled fish, crusted with honey and salt. Sharp and sweet and elegant, half disgusting, half perfect. Apples, still fresh from the orchards, the last of the year, their skin mottled with stars. If you cut one the right way you made a star pattern. Venison, burned black without, bloody raw within. Thalia ate with a look of astonishment on her face. Loathed the food. Loathed the place. Probably loathed him, after what he'd done to her. But I love you, Thalia, he thought. Please love me. Hippocras to drink, green and heavy, stinging his tongue. Kind of Deneth, to remember his liking for it. He drank it and it was bright and sweet. His head was getting heavy. I'm so tired, he thought. Help me, Carin. Help me. Make everything go away. Landra was glaring at him. She hates me. She's always hated me. He raised his glass to her, green liquid slopping over his shaking hand. "Old times, Landra. Don't tell me you haven't missed the sight of me vomiting onto my plate." His voice sounded distant. Hippocras, green and heavy, stinging his tongue.

At the end of the meal, Deneth rose and gestured to him to follow. Thalia stared at him helpless as he staggered to his feet, collapsed, tried again and finally stumbled out.

Woke the next morning with a groan, his head pounding. Seemed at least to have made it back to his own bed. Thalia stood at the window, looking out toward the sea. She turned as she heard him stir. Marith looked down at himself, still dressed in rumpled finery, and smiled ruefully at her.

"I really should mend my ways and stop waking up in bed with something like you fully dressed and horribly hung-over. You're too forgiving, lovely thing. You could have at least helped me take my boots off, though. So, I take it I signed my kingdom away last night. What did I offer him, the blood of my first-born and all five fingers of my right hand?" He saw her horrified expression and laughed. "I'm joking, lovely girl." Considered a moment. "Half joking anyway. I admit, I was possibly in a weaker negotiating position than was entirely wise. But it's no more than I was expecting. Less, perhaps. I don't think he actually wants me to kneel in the mud and publicly beg his forgiveness. It's nothing I wouldn't have gone into sober: the fact he felt the need to indulge me was simply an added good. It all went off rather well, in fact, given I'm not entirely sure I was capable of intelligible speech by the end of it."

Thalia turned back to the window, staring out at the sky and the sea. She looked so fragile, so lost here. So afraid. There's nothing to be afraid of, he thought. Can't you see? Everything will be fine now. It's done and can't be avoided and I'm almost glad of it.

She said, "You can't mean to trust him. You can't."

"Trust him? Of course I don't trust him. He doesn't exactly trust me, either. But I need his support, and he wants what he's always wanted. Thinks I'll give it to him. And so we are allies."

"Allies?" She looked puzzled. Ah, gods, she was so innocent still.

"King, Thalia my beloved." He came over to the window beside her and kissed her. She smelled of honey and milk and fresh flowers, and he felt her wince at the reek of sour alcohol on his breath.

You smell like a distillery. "He'll make me king." So glorious, saying it to her.

It's done, he thought, saying it. It's done. Everything that's happened...it's done.

"King?"

"I knew he would." He laughed giddily, kissing her face. "Whatever I...I've done to him"—a stumble in his speech, pain shooting through him, then he shook himself—"whatever I've done, he knows I'm the only way he can get what he wants. He was furious when...when Carin...when it happened, but this is what he's been working toward all these years, after all. Power. Strength. His hand pulling my strings. His family ascendant, his enemies crushed in the dust. And so he'll help me. Should have just asked directly, years ago, and spared us both some pain."

"King?" she said again.

Marith went over to a table and poured himself a drink from the flagon waiting there. A toast to himself. Happiness welling up within him: All hail Marith Altrersyr, *Ansikanderakesis Amrakane!* "King. I'll have my father butchered. Or keep him alive, locked up, in pain. And Tiothlyn...He'll suffer, for taking my place. And that bitch his mother, and her kin..." He gulped down the cup in one go, laughing. So much easier it all felt, now it was settled and done. Why had he kept running from it? Everything would be fine now. Fine and good. "I'll wrap you in all the jewels in my father's treasury, place the crown of Eltheia on your head. I'll make every man, woman and child on the Whites grovel at your feet. And I'll kill every person who was there when my father abandoned me. Hang their heads on Malth Elelane's walls."

"King..." Her eyes were very wide. "King..."

He smiled and kissed her face again. I love you. I do. And you love me. And everything will be fine now. It's all so good! Looked where she had been looking, out over the green and gold walls down to the knife-gray sea. White horses racing, spray breaking on the dark rocks of Caltrean Head. *Saleiot*: to shine, to sparkle, to dance like the sunlight on fast-flowing water.

He went to pour himself another drink and then hesitated, frowning at himself. Half ashamed. No more. Not now. Not today. Today they would go out to the wild country, and he'd show her indeed the beauty of the White Isles, beauty and living and sunlight on hard frost. She should share them. The world's such a beautiful place! he thought. He bathed and dressed hurriedly, forced himself to eat a little, ordered a horse fetched. The day cold and clear, washing the pain in his head away, riding fast into the wind while the gulls wheeled and shrieked above them.

Chapter Fifty

I do not like him, the way he was last night, so full of himself and his pride, so full of cruelty and hate. Selfish and vile. Self-pitying. Half-drowned in ceremony and status. Rather more than half-drowned in other things.

But then he takes me out into the wilds, riding fast with the wind in our faces. The land is hard with frost; his face shines and he reminds me of the frost. We go down to the sea and he rides the horse out into the waves and laughs when the water soaks the hem of my gown. The seabirds scream, and where last night they were terrible, the cries of things in pain, now they are poignant and lonely and catch my heart with grief. The most beautiful sound in the world, he says. They sound like the dragon's eyes were as it lighted on the ground.

We sit on the beach, in the cold wind. He looks at me as he did in the desert, when we sat beneath the stars, when he told me his heart and wept for what he was and is and will be.

The landscape here is wild and strange like nothing I could imagine, bare rocks and barren trees and bitter cold, cold through to my bones, gray sea and gray sky and gray earth, pressing with life, calling despair. The sea! I could not conceive of it, he could not describe it, and now I see it it near breaks my heart. All my life behind high walls, dark enclosures or burning, blazing light,

Great Tanis, who rules all things, but whose world is constrained to one building alone on the face of the earth. And now I am here in a place where the light is pale as water and the sky and the land and the sea go on forever.

We ride into the sea and the water splashes my skirts and I feel washed clean. Scoured by the wind and the water.

I could live here, I think. I could live here with him.

Chapter Fifty-One

In the cool sunshine of an autumn afternoon, they turned the horse away from the surf and rode inland, following a little muddy creek trickling its way through thick reed beds. Wild duck started up as they passed, and once a great white and black goose, honking mournfully. "Snowgoose," Marith said with satisfaction. "Means a hard winter." The sedge grew up almost as tall as a man, pressing in close around them with a hiss like whispers. They rode on a small raised track, thick old planks banked up over the creek. Another old road. Old as the keep. Old as the lich road. Older than dragon blood and black-red hair. Still and rotting, the land seemed in the frost. Heavy with bleak gray life. Another duck burst up, startled by their approach, wing beats vast in the still air. Then silence again save the whispering of the reeds.

After a while, when the sedge and the salt seemed to Thalia to become oppressive, they came to a fork in the narrow trackway, a meeting of ways, one running on up the creek toward the hills, the other turning off to the left toward a wood and dry ground. Marith paused the horse a moment, then took it left. Thalia breathed a little sigh of relief. These silent marshes: she thought with deep fear what they would be like at night. In the twilight, the between time. Between land and water, salt and earth. In her bed in the chambers of Malth Salene, she would not want to think of this place and that it was near.

The track they took led out of the marsh quickly enough, the wooden walkway giving way to solid beaten ground, the sedge to gorse and heather and thick coarse grass and small tangled trees bright with scarlet fruit. The way turned up and back toward the sea; they were coming to the tip of a low headland, where the cliff tumbled down in jumbled rocks to tiny coves.

"Here," Marith said, pulling the horse to a stop. They had not spoken for a long time, riding together without needing to speak, together and alone. He dismounted, helped Thalia down, tethered the horse to a tree. They went on on foot for a little, to the end of the headland where the sea and the sky and the earth met and were all three things together. Gray rocks, rough and leprous with barnacles, slippery and shiny with green-black seaweed, worn and eaten into lacework and worm tracks and smooth flat surfaces like altar stones. The water white with foam, swelling and booming in hollows and caves.

"Wait here." Marith scrambled down onto the rocks, carefully picking his way over the thick clumps of seaweed, between dark rock pools. He reached the very end of the point, where the sea washed over the rock and there was nothing around him but swirling water. He raised his arms, white and black against the gray rock and the gray sea and the gray sky. Shouted in triumph, the shout of a boy: "Hah! Hah!" Stood frozen, breathing in the scent of freshness and wildness, salt and stone and decay, tiny, vast, alive like the water and the rocks and the sky. Then he made his way back up to Thalia, cursing and laughing once when he slipped and soaked one foot in a rock pool, cursing without laughing when he slipped again and struck the heel of his hand on a barnacled rock.

"I drink too much to be scrambling out over rocks," he said ruefully. "Once I could climb anything and anywhere." He grinned and grinned like a child.

They rode on, and came to a small fishing village huddled beneath the cliffs in the next bay, a bare handful of gray houses clinging to the land behind a shingle beach where the water churned up the pebbles with a sighing whisper, so close to Malth Salene but as far distant from it as the tiny villages of the desert were distant from Sorlost.

So many voices, Thalia thought, listening to the waves breaking. All this silent land is alive with voices.

"Hungry?" Marith asked.

Thalia nodded. Marith steered the horse down the track to the edge of the village, dismounted and tapped on the door of the first house. It was low and dark, crouching into the earth, windows looking out bleakly onto the sea. The roof was of reeds, black with pitch. Nets and small domed baskets were piled about. "Lobster pots," Marith said, seeing Thalia looking curiously. The corpse of a bird, dried and mummified, hung by the neck next to the door, beside a long pole of driftwood, salt-white, so bleached dry it made Thalia's hands crawl. Rune markings were carved into it, black on white.

"Protection against death by drowning, death by starvation, death by thirst in the midst of the sea," Marith said, seeing her look at it with the knowledge of its power. "Cheerful folk, hereabouts. But you'll see."

The door opened. A woman gazed at them. Middle-aged, thin and gaunt-faced, but so beautiful she made Thalia draw breath in astonishment. Long hair, still dark and shining, great dark eyes, soft white skin tinged with gold. She blinked at them; when she spoke, her voice was low and guttural and harsh. Pebbles shifting in the waves. Water booming on rocks. So strange, hard for Thalia to understand, the cadences wrong.

"Yes?" The woman looked at Marith. "I know you. I've seen you here before. They said you were dead. Come back, are you?"

Marith merely nodded. He did not seem to expect, or want, her deference. "We'd buy bread, if you have some," he said simply. "Milk, if you have that. Or just water."

"Sweet water or salt?" she said in response, and laughed a harsh laugh. "You're in luck, for I have milk, and bread, and curd cakes hot from the oven. If you've money for it."

Marith handed her a few coins. She weighed them carefully, then ushered them in. The room was larger than Thalia had expected, very low and gloomy but warm, furnished with a heavy table, benches, a great chest with a huge iron lock. More fishing nets hung from one wall, giving the place a strong smell of fish and brine over the peaty smoke from the fire. Marith tethered the horse then stepped in after them. The woman set bread and bowls on the table, disappeared through a doorway. Through the door came the babble of a child's voice. Thalia looked questioningly at Marith.

"Not now." He smiled at her puzzled expression. "Later." The woman came back with a jug of milk and a pat of gleaming yellow butter, warm bread, small yellow apples like those they had eaten the previous night, a long side of cured fish, gelatinous and silky as Thalia's gown. Thalia ate hungrily, enjoying the food far more than the dishes she had been served at Malth Salene. Marith seemed to enjoy it too, ate better, his face filled with a simple pleasure. She remembered him eating the burned bread and meat he had cooked at dawn in the desert, proud of himself for trying. Perhaps he remembered it too, for he reached out and took her hand.

After they had eaten their fill, Marith walked over to the chest. He bent down and touched the heavy lock, raised his eyes quizzically at the woman. She looked back at him, then shook her head. He breathed out a little "hah" sound between his teeth.

They thanked the woman and left the house. A sense of strange calm descended on Thalia as they crossed the threshold. The bird hung there, twisting in the wind.

"Come down to the beach," Marith said. They walked down and sat on a rock looking at the tide coming in and the boats on the water. The sea shone pale silver in the light, the waves like ripples in a skein of long hair, moving slowly with the heavy liquidness of dreams. A knife blade of sunlight struck the sea far out, brilliant as fires, making the waves sparkle. To shine. To sparkle. To dance like the sunlight on fast-flowing water.

"What is she?" Thalia said at last.

"Not my lover, if that's what you're worried about." Marith

grinned at her. "You could tell, then, could you? I wondered if you might. She's a selkie, beautiful girl. A seal woman. One of the mer folk. A tiny wild sort of a god. Most of the women in this village are such, and in several of the villages round about. The men go out with nets, at night when the moon is full, over to the sands that can only be reached at low tide where the seal maidens shed their skins to dance as human women beautiful as stars. If a man catches one and steals her seal skin, she has no choice but to stay with him. As long as he holds her skin, you see, she can't go back into the water. So she marries him, and keeps his house for him, and bears his children. And because she is a god of a kind, he has great luck with his fishing. Until she can get back her seal skin, when she will leave him and go back into the sea, and curse his nets so that he will never catch anything but seaweed and sand." He thought for a moment. "It's a kind of wager, I suppose. How long he can keep her, how much money he can save, how old his children can grow to be, before she leaves him to starve."

Thalia was silent for a while, looking out at the sea. "That's cruel," she said at last.

"Yes," Marith said simply. "It is." He picked up a stone, weighed it in his hand and sent it skimming across the water. He got up and dusted sand from his coat. "We should go back."

They walked up into the village and reclaimed the horse. It seemed quite contented, cropping grass in the shadow of an apple tree. Marith searched in his pockets and offered it a few raisins. "Stroke her nose," he suggested. Thalia raised her hand tentatively, touched the soft velvety muzzle. The horse snorted and flicked its eyes, then went back to munching grass. Marith swung up and lifted her up gently in front of him.

They rode back inland, through beech woods brilliant with dried leaves. Something else Thalia had never seen. Something else that delighted and astonished her. "Trees made of fire," she said, "or gold, like a storybook." Marith reached up and pulled a handful of leaves from the tree, shook them into her hair.

The ground was heavy and soft with moss. Squirrels chased in the trees; once they disturbed a herd of pale tawny deer, one white stag among them with great antlers twining like the branches of a tree. Marith caught his breath at the stag: struck by its beauty, Thalia thought, as she was. He made a little hissing noise, sharp in his teeth, and the stag started up and was gone in a flash. He breathed out slowly, and spurred the horse on.

It was full dark when they arrived back at the keep. It confused Thalia how early the night came here. It must be so very late, she kept thinking. As the dusk fell, she had thought drowsily that she had lost track of time and days, on the ship, in the never-ending dark. Perhaps she should have been killing a man, tonight. Now it was night, and the stars shone down. The great red star of the Dragon's Mouth was clear, but in a different place in the sky, so she had to search for it. The Maiden and the Tree had vanished, other stars she did not know shone in their place. Only the Fire Star she recognized. She would have to ask him the others' names. But not tonight: it seemed so late and the sea air had made her so sleepy; Marith too yawned.

They came into the great main court of Malth Salene, riding under the vast gatehouse of whalebone and bleached white wood, and three men in the deep red livery of the Altrersyr stepped out to meet them.

Marith drew the horse up hard, his hand going to his belt. No sword, but a long knife. His fingers itched on the hilt as he drew it. The horse moved uncertainly under him, sensing his tension. Not a warhorse, not trained to fight, but he could feel it was ready to kick and lash out if he bid it to. Its ears flicked, maddened.

"My Lord Prince!" Aris's voice, ringing out loudly, full of fear. Marith turned his head in irritation, the horse skittering sideways. Thalia's body was rigid. "My Lord Prince, these men are...are sent by the king. No harm, I swear. But My Lord Relast—My Lord Relast would see you, urgently, if he might."

I'll bet he would, Marith thought wearily. His eyes burned again, the skin around them crawling. He rubbed violently at his face.

"Here, then." He gestured to Aris to help Thalia dismount, pushed the horse's reins into the hands of a waiting groom. "Take Lady Thalia to my quarters. See she has food, wine, a bath drawn, anything else she might desire. Place a guard at the door." Thalia's face was pained, as servants bustled her away. Dried beech leaves still caught in her hair. I'm sorry, he thought. We had one day, at least, you and I. One day. He walked with Aris into the keep, the three men behind them. "Water, to wash my face. And a drink of something." And then we'll see.

Lord Relast was waiting in his study, seated by the fire. He rose as Marith entered. Lord Carlan Murade, the queen's brother, was seated at Deneth's left. He did not.

"Deneth. Carlan." Marith nodded to them, ignoring the insult. He took a proffered cup of wine from another wide-eyed servant, gulped it down then pushed the cup into the man's hands and ordered him to bring him something stronger. He still had leaves and sand in his hair himself. Felt half a fool.

Deneth Relast coughed. "My Lord Prince," he said calmly. Marith sat at his right, trying not to glower at Carlan. There was another bustle at the door, whispered voices. A servant hurried in with a bottle, then the doors closed and the three men were alone.

"So," Carlan Murade said carefully after a moment. He watched as Marith poured himself a large cup of brandy, drained it and refilled it. "Being dead for several months doesn't seem to have led to any noticeable change in habits, I see."

Deneth Relast snorted at that. Marith tried to smile.

Carlan rearranged the material of his coat with a fussy motion. Cleared his throat. "Now we are all finally assembled, I suppose we'd best get this over with. So, then: My Lord Relast, I am sent by our King and Master, Illyn Altrersyr, Lord of the White Isles and of Illyr and of Immier and of the Wastes and of the Bitter Sea, the heir to Amrath and Serelethe, the Dragon Kin, the Demon

Born." "*My good brother*" implicit in his smug face, his fur collar, the way he gestured with his hands. "As we both know, the king's older son is tragically and grievously dead. Buried. Mourned. This...imposter, this pretender, this false prince, is to be killed. Immediately. I am commanded to bring his head back with me to Malth Elelane, where it will be set before the gates as a warning to all other traitors. Obey me in this now and the king will be...merciful. He does appreciate that your recent grief may have affected your judgment somewhat. Being a father himself, who has himself so recently seen the death of one of his own sons. Your elder daughter's head in a bag beside the imposter's, the corpse's weight in gold and jewels, an oath of fealty delivered at his feet. Nothing more than would be expected."

Deneth rolled his eyes and poured himself a drink. He refilled Marith's cup too, while he was at it. Marith gulped it down gratefully. A very good cellar, the Relasts kept.

"My father can go hang himself," Marith said after a moment. "I'll do it myself, otherwise, after I've ripped the crown from his head."

"Your father should have had you strangled the night he married my sister," Carlan snapped back. "I told him so at the time."

Marith refilled his cup again. I'm more than them, he thought desperately. More than them. The knives in his head, blunt, rusty, cutting him raw. I'll skin you alive. Take out your guts and make you watch me do it. He shut his eyes for a moment, trying to see Thalia's face garlanded in beech leaves, the light and the warmth, her eyes like the summer sky. Shadows crawled around him, drowning it out.

I'll never be happy, he thought suddenly. Tobias was right. I was right.

"My Lords, please," Deneth said weakly. Very far away, his voice sounded. Distant as stars.

Marith opened his eyes again. Carlan blinked and jerked his head. Very cold in the room. The seabirds screamed, louder and louder. Death! Death! Death! He got up and walked over to Carlan, his hand on his dagger. Drew his dagger, stared into Carlan's face. Cut Carlan's throat in a great spray of scarlet blood. So cold in the room that the blood froze, tiny droplets clicking onto the smooth oak floor.

"You would appear to have burned my bridges for me, My Lord Prince," Deneth said at last. His face was very white. His voice shook. "Rather definitively."

"My father's troops can't be more than a few days behind him anyway. Waiting just off-shore, even. Whatever was said here tonight would have made no difference. Even my head on a stick. You pushed him to it when you had him abandon me." Marith gave the corpse a push, so that it fell with a hard thump to the floor. Ice crystals crunched underfoot. He felt absolutely sure, absolutely certain. Could see, clear as if it stood before him, how things were and would be. "You'll be dead soon enough, I should think, one way or another. And I'll be king."

Deneth took a deep, long breath. For a moment, Marith wondered if the man would be fool enough to try to kill him. He bent down, gathered a handful of Carlan's blood, poured two cups of brandy, divided the frozen drops between them, gave one to Deneth. "Death and all demons, Lord Relast. You agreed to back me." The shadows clawed at the walls. He smiled. Deneth drank slowly. Bent and knelt at his feet.

Marith did not sleep that night. He walked down onto the beach, out onto the moor, stood by the stones that marked the lich road and looked up at the night. The weather was changing, clouds coming in blocking out the stars. Ragged across the sky, great reaching, tearing hands dark beyond dark. Like the cloud was the edge of the world, the stars beyond a crack from which all the life was pouring out.

No longer frightening. Nothing was frightening now. Marith walked the walls of the fortress, paced the corridors and halls.

In the gray light of dawn he came back into his chambers. In the bedchamber Thalia lay asleep, her face crumpled and strained.

A few beech leaves were scattered on the floor by the bed. Marith sat down and looked at her. Her hair hung across the pillows like a stream of black water. She was wrapped heavily in the blankets, hunched with cold. But her left arm showed. Her scars. Like writing, she had said one night when he had pressed his face against them, kissed them one by one, held his own marred left hand beside them. Writing that told her guilt and her power in jagged marks on her perfect, luminous skin.

It can't be stopped. Can't be undone. It's too late. He kissed her hair, took a bottle from the sideboard, went out. He walked back through the doors of the keep into the gardens. Over to the edge of the cliff, where a small mound rose, bare earth still being reclaimed by the grass and the moss. A rough stone at its top, carved with the crude image of a horse. A very old stone, far, far older than the grave it marked.

The clouds were thicker, sea mist and drizzle. The sky was lighter now, almost full morning, but the sun was hidden. The sea the color of a drawn sword.

In the court of kings he was victorious,
Fair-haired, fair-mannered,
Horse tamer,
Gold wearer,
Strong young tree branch,
Fierce to his enemies, kind to his friends.
No man can say of him,
That he did not fight his share or give it.
No man can say of him,
That he did not deserve his renown.

The old songs, the laments for dead heroes. We drink and fight and kill and die.

What would Carin think of this? he wondered. Laugh? Weep? Try to kill him in his turn, to stop it? Ride out beside him, hating him but loyal to the end of everything? Nod, and smile, and look at him in silence? Shake his head, and say he'd always known?

The wind blew a cold squall of spray into his face. He poured some of the contents of the bottle onto the earth of the grave. He sat down leaning against the headstone and drank the rest in long, leisurely mouthfuls.

Chapter Fifty-Two

Fire and smoke. Fire and blood. Over and over, endless. The smell was coming into Orhan's dreams, there in his bedroom, his dining room, when he was taking a piss. Smelled it last night in Darath's arms, fucking him and suddenly cold with the sick stench of burning.

Bil had talked about a taste in her mouth, a smell in her breath, caused by the child within her. Common, she said, in pregnant women. Meant a healthy child, more likely a boy. Meant good.

The roof of Tam's house collapsed in a shower of sparks, wild dancing like Year's Heart magery. A great gout of smoke went up. A few ragged cheers. A beautiful building, the House of the Sun in Shadow. Gold columns and white marble, a window of mage glass in green and deep blue. Roses in pots on the balconies, the central courtyard a grove of magnolia and cherry trees with a little pool lined in black china to make the water as dark and cool as sleep. He'd been to parties there. Sucked Darath's cock there, on one memorable occasion.

A crash and the windows of the upper floor fell in, sending several large pieces of burning timber down. More cheers, mixed with a few screams. He should probably have some soldiers sent over here. Someone was going to get hurt.

Someone had, of course, already been hurt. Several someones, in fact. Orhan had been sure he could hear them screaming, for a while, even over the roar of the flames. One middle-aged woman. A girl of marriageable age, a boy a few years younger. A very old man. Nobody anyone would miss. Beggars. Street whores. Hatha addicts. Daughters and sons and mothers and lovers. And then the servants and the bondsmen and the hangers-on and Tam's boy and a couple of people whose names got dragged in because, well, just because…

Ultimately, he'd killed every single one of them.

He could blame Tam. Darath did. He'd betrayed them, and had surely planned to do the same to them. Orhan and Bil and Darath and Elis and Elis's myriad mistresses and the boy Darath had been screwing last month. All of them, burning. Would Tam have felt guilt about it? Cared?

Probably yes, Orhan thought, watching the flames. Tam wasn't a monster, any more than he was. The law was the law. He didn't want any of this to happen. It just had to be done.

The worst thing he'd ever done. Though possibly not the worst thing he would ever do.

Thank the Lord of Living and Dying the child's not mine, he thought.

A very long time he stood there, watching the fires. The house finally collapsed completely, caving in like a gutted ox. Bil left early on, pleading sickness and weariness, carried back in her splendid new litter, green silk shimmering like leaves, its bearers white robed like new bones. She had begun preparations for the baby, opening the house's nurseries, interviewing wet-nurses and servants, exploring the relative merits of silk and silk velvet as material for clout cloths. Found it tiring, she said, in her current state.

Darath stayed for longer, standing gravely beside Orhan, cynically dressed in old clothes to dump afterward rather than try and wash out the stink.

"Come and get drunk with me," he said to Orhan after the front wall came down with a roar and a burst of morbid applause.

"Maybe not a good idea."

"No, but a necessary one." He shrugged. "Suit yourself. Come round tomorrow. Well after noon. And don't spend too much time brooding."

"I'll try not to." Orhan grasped his lover's hand suddenly, almost hungry for him to stay. "I would come. But..."

"What do you think I see in you, Lord Emmereth? I don't just marvel at the beauty of your cock, you know." Darath squeezed his hand back, smiling at him ruefully. "Necessary evil, Orhan. I'll fuck you tomorrow, make you happy again."

And so he was alone, with the last of the crowd of voyeurs and carrion crawlers and those with nothing else to see and nowhere else to go. The night drawing in. Night comes. Some of us survive. No desire to go home and look at his own walls and imagine them burning instead.

He walked away aimlessly into the city. Another hot day. Thin high clouds making the evening sky gray and yellowed like diseased skin. In the Street of All Sorrows women had been pouring water to keep down the dust and the air smelled sweet with it. A street trader stood in a shady alleyway with a tray of little paper kites that bobbed in the air on strings hung with copper bells. Strange, to think that one day soon he'd be buying such toys for Bil's child.

Camellias blossomed all down the sides of the street, red and pink and pallid white. Pethe birds flickered in the branches, chasing butterflies. The leaves on the bushes were curling and browned, dropping to the ground, trampled to a mush underfoot, soiling the stones.

That's another good omen, Orhan thought. My, my, I'm melancholy this evening. Too many late nights and early mornings. Too much time spent with old books. A thinness of the blood, a confusion of the red and yellow humors. Burn sage and lemon peel and tallow candles, take hot baths regularly, avoid milk and sweet things. Try not to kill people, and, if you do, try not to think too much about the fact they're dead.

He turned off All Sorrows into Beating Heart Lane, where there were no flowers and nothing was currently dying. A small, thin alley, a cut-between housing a quiet wine shop and a baker's, leading to the Street of the Butchered Horse and then the Street of Flowers. Down the Street of Flowers itself, sweet with yellow lilies, where fashionable crowds were strolling before a late dinner, making eyes at each other, smoothing down their silk dresses, raising their arms casually so that golden bracelets and heavy gemstones best caught the light. A beautiful boy slunk past him, red hair, a mouth like a rose. Orhan stared. Should have gone with Darath, he thought mournfully.

His footsteps were leading him to Darath's house. Darath wasn't even there. He turned away, wandered aimlessly for a while, had almost reached the Court of the Broken Knife when one of his guardsmen raised his hand to stop him.

"Someone's following us, My Lord. Someone—"

An explosion of white light. No sound, but a sudden strong, sweet smell. Orhan fell backward, his head striking the marble paving stones. Blind: brilliant silver in his vision, black patterns moving. Another burst of light, and then silence, and then someone was helping him to his feet.

He stood up dizzily, his clothes feeling hot and dry, flaky and rough on his skin. The square smelled of other things now, scorched stone, burned things. Always burned things. Two of his guards were dead on the ground, black and bloodied. Smoke and flames rose from their clothes. He regarded them gravely, as his remaining guards began to pull him away. More dead.

"Run! My Lord! Run!"

More light, licking around the square. Quicksilver, pouring in thick trails. Melting the stone. Orhan screamed. Began to run with his guards, swords drawn uselessly, shouting prayers. A great burst of green-gold fire caught him on his arm and his shirt was burning, pain tearing up his skin. He staggered, knocked off balance, white light pulsing behind his eyes. Endless voices screaming. All he could smell was burning flesh. He fell to the ground again, beating at his burning clothes. A guardsman dragged at him, hauled him toward the nearest doorway. Wood and stone exploded above their heads.

The tinkling of shattered stonework falling in tiny fragments like glass beads, making music on the paving of the street.

A figure leaped forward in the corner of his vision, threw itself at another, slighter man standing in the corner where two houses met. A howl and a burst of light, suddenly extinguished. The two men rolled on the ground, grappling with each other. Light burst up again, and a scream. Blind. Silver. The outline of a man's body flashed black in Orhan's closed eyes, bones and heart visible through the skin. Writhing like water. Like the way the rain had beaten on the ground. Men can't move like that, he thought somewhere in some distant part of his mind. Can't move like that. His vision flickered back slowly, light and shadow dancing around in his eyes. When he could see again his guard lay sprawled at odd angles, his body jerking. The mage was gone.

Orhan crawled forwards. Tried to stand. The pressure of his weight on his arm made him scream: he fell back down, dazed with pain. Hands reached for him. He felt himself pulled up gently, helped into a nearby shop. Sat gasping and shaking in a small bookseller's. Two guardsmen sat flanking him, swords on their knees.

They sat like that for a long while. The third guard lay in the street. Should go and see him. Should check he was alive. Should help him. But Orhan's body shook uncontrollably. Couldn't move.

People came creeping back into the street, staring with awestruck faces at the burned stone. At the bodies. The owner of the house that had been hit came out and wept, cursing man and God. Blood trickled from a wound to his face where he had been hit by flying glass. Lucky to be alive. The bookseller brought Orhan water and wine and a cloth to bind his arm.

"My man," Orhan whispered. "My servant—the one who fought...The one there...Help him." The bookseller stared at him dumbly. Backed away, muttering a prayer. Orhan drank the water. His arm was burned. His hands shook too much to be able to bind up the wound. The guard lay in the street, still jerking a little now and again. "Help him," Orhan said to the two men by his side. They too stared at him dumbly. They were paid to guard him. So would not leave him. So sat and watched their comrade die.

A group of Imperial soldiers arrived, terrified, no idea what to do or why. Orhan spoke to them haltingly, his voice distant in his head. A mage. Yes, a mage. Yes, mage fire. Yes, he was certain. They gathered up the bodies. The guard who'd attacked the mage was now dead. One of the soldiers cut the dead men's throats just to be sure. They'd sew up their mouths and sew up their eyes and bury them in the shadow of the city walls with wreaths of copper-stem around their necks. And still they'd be afraid of them. Orhan was a rational man. But he shuddered, looking at the crumpled bodies. A bad death. Unnatural and wrong.

The new litter was fetched: Orhan shook so much he was unable to walk. Fortunately the litter hadn't been made by the man who'd just tried to kill him. Orhan gave a couple of gold talents to the bookseller and the man with the ruined house. Then he crawled into his litter, feeling horribly exposed and imprisoned behind its curtains. The journey home seemed to take an eternity. His arm hurt. His whole body hurt. His head ached. He could still see lights dancing in his vision, burned onto his eyes. Janush his doctor bound his arm with feverfew and calendula flowers and muttered a prayer. Finally he collapsed into bed, smoke-stained and exhausted and shaking.

It all just went on and on and on. Never ending. What have I done? he kept thinking. How could it possibly have been worth it? What have I done? What have I done?

Chapter Fifty-Three

Woke the next morning to find Darath sitting at the end of his bed.

"I don't think much of your security arrangements," said Darath. He was munching candied apricots, held out the dish to Orhan. "I could have cut your throat a dozen times while you snored. Didn't even bother to take my dagger. Want one?"

Orhan sat up and rubbed his face. "I think they make a special dispensation for you. You'd probably persuade me to flog them if they tried to strip-search you on the way in here."

"Such tender signs of affection." Darath leaned over and kissed him, bits of apricot stuck to his lips and getting into Orhan's mouth.

"So…" Darath shuffled up, lay down beside Orhan, who curled himself gratefully into his lover's shoulder, closing his eyes. So good, having him here like this. They should live together properly. He'd suggest it. Yes.

"So," said Darath. "Someone tried to kill you last night. Does nobody in Sorlost have the decency just to die when someone tries to kill them any more? If you'd come drinking with me, you'd have escaped completely, you realize?"

"If I'd come drinking with you, we'd both have been burned to pieces. It was a pretty close thing as it was."

"No, you'd have woken hung-over in my bedroom, wrapped in my ardent arms and in a considerably better mood than you seem to be. Understandably so, I grant you. Anyway." Darath chewed another apricot. "March, I assume?"

"I'd think it most likely." Orhan raided the plate, realizing he was starving. "It was painfully crude. And stupid." He shuddered. "I don't want to think about it."

Darath wrapped his arms around him, kissed him again. Kisses literally sweet as honey. "Thank Great Tanis for stupidity."

"Oh, I intend to. A big show of thanks, a thaler's worth of candles, rub March's nose in his failure. Come with me?"

Darath sighed. "If I must. No, no, of course, I'll come. A thaler's worth of candles burning will be quite a wonderful sight with an aching head and not enough sleep. Your assassin had consummate timing: I'd only just got off after a night of pitifully mild debauchery when one of my servants woke me up again to let me know you weren't dead. God's knives, Orhan."

Orhan bathed and dressed slowly. His body hurt as though he was a thousand years old. He was bruised and battered, thick red burns on his arm. But surprisingly unharmed otherwise. Or not surprising: he was beginning to suspect that March hadn't actually wanted him to have died. He came back to his bedroom to find Darath sprawled on his bed still eating apricots and reading one of the Treasury ledgers he'd brought home.

"Fascinating stuff," Darath said. "You cut my stipend as Lord of the Golden Mask of the Furthest West, I see. My great-great-great-great uncle bribed and blackmailed one of the under-secretaries for months to get that. Five thalers a month, it pays."

"You're not supposed to be reading that. And you've still got the title, so don't complain."

"I'm not complaining. I'm just observing. But don't be surprised if I can't afford to buy you a gift on your birthday this year. So." Darath sat up cross-legged, shoving the book away. He'd got honey smears on the cover. Honey and human skin: Lord of Living and

Dying have mercy. Orhan felt nauseous looking at it. "So. What the fuck do we do about March, then?"

Orhan sighed wearily. "I don't want to talk about it. Really. Not now."

"You know why he's doing it like this, of course?"

"We discussed this, I thought. Because he's an idiot."

"Because it makes you look an idiot, Orhan."

That stung. "And why is that, exactly?"

"Why? You know why. Your big triumph, your enemies dead and your power displayed, and you can't manage to walk home without someone trying to burn you to a crisp with mage fire. Do you know how long it's been since anyone was assassinated using magery? It's so dramatically overblown it stops even being frightening. Just goes straight to utterly and totally absurd."

"But it failed."

"But that hardly matters. You think you can keep a grip on the city with this going on around you? People will start to laugh. You can't ignore it."

All true. All quite correct. He'd worked that out for himself, in the dark, trying to sleep, listening for the sound of an assassin's knife. If March had killed him, he would be some kind of Imperial hero, tragic and mourned, the Emperor clinging on to his wise words. The very absurdity of the attempt instead made him look ridiculous. He'd squirmed himself, talking about it. As thought it was a failure on his part. As though it was somehow embarrassing. *Listen to this man, oh people of the Sekemleth Empire! Pay more in taxes! Stamp out corruption! Build up the army and feed the poor! He has a plan to make us great again! It will all be worth it! It will! Just ignore the fact that he can't walk down the street without his own bodyguards being magically burned to death!*

What was that I said? thought Orhan. That one child's life is worth half a hundred other lives? That it would be different if it were my own child?

Darath said: "So, we go after him then?"

Ah, God's knives, thought Orhan. What has become of us? "We'll have to, I suppose."

"Poison? A quick knife while he sleeps? Poison would be easiest, surely?"

What has become of us? Orhan thought. What we did was supposed to be the end of it. A change, a remaking of Empire. A good thing. Now it's begun, and it will just go on and on and more and more people will die until everything has slipped away into bloodshed.

You knew this would happen in the end, he thought. Just hoped otherwise.

"Poison," he said.

Darath astonished him then by saying, "What about Elis's wedding?"

"Elis's wedding?" God's knives. It would have to go ahead. Everybody pretend everything's all right with the world. Elis's wedding, Bil's child...

"So does March die before the event, or after it?"

Orhan thought suddenly that he was going to be sick. How have we come to this? How have we come to this? What have I done? It all just happened, so easily.

"After. It will have to be after. Tie things together before pushing everything apart again. If I live that long...If March doesn't try to again..." He felt the blood rush to his face. It hadn't been like this, before, plotting the death of an Emperor and all his servants. All they'd known of death was stories, and the white-clad men in the Court of the Fountain, empty and ready to die. Abstractions dying behind a curtain, a beautiful woman with blood-red hands. His own father dying, sick with fever, stinking, sweating, everyone relieved that it was so quick at the end. But once you had seen, it was so full of shame.

Darath said, "I'll handle it." He squeezed Orhan's hand. "Don't think about it. You'll just wake up one morning and it'll be done."

"Don't use anything too nasty."

"I'll handle it, I said." A nasty gleam shone in Darath's eyes, like the way he'd looked at Orhan after they'd broken up the last time, meeting at a party with a pretty thing in a diamond collar on his arm. I broke his heart, Orhan thought. I took him back and got him stabbed in the gut. And now this, because I'm too high and mighty to do it myself.

He pulled on a jacket to cover the sore red burns on his arm. "Let's go to the Temple, then."

Chapter Fifty-Four

A thaler bought an awful lot of candles. The Great Chamber of the Temple blazed with them, gold on the bronze walls. Even the black stone of the floor was golden. Orhan's skin, and Darath's, and the light reflected in Darath's dark eyes. They ran over the altars, the wall sconces, the floor, serried ranks of flame. Perfumed with cloves and cinnamon and rose, the smell of sun and warmth and living in the old symbolism of the body's senses. The most expensive candles possible. But still, a thaler bought an awful lot of candles. The heat made Orhan's eyes water; he could see Darath was sweating.

The High Priestess knelt before the High Altar. Her hair hung over her face, her hands were raised to her mouth. She looked so tiny. So fragile. Orhan stared at her until Darath shoved him away. One life.

"She's fine," Darath whispered to him. "It's what she does. Was born to do. Stop."

She did draw the red lot, thought Orhan. If the God hadn't wanted her...The God chose her. Just as the God spared me. Another priestess came up to the girl, said something to her. She moved her head, replied something, got up and walked away. He caught a glimpse of her face, pale and pinched with big eyes. It will be all right, Orhan tried to tell himself. And if it isn't...One more life, he thought. What's one more? The Treasury ledgers were terrible but he had some hope of improving them. Made some changes already. More to come. The letter to the Immish High Council had been answered almost respectfully. He'd had a very good idea about including better houses for the destitute and starving poor when rebuilding some of the streets damaged in the uproar. *Listen to this man, oh people of the Sekemleth Empire! He has a plan to make us great again! It will all be worth it! It will!*

Tam was dead. March was going to die. If March didn't kill him and Darath first. What was one more life? Hers, or March's, or his own? The city might yet be made better. And others might yet have better lives.

Human skin and honey. It sickens you, but it's what's needed to go on.

Other worshippers stared at them. Stared more when Orhan handed over a gleaming gold coin, voiced his desire to make offering in a loud, clear tone that carried around the muffled silence of the chamber, echoing on bronze and stone. The priestesses milled about him gasping and mouthing platitudes. Murmurs all around them: rumors of what had happened last night would be everywhere. So outré. So...bizarre. Louder, bolder murmurs when he explained that he had been saved from death at the hands of an assassin only by the great mercy of the God who smiled down on him. Darath smiled at him: you're learning, Orhan. Showmanship is all.

In the golden light, so bright there were no shadows, Orhan knelt down before a small altar and prayed. "Great Lord Tanis, I come before You, to ask Your blessing of my life." A rational man. But a thankful one. It's good, he thought, even with what I've done, it's good being alive.

"We live. We die. For these things, we are grateful," Darath repeated beside him. The scent of the candles was so strong, spice and flowers and the sweet honey of the wax. So he had knelt here before, with Bil, giving thanks for her child. So he had sat and given thanks for the life of the man he'd tried to kill. Strange and strange again, all the ways of the world. God forgave him, it seemed. Or did not altogether despise him, anyway. The first time since that night that he had set foot in the Temple without shuddering. The golden light danced around him, the movements of the worshippers making the candle flames flicker. A young woman heavily pregnant, a young man with the scars of the knife, an old couple with thin shaking hands like the branches of a dead tree. Priestesses, masked in silver and lapis, shapeless as rain clouds in their gray robes. He'd killed several of those.

No, not killed. Killed suggested action, danger, personal involvement, playing a role. Better to say he'd ordered several of them dead. More callous put that way, and more true.

He took Darath's hand as they walked back through the thin high dark passageway out into the world beyond. When Bil's child is born, he thought, I will love it as if it were my own. The thought made him suddenly deeply happy. Bil will have a child. I will be a father. I will raise a life. Only a few months now. A child! he thought.

Gray Square was hot and muggy. Crowded, too. The city seemed noticeably more pious with all that had happened. The kite seller had moved there, the tinkle of copper bells followed Orhan as he walked past. Another man was selling waxed silk balloons in bright colors that floated up into the sky when a tiny candle was lit beneath them. Very pretty, they must look at night. Flying things up to the heavens seemed a new fashion, a childish distraction from the chaos that had almost engulfed them, an attempt to reach the numinous glories of the light whilst trapped in human decay.

Orhan bought a blue balloon for Bil. Nice and symbolic. She'd like that.

They skirted the Court of the Fountain, heavy with street merchants and whores and all the music of the city that shifted around them, the crowds parting almost unthinking before them in deference to great men. A few people still cheered for Lord Emmereth, the savior of the city. Darath snorted but squeezed Orhan's hand. In the Street of Closed Eyes, a man was breathing fire, watched by a small circle of children and stupefied drunks. He wasn't very good: the fire was barely coming out more than a hand's width from his mouth. His torch smelled oily and rank and his clothes were shabby. Imitating a dragon. The tell-tale marks of hatha cravings around his smoke-sore eyes.

"Always wanted to be able to do that," said Darath. He turned to Orhan. "Let's go and do something pleasant, then."

"I should go to the palace. Work."

"No. You almost died last night! You should enjoy yourself a bit."

Orhan looked at him, and laughed, and took his hand.

They went to Darath's bathing house, swam in the cool water of the shade pool. The room was kept in darkness, its walls and ceiling gilt in silver, the water heavy with rose oil. Larks and heart doves in cages buried in the walls. The hot pool next door was heavily salted so that one floated on the surface of the water. It stung sweetly on Orhan's injured skin. Thick steam pumped up from the floor was scented with frankincense, the atmosphere so humid it was hard to see clearly and the water upon which one rested seemed to merge into the heat of the air. Finally the cold plunge, icy sweet. Afterward they sat in a rooftop garden walled in lilac trees, listening to a boy sing. A servant girl brought milk curdled with vinegar and spiked with brandy. The twilight bell rang across the city. Ferfews began to fly and to call. Great green moths circled their heads, drawn by the flicker of the lamps.

Night comes. We survive.

Orhan thought: I may just have saved the Empire.

Or at least I've done the best I can.

A dark clear night and the stars were out, looking down on them.

Lord of Living and Dying, Great Tanis Who Rules All Things, thank you.

Thank you.

Chapter Fifty-Five

Illyn Altrersyr's troops reached Third ten days after Marith did. Great chains had been raised at Toreth Harbor to keep out the ships, but the people of Escral turned on the Relast men sent to do likewise. Two died, the rest were imprisoned. Five great ships with sails the color of clotted blood swept down into the harbor there only a few hours afterward. A day's march from Malth Salene, and no time to call for aid. They reached Toreth with the dusk, and the city reluctantly opened her gates to her king.

Thalia saw them in the morning light, drawing up before the walls, pennants fluttering in the wind. Cold winter sunlight shone on their armor. Another hard frost, painfully beautiful: the dark shapes of men and horses stood out harshly against the silver white of the world, looking false and unreal.

Marith was closeted with Lord Relast, had been since the message came in the gray cold of first light that his father was present in person and the men of Third were uneasy with it. The set of his face as he left her had been terrible; when he had been told his father had come, he had laughed.

I wish I was back in Sorlost, Thalia thought. That this was all a dream. He's a beautiful boy, he shines like the moon. Kingly. And myself a queen. A golden throne and a crown of silver...But this! This! She looked at the men outside the walls. A bit late now to think she might leave.

Just after noon, there was a stirring in the men outside the walls. Voices shouted, too far away to make out the words. She craned her head out of the window, trying to see what was happening. Figures milled around in a tight knot of action; someone brought up horses, raised a standard with a deep red flag worked with gold stars.

A tap at the door. A servant entered, flushed and out of breath from running.

"My Lady," he said hurriedly, "My Lady, My Lord Prince desires your presence in the great courtyard. He said as quickly as you can."

Thalia picked up the black cloak. Desires your presence? An order. His face, once, in the desert, afraid to go near her, afraid she might push him away. And so now we come to this. Your woman, the dragon had called her. The holiest woman in all Irlast, and no one would ever say he was her man. A trophy. A thing to display. *Look, look, Father. Look what I've got.*

They walked through the corridors, the serving man dancing impatience, wanting to go faster. I will not run for him, Thalia thought. People bustled aimlessly around them, fear in their eyes, drawing back as she passed.

In the courtyard, Marith stood in the midst of a mass of armed men. He was dressed in a shirt of fine silver armor, a sword at his hip, a deep red cloak spilling out behind him. In the bright clear pale light of the winter sun he was as beautiful as dreams, as shining as frost, with a shadow behind him that stank of pain and despair and death.

The serving man led Thalia through the press of people to his side. For a moment she thought that she should kneel.

"You are to come with me," he said shortly. His eyes sparkled, a boy's glee in which maggots writhed. "We're to ride out, to meet him. I want you to see them. I want them to see you. Ti will be so jealous."

A groom stepped forward with horses, a great white stallion saddled in red and gold, gold ornaments at its head and mouth, a honey and cream palfrey with a side-saddle in black velvet and silver gilt.

"She's very tame, My Lady," the groom said gently. A kind man, sensing her fear. "No harm come, mounted on her. And I'll be with you, see, walking at the rein."

Lord Relast gestured impatiently. "We need to go out, My Lord Prince. They'll be waiting." Deference fighting terror in his voice.

Marith nodded. He mounted eagerly, smoothing his cloak back behind him in a great streak of deep red. Deneth Relast and Aris did likewise; the groom helped Thalia up and arranged her skirts. Ten men around them, also mounted, armed and helmeted, their horses caparisoned with leather around their heads to make them look almost like skulls. Ten men on foot, with long spears. In front, standard bearers with a green and gold banner that must be Lord Relast's, and the dark red of the Altrersyr.

They moved forward slowly, at walking pace. A sudden cry, sharp as the gulls' screams, caught Thalia. She looked up and saw Landra and her mother and sister standing on the wall. Lady Jora was weeping: it must have been she who had screamed. Landra's face curled with hatred. Savane, still barely more than a child, clapped her hands to her mouth in awe.

They came out through the great gates of Malth Salene, onto the road that led down into the town, bordered in brown heather and the last of the gorse. The sea roared below them, churned white. The sun shone brilliant in a sky clear as liquid. The shadows rose up before them as they went.

Men came forward to meet them, beneath the same dark red banner, armed and mounted in the same style. A tall man in their midst, dark-haired and dark-eyed with skin as white as the foam. A young man beside him, dark-haired and dark-eyed also, his hand on the hilt of his sword. The two groups stopped, regarded each other in silence. Horses nickered and shifted. The waves roared. The seabirds screamed.

Marith rode forward, right up to them, drawing his horse up almost nose to nose with the king's.

"Father. Ti."

Illyn Altrersyr regarded him. Tiothlyn started to speak, but his father's hand raised and the boy fell silent. A cold, sullen look on his face. So like and unlike Marith's face.

"Marith." Illyn Altrersyr's voice was bitter, grating like metal on stone. Weariness and love and despair underneath it. A man who knew as clear as the rising sun that he had lost something precious, and that there was nothing he could have done to avoid it, but that he should still at least have tried. He studied his son's face a long time, while the banners snapped and creaked in the wind and the horses stirred.

"You failed to kill the Asekemlene Emperor, then?" King Illyn said at last. "Dragonlord, I hear you are, and a killer of babies." His eyes flicked to Thalia. "This is the woman, of course. The Priestess."

"Dragonlord and dragon killer, Father. Mage killer, too. And, yes, killer of babies. Women. Old men."

Tiothlyn stirred again, trying to speak. Again, his father silenced him with a motion of his hand.

"Why?" Illyn asked. For a moment, Thalia thought he was referring to the Emperor, or the dragon, or herself, then she saw where his face looked. She turned in the saddle. Saw the body of a man, richly dressed in silks and furs, raised up on spears above the carved wood of the gates.

"Because he bloody deserved it," said Marith. "Bloody stupid bastard that he was."

"He was my mother's brother and a loyal servant of the crown," Tiothlyn shouted. The horses snorted and twisted their heads, stamped their hooves. Men shifted in the drawn-up columns, awaiting something. The look on Illyn Altrersyr's face was unreadable. His eyes moved from Marith's face to the man's body and back again. He would have forgiven him, Thalia thought then. He would have taken him in again. He was proud, to hear of the dragon and the things done in Sorlost. *Really, as drinking boasts go, it's pretty impressive, you know*. He loves him. Of course he does. He's his father.

But it's all done and over now, and neither can go back.

Marith perhaps sensed something, also. He raised his hand and rubbed at his face, weak and weary.

Then he drew his sword.

There was a sudden shouting, metal flashing in the light. Screams in the air loud as thunder. Shadows vast in the low sun. Thalia cried out in panic as the men around her began fighting, swords out, blood spurting up. Her horse tried to back away, the groom at the lead rein shouting something and then the groom was cut down. Thalia clutched at the reins, trying to make the horse turn around, get away. All there was was blood and dark and screaming, so loud it drowned out her vision, horses screaming, men screaming, the world screaming like a dying child.

Marith swerved his horse toward her. His face was rapturous. Ecstatic. So beautiful her heart leaped. He raised his sword and for a moment she thought he would kill her, and for a moment she thought that she would welcome it if he did. So beautiful and perfect his face. So joyous and radiant his smile.

"Get back to the gates," he said shortly. Not loud, but his voice was clear over the roaring, screaming dark. For a moment they were alone in the world, and then he wheeled away and Thalia found her horse galloping toward Malth Salene, through the gates and beneath the dead body that hung there, against a tide of men running out with swords in their hands.

In the courtyard, Thalia almost fell from her horse, her hands shaking. A young groom came to help her, tried to quieten the horse. It gnashed its teeth at him, shrieked and kicked out its hind legs. Its body was lathered with sweat as though it had run a race. Blood dripped from its mouth where it had torn itself on the bit. Thalia staggered away from it. Hands caught her, holding her up.

"You're not hurt? Help her to her chambers." Landra's voice, shaking like Thalia's body and mind.

"No...I want...to see." Thalia gestured weakly to the walls where the other women still stood looking out. "I need to see."

Landra looked at her. Nodded. Her eyes too were filled with tears. They climbed the steps of the wall, Thalia holding Landra's arm. Don't let go. Hold on to something. Grief and fear. Shame. The absolute certainty of what was to come. Lady Jora turned briefly as they joined her. Her hands gripped the stone so hard they were bleeding. Savane's face was rapt.

A trampling mire of men and horses. In the maelstrom of the fighting, loyalties and allegiances were long lost, men hacking at comrades and commanders and lovers, nothing in them beyond killing and being killed. King Illyn's army surged forward, formless, swords shaking in their eagerness. Men came riding or running out from Malth Salene, some barely armed, bareheaded and clad in servants' liveries, clutching swords and spears and wooden sticks. A madness overtaking them all, bloodlust and deathlust, hacking and stabbing with no thought to self-defense. The hard ground churned to mud. The horses rearing, exposing their soft underbellies, falling dying and crushing their riders beneath them, men and beasts treading them into the ground. In the midst of it all, Marith Altrersyr, dragonlord, dragon killer, dragon kin, demon born. King of Dust. King of Shadows. King of death and emptiness and despair. His sword flashing, his face alive with radiant shining light.

Blood! Oh blood! Oh blood and killing! He struck out with his sword and a man fell before him, cut open, gutted like a fish. A stink of shit. He spurred his horse forward and a young man was there, mounted on a warhorse, expensive silver armor, his helm crested in peacock feather plumes. Kamlen Jurgis, the younger son of his father's best friend. Kam lunged at him. Marith parried the stroke easily, struck back. Kam was good: parried, twisted himself sideways in the saddle, struck again. A shriek of metal as the sword grated on Marith's armor. Green eyes stared at him, hating. Gods, this was wondrous! Everything, even the joyful slaughter in the palace of Sorlost, everything in his life was as nothing compared to this! Power. Such power flowing through him. They died at his asking. All of them. He'd kill them all. So futile, their little lives. The thin fine skin of life, suspended over the eternity of emptiness. They all deserved to die, surely? Death and death and death! The one true thing! The only thing! He drew first blood on Kamlen, making a mess of the man's left arm. Kam howled at him and got a stroke in in return, not managing to wound but the flat of his sword smashed into Marith's head by his temple, making his ears ring. You can die badly for that, Marith thought. For hurting me. He'd never liked him when they were children together. Nasty, lazy boy two years his senior. He wheeled and struck again and Kam lost his helmet. Hah! Marith raised his sword. Drove it in across the boy's face. A gash opened where the eyes should be. Seemed to stay alive for a moment, blinded, raw, opened up. Puzzled at what had just happened to his world. Made nothing as he died, a broken thing lacking the power of sight and speech, unrecognizable so that no one would know it to mourn. He killed the horse too and rode his own horse over their bodies, just to be sure, bringing its front hooves down hard on what was left of Kam's face. A funny loud hollow crunching sound, it made.

He could hear it, clear and fine, over the roar of battle around him. Could see everything, hear everything, every detail, the pattern, the logic of it. Everything. Ti was swinging and hacking. His face was bloody, he seemed to be wounded. You can't die, Marith thought suddenly as he watched. You can't die. I need to kill you. He steered his horse over toward his brother, cutting men out of his path as he went. Couldn't see his father. Ti looked up and saw him coming toward him, stared, mouthed something, turned his horse and was off down the field away from him. Coward! Coward! Come back and die! Marith turned his own horse to follow, but then suddenly two men were in front of him, drawing up swords. He recognized them too, men of his father's guard, good fighters, men who'd helped teach him to fight. They knew what they were doing, they came on together, one on either side of him, swords swinging in concert, heavy thick broadswords, their horses getting in close so he couldn't turn away. Stank of sweat.

No fear in him. No concern. He knew perfectly and absolutely that they could not kill him. "Amrath!" he shouted, parrying off one blade, ducking and twisting to avoid the other. "Amrath! Amrath! Amrath and the Altrersyr! Death and all demons! Death! Death! Death!" The air screamed around him. Things tore through the skies, shrieking, clawing at the light. He parried another sword thrust, avoided another, struck out. His sword met his opponent's with a crash. Garent. The man's name was Garent. Had helped teach him to fight. The other's blade came for him, he couldn't move in time but it rang on his armor and he knew he was unhurt because here nothing could hurt him. The screams were so loud, a maelstrom of noise, waves hammering on rock, seabirds shrieking, hungry, angry, maddening, maddened, voiceless, beyond speech, beyond anything. So loud it was almost blinding. But he could see. He could see everything. This was all he was. This was all that was real. Everything would die. "Death!" he screamed over the shrieking voices. "Death! Death! Death and all demons! Death!" He lashed out and Garent was dead, his head hanging from his body. Lashed out again and the other was broken, arm cut off at the elbow, staring bloodied and astonished at his wound, horror in his eyes as Marith killed him.

Garent's horse went screaming off toward the cliff top, Garent's body flopping over it, the head hanging on by a few shreds of sinew and bone. Jogged up and down as the horse bucked, like Garent was laughing. The horse's eyes were so wide. The body slipped and went down hanging upside down tangled in reins and stirrups, arms dangling. The head was torn off, rolled away and was crushed in the melee of men fighting. The horse went over the cliff top, still screaming, taking Garent's headless flopping body with it.

Hah!

He needed someone else to kill. Everything around him was red and bleeding. The men seemed to be fighting so slowly, like they were too worn out to move properly, like they were fighting underwater, like the air was too thick. Their mouths opened and shut but he couldn't hear them. All he could hear was the screaming. Crows and gulls thick in the sky, wheeling, shrieking, heads red with blood. A man in white armor careered toward him, running on foot, holding his sword in both hands like a woodman's ax. Laughing. Marith killed him in one stroke. A ragged boy with the dirt of the kitchens on him, a meat cleaver in one hand, a poker in the other. A lord on horseback who recognized him at the last breath, pulled away and ran until Marith cut him down. Another man on horseback. Another man on foot. A serving girl. Another man on horseback. Another man on foot. More. More. More. Killed and killed and killed and killed. His heart sang with killing. His mind was empty, dancing light, pure and utterly perfect joy. *Saleiot*: to shine, to sparkle, to dance like the sunlight on fast-flowing water. Joy absolute in his heart. The things in the air screamed, tearing at the light. He killed and killed and killed and killed.

Death! Death! Death!

Evening drew in, and surely none of Lord Relast's men remained alive by now. Illyn's army turned in upon itself, eating itself alive. The battlefield was meat like a butcher's counter, the men fighting no longer recognizable as men. Half-living fragments hacking at each other, tearing with nails and teeth, drowning in their own blood. Endless bodies trampled in the dirt, a mass of dark and red and brilliant metal like a mosaic floor. All the banners brought down and scattered, most of the horses dead. Crows and seabirds everywhere, beaks crimson, drunk on blood, too sated to fly.

The sky burned with the awful, terrible beauty of sunset, turning the sea to liquid flame. Beyond the cliffs the seal women swam in the harbor, watching with pebble eyes the insanity and cruelty of men. Far off, around the high peak of Calen Mon, eagles were dancing on the wind. Somewhere in the west in the desert a dragon flew. Always a perilous time, this borderline between the realms of life and death, light and darkness. Thalia raised her face to the west and prayed. From the fear of life, and the fear of death, release us.

The words faded in her throat, empty.

No one wants to die, she thought. Not truly. At the moment of death, all regret that it comes. All see that they were wrong, and fools. All see the glory of living, even in pain, even in sorrow, even in the dark. The men out there fighting will regret, in the moment of dying.

I pray they will, she thought. It is too horrible otherwise. Too horrible to bear.

Finally, two figures broke away from the heaving mass, which now resembled only maggots wriggling in the filth. Two mounted figures, riding for the gates, flashing light and shadow as they came. A cry from one of the riders, answered by men at the gatehouse. The gates opened, the riders came in and the gates swung shut behind them with a crash.

Silence. No more screaming. The air stilled. The sea and the seabirds fell silent. Calm.

Marith dismounted his horse in the courtyard and Thalia came down to meet him. He was mired in blood to his eyeballs, his drawn sword still clutched in his hand. Light shone in his eyes. Unharmed, of course. Bareheaded, lightly armored, even his horse unscathed. Lord Relast beside him, as caked in gore and as radiant.

Every man, woman and child in the courtyard apart from Thalia went down on their knees before him. Lord Relast shouted in a great voice, "All hail King Marith! King Marith! He is king here! The true and only king!"

Lady Jora shouted, "King Marith! King Marith! *Ansikander-akesis Amrakane!*"

Marith looked at them. His eyes were like knife blades. His face was a rotting wound. He looked, thought Thalia, as though he might kill them.

The people around took up the cry. Every voice, of all those left alive in Malth Salene. "King Marith! King Marith! *Ansikanderakesis Amrakane!* Death! Death! Death!"

What does it mean? Thalia wondered.

Ansikanderakesis: Great Lord. King.

Amrakane...

She saw his silver armor. His red cloak. His shadow. His face.

Lady Jora shouted, "All hail King Marith! Marith *Ansikanderakesis*! King Marith, who is Amrath come again!"

Thalia began to weep. Marith was weeping. Grief and wonder perfect in his face.

Landra lowered her face into the dust and shouted, "All hail King Marith! King Ruin! King of Dust! King of Shadows!" Her voice dripped hatred. Grief. "I brought him back to you! King of Death!" The people of Malth Salene took up the cry with joy. "King Ruin! Amrath returned to us! Death and all demons! Death! Death! Death!"

Outside the gates, the shattered remnants of the army of King Illyn stumbled over the battlefield, bloodied and broken, filled with shame. Searching out fallen comrades. Brothers and friends and enemies and lovers. Men they had themselves killed.

Out of a clear bright sky it began to snow, the white flakes like feathers, white and perfect, covering the bodies of the dead.

But he's so beautiful, Thalia thought, looking at Marith.

He took her into his arms.

"King Marith! King Ruin! Amrath come again!"

Chapter Fifty-Six

Bright they rode out in the sunlight,
They did not fear to ride out to slaughter
Nor did they fear to ride out with drawn swords.
Bright their armor,
Bright the jewels on their arm-rings,
Bright their shining hair.
The wolf ones, the bold warriors, the thieves.
Happy they feasted in our halls,
Happy they fought and bested each other,
Smiled at women, groomed their horses,
Drank wine in gold cups.
At Amrath's command they rode out in sunlight,
Swords drawn, spears poised, hair bound.
Every man they met, they slew and left dying.
Red the blood they shed, and red their bleeding.
They did not ride back.

The great chant, sung by the men of the White Isles at the crowning of kings. The burial song of the last of Amrath's followers, composed on the battlefield of Malth Ethalden where the ground was burned black with dragon fire. The last men of His Empire. The few who were loyal to the end.

They say, anyway. Who can tell what it's about, or when it was written? Just men who died.

And with that, they crowned Marith king.

Chapter Fifty-Seven

That fucking poisonous bastard Marith. That sick, vile, diseased, degenerate fucking bastard shit. Gods and demons, he should have knifed him.

In a stinking tent most of whose other occupants were now dead, Tobias sat gnashing his teeth.

Join King Illyn's army. March on Malth Salene to see Marith get his comeuppance. See Lady pox-on-her Landra get hers too. Find some closure on the whole fucking disaster then bugger off to Alborn to sit and drink beer. Maybe even find Thalia to apologize.

Yeah. Good plan, Tobias, me old mucker. Really good plan.

King Illyn had been really very nice to him when he turned up at the gates of Malth Elelane the never-was-anything-more-aptly-named Tower of Joy and Despair. As in: hadn't killed him on the spot. Listened oh so politely, not asked the obvious questions about how exactly he came to have run into Lady gods' damned Landra whilst in the company of beloved former son and heir wacked out and tied up in a cart. Nodded, said "I see" a couple of times. Frowned. Barked orders about ships and swords at people. Made Tobias a nice generous choice of rewards for his services to the throne.

Option one: Stand in the front line when they marched on Malth Salene.

Option two: Have his throat cut right there and then.

Same old same old. Never ever turned out to be a choice any-way. He'd only survived what was politely being referred to as the battle at all because he'd run screaming and stuck his head in a lousy horse blanket the moment Marith drew his sword.

So now here he was. In a stinking tent most of whose other occupants were now dead. Besieging a fortress. Front line to what now seemed to be a civil war. Freezing his nads off. Being driven half-insane by seagulls. Listening hilariously to the hilarity going on just the other side of the besieged fortress wall.

Such hilarity! Cheering and laughing and dancing and big warm-looking bonfires. A great big feast where they emptied every store-room. Days, it seemed to go on. People occasionally stumbled onto the ramparts waving drink cups, shouting "King Marith! Hail to the king!" One girl flashed her nipples at them, yelled they'd see a lot more where that came from if they came over to the side of the true king. Dead drunk: she slipped and fell off the wall. It was a long drop, the outer wall of the fortress of Malth Salene. The bloke who found her body did indeed see a whole lot more.

King Illyn the actual/ex true king's soldiers, meanwhile, scraped up meat slurry with shovels and poured it onto funeral pyres. Days, it seemed to go on. Tobias's arms ached. His back ached. The pools of dead people never ended. Then they broke for dinner and it was roast pork and whichever fucker thought roast pork was a good idea right now should be disemboweled. He sat staring at it trying to eat it without breathing in. Until a seagull swooped down and crapped in it. Bloody bird shit dripped down his arm and onto his food.

Gnashed his teeth at it. Oh hell yeah.

Tense days passed, dusk and dawn and dusk and dawn again. The party in Malth Salene finally ended. The keep before them fell silent, men were occasionally glimpsed walking its ramparts, hoisting red banners, cheering their king. Tobias's few surviving tent-mates sat and tried to pretend they weren't all thinking "King Marith" and shivering with something and simultaneously almost pissing themselves with terror and creaming their breeches with lust. Fresh troops and siege engines arrived by fast ship from Malth Elelane, trundled up the cliff road. They all watched them, awe-struck. A thousand soldiers. A hundred horses. Seven trebuchets. A whole load of big, carefully handled barrels. One old bloke in fancy robes.

Banefire and mage fire. The men were halfway between terror and climax at the thought of that, too.

The men were a fine lot. His squad. Not that he thought of them as that. Maerc and Brand and Mish and Acoll. Mish was two heartbeats away from killing himself. "I trained and trained to be a soldier," the kid kept muttering under his breath. Brand and Maerc spent their time trying not to kill each other. San spent his time doing something nobody wanted to ask about in his tent. Tobias mostly sat about feeling sick.

Good lads. Handy with the shovels. Kept their armor polished to a mirror shine. Didn't even seem too bothered by the smell of roast pig.

Join King Illyn's army! Gods and demons, he bloody missed Alxine and Rate.

Finally, at noon on the sixth day, trumpets sounded and the men were drawn up in files close to the funeral mound.

"Here we go, then," said Maerc. "Meat slurry time again. Hope you've all been sharpening your swords."

The king trotted up on his warhorse, Prince Tiothlyn by his side. He'd aged ten years in the last few days. Prince Tiothlyn beside him also looked changed, his face worn and gray. Never seen real bloodshed before, Tobias would guess. Like poor Mish.

That wasn't a battle, he kept telling Mish. That was...I don't know what that was. But definitely not a battle. Not even berserk barbarians wacked on horse milk and dodgy mushrooms tend to fight quite like...whatever that was.

Fun, something in him kept saying. It was fun.

Then he'd go away and almost puke with shame at himself.

"My loyal soldiers," Illyn began. Poor bastard, thought Tobias.

Knows he's beaten. You don't start a speech to your troops like that unless you already know you're totally screwed. "King Marith", the whisper had gone around the men that morning in eager voices. A tone in the voices that made the skin crawl even as it made the heart beat.

"My loyal soldiers. What has happened here on this field cannot be allowed to stand unavenged. The dead demand it of us. Honor demands it of us. And so I say to you now: this is war. We will crush this place and all within it. The pretender and all those who support him will die. The dead demand it. Our honor demands it. In Amrath's name, I swear this will be so."

Coughing. Shifting of men's bodies. Muttering in the ranks. Then one of the big nobs raised his sword and shouted "King Illyn!" in a weak voice. The men around him stamped and cheered half-heartedly. After a moment Tobias joined in. Mostly out of pity for the poor bloke. The trumpet blew the call to form battle lines. Slightly more rousing than the lame-duck stutter that had just passed for a speech.

And that's it then. Meat slurry time again.

The king stomped off into his command tent. Big fancy silk thing, dark red with gold trim in case someone, somewhere forgot for one moment who the Altrersyr were descended from. Like everything around the battlefield, it was covered in bloody seagull shit. Didn't show quite so badly on the red, at least. You stupid fool, Tobias thought, watching him go. He was your son. He had so much in him. Even I can see that. Now he's...whatever it is he is. Your murderer, for one. A whole lot of us did things that led up to this, and you did more than most. Couldn't you just have told him you were sorry? Had a pint and a man-to-man chat and made up?

The soldiers formed up in columns. Tobias was somehow humorously close to the front. A group of particularly hard-core guys shuffled forwards with a battering ram. The trumpets sounded. The war drums began to beat.

Oh fucking fucking fuck, thought Tobias. What am I doing

here? Why did this seem a good idea? Why didn't I just leave everything well alone?

King Marith. I want to kill him. I have to kill him. He needs killing. He can't be allowed to live. That's why I'm here.

Yeah?

King Marith...The skin crawled but the heart beat.

The trumpets sounded. The trebuchets heaved into action. A crash, a scream and a spout of fire as the first round hit Malth Salene's walls. The battering ram began to hammer against the gates. The trebuchets loosed again and the ground shook. A section of wall dissolved in green liquid fire. Molten fire. Molten stonework. Molten men.

A voice screamed, "Take the fortress! Destroy the traitors! Surrender or die in the name of the king!"

The soldiers of King Illyn pressed forwards. A burst of mage fire caught the gatehouse. White flames, as well as the green.

See it through. See it through. Kill the boy.

King Marith. Ah, gods...

The trebuchets loosed again. Shattering the walls. Running, running with fire. Eating away the gilded stone.

The gates of Malth Elelane burst open. A troop of horsemen burst out. At their head a silver figure. Shining. Blazing. His sword flashed rainbows. His cloak was red. Shadows circled over him.

King Marith.

The most beautiful thing in the world.

Tobias's mouth fell open. The men at the battering ram went down beneath the charge. A spurt of blood. King Marith's sword flashed like lightning. Rainbows. Stars. Pure perfect silver light. The attack stopped in mid-sword stroke. A last trebuchet missile shattering on the keep walls. Then a long pause and silence. The army of King Illyn staring. The beautiful figure. King Marith! Amrath! Amrath come again!

Marith's horse reared. He cut the men around him down. They did nothing. Stared at him.

Amrath! Amrath! Amrath returned!

There were a couple of villages in Chathe whose inhabitants believed the world was one vast rotting corpse, people the maggots crawling in its flesh. You could kind of see that, looking at Marith. Suddenly really made sense.

The men stood and let him kill them. Smiled at him as they died. So godsdamned beautiful. Radiant. The most perfect perfect thing in the world. The thing that had entered them all and never quite left them, worn its traces like scabs. A little bit of him in all of us, Tobias thought. Like a man who's drunk tainted water and got the fluke.

He hurled himself on the man next to him.

The man next to him hurled himself back.

And we're all fighting and fighting and fighting together, he thought. Fighting and fighting and fighting till the world ends.

What men are made for. Killing. Dying. Being killed.

A song came into his head suddenly. Old, old song. Knows the words right as breathing. Better than he knows himself. His own name.

Shouts it out, stabbing at the bloke next to him. Bloke next to him dies shouting it back. They all take it up, dead men and dying. And we're all dying, aren't we? he thinks. Just some quick, some slow. What we're born for. Killing. Dying. Shouts it loud and clear, while he's killing. Kill and kill and kill! Keep killing until we're all dead.

Why we march and why we die,
And what life means…it's all a lie.
Death! Death! Death!

Chapter Fifty-Eight

A rock slams over the walls and smashes into the courtyard. A shower of dust and shattered stone. Green liquid fire drips off it, liquid and burning, a cry from the courtyard where it strikes. Men fall with fire coursing up their bodies. Like insects swarming over them, climbing legs and arms, making for the face. Where it meets skin it hisses and steams, eating away flesh and bone, melting leather and metal, worming its way into the bloodstream and making the blood boil. White fat runs in streams across liquefying flagstones, bubbling and smoking as it runs. The towers of Malth Salene shake and tremble. The towers are burning and falling. The walls break apart. Destroyed.

I could live here with him, I thought.

Deneth Relast is putting on his armor. Jora Relast sings with pleasure as she straps it on. Savane blows kisses at the soldiers arming. Landra stands in the doorway and weeps.

"Here we are then." Marith looks around at me. "It's done."

He takes my hand. Kisses me, gently and softly, a kind protective kiss.

"Ride out of the back gate by the middens. Take the lich road onto the moors. Wait there until it is done. You will be safe. No one will come near you. No one will be there. I swear it." He smiles. "My Queen."

I kiss him back.

I see the thought in his eyes: She loves me! She loves me!

I don't know. I think perhaps I do.

Shame in my heart like the light on the water.

But he's so beautiful, I think.

The towers rock and tremble. Mage fire and banefire eating at the walls. Another missile strikes the courtyard. Men standing rapt with worship as they burn.

"King Marith! King Marith!" Their voices are prayers. Like the Great Hymn to the rising sun.

A burst of mage fire shoots over the walls into the courtyard. Catches Landra. Catches Savane. Savane's dress shimmers silver. Her skin sparkles. She burns. Jora their mother shrieks with horror. Deneth her father shouts "Kill them!", pulls his helmet onto his head, grips his sword.

I think of what Landra Relast did to me, dragging me here, wanting to kill me, wanting to kill him.

His father wanted to kill him. Was glad to say he was dead. Deneth Relast and his son and daughter tried to destroy him.

Landra survives.

Savane is dead.

A wave of banefire crashes across the courtyard. Drowning men even as they burn. A voice is screaming somewhere "Destroy it! Destroy it!." From inside the walls or outside, I don't know. Destroy it, I think. Yes. Jora Relast turns toward the fire. Holds out her arms. The fire embraces her. Surges over her body. Runs like insects over toward her husband. I do not want to watch them die.

Landra screams something. Runs toward her mother. Her hair is burned off. Her skin is burned off. Soldiers turn toward her. They are turning on each other. Beginning again to kill each other. Deneth Relast stares at his wife and his daughters. His home burning. He does not seem to understand what to do.

"Destroy it!" the voice shouts. Marith's voice. "Destroy it! Kill them all!"

Landra's eyes meet Marith's for a moment and they are worse

than his own. She screams a curse at him. Then she is gone inside the burning building, and a handful of soldiers are chasing after her, and the rest are killing each other at Marith's feet.

"Ride out of the back gate!" he shouts at me. "Wait on the lich road! You will be safe! I swear it!"

The walls explode in white and silver. Marith forms up a group of horsemen behind him. "Destroy it!" he shouts again. "Kill them!" Then he shouts, "Open the gates!"

The fire is burning in him. In his eyes. His face. His cloak is still stained with the blood of his last battle. Blood runs off it as he goes.

He is death. He is ruin. He is Amrath.

But he is so beautiful.

Chapter Fifty-Nine

The gates opened. He rode out through them, killing men as he went. The fire burned in his head so bright it sang. He could see everything. Hear everything. Feel it all as it moved around him. Every life. Every death. The men surged after him, shouting his name. *"Ansikanderakesis! Ansikanderakesis Amrakane!* King Marith! King Marith!" Beauty and joy to break the heart.

His father's soldiers stood and died for him. Worshipped him as they died. Loved him. He cut them down. Rode through them to the ranks of men gathered around the siege engines. Waiting for him. All of it waiting for him.

He pointed at the walls of Malth Salene behind him. "Destroy it! Kill them! Kill them all!"

The trebuchets loosed. Banefire flying. Men turning to fight each other. Overwhelming themselves. The earth trembled. His sword danced in his hand.

Fire and stone and blood and bone as the gatehouse gave way, shattering like the glass had shattered in Sorlost, fragments shining glowing falling through the air like jewels. Like eyes. Falling through the air like colored stars. Look! There's the Worm, and the Maiden, and the Crown of Laughing, and that big green one is the Tear.

"Death!" he screamed to them. "Death! Death!"

He crashed through the ruins of his father's army, standing staring at each other, staring in adoration at him, turning in confusion to fight the men following him and each other and themselves and everything. Had to find his brother. His father. Decide how best to kill them.

Ti was probably on his way back to Malth Elelane, he thought then. Weak and hiding. Resentful and scared. But his father was here somewhere.

A burst of white light smashed into the ground near him. Mage fire. And so his father was with the mage. Marith spurred his horse in the direction the mage fire had come from, charging against the tide of the men. One of them went down under his horse's hooves. Should have got out of the way then, you fool, he thought.

Another burst of mage fire. Aimed at him this time. Marith pulled the horse up short. It let out a scream as the ground around it exploded. He shouted angrily, spurred the horse on hard over the burned earth. Flickers of white flame darted around its legs.

A man came rushing toward him, howling something, armed with sword and knife. One of the few who still tried to fight him, hadn't yet seen him, seen what he was. He warded off a blow from the man's sword. The knife came up too, trying to stab at his leg or at the horse's flank. He felt a sudden shriek of pain rip up his side. Another man, behind him, smashing at him through his armor, a hard vicious blow to his hip and another to the small of his back. The horse screamed. Reared up so that he almost lost control of it. Thrashing about maddened with pain, one leg limp.

He forced it to run on, brought it round in a circle. They couldn't kill him. Nothing could kill him. It wasn't fair that they'd hurt him. Another burst of green fire shot up over his head and despite everything he stopped a moment to watch it land. The wall of the keep swayed, its stones hissing, sweating flame.

"Destroy it!" he screamed.

He struck one of his assailants hard on the side of the head, hitting down to the bone. The blade stuck: he had to kick the man and the body fell back off the sword with its head all in pieces like it was a dead pig being made into brawn. The horse was still screaming, its leg flopping about. It shouldn't be up any more. Should be collapsed in a heap with him cutting its throat. He pulled it round again, slashing at the first man, aiming again at the head. An explosion of white light, everything so bright he could see through it. The horse shrieked and tried to twist away.

Rethnen Jurgis. The man who'd run at him jerked back with his helm knocked askew and his skin burning, and Marith saw Rethnen Jurgis's face staring, all angry and weeping and fervent. He'd killed Kam. Cut his face to pieces and ridden his horse over him. So now he'd kill Rethnen, Kam's father, too. Rethnen howled as he swung at Marith. Marith cut back at him, catching his blade on Rethnen's armor, the metal screeching and Rethnen flinched. Hacked down again, harder and angrier. The horse shrieked, its leg going, bleeding now where one of their blades had caught its flank. Weak. Weak thing. Stupid thing of flesh and bone. Thalia had been frightened of horses. Too big, she'd whispered. Her lips close to his face. Too big. How do you control it? Know it won't run? Another explosion of mage fire, dancing over Marith, filling his vision, beautiful as stars. Rethnen was burning, lit up and filled with light. Closed his eyes and he could still see, liquid silver and the man's figure black against it, see Rethnen's heart red and beating, failing, breaking in the heat of the fire. Opened his eyes and the world was shadows, pale and jagged and raw. He got Rethnen again in the shoulder, smashing with the flat of the blade, watching the man stumble back a pace. Spurred the horse and Rethnen stumbled and the horse crashed into him and he went spinning and falling backward dropping his sword, blood welling at the shoulder joint, back and down, stupid weak thing like the horse.

No point staying to see if he died. Marith kicked the wounded horse on and galloped looking for his father, thinking how to kill him.

Found him by one of the trebuchets, guarded by a troop of soldiers and the mage. They'd killed several men who'd tried to take them. Good. His father was for him and him alone.

Illyn's guards drew up around him. And the mage. The horse paced and snorted. Just like Sorlost, the king cowering behind some stupid magician, thinking that might keep him alive. He cut down the soldiers. So small and helpless they seemed. Their swords nothing. They came at him together in a rush, striking at him. You shouldn't be fighting me, he thought. You're fools. He got one in the chest, through the armor, seeing the look of shock on the man's face that the bronze didn't protect him. Another in the head, a good sound it made as his sword smashed into the skull, cracked it open and crushed it. His blade like hands tearing things apart. Breaking them. Rending them down.

White fire crashed over him as he fought, great white waves of it like breakers. Swimming in light. The horse was bleeding in a thousand places, leaching blood, hacked open and black as cinders, its heart beating slow, its head flopping and moving like a toy horse. Not real. Not real any more. Nothing's real, apart from death. He turned on the mage who was screaming and howling at him. A glorious thing, magic. A wonder. A marvel. But it can't stop a man dying in pain. He struck home and the mage was bleeding. Hacking and slashing in wild strokes. White fire blazing on everything, lit up so bright he can't see. Swimming in light. Shattered glass and stars and snow. Everything dying. Everything burning. Nothing but death in all the world. In his mind. He hits and cuts and stabs and the horse is screaming and the mage is screaming and he laughs and shouts and hits out again, everything's white, so brilliant it's like his heart's singing, he can see everything even with his eyes closed and he kills and kills. His skin is hurting from the light, it feels like salt water on a wound, I will not burn he thinks, the mage is burning with fire hissing out of him, his skin is hurting now from the light, I will not burn and he strikes harder, and the light is so bright, the world's fading, he's almost frightened for a moment, his sword hurts in his hand, I will not burn, I will not burn, striking harder and harder even as he's tired, just killing, just kill them, and then onwards and onwards and everything will die and he'll be king. Killing and killing and killing. Death and death and death. He's blind and the light's too bright and he's tired and everything's bleeding and everything's burning and his heart is so full of joy.

The scent of wild thyme and wild garlic in the hedgerows. The song of a blackbird in the west gardens where the may tree grows. Eating apples straight from the tree in the orchard, the juice running down his chin, then washing his hands in the little stream that flows there, thick with yellow irises and bulrushes that leave their down on his clothes. Hoarfrost crunching beneath his feet on the uplands, the sky white with coming snow. Riding through a meadow when the hay is being cut. Riding through green summer trees. Reading a book by the fireside. Swimming in the sea.

I know what I am, he thought. And I know what I've given up. Sometimes I even wonder why.

And he stops, and the soldiers are dead, and the mage is dead, and his father is dead, face down in the dust and broken apart.

Death! Death! Death!

Chapter Sixty

Thalia sat on a low flat rock surrounded by brown and purple heather. The wind was blowing in her face, bringing rain. She could see the high peak, the mountain he had told her was called Calen Mon. Eagles' Seat. Eagles flew around it, or what she guessed were eagles. They looked like the dragon dancing on the wind. She almost imagined she could hear them calling. What a beautiful thing it would be, to see them close up. Turning with the air, the long soft beating of their wings. He'd climbed right to the top, he'd told her. There were old carvings up at its summit, and little gray stone cairns. You could see all the way to Seneth and Malth Elelane, when the sky was clear. The ground shook again and she started, turned back to look at the flames rising behind her. He'd keep her safe. He'd promised he'd keep her safe. The honey and cream horse cropped at the grass a little way away, unconcerned. The sound of its pink mouth tearing up the grass stems was pleasant. Her cloak was thick and warm.

The ground rocked again, a great crash and a roaring, a vast wild shriek of gulls. A gust of hot wind blew around her. Why does he want to destroy it? she wondered. Because of the boy. Because he'd been hurt there. No, she thought then. Because he'd been happy there. She wondered how long she had been sitting looking away at the peak of the mountain. A long time, she thought. A long time.

What do I know of life? she thought. All I know is death and a dark room that stinks of blood. I vowed to live once. Am I not living? Look! The grass is alive. The sky is alive. Eagles are flying. I have seen a dragon. I have seen the sun rise in the desert. I have seen the sea.

It was getting colder. The sky had cleared in the far west, bringing long golden beams of light. She pulled her cloak more tightly around her. It must be over soon, she thought. But it was good, to sit there with her face to the wind looking at the mountain and the eagles and the sky.

A silence was coming into the air, the screams dying away. A tired weary peace. Thalia stood up slowly, her body stiff. Stretched. She walked over to the horse, still quietly cropping the grass, its head bent. Smelled warm. It pricked up its ears as she approached and she was briefly frightened, but it shook its head and snorted and sniffed at her hand in the hope she might have something for it.

"Nice horse," she said, remembering how Marith had spoken to the mage's horse in the desert. "Nice horse. Good horse." She took the reins carefully, tried to remember how to mount it. She couldn't remember so had to lead it instead, going slowly back toward the fortress over the crest of the hill. The fires still burned, a great plume of smoke blowing on the wind.

They had to cross a stream, clear water running over stones, cutting deep in the turf. It ran very fast and bright, down from the high moor. It sang as it came down. The horse stopped and drank. Thalia drank also, bending her head and cupping her hand. Drops dancing through her fingers. The water was clean and cold, tasting of leaves and stones and earth and rain.

A noise caught her, a snort like the horse's snort. A rider? Marith? She raised her head.

A deer. A white deer, like the one they had seen in the woods. A stag, crowned with great antlers that stretched up like branches. Like the canopy of a tree, all its leaves dancing. It stared at Thalia with great sad dark eyes. Snorted again, its nostrils flaring. Pawed the earth. Thalia stared back and their eyes held together, woman and animal, and it looked so very sad. Its nostrils flared and trembled, so delicate. It bent and drank, the water dripping from its muzzle, its antlers shivering slightly with the movement of its head. Then it snorted again, rushed away over the moors toward the mountain of Calen Mon. Thalia stared after it.

Run after it. Run off into the wilds. Running water and trees and earth and the sea and the sky. Leave.

She took up the horse's reins and began to walk on. It trotted behind her patiently, its harness jingling.

After an hour's walking, she came to Malth Salene. The place where Malth Salene had been. She stopped. An emptiness on the sky in front of her. A gash in the world. A scar. Like her scars. Like Marith's hand. Ragged and ruined beyond all healing.

But he's so beautiful, she thought.

A man came up the slope of the moor toward her. He was dressed in battered armor, blood on his face.

"My Lady." He bowed low to her. How many did you kill? she thought.

"My Lady, My Lord King is looking for you. Awaiting you. If you will follow?"

I should be glad, she thought. We are King and Queen. Crowned in silver. Throned in gold. And they hurt him first. They hurt me. They were cruel. They have brought this upon themselves. Crowned him. Called him Amrath and King. So they deserve it. They could have left us as we were, in the desert outside Sorlost. They did this, not him.

She walked slowly following the soldier across the burned grass, looking and trying not to look at the ruins. Impossible to tell what was flesh and what was stone. All bound together, formless filth and rubble. Like Ausa's bones had been, ragged and snapped. Crows and seabirds crouched everywhere, glaring at her as she walked. As she passed they flew up, calling out their lonely pained cries. The most beautiful sound in the world, Marith had told her.

Fierce bright burning joy, like the fire in the dragon's eyes as it lighted on the ground. The terrible, beautiful pain of being alive.

Marith came out to meet her, standing at the edge of the ruin. It made her think of the mer woman's house, looking bleakly out to the sea, bound around with charms against death.

"Thalia!" Marith's face leaped when he saw her. His eyes were so wide and laughing. "Oh, Thalia! Do you see? Do you see? What I've done! And this is nothing to what I'll do!" He clasped her hands. "I love you so much! I swore I'd be avenged on them for harming you! I swore I'd make them all kneel at your feet! King and Queen!"

The soldier with her bowed down to him. "King Marith! King Marith! *Ansikanderakesis Amrakane!* Amrath returned to us! Amrath come again!"

Marith beamed at her. Radiant with happiness. "You see?" he said again. "You see? Isn't it wonderful? What I've done? What I'll do?"

"I see," she said. She smiled back at him.

The men danced in the ruins. Beat their swords on their shields. "King Marith! King Marith! Victory to the King!" They sang the songs they had sung at his crowning. Stamped their feet, leaped the fires, leaped and danced over the bodies of the dead. Stamped out the war dance, treading patterns of glory. Singing the paean, the praise song. The bronze rang out in triumph. Swords and shields crashing. Armor crashing as they danced. The clear blue sky shone above them. The golden light of the evening sun.

Marith smiled at them in wonder. His face looked as he had looked in the desert. Amazed and frightened. Alive with hope.

"King and Queen," Thalia said. It made her breathless.

Marith said, "We'll go to Malth Elelane. Marry there. Be properly crowned. You'll stand in the chapel of Amrath my ancestor where I will place the crown of Eltheia on your head. I told you we'd be there by Sunreturn! We'll have a great banquet, with sledging and skating and bonfires on the ice."

"You did tell me."

The boy's grin. "I knew it would happen, you see? It's too beautiful for us not to be there by then. We'll have pavilions built, gold and silver. Three days of feasting. Horse races, dances in the snow." He caught her up in his arms. "Come riding with me now! Let's look over everything. Our kingdom. The hills, the marshes, the trees. The air stinks here. We'll ride away into the wind until it's clean. There's still so much I need to show you. So much in the world that's mine."

"I'm tired," she said. "You must be tired. I don't want to ride anywhere. I want to sleep."

I should be killing a man, she thought then. Somewhere far to the west Demerele will be killing a man.

It always comes back to death and dying. Always. Everything. In Sorlost a man is dying in the dark so that the dead may die and the living may live.

Death is terrible, she thought. Terrible and to be feared.

But he's so beautiful, she thought.

Marith smiled at her grave face. "But all you did was sit and watch it! And it's still only just evening...Come a little way? Please?" His eyes glittered with life. "Please?" Then he paused, looked at her. "I'm sorry. You're cold and tired. And I'll probably collapse from exhaustion in a moment. Battle joy wears off worse than drink, and I'll realize I hurt and my head aches." Looked around at the ruins of Malth Salene, and a realization seemed to come to him. "And we'll need to find somewhere to sleep, I suppose..." He laughed. "All those beautiful things, that beautiful place. All gone."

A horse was brought up, a warhorse, roan-colored, harnessed and plumed in silver, snorting and tossing its head. It lashed out, tried to bite at the man leading it. Its flanks were cut and bloodied. Burn marks on its strange thin legs.

"Father's horse," said Marith. He came toward it, stroked its nose. The horse snorted, stamped its feet, then calmed at his touch. "There, that's it," Marith said, stroking its nose. "Good horse. Good horse."

So are we going…somewhere now? Thalia thought. The men still danced around the ruins, shrieking as they danced. The evening was coming in now and they looked like monsters, bronze and silver and all stained with smoke and blood. The drums and the clash of swords and shields grew louder and louder. The fires rose. They were starting to burn the dead. They would soon begin again to kill each other, she thought. Kill and kill and kill! They leaped the fires, singing the paean. Their feet drummed out war chants on the ruined ground.

"Amrath! Amrath! Amrath!"

A voice shouted, "Trained and trained for it! And that was a battle! What all battles should be! I trained!" The sound caught her, a young voice, raw, madly on edge. She turned toward it, saw a young man's face. "A battle!" he shouted again. His face strained with disgust. Another man, older, clapped a hand to the boy's shoulder. "It's all right, lad. You know that." She thought, confusedly, that she saw Tobias with them. Behind them. Helping the older man lead the younger man away. It can't be Tobias, she thought. The three all shouted together, "King Marith! Hail King Marith!" She wasn't sure, it did look like Tobias. But…

If it is him, she thought, this is a good punishment for him. Fighting and dying in Marith's army. It did look so much like Tobias. But the face was so shining with happiness. Lit up like a candle with love for the king.

"Thalia!" Marith was waiting for her. He led the horse to the very center of the ruins. The blackened, melted ground where the Great Hall of Malth Salene had been. Where they had crowned him king. Marith drew his sword. Killed the horse. Blood spurted out all over him. Covering the human blood. The soldiers went down on their knees before him shouting "Victory!." She was sure she saw Tobias, kneeling between the older man and the boy.

Marith hacked off the horse's head. Raised it aloft.

"Victory!" Marith shouted. The evening sky rang with it. Shadows in the sky shrieked and danced.

He turned to Thalia. His eyes were silver with tears. Grief and joy together to break his heart.

"It's done, then," he said.

Chapter Sixty-One

We ride down to Toreth together. The soldiers march behind us, still singing and clashing their swords. At the gates of the town we stop. The gates are closed. Marith frowns. Then a great cry, a cheer, "The King! The King! Amrath returned to us! Open for the King!" The gates swing open, the townspeople flood out, shouting, singing, holding out their hands in greeting, filled with happiness.

"King Marith! King Marith! Hail to the King!"

The wealthy men of the town argue among themselves for who should have the privilege of giving up their home to us. Marith chooses a fine tall house near the harbor, windows looking out over the sea. Inside, more people bustle and shout and fall over themselves crying out "King Marith! The King! The King!." Hot baths hastily prepared, sweet with lavender and dried mint. Hot food. Wine. Clean clothes dragged from some rich merchant's wardrobe, a gray silk gown for me, even a necklace, gold flowers set with pale green stones. Everywhere people kneeling, eyes cast downwards, calling me "My Lady", "My Queen." More cheering. More singing. Dancing. Happiness. "The King! The King!" It seemed to last forever. This moment burning in my heart. Marith drinks it in, stares with eyes wide as the sea. His triumph. Truly, now, he is King.

Until at last even he is exhausted, admitting he wants to sleep a while. The candles burning low. The first scent of dawn in the air. He aches, he says. His head hurting. Battle joy wearing off. The last dregs of it. Wants to go to bed.

So finally I am alone with him. The bedroom door is closed and guarded, shutters bolted against the world. Yellow candles burning. The room blazing with light. Red cloth hanging around the bed.

"Here we are, then," he says. Smiles a sad smile. Things crawl behind his eyes, in the darkness beyond the dark. Things that beat like wings, clamoring to get out. Maggots and scars and the sound of a knife. I cannot tell, now, looking at him, whether he is happy or so grief-stricken his heart will break. He sits down on the bed, stares at his hands. "It's done," he says.

A crown of silver. A throne of gold.

A sound of weeping. A scent of blood in the air.

King Ruin. King of Dust. King of Shadows. Amrath returned. It's done.

Afterward, I lie awake in the darkness, listening to his breath. The wind has risen. I can hear the sea, the waves breaking on the shingle, the gulls. Faint noises outside the window, a woman's voice calling, drunken singing and a shriek and a crash. A woman's laugh.

I have seen a dragon dancing on the wind. I have seen the sea. The sky. The cold of frost. The beauty of the world.

I have felt the sun on my face as it rises over the desert. I have felt clear water running beneath my feet.

I have known sorrow, and pain, and happiness, and love.

Love.

I bring one of the candles to burning. Marith stirs at it, claws roughly at his face. Mutters something. Pain in his voice. I smooth my hand over his forehead and he sighs and relaxes back deeper into sleep.

King Ruin. King of Death.

I go over to the wall where his sword hangs, take it up, walk back over to the bed.

The gulls scream at the window. Shadows crawl on the walls.
I raise the sword over his heart.
Look down at him.
A kindness. That was what Tobias said.
A kindness. To him and to me.
I put the sword down. Curl back beside him.
Sleep.

Chapter Sixty-Two

Two young men, boys really, sit side by side against a large gray boulder on the moorlands north of Malth Salene. Marith leans his head on Carin's shoulder, Carin's arm rests lightly around Marith's waist. They sit on the edge of a low cliff, looking out over a tumble of rocks to the sea. Still and calm weather, gulls bobbing on the water. A seal head watches them. Far above a kestrel hovers. In the distance the sound of goats being called in to milk. They pass a bottle leisurely between them, warm and comfortable in a summer evening. Their horses graze contentedly a little way off, tethered to a hawthorn tree still bearing the last of its blossom.

"We should get back," Carin says.

"Why?"

"Well...I don't know. Maybe we just should."

"No."

"Fair enough." Carin kisses Marith's hair. "You're hogging the bottle again."

"Of course I am." Marith passes it over to him, curls himself more comfortably into Carin's body.

They watch the gulls soaring on the wind, a fishing boat out in the bay.

Carin says, "You'll be king, one day."

"Just realized that, have you?"

"No, but, I mean…When you are…" Carin shakes his head. "Never mind. I'm just being maudlin."

"Don't be." Marith sits up a little, looks at Carin. "What?"

"You as king…I don't know…It can't be like this when you are, I suppose."

"I'll have to stop sleeping in gutters, you mean?"

"Ha, yes. But more than that. All of this. You'll have to do things. Rule."

"You'll be Lord Relast of Third. You'll have to do things, too. The same things, really. Only smaller."

"Oh, thank you."

"Now you're making me maudlin." Marith rests himself back against Carin. "So stop it. We'll find time for this. I'll order it."

"And we'll be old and boring by then anyway."

"We will. You're hogging the bottle now."

"I'm not." Carin kisses Marith's forehead. "Just not letting you hog it."

"That comes to the same thing." Marith sighs, runs his hand idly down Carin's arm. "Do you want to be Lord Relast of Third? Really want to be, I mean?"

"Really want to be how? I will be. I can't want it or not want it." Carin kisses Marith's forehead again. Can tell Marith's becoming troubled again. The happiness lasts so briefly, now. He shouldn't have started this conversation. But it bothers him. The thought of Marith being king. "It's probably all much less interesting than it looks anyway," he says. "Signing papers. Listening to people boring on. Having people executed. A lifetime of tedium, I should think."

"Should you?" Marith smiles sadly. "Perhaps tedium would be good for me. A long and tedious reign in which nothing happens and about which the historians have nothing to say."

"King Marith the Eminently Forgettable."

"Indeed."

They look at each other and something passes between them and Carin turns away and squeezes his eyes shut for a moment like he's in pain. "I suppose we could always run away," he says. "Become traveling minstrels."

Gratitude in Marith's face for the things unspoken. The things they both know but never say. He smiles again his sad smile. "Bandits. We'd have to be bandits. Because you can't sing."

"My love is like a lily fair, White her skin and gold her hair… You're quite right, I can't." Carin gets up and pulls Marith up after him. "Bandits, then. Shall we start tomorrow? Go roving across the wild woods in search of dragons and damsels and rich caravan trains?"

"We could. Why are we getting up? It's comfortable here."

"Because I want to go down to the sea." Carin scrambles down the rocks and splashes into the water, waves breaking over his boots. "Let's catch a selkie!" He steps backward and the water hits him around his waist. "Gods! It's cold!"

Marith follows him, laughing.

They clamber around on the rocks, and Marith almost slips and falls in, and when they eventually make their way back up to their horses they're wet through and breathless and happy, and when they ride back to Malth Salene they're scolded for arriving at dinner late and disheveled and caked with wet sand.

Acknowledgments

There are so many people I need to thank for helping in the making of this book.

First off, my agent Ian Drury and everyone at Orbit, who between them changed my life by taking this book on.

The writers and readers who have inspired and supported me. Mike "Beyond Redemption" Fletcher. Mark Lawrence. Daniel Polansky. Rjurik Davidson. Christian Cameron. Graham Austin King. Andy Remic. Adrian Tchaikovsky. Marc Turner. Mike Brooks. Joanne Hall. Steve Poore. Tej Turner. Sammy K. Smith—go Grimbold! Leona Henry—your time will come, my friend! Quint VonCanon, creator of beautiful pictures. Sophie E Tallis, creator of beautiful maps. Adrian Collins and the team at Grimdark Magazine. Rob Matheny and Philip Overby at Grim Tidings. Marc Aplin at Fantasy Faction. M. Harold Page at Black Gate. Mike Evans, Thomas Clews, Laura M. Hughes, Kareem Mahfouz and everyone at Grimdark Writers and Readers, my special spiritual home-from-home.

Allen Stroud and Karen Fishwick. Jo Fletcher. Helen Smith. Ben O'Brian. Nic Davis. Coffee Corner. My local Waterstones.

Gareth Thomas and Julian Barker and everyone in PP, who put up with me living in Irlast rather than at my desk.

Judith Katz. Melanie Wright. Kate Byers.

My family, above all.

This book is dedicated to my father, who introduced me to fantasy and history and mythology, and who taught me how to write.

The story continues in...

The Tower of Living and Dying

Book Two of the Empires

of Dust trilogy

extras

orbit

meet the author

ANNA SMITH SPARK lives in London, England. She loves grimdark and epic fantasy and historical military fiction. Anna has a BA in classics, an MA in history, and a PhD in English literature. She has previously been published in the *Fortean Times* and the poetry website greatworks.org.

if you enjoyed
THE COURT OF BROKEN KNIVES
look out for
THE TOWER OF LIVING AND DYING
Empires of Dust
by
Anna Smith Spark

Marith has been a sellsword, a prince, a murderer, a demon, and dead. But something keeps bringing him back to life, and now there is nothing stopping him from taking back the throne that is rightfully his.

Thalia, the former High Priestess, remains Marith's only tenuous grasp on whatever goodness he has left. His left hand and his last source of light, Thalia still believes that the power that lies within him can be used for better ends. But as more forces gather beneath Marith's banner, she can feel her influence slipping.

A powerhouse story of bloodshed, ambition, and fate, **The Tower of Living and Dying** ***is a continuation of Anna Smith Spark's brilliant Empires of Dust trilogy.***

Chapter One

In the tall house in Toreth Harbor, the High Priestess Thalia lay awake in the darkness, listening to her lover's breath. Faint noises outside the window: a woman's voice calling, drunken singing and a shriek and a crash. Laughter. The wind had risen again. She could hear the sea, the waves breaking on the shingle, the gulls.

I have seen a dragon, she thought. I have seen a dragon dancing on the wind. I have seen the sea. The sky. The cold of frost. The beauty of the world. I have felt the sun on my face as it rose over the desert. I have felt clear water running beneath my feet. I have known sorrow and pain and happiness and love.

She sat up and brought a candle to burning. The man beside her stirred at it, clawing roughly at his face. She smoothed her hand over his forehead, and he sighed and relaxed back deeper into sleep.

King Marith Altrersyr. Amrath returned to us. King Ruin. King of Shadows. King of Dust. King of Death.

Dragonlord. Dragon killer. Dragon kin. Demon born.

Parricide. Murderer. Hatha addict.

The most beautiful thing in the world.

She went over to the wall where his sword hung, took it up, walked back over to the bed. For a moment her hands shook.

A kindness, she thought.

The gulls screamed at the window. Shadows crawled on the walls.

She raised the sword over his heart.

Looked at him.

A kindness. To her. To him.

But he's so beautiful, she thought.

476

She put the sword down and curled back beside him.

Slept.

When she woke again, the first light was coming in the east, over
the sea out beyond all lands, at the edge of the world. Pale gray
faint light that made no shadows. Always a perilous time, this borderline between the realms of life and death. The light coming in
at the very edges, at the very furthest point of everything, the iron
sea moving. So attuned she was, after so many years kneeling in the
darkness, to the small changes before the dawn. So well she knew
the dark and the light.

She got up slowly, opened the shutters, looked out over the water
and the sky. The clouds parted a little, ragged; the stars appeared. The
Fire Star. The Maiden. The Dragon's Mouth. She looked again at the
sword hanging on the wall by the bedside. At her lover curled sleeping, white in the dawn light. For a moment she could see his heart
through the skin of his body, red and beating. Beating like wings.

She was the Chosen of Great Tanis, the One God of the Sekemleth Empire of the Golden Sun Rising, the Lord of Living and
Dying, He Who Rules All Things. She was the holiest woman in
all the Empire. The holiest woman in all Irlast. All of her life, she
had lived in the Great Temple of the God, in the heart of a great
city, killing those who offered themselves up to her knife. She had
killed men and women and children. She had cut out the eyes and
cut off the hands of one of her own priestesses. Her friend. She
had seen her successor chosen, and now knew that she herself must
one day soon die.

She had left her city. Her God. Her maimed friend. Left them
for this man, her lover. This boy, who was the King of Death.

Everything has a price, she thought. I killed for the God, because
lives given in sacrifice are the prices of the dead dying and the living being born and the sun rising in the sky. Now I lie in my lover's
arms, and he is happy, and I am happy, and I will be a queen. A
crown of silver. A throne of gold. Life. Love. The world, he has

promised me. He will show me the world. So long I lived closed up and helpless. Now I will truly be alive.

Marith rubbed his face. Mumbled something. His voice was raw with pain. "Father," he whispered. "Mother. Please." He whimpered something strained and angry. "Kill them. Kill them all. Death!"

She ran her fingers over his forehead. He sighed.

"That's good," he said.

She looked again at his sword, its blade shining.

He's so beautiful, she thought.

Chapter Two

Marith yawned and stretched and sat up. Full morning, golden
sunlight streamed in through the open window, catching Thalia's
hair. She was standing by the window, looking out over the water,
the sun on her face. She wore the white dress with the pink and
green flowers on it: in the golden light, with her brown skin and
black hair, she looked like a may tree in bloom.

"Thalia! Thalia, Queen of the White Isles!"

She turned and smiled at him. "Good morning."

"What's wrong?"

Her smile brightened. "Nothing."

"That's good. Look—even the sun has come out to celebrate!"
She moved toward him and the morning light struck him full in the
face. Ooff. Very bright. His head was feeling a bit, um, fragile. His
body was rather aching after all the fun and games yesterday too.
He rubbed his eyes. "Maybe you could close the shutters for a bit?"

"I did suggest several times last night that you go to bed."

"You did."

She still looked tense. Marith took her hands. "What's wrong?"

"Really, nothing."

"Really?"

"Really."

"This is the best day in the world, Thalia! I'm king! King! By
name and blood and right of the sword! King!"

I killed my father yesterday, he thought. That's why I'm king.
Because my father's dead.

I hated him, he thought. I did. I did. And he hated me.

He must have, he thought.

"It's nothing," said Thalia. Kissed him. "You're not the only one
who went to bed too late after drinking too much wine. That's all."

Marith looked out of the window where she had been gazing. Fishing boats in the harbor, their sails green or vivid blue. A garden of fruit trees. A little beach of yellow sand. The view was soothing. Cheered him up again. This is what I'm king of, he thought. This beautiful place. There were ringdoves on a cot in the garden; the lavender was still flowering; a girl with sand yellow hair was gathering early apples, perhaps even for their breakfast. You could half forget, looking at the scene, what he'd had to do to make it his. All so pretty and charming. Their host, the future Lord Fishmonger, the best herring merchant in Toreth Harbor, might almost be accused of having good taste.

Well, Lord Fishmonger been very vocal about having his king turf him out of his house for the night, literally thrown himself at Marith's feet begging for the privilege, indeed, so he must have some degree of good taste, mustn't he?

"Breakfast?" he asked Thalia. Her beautiful blue eyes glittered back at him. She was crying. Trying not to cry.

"I'm sorry," she said. "It's nothing. It was a...a strange day, yesterday. That's all."

He smiled at her. "I suppose it was."

Marith and Thalia were eating breakfast in something like strained silence when a servant announced that one of the lords of Third had come to do homage to his king. Had told the servants that he was the king's particular friend, indeed. Thalia went back up to the bedchamber. Marith received him in as much state as could be managed in borrowed cloths in a borrowed house. Osen Fiolt knelt at Marith's feet, his sword held out with the hilt toward Marith in offering. Had the sense at least not to look at the crudely carved chairs, the plastered walls, the pewter jug and clay cups. The fact that his clothing was so much richer than the king's own.

"You have my loyalty and my life, My Lord King. My sword is yours."

A young man, only a few years older than Marith. Dark haired, dark eyed, handsome, with a clever face. Marith looked at the proffered sword but did not take it or bid its owner rise to kiss him.

"Your life and your loyalty. Your sword." Marith raised his eyes, looked at the whitewashed ceiling. A stain up there where the winter storms had got in. "Yet you did not come, my Lord Fiolt, when my father was besieging Malth Salene. One thousand men and seven trebuchets and a magelord, and you did not come to my aid. So should I not kill you? For abandoning me? For not coming to my aid? Where was your sword then? Your loyalty? Your life?"

Osen's face went as white as the ceiling. "I...Marith...My Lord King...Marith...I..." He blinked, his hands working on the blade of the sword. He'd cut himself in a minute, if he wasn't careful. "I..."

Men's voices drifted in through the windows, soldiers being drilled into order. The army of Amrath. Marith's army. Marith's loyal and beloved men. Osen raised his eyes to Marith's face and Marith could see the thoughts there moving. Going to stake it all on one throw.

Osen said slowly, "For as long as I have known you, I have loved you as my friend. You know that. But I am the Lord of Malth Calien. I am sworn to Malth Elelane, to the throne of the White Isles, as a vassal of the king. I swore an oath to your father. While he lived, was I not bound to keep it? Whatever my true feelings might have been? Without loyalty, there is chaos. So where does a man's loyalty lie, then, if not to his king above all else?"

Marith thought: We were friends, once, I suppose. I killed my best friend. I killed my father. I'll kill my brother and the woman I've called mother since first I learned to speak. I suppose I may need some friends. He looked down at Osen. "As far as I can remember, we decided it rather depended on the king."

"And on the all else. Though as far as I can remember, we never reached a definitive conclusion, since we had to break off discussing it for you to be sick."

481

Their eyes met. The tension broke.

Friends.

Marith reached out and took the proffered sword. "Very well then, my Lord Fiolt. I take your loyalty and your life and your sword."

Twisted the hilt in his hands a moment, beautiful old iron, dark tempered, bone plaques on the guard, the pommel carved with worn yellow birds' heads. *Calien Mal*: the Eagle Blade. Old and beautiful, passed in trust from father to son. Often enough its bearer died in pain and weeping, but still it was treasured and passed on. One almost heard the metal whispering: Kill! Kill! Kill!

"Keep it sharp, Osen. You'll need it." Raised Osen up and kissed him. "Drink to the fact I'm still alive?"

"Like I drank to the fact you were dead?"

"You drank to my being dead?"

"Drowning my sorrows. It's what you would have wanted, I'd assumed, no?"

They grinned at each other and sat down by the fire, and Marith sloshed wine into two of the cups. "It's utterly vile, of course. Half vinegar. But it was this or goat's milk.... We'll be in Malth Elelane soon, and then we'll have a proper feast to celebrate."

Osen looked around the room. The rough furniture, the crude wall hangings, the ugly bronze lamp. "We can have a proper feast quicker than that, at Malth Calien. My loyalty, my life, my sword, and all the contents of my wine cellars, I'll pledge you." Raised his cup. "King Marith. May his sword never blunt and his enemies never cease to tremble and his cup never be empty of wine."

"King Marith."

They sat in silence a little while, drinking bad wine and thinking of things passed and gone. They had never been close friends really. Never anything near what he and Carin had been. Two young men around the same age, who drank together occasionally because they were young and men and liked to drink. But the strange grief of it burned in Marith, to be here with someone he had known and half trusted. As if all that had happened had not been. Three young men once in a tavern, arguing into the dawn about loyalty and honor and love and the nature of command. A petty lord's heir and a great lord's heir and the heir to the kingdom, shaping a court and an army in the air before them, tracing plans on the tabletop in the wine lees, making promises of fealty and reward. An inseparable pair and an outsider, clinging on in the hope of gain. So now look at them. A king and a petty lord and a dead man. A parricide and a likely parricide and a man who had loved his father and died for it. The bright fiery dreams of youth. Filth and ash and slag.

Osen said, "You'll need captains. And someone to hold Third for you. Now the Relasts are gone—" He broke off, staring nervously at Marith. Relaxed too much. His ambition running on too fast ahead of him. The shadow leapt up at them, dark and clawed. Carin Relast of Third, first, dearest, best of all the king's companions, the king's one true and beloved friend. . . . Marith gulped down his cup, refilled it. His hands shook. You should be grateful, Osen, he thought. Be grateful it was Carin I killed and not you. Or would you still change places with him?

A long silence, then Osen raised his cup again with a bitter, frightened half smile. "Lord Fiolt of Third, then. He Who Will Stand Forever in the Shadow of a Dead Man."

Marith too raised his cup. "Lord Fiolt of Third." He drank and drank again and breathed deeply, trying to stop the trembling grief in his hands. "Lord Fiolt of Third."

"May my sword never blunt and my life's blood be shed at my king's asking."

"And your cellars hold better things than this muck."

"That I can pledge you unfailingly." The tension broke again. "If we ride today, I'll have you drinking hippocras by my fires tomorrow evening. And your beautiful priestess, too. Her I am certainly looking forward to meeting." Smiled more easily. "Did you really drag her screaming from her temple?"

Marith almost choked on his drink. "Is that what they're saying?"

"Why, would you like them to be? No, no, of course not. General agreement is that she caught one glimpse of your ridiculously pretty face and abandoned God and empire out of love. And that by the time she first saw you unconscious in a pool of vomit, it was all tragically too late."

"Tragically! I'll have you know she loves me in any condition."

Osen refilled both of their cups. "Does she indeed?"

if you enjoyed
THE COURT OF BROKEN KNIVES

look out for

MALICE

The Faithful and the Fallen

by

John Gwynne

The world is broken...

Corban wants nothing more than to be a warrior under King Brenin's rule—to protect and serve. But that day will come all too soon. And the price he pays will be in blood.

Evnis has sacrificed—too much it seems. But what he wants—the power to rule—will soon be in his grasp. And nothing will stop him once he has started on his path.

Veradis is the newest member of the warband for the High Prince, Nathair. He is one of the most skilled swordsman to come out of his homeland, yet he is always under the shadow of his older brother.

Nathair has ideas—and a lot of plans. Many of them don't involve his father, the High King Aquilus. Nor does he agree with his father's idea to summon his fellow kings to council.

The Banished Lands has a violent past where armies of men and giants clashed in battle, but now giants are seen, the stones weep blood and giant wyrms are stirring. Those who can still read the signs see a threat far greater than the ancient wars. For if the Black Sun gains ascendancy, mankind's hopes and dreams will fall to dust…

…and it can never be made whole again.

CHAPTER ONE

CORBAN

The Year 1140 of the Age of Exiles, Birth Moon

Corban watched the spider spinning its web in the grass between his feet, legs working tirelessly as it wove its thread between a small rock and a clump of grass. Dewdrops suddenly sparkled. Corban looked up and blinked as sunlight spilled across the meadow.

The morning had been a colorless gray when his attention first wandered. His mother was deep in conversation with a friend, and so he'd judged it safe for a while to crouch down and study the spider at his feet. He considered it far more interesting than the couple preparing to say their vows in front of him, even if one of them was blood kin to Queen Alona, wife of King Brenin. *I'll stand when I hear old Heb start the handbinding, or when Mam sees me*, he thought.

"Hello, Ban," a voice said, as something solid collided with his shoulder. Crouched and balancing on the balls of his feet as he was, he could do little other than fall on his side in the wet grass.

"Corban, what are you doing down there?" his mam cried, reaching down and hoisting him to his feet. He glimpsed a grinning face behind her as he was roughly brushed down.

"*How long*, I asked myself this morning," his mam muttered as she vigorously swatted at him. "*How long before he gets his new cloak dirty?* Well, here's my answer: before sun-up."

"It's past sun-up, Mam," Corban corrected, pointing at the sun on the horizon.

"None of your cheek," she replied, swiping harder at his cloak. "Nearly fourteen summers old and you still can't stop yourself rolling in the mud. Now, pay attention, the ceremony is about to start."

"Gwenith," her friend said, leaning over and whispering in his mam's ear. She released Corban and looked over her shoulder.

"Thanks a lot, Dath," Corban muttered to the grinning face shuffling closer to him.

"Don't mention it," said Dath, his smile vanishing when Corban punched his arm.

His mam was still looking over her shoulder, up at Dun Carreg. The ancient fortress sat high above the bay, perched on its hulking outcrop of rock. He could hear the dull roar of the sea as waves crashed against sheer cliffs, curtains of sea-spray leaping up the crag's pitted surface. A column of riders wound their way down the twisting road from the fortress' gates and cantered into the meadow. Their horses' hooves drummed on the turf, rumbling like distant thunder.

At the head of the column rode Brenin, Lord of Dun Carreg and King of all Ardan, his royal torc and chainmail coat glowing red in the first rays of morning. On one side of him rode Alona, his wife, on the other Edana, their daughter. Close behind them cantered Brenin's gray-cloaked shieldmen.

The column of riders skirted the crowd, hooves spraying clods of turf as they pulled to a halt. Gar, stablemaster of Dun Carreg, along with a dozen stablehands, took their mounts toward huge paddocks in the meadow. Corban saw his sister Cywen among them, dark hair blowing in the breeze. She was smiling as if it was her nameday, and he smiled too as he watched her.

Brenin and his queen walked to the front of the crowd, followed closely by Edana. Their shieldmen's spear-tips glinted like flame in the rising sun.

Heb the loremaster raised his arms.

"Fionn ap Torin, Marrock ben Rhagor, why do you come here on this first day of the Birth Moon. Before your kin, before sea and land, before your king?"

Marrock looked at the silent crowd. Corban caught a glimpse of the scars that raked one side of the young man's face, testament of his fight to the death with a wolven from the Darkwood, the forest that marked the northern border of Ardan. He smiled at the woman beside him, his scarred skin wrinkling, and raised his voice.

"To declare for all what has long been in our hearts. To pledge and bind ourselves, one to the other."

"Then make your pledge," Heb cried.

The couple joined hands, turned to face the crowd and sang the traditional vows in loud clear voices.

When they were finished, Heb clasped their hands in his. He pulled out a piece of embroidered cloth from his robe, then wrapped and tied it around the couple's joined hands.

"So be it," he cried, "and may Elyon look kindly on you both."

Strange, thought Corban, *that we still pray to the All-Father, when he has abandoned us.*

"Why do we pray to Elyon?" he asked his mam.

"Because the loremasters tell us he will return, one day. Those that stay faithful will be rewarded. And the Ben-Elim may be listening." She lowered her voice. "Better safe than sorry," she added with a wink.

The crowd broke out in cheers as the couple raised their bound hands in the air.

"Let's see if you're both still smiling tonight," said Heb, laughter rippling among the crowd.

Queen Alona strode forward and embraced the couple, King Brenin just behind, giving Marrock such a slap on the back that he nearly sent his nephew over the bay's edge.

Dath nudged Corban in the ribs. "Let's go," he whispered. They edged into the crowd, Gwenith calling them just before they disappeared.

"Where are you two off to?"

"Just going to have a look round, Mam," Corban replied. Traders had gathered from far and wide for the spring festival, along with many of Brenin's barons come to witness Marrock's handbinding. The meadow was dotted with scores of tents, cattle-pens and roped-off areas for various contests and games, and *people*: hundreds, it must be, more than Corban had ever seen gathered in one place before. Corban and Dath's excitement had been growing daily, to the point where time had seemed to crawl by, and now finally the day was here.

"All right," Gwenith said. "You both be careful." She reached into her shawl and pressed something into Corban's hand: a silver piece.

"Go and have a good time," she said, cupping his cheek in her hand. "Be back before sunset. I'll be here with your da, if he's still standing."

"Course he will be, Mam," Corban said. His da, Thannon, would be competing in the pugil-ring today. He had been fist champion for as long as Corban could remember.

Corban leaned over and kissed her on the cheek. "Thank you, Mam," he grinned, then turned and bolted into the crowd, Dath close behind him.

"Look after your new cloak," she called out, smiling.

The two boys soon stopped running and walked along the meadow's edge that skirted the beach and the bay, seals sunning themselves on the shore. Gulls circled and called above them, lured by the smell of food wafting from the fires and tents in the meadow.

"A silver coin," said Dath. "Let me see it."

Corban opened his palm, the coin damp now with sweat where he had been clutching it so tightly.

"Your mam's soft on you, eh, Ban?"

"I know," replied Corban, feeling awkward. He knew Dath only had a couple of coppers, and it had taken him moons to earn that, working for his father on their fishing boat. "Here," he said, delving into a leather pouch hanging at his belt, "have these." He held out three coppers that he had earned from his da, sweating in his forge.

"No thanks," Dath said with a frown. "You're my friend, not my master."

"I didn't mean it like that, Dath. I just thought—I've got plenty now, and friends share, don't they?"

The frown hovered a moment, then passed. "I know, Ban." Dath looked away, out to the boats bobbing on the swell of the bay. "Just wish my mam was still here to go soft on me."

Corban grimaced, not knowing what to say. The silence grew. "Maybe your da's got more coin for you, Dath," he said, to break the silence as much as anything.

"No chance of that," Dath snorted. "I was surprised to see this coin—most of it fills his cups these days. Come on, let's go and find something to spend it on."

The sun had risen high above the horizon now, bathing the meadow in warmth, banishing the last remnants of the dawn cold as the boys made their way among the crowd and traders' tents.

"I didn't think there were this many people in all the village and Dun Carreg put together," said Dath, grunting as someone jostled past him.

"People have come much further than the village and fortress, Dath," murmured Corban. They strolled on for a while, just enjoying the sun and the atmosphere. Soon they found themselves near the center of the meadow, where men were beginning to gather around an area of roped-off grass. The sword-crossing ring.

"Shall we stay, get a good spot?" Corban said.

"Nah, they won't be starting for an age. Besides, everyone knows Tull is going to win."

"Think so?"

"Course," Dath sniffed. "He's not the King's first-sword for nothing. I've heard he cut a man in two with one blow."

"I've heard that too," said Corban. "But he's not as young as he was. Some say he's slowing down."

Dath shrugged. "Maybe. We can come back later and see how long it takes him to crack someone's head, but let's wait till the competition's warmed up a bit, eh?"

"All right," said Corban, then cuffed his friend across the back of the head and ran, Dath shouting as he gave chase. Corban dodged this way and that around people. He looked over his shoulder to check where Dath was, then suddenly tripped and sprawled forwards, landing on a large skin that had been spread on the floor. It was covered with torcs, bone combs, arm-bands, brooches, all manner of items. Corban heard a low rumbling growl as he scrambled back to his feet, Dath skidding to a halt behind him.

Corban looked around at the scattered merchandise and began gathering up all that he could see, but in his urgency he fumbled and dropped most of it again.

"Whoa, boy, less haste, more speed."

Corban looked up and saw a tall wiry man staring down at him. He had long dark hair tied tight at his neck. Behind the man were all sorts of goods spread about an open-fronted tent: hides, swords, daggers, horns, jugs, tankards, horse harness, all hanging from the framework of the tent or laid out neatly on tables and skins.

"You have nothing to worry about from me, boy, there's no harm done," the trader said as he gathered up his merchandise. "Talar, however, is a different matter." He gestured to an enormous, gray-streaked hound that had risen to its feet behind Corban. It growled. "He doesn't take kindly to being trodden on or tripped over; he may well want some recompense."

"Recompense?"

"Aye. Blood, flesh, bone. Maybe your arm, something like that."

Corban swallowed and the trader laughed, bending over, one hand braced on his knee. Dath sniggered behind him.

"I am Ventos," the trader offered when he recovered, "and this is my faithful, though sometimes grumpy friend, Talar." Ventos clicked his fingers and the large hound padded over to his side, nuzzling the trader's palm.

"Never fear, he's already eaten this morning, so you are both quite safe."

"I'm Dath," blurted the fisherman's son, "and this is Ban—I mean, Corban. I've never seen a hound so big," he continued breathlessly, "not even your da's, eh, Ban?"

Corban nodded, eyes still fixed on the mountain of fur at the trader's side. He was used to hounds, had grown up with them, but this beast before him was considerably bigger. As he looked at it the hound growled again, a low rumble deep in its belly.

"Don't look so worried, boy."

"I don't think he likes me," Corban said. "He doesn't sound happy."

"If you heard him when he's not happy you'd know the difference. I've heard it enough on my travels between here and Helveth."

"Isn't Helveth where Gar's from, Ban?" asked Dath.

"Aye," Corban muttered.

"Who's Gar?" the trader asked.

"Friend of my mam and da," Corban said.

"He's a long way from home, too, then," Ventos said. "Whereabouts in Helveth is he from?"

Corban shrugged. "Don't know."

"A man should always know where he's from," the trader said, "we all need our roots."

"Uhh," grunted Corban. He usually *asked* a lot of questions—too many, so his mam told him—but he didn't like being on the receiving end so much.

A shadow fell across Corban, a firm hand gripping his shoulder.

"Hello, Ban," said Gar, the stablemaster.

"We were just talking about you," Dath said. "About where you're from."

"What?" said the stablemaster, frowning.

"This man is from Helveth," Corban said, gesturing at Ventos. Gar blinked.

"I'm Ventos," said the trader. "Where in Helveth?"

Gar looked at the merchandise hung about the tent. "I'm looking for harness and a saddle. Fifteen-span mare, wide back." He ignored the trader's question.

"Fifteen spans? Aye, I'm sure I've got something for you back here," replied Ventos. "I have some harness I traded with the Sirak. There's none finer."

"I'd like to see that." Gar followed Ventos into the tent, limping slightly as always.

With that the boys began browsing through Ventos' tent. In no time Corban had an armful of things. He picked out a wide iron-studded collar for his da's hound, Buddai, a brooch of pewter with a galloping horse embossed on it for his sister, a dress-pin of silver with a red enamel inset for his mother and two sturdy practice swords for Dath and himself. Dath had picked out two clay tankards, waves of blue coral decorating them.

Corban raised an eyebrow.

"Might as well get something my da'll actually use."

"Why two?" asked Corban.

"If you cannot vanquish a foe," he said sagely, "then ally yourself to him." He winked.

"No tankard for Bethan, then?" said Corban.

"My sister does not approve of drinking," replied Dath.

Just then Gar emerged from the inner tent with a bundle of leather slung over his back, iron buckles clinking as he walked. The stablemaster grunted at Corban and walked into the crowd.

"Looks like you've picked up a fine collection for yourselves," the trader said to them.

"Why are these wooden swords so heavy?" asked Dath.

"Because they are practice swords. They have been hollowed out and filled with lead, good for building up the strength of your sword arm, get you used to the weight and balance of a real blade, and they don't kill you when you lose or slip."

"How much for all of these," Corban asked.

Ventos whistled. "Two and a half silvers."

"Would you take this if we leave the two swords?" Corban showed the trader his silver piece and three coppers.

"And these?" said Dath, quickly adding his two coppers.

"Deal."

Corban gave him their coin, put the items into a leather bag that Dath had been keeping a slab of dry cheese and a skin of water in.

"Maybe I'll see you lads tonight, at the feast."

"We'll be there," said Corban. As they reached the crowd beyond the tent Ventos called out to them and threw the practice swords. Instinctively Corban caught one, hearing Dath yelp in pain. Ventos raised a finger to his lips and winked. Corban grinned in return. *A practice sword, a proper one, not fashioned out of a stick from his back garden. Just a step away from a real sword.* He almost shivered at the excitement of that thought.

They wandered aimlessly for a while, Corban marveling at the sheer numbers of the crowd, at the entertainments clamoring for his attention: tale-tellers, puppet-masters, fire-breathers, sword-jugglers, many, many more. He squeezed through a growing crowd, Dath in his wake, and watched as a piglet was released squealing from its cage, a score or more of men chasing it, falling over each other as the piglet dodged this way and that. They laughed as a tall gangly warrior from the fortress finally managed to throw himself onto the animal and raise it squeaking over his head. The crowd roared and laughed as he was awarded a skin of mead for his efforts.

Moving on again, Corban led them back to the roped-off ring where the sword-crossing was to take place. There was quite a crowd gathered now, all watching Tull, first-sword of the King.

The boys climbed a boulder at the back of the crowd to see better, made short work of Dath's slab of cheese and watched as Tull, stripped to the waist, his upper body thick and corded as an old oak, effortlessly swatted his assailant to the ground with a wooden sword. Tull laughed, arms spread wide as his opponent jumped to his feet and ran at him again. Their practice swords *clacked* as Tull's attacker rained rapid blows on the King's champion, causing him to step backward.

"See," said Corban, elbowing his friend and spitting crumbs of cheese, "he's in trouble now." But, as they watched, Tull quickly sidestepped, belying his size, and struck his off-balance opponent across the back of the knees, sending him sprawling on his face in the churned ground. Tull put a foot on the man's back and punched the air. The crowd clapped and cheered as the fallen warrior writhed in the mud, pinned by Tull's heavy boot.

After a few moments the old warrior stepped away, offered the fallen man his hand, only to have it slapped away as the warrior tried to rise on his own and slipped in the mud.

Tull shrugged and smiled, walking toward the rope boundary. The beaten warrior fixed his eyes on Tull's back and suddenly ran at the old warrior. Something must have warned Tull, for he turned and blocked an overhead blow that would have cracked his skull. He set his legs and dipped his head as the attacking warrior's momentum carried him forwards. There was a crunch as his face collided with Tull's head, blood spurting from the man's nose. Tull's knee crashed into the man's stomach and he collapsed to the ground.

Tull stood over him a moment, nostrils flaring, then he pushed his hand through long, gray-streaked hair, wiping the other man's blood from his forehead. The crowd erupted in cheers.

"He's new here," said Corban, pointing at the warrior lying senseless in the mud. "I saw him arrive only a few nights ago."

"Not off to a good start, is he?" chuckled Dath.

"He's lucky the swords were made of wood, there's others have challenged Tull that haven't got back up."

"Doesn't look like he's getting up any time soon," pointed out Dath, waving his hand at the warrior lying in the mud.

"But he will."

Dath glanced at Corban and suddenly lunged at him, knocking him off the rock they were sitting on. He snatched up his new practice sword and stood over Corban, imitating the scene they had just witnessed. Corban rolled away and climbed to his feet, edging slowly around Dath until he reached his own wooden sword.

"So, you wish to challenge the mighty Tull," said Dath, pointing his sword at his friend. Corban laughed and ran at him, swinging a wild blow. For a while they hammered back and forth, taunting each other between frenzied bursts of energy.

Passers-by smiled at the two boys.

After a particularly furious flurry of blows Dath ended up on his back, Corban's sword hovering over his chest.

"Do—you—yield?" asked Corban between ragged breaths.

"Never," cried Dath and kicked at Corban's ankles, knocking him onto his back.

They both lay there, gazing at the clear blue sky above, too weak with their exertions and laughter to rise, when suddenly, startling them, a voice spoke.

"Well, what have we here, two hogs rutting in the mud?"